CW01636340

KNOCK KNOCK

A DCI ROBERT KETT NOVEL

ALEX SMITH

RELENTLESS MEDIA

KNOCK KNOCK
Published Worldwide by Relentless Media.
This edition published in 2022.

Edited by Hanna Elizabeth

978-1-913877-09-5

www.alexsmithbooks.com
relentless.media

ALSO BY ALEX SMITH

The DCI Robert Kett Thrillers

Paper Girls

Bad Dog

Three Little Pigs

Whip Crack

Run Rabbit Run

Stone Cold Dead

Every Mother's Son

Sweet Briar Rose

Jaw Breaker

Knock Knock

Cry Baby: A Novella

The Softley Softley Thrillers

The Harder They Fall

Hard Luck House (Coming Soon)

Other Books

Six Days, Six Hours, Six Minutes

Dedicated to my little sister Kate,
And to her many past, present and future bestsellers!

PROLOGUE

Wednesday

It was official.

She was going to murder him.

Merletta Shaw threw down her pen hard enough for ink to splatter the surface of the desk. Rocking back in her chair, she screamed at the ceiling. Not that anyone would hear it over the sound of music from downstairs. The house was literally vibrating as Duggie's industrial-grade subwoofers pumped out their tuneless ear poison. It was the same drum and bass crap he always listened to, each note like a cannon shot that travelled up through the floorboards and into her legs. She could feel it in her teeth.

She was *definitely* going to murder him.

Merle took one more look at the sad collection of textbooks that sat open in front of her, then pushed herself out of the chair. Her body was tight with panic because her first sociology exam was tomorrow and literally everything she'd learned this year at uni had drained out of her mind in the last twelve hours. There was nothing up there anymore, no memory of culture or identity, or of families and households, and certainly zero resembling *the self, identity and difference as both socially caused and socially constructed*, which was what Professor Nguyen had all but told them the first question would be.

Nothing. Her head was empty. Everything had been shaken out of it by that infernal bloody noise.

"Duggie!" she shouted as she crossed her room.

She opened the door and the noise became a solid wall that she almost couldn't bring herself to walk into. Duggie's bedroom was empty—at least she assumed it was, although it was so cluttered she couldn't be sure. Jozef's door was closed, but she was pretty sure he was at his girlfriend's house, and Carolina had moved out of her box room at the end of the house a couple of weeks ago.

Merle walked to the stairs and looked down, seeing the front door open. Sunlight poured through, the summer seeming to call to her. She was tempted to grab her books and leave the house, head over to the university lake and do the last of her revision by the water. But there was just no time, and she had to stay in because one of her textbooks hadn't even been delivered by Amazon yet and she didn't trust anybody else to answer the door when it finally came.

"Duggie?" she shouted again as she clattered down the stairs. She could barely hear her own voice over the concussive thump of the speakers. "Turn it down!"

She poked her head into the kitchen to see a couple of women there she half recognised from Duggie's social circle, third-year students. They were propped up on the short breakfast bar. One was pouring vodka into Merle's favourite mug, the other—a ridiculously attractive Barbie look-alike who was called Mandy or Candy or something stupid like that—holding a champagne glass to her chest. Neither even bothered to look at her.

"Hello?" Merle said. "What are you doing?"

They *still* didn't acknowledge her. Mandy or Candy said something that Merle couldn't catch and the other woman burst into laughter. The panic was fast becoming something hotter, an anger that made Merle storm across the kitchen and grab her mug. Vodka splashed over her hand as she yanked it off the counter.

"Hey!" snapped the girl. "What the hell?"

Merle didn't bother to explain, tipping the contents of the mug down the sink and carrying it out of the room. She'd had the Boost mug for nigh on a decade, back when they'd come free with your Easter egg, and so far it had survived two moves, her mum and dad's divorce and one year in a student house full of dickheads. She wasn't going to lose it now.

Two more women were walking through the front door, followed by a guy who was holding a carrier bag full of clinking bottles.

"No," said Merle, more to herself than to them. "No, no, no."

She barged in front of them, entering the living room to see Duggie on the sofa with his two mates whose names she could never remember. He was holding a spliff and the air was heavy with the cloying stench of weed. She held her breath, then realised she needed to speak, accidentally sucking in a lungful of air that made her feel instantly giddy. The music was deafening. It felt loud enough to bring the entire house down around them.

"Duggie!" she said, her voice just a whisper.

She flinched as somebody pushed past her, one of the

girls from the kitchen. She had a fresh mug now—which was also Merle's—and she started dancing in the middle of the room. Duggie grinned at the woman, as did Tweedle-Dumb and Tweedle-Dumber, but it was like Merle was invisible. More people entered the room, their laughter seeming to blend with the smoke, with the pulse of the music. There was something almost nightmarish about it, it was suffocating, and the anger and the panic boiled to a frenzy inside her skull.

She spotted the speakers beneath the window and charged towards them, weaving through people who didn't seem to know she was there. She felt like she could be on fire right now and still nobody would notice her.

The plugs were underneath the TV table and she had to get down onto her knees to find them, scratching her shoulder on a nail as she reached into the dark with her free hand. The music pummelled her ears, made her feel like she'd never be able to hear anything again.

"Come on!" she said, finding the first switch and pressing it. Nothing happened, but when she clicked the second one the silence fell like a hammer. It was almost worse than the noise, her ears ringing with the shock of it.

"What the fuck are you doing?"

The voice felt weirdly *numb*. Merle tugged her arm free of the TV table, catching the nail again. Everyone in the room was staring at her, not a single friendly face amongst them. Duggie was halfway out of the sofa, already drunk or high, or possibly both. One of his friends had to brace a hand on his backside and give him a shove to stop him from collapsing back onto the cushions. He lifted his hands in the air in a shrug, ash dropping from the spliff onto the carpet.

"Merley, I said what the fuck are you doing?"

"I've got an exam tomorrow," Merle said, using the table

to push herself to her feet, still clutching the mug like it was a weapon. "I told you. I need to revise."

"So revise," Duggie said. "Put some fucking tissue in your ears if it's too loud."

Merle felt her jaw drop, then the anger made her clench her teeth. Everyone was staring at her, and they all had stupid little smirks on their faces. The two girls from the kitchen were whispering something to each other and Merle would happily have cracked them both over the head with the mug, even if it meant breaking it into a million pieces.

"You can't have a party," she said, speaking slowly, deliberately, because she didn't trust her voice not to shake. "Not tonight. Not this week. It's important."

Duggie grinned, taking a hit on the joint.

"Not my fault everyone else has finished their exams," he said, his words made of smoke. "Bring it up with the psychology department, sweetheart."

Sociology, she thought, and God, how she hated him. She didn't think she'd *ever* felt this much hate towards another living person. She'd been in the shared house for less than a year, just since the start of term in September, and Duggie had never been nice to her, never been kind. He was a member of the university football team, athletic, irritatingly handsome, good genes and plenty of money. And he knew it. He was an arsehole, an arrogant, selfish prick, and she *hated* him.

"Aw, diddums," Duggie said, pretending to rub the tears from his eyes. Everybody laughed and Merle once again had the idea that she was trapped in some kind of fever dream. "Nobody cares, so please just fuck off back to your shitty room and your boring books, you absolute loser."

"Loser!" parroted Tweedle-Dumber, putting two fingers to his forehead in the shape of an L.

"Turn the music back on," shouted one of the women, and the guy who'd been carrying the carrier bag lurched past Merle hard enough to ram her arm with his shoulder. She dropped the mug and it hit the TV table, spinning onto the carpet. It was a miracle it didn't shatter. It was a miracle that Merle hadn't shattered, too, because she felt like she was made of glass.

"That's not fair," she said, grabbing the mug. "That's not—"

And the music thumped back to life, a fist around Merle's heart, actually painful. There was nothing to do but leave, her walk becoming a run by the time she'd escaped the room. She glanced through the open front door as she went, seeing another person outside, the shape of them dulled by her tears.

Her heart seemed to tumble all the way into her feet, her chest hollow. It was hopeless. Duggie's parties were always huge, and they went on until the early hours, sometimes even past dawn. She wouldn't be able to revise, she wouldn't be able to sleep. She was going to fail her exam, and it was his fault. It wasn't like she had wealthy parents to fall back on, or a job lined up ready and waiting as soon as she graduated. People like Merle didn't get those kinds of things, only people like *him*.

Merle scrubbed her eyes as she climbed the stairs, making it halfway back to her room before she heard it over the drum and bass.

Knock knock.

More people for the party, and she was half tempted to run back down and tell them where to go. Not in a nice way, either. Maybe she could say there was a gas leak, or a fire. Then she could call the police, make them shut everything down.

Knock knock.

Somebody was properly thumping the door. She paused, wondering why they didn't just come in. It was open, after all.

Maybe it was her book? Merle doubled back, ducking down so that she could see the open door. There was nobody there, but a parcel sat on the mat.

Yes!

That was one piece of good news, anyway. She galloped down the stairs and crossed the hall, glancing down the short path to see that the delivery driver had already gone. She had to step into the little puddle of sunlight in order to reach the box, and the warmth did even more to dispel the panic and the anger. It made her think that she could take her new book upstairs, put on her headphones, burrow beneath her duvet and actually do some revision. Maybe she wasn't doomed.

She picked up the box, turning it in her hands. It was brown cardboard wrapped tight with parcel tape and a pale pink ribbon, tied in a bow. Something heavy slid back and forth inside, something that didn't feel quite bookish enough. Then her eye caught the neatly handwritten label and she swore silently.

Douglas Ireland.

It was for Duggie.

Unbelievable.

She almost dropped it back onto the mat, then hesitated. If Duggie was going to be such an arsehole to her, then why shouldn't she be an arsehole right back? A quick look over her shoulder told her she was alone, so she snuck into the kitchen and dumped the box onto the counter. The room stank of vodka, and the cardboard was instantly soaked through from the puddle that had been left on the worktop.

"Whoops," Merle said with a smile.

It would be such a shame if whatever was in there was ruined, right?

The ribbon was easy enough to undo and she tugged it free, tossing it to the floor. She fetched a knife from the sink, not bothering to wipe off the peanut butter before jamming it into the flap. It was bound in parcel tape, but the knife made short work of it. The music played as she worked, so loud that she didn't realise she wasn't on her own until somebody cleared their throat right behind her.

She almost shrieked, whirling around with the knife clenched in her hand. The woman called Mandy or Candy was right there and she stepped back, her eyes wide, her hands up.

"Jesus," she said. "Don't stab me."

"Then don't sneak up on me," Merle shot back, her heart playing its own drum and bass tune behind her ribs. "You almost scared me to death."

Mandy or Candy frowned, glancing back. When she turned to Merle again, she looked sheepish.

"Look, sorry about Douglas," she said, her voice raised so that it could be heard over the music. "He shouldn't have said all that. He can be a real prick sometimes."

Merle shrugged, unsure what to say. The box sat behind her, Duggie's name as clear as anything.

"I'm just over the road," the girl went on. "I'm the last one in my house, everyone else has gone home for the summer. If you want to revise, you're welcome to hang out there. I'll give you the key."

"Oh," said Merle, and she didn't know what to follow it with.

"It's up to you," said the woman. "I'm easy either way. I

just know how stressful it can be, exams and all that. You in your third year?"

"First," said Merle, and the woman smiled.

"Well, just remember that first-year exam results don't even count. You're going to be fine. I'm Jane, by the way. I don't think we've ever been properly introduced."

Not Mandy or Candy, then, thought Merle.

Jane gave Merle a smile that seemed perfectly genuine as she walked to the counter. Merle tried to block her, but there was nowhere to go. Jane reached for the bottle of vodka and caught sight of the box.

"Anything exciting?" she asked.

"I, uh, I don't know," Merle replied. "I don't think it's mine."

She twisted her arm behind her back to hide the knife, but she wasn't fooling anybody.

"Sure," Jane said. "That's why there's peanut butter all over it. Go on, don't mind me. Is it something, you know..."

She smiled again, this one loaded with meaning. Merle felt her cheeks blaze.

"No," she said. "Gosh, no. I thought it was... you know, I thought it was a book of mine, a sociology book I need for my exam, and I started to open it but then I saw Duggie's name just as you were walking in and... sorry."

She didn't even know why she was apologising, and Jane laughed—although there was nothing unkind about it.

"It's Duggie's?" she said, waving Merle out of the way. "Let's open it. I bet it's a bunch of second-hand nudie mags or something, knowing him."

"We, uh..."

Merle took a step to the side as Jane lifted the flaps of the box. Inside was a carefully folded layer of white tissue paper, held with a delicate pink sticker.

"I think he's bought himself some lingerie," Jane said with a snort of laughter. "Always knew he was a perve."

"Do you think we should leave it?" Merle said, glancing through the door. From here she could see the living room, and the mass of people who danced there now reminded her of an engine of pistons. Duggie didn't just make her angry, he scared her a little too. Guys like him lost their temper way too easily. "What if he gets mad?"

"He won't," said Jane. "Not with me."

She unpicked the sticker, the tissue paper tearing as she peeled it free. They leaned over the box together, close enough that Merle could smell the vodka on the other woman's breath. She felt almost dizzy with it, like *she* was drunk.

"Right then," said Jane, lifting the tissue paper. "What have we got here?"

It wasn't immediately clear, because whatever it was had been mummified in cling film. It sat in a little nest of paper and packing chips, just a flash of something marbled and red visible at the top.

"What do you think it is?" said Jane. "Sex toy?"

A laugh slipped its way out of Merle's mouth before she could stop it. Jane poked a finger into the box and pushed some of the packing chips away. The object was pink, and there was something fleshy about it, something meaty.

"Oh gross," said the woman. "It's definitely a sex toy, and it's a..."

She grabbed handfuls of chips, shovelling them out of the box. Merle leaned closer, trying to make sense of what she saw there. It almost looked like a...

"It's a *foot*," Jane said, laughing. "Oh Jesus, Duggie bought himself a sex foot."

"A *what*?" said Merle.

"A sex foot, like a dildo or something. Look."

She grabbed the object and hefted it out of the box, packing chips scattering to the floor like hail. She held it up between them, and Merle found herself ready to laugh again at the idea they'd uncovered Duggie's shameful secret, a disgusting truth about him that would almost certainly mean the end of his reign as the king of the house. She saw Jane grin as well, but only for a second. Then the grin fell away, and Merle's laughter was extinguished like a candle in the bath.

Because the foot wasn't a toy. She could see that now, in the crooked angle of the toes and the too long, too-yellow nails that curled out from them, almost piercing the cling film. She could see it in the faint tattoo that ran along the cracked skin of the heel, and most of all in the twin circles of bright white bone that formed a cross-section through the marbled meat of the ankle.

"Oh Jesus," Jane said, and she hurled the foot to the floor. It landed with a thud, sliding beneath the table. The cling film must have split because it left a trail of blood behind it. "Oh shit, shit shit shit."

Jane staggered into the breakfast bar, rubbing her hands down her dress. Merle was moving too, even though she hadn't given her body any orders to do so. She backed into the wall, papers scattering loose from the cork notice board.

"It's a foot," said Jane, her face a hundred years old. "It's a fucking foot."

Merle didn't reply. She couldn't. The music was forgotten. The party was forgotten, every thought obliterated. Once again, her head was empty.

There was just the foot that lay on the kitchen floor—pink and shrivelled and ugly.

And unmistakeably real.

CHAPTER ONE

It was one of the undeniable facts of life: a cup of tea could make everything right with the world.

DCI Robert Kett closed his eyes and took a sip, the tea a little too hot but all the better for it. It was just a standard PG Tips teabag, but he'd brewed it himself and it was just the way he liked it—on the strong side, steeped for two minutes, finished with a dash and a half of milk. When he swallowed, he could feel every muscle relax, every stress float out of his head. It was like he'd learned to breathe all over again, and he kept the mug against his lips and took a lungful of that unmistakable scent.

"Get a room, will you?"

Kett opened his eyes, peering over the top of his mug, through the rising steam, to see DI Keith Dunst on the next desk over. He was one of five other coppers in the entire bullpen, the station weirdly deserted. Part of that was because of the weather, Kett knew. Norwich was in the middle of a glorious fortnight of continental June sunshine, and most of his colleagues had found an excuse to leave HQ and get out into the heat. Kett would be right there with them, under different circumstances.

But it wasn't just quiet because it was summer. There was no denying it had been strangely peaceful in the county of late, especially for the Extreme Crime Task Force. So peaceful, in fact, that Superintendent Clare had temporarily moved both DC Savage and DI Porter out of the unit so they could catch up on other things. There was still plenty of crime, of course. There always would be. But fortunately, nothing that could be labelled *extreme.*

For that, Kett was infinitely grateful.

"What?" he asked when he realised Dunst was still looking at him.

"You and that mug, sir," the old DI replied, shovelling a piece of cake into his mouth. "Get a room. Nobody wants to see you snogging the crockery."

The mug was still resting against Kett's lip, comfortingly warm, and he took another sip before lowering it to the desk.

"What I do with my crockery is none of your concern, Keith," he said with a smile. "So kindly mind your own business."

Dunst coughed what sounded like a pint of mucus into his hand, wiping it on his trousers. He picked up another slice of cake from the plate on his desk and devoured it in one go.

"You really should try it," he said, spraying crumbs like he was feeding the birds.

"Is that Superintendent Clare's cake?"

Dunst nodded. It had been the Super's birthday three days ago—although nobody had a clue how old he actually was. On a good day, Clare could be in his late fifties. On a bad day, he looked like the angry, wrinkled ghost of an Elizabethan witch hunter who'd been dug from his grave and badly resurrected. He'd made himself a birthday cake, and when nobody at home had dared to eat it, he'd brought it to work. It had been sitting on the worktop in the kitchen ever since looking like a monstrous turd.

"It's delicious," Dunst said, or something like it—Kett couldn't really understand him as he chewed.

"It's a Bounty cake, Keith. *Bounties.* That's so wrong." Kett shook his head. "Not to mention the fact I think I can smell those uncooked eggs from here."

"It's fine," Dunst said, collecting crumbs with his fingertip. "You still planning on moving house?"

Kett nodded, sitting back in his chair. He and Billie had been talking about it a lot since the end of the last case. They'd barely talked about anything else, in fact. Their kitchen table was a monument to Right Move, dozens of print-outs stacked into piles based on price and suitability and all covered in doodles from the kids.

"I'd want to move too, if I were you," Dunst said. He glanced at his hand, at the stump of the finger that had been taken by Hollenbeck. "First thing I did after that was move house. Too many bad memories."

Kett nodded, looking at the screen in front of him. It was blurry, and with a sigh he picked up his reading glasses from the desk. After weeks of being nagged by Savage, he'd finally given in, and even though he was still adamant that his vision was perfect, there was no denying they made everything sharper. He'd had the girls with him when he went to his appointment, and they'd bullied him into getting a pair of cheap, bottle green frames from Specsavers, boxy and uncomfortable. He was still getting used to them.

The image on his computer was what had kept him

inside, even on a day like this. It's why Billie was so keen on getting out of their house. It was the security feed from a city garage, dated November last year. The car in the middle of the footage was a black Peugeot 407, the same one that had been parked outside his house when he'd got home from Superintendent Clare's ill-fated weekend away.

The car hadn't stopped at the garage, it had just idled on the street while it waited for the lights to change. The driver was a hunched shadow in the windscreen, not a single identifiable characteristic in sight. But Kett could still see him, as clear as if he was sitting on the other side of the desk. The man had been staring at the house, staring at *his* house, his grin sharp enough to cut through time.

What if it's them? Billie had asked.

The man had driven off before Kett could talk to him, but everything about him, every single thing about his actions and about that smile, meant there could only be one answer to his wife's question.

Yes. He had been part of Hollenbeck. The same people who had controlled the monster who had kidnapped Billie, the same group who had tried to frame him for murder, the same arseholes who had trained the man who had tried to murder all of those women during the Sweet Briar Rose case. The driver of the Peugeot was one of Hollenbeck's ghosts, Kett was sure of it.

But the real question was, what the hell had he been doing at Kett's house?

"We don't have anything on him," he said, cradling his tea against his lip again in the hope the warmth of it would chase away the sudden chill. All it achieved was steaming up his glasses, so he took them off and rested them on the desk. "The Peugeot was a hire car, taken out under a false name. The driver knew what he was doing, wore a cap to hide his face from the cameras, didn't stop anywhere other than my house. We've got the car on two dozen NPRCs but his face isn't visible on any of them."

"Forensics ever pull anything from the wreck?"

They'd found the Peugeot two days later, or what was left of it. It had been left in a field down by Whitlingham Broad, not far from the house where they'd found the newspaper girls all those summers ago. The accelerant they'd used had been so fierce that the fire had been visible across the whole city. The car burned to its bones.

Kett shook his head again, sighing so loudly that tea sprayed from the cup. He put the mug down, closing the footage on-screen. It was June now, over six months had passed. He was chasing ghosts.

Literally.

"It's probably nothing," Dunst said, leaning back in his chair. "If it was them, they'd have made a move by now. Quit worrying."

Easy for you to say, Kett almost replied, but he was cut off by his phone.

"Pete," he said as he answered it. "What's up?"

"You busy, sir?" said DI Pete Porter.

"That depends entirely on what you need me for," he said. He thought he could hear shouting down the line, and car horns blaring.

"We're in the middle of something down here. I don't think you want to miss it."

"Is it an emergency, Pete?"

Porter laughed.

"It's a *comedy* emergency."

"A what?"

More honking, and what sounded like a squeal.

"Just get down here, sir. You won't regret it."

Porter ended the call and Kett stood up, polishing off the rest of his tea in one go.

"Something tells me I'm totally going to regret it," he said as he took his jacket from the back of the chair and slid his glasses into the inside pocket. "Catch you in a bit, Keith."

TWENTY MINUTES LATER, Kett turned a corner on the A47 to see a wave of rolling blue lights ahead. Two uniformed constables stood in front of the first IRV diverting traffic down a side road, and Kett pulled out his warrant card as he slowed the orange Volvo V60 to a halt.

He wound down the window, instantly assaulted by what sounded like an ancient battle. Shouts and screams rang out from behind the vans that blocked the road, the clang of ringing metal like clashing swords. The smell was equally horrific, the air heavy with something pungent and unmistakably *farmy*.

"What on earth is going on?" he asked, showing the constables his warrant card. "Sounds like we're under attack."

"You're not far wrong, sir," said the first PC, a young woman whose face was almost scarlet from the sun. "You wouldn't believe it even if I told you."

"Kind of have to see it for yourself, sir," said the older man beside her as he waved another car away from the scene.

Kett nodded, moving the Volvo up to the line of parked

vans before climbing out. The afternoon was hotter than ever, no shade here at all. The road was sticky, pockets of hot air making it look like there were shimmering puddles along it. It was glorious, despite the smell.

He walked around the first police van, seeing a row of constables standing with their backs to him—almost like a line of defenders waiting for a free kick. More shouts rose from behind them, more screams and snorts and the drumming of feet on asphalt. Porter was there too, his phone up like he was recording the scene.

"Pete?" Kett said as he squeezed past the constables. "What..."

And he didn't need to finish, because it was clear enough. At least a dozen enormous pigs were loose on the A47, bolting back and forth across the dual carriageway in a complete panic. Twice as many coppers were doing their best to herd them, along with a few civilians who were probably farmers, but it wasn't going particularly well. The pigs really were huge, and they were showing no sign of coming quietly.

"Bloody hell," said Kett.

He felt a pain in his chest, like his heart had been struck with a sculptor's hammer. For a moment, all he saw was the Pig Man in that awful mask, staring at him from the dark hollows of its eyes.

Then he blinked, and they were just pigs.

"What happened?" he asked, just a croak.

"There's a farm just over the hill there," Porter said. "Somebody must have left a gate open and they all ran down here. There were three times as many when I got here. These are the last ones."

"Why are you filming it?" Kett said.

"Why do you think?" Porter replied, grinning. "Look."

He pointed his free hand to the middle of the crowd and Kett saw PC Aaron Duke there, his jacket off and his face streaked with sweat and mud. He was squatting like a rugby player, his tree-trunk arms wide and his eyes wild as he tried to outmanoeuvre a charging pig.

"Go on, Duke!" Porter yelled. "You can do it!"

Duke glanced up, distracted, and the pig clipped him as it ran past. Duke made a wild lunge for it but missed, his boot slipping on a little mound of manure and depositing him onto his face. Porter's laugh was so loud that every single person on the road turned to look at him, and half of the pigs as well. The DI snapped a photo.

"Brilliant," he said, laughing so hard there were tears in his eyes. "Another one for the wall."

Duke shot Porter a death stare before running off after the pig.

"I'm surprised he hasn't started Tasering them," said Porter.

"They gave Duke a Taser?" said Kett.

"Yeah. Scary. It's like trusting a goat to work a..." Porter shrugged. "A Taser, I guess."

"That's just mean," said Kett. "Shouldn't you be helping?"

"I'm an important part of the perimeter wall," Porter replied, putting his phone back in his pocket. "Besides, they've got it covered. Savage is out there, too."

It took Kett a moment to see her further down the road, working with a couple of farmers to corral a colossal black and pink pig against the central divide. They were coaxing it gently, which seemed like a much better technique than the one Duke was using. One farmer slipped a collar around the pig's neck while another offered it a treat. Savage stood up, her hands on her hips, her expression one of exhaustion. She spotted Kett and smiled, throwing a wave his way. He threw one right back.

"Shouldn't be much longer now," Porter said, checking his watch. "I'm just glad you caught it. It'll be on the news, anyway."

He nodded to the gaggle of reporters who stood on the raised verge, their cameras rolling.

"If they show the bit where Duke slipped in shit, I'll be the happiest man alive," the DI said.

"Pete, give him a break," Kett said.

"He's a big boy, he can take it."

"He is," said Kett. "Bigger than you anyway, which probably explains a lot."

Porter gasped, genuinely outraged.

"Clare here?" Kett asked.

"For this? Nah. Bit below his pay grade, this one. He said he was on the way to something else, something urgent."

"More urgent than escaped pigs?" Kett said. "I—"

And he had to stop because his phone was ringing. He pulled it out, seeing Clare's name on the screen. He showed it to Porter, who shook his head.

"You *summoned* him," he said quietly.

Kett laughed as he answered it.

"Sir?"

"Kett," Clare boomed. "Where are you?"

"With the pigs, sir."

"I need you back in the city, now."

"Sure thing," Kett said.

"I need Porter and Savage too."

And just like that, the smile fell from Kett's face.

"The Task Force?" he asked. Clare's sigh roared down the line.

"Yeah, the Task Force," he said after a moment. "Something's happened. Something bad."

"Something *extreme*," Kett said with a sigh of his own. "We're on our way."

CHAPTER TWO

KETT DROVE WITH THE WINDOWS OPEN, BUT EVEN THEN it was a struggle. Savage sat in the passenger seat and the smell coming off her was unreal, enough to make Kett's eyes water. He had to keep checking the back to make sure one of the pigs hadn't climbed into the car with them.

"Sorry, sir," she said for the twentieth time. "It really won't take me a second to go and change."

It would, though, because they were on the wrong side of town for Savage's flat. It would take them another hour or so to make the round trip, and Clare hadn't sounded like he was in the mood for waiting.

"You'll be fine," Kett said as they pulled off the A47. "I'll drop you off after."

"Wonder what's got the boss so spooked," she said.

Kett glanced at her, seeing the lines of worry that were etched on her young face. They had been there since the last case, although she did a good job of hiding them. The deaths over in Toltham had been bad, and what had happened afterwards was worse. Kett knew that Savage had stayed in touch with Catherine Cavaney, and he knew Cat was doing okay—not *okay*, as such, although better. But the scars of that weekend were deep.

And now here they were again, on the edge of something bad.

Something extreme.

Kett didn't know how to answer her question, so he just drove, passing the sprawling hospital and then the equally immense university before taking a left. If it hadn't been obvious that summer was here before, then it was now. The street was mobbed with students, most of them already drunk even though it wasn't quite six. They paraded towards campus like they were heading to a music festival, the girls in skirts so short they would have been better served as belts, half of the guys shirtless and everyone plastered with glitter. Kett counted more than one open bottle being passed between them, as well as a couple of joints, but there was no time to stop.

"Did you go to uni, sir?" Savage asked.

"It was so long ago I can barely remember," Kett said. "But yeah, I did. You went too, right?"

"Criminology, down in Suffolk."

"Did you go out like this?" Kett asked, swerving the car as a young man toppled into the street.

"Nah," Savage said. "Kept my nose in the books."

But there was a smile on her face that made Kett think that wasn't entirely true.

"Wish I had a book to put my nose in right now," he said, still trying to breathe through his mouth to avoid the unspeakable stench.

There was a shallow hill ahead, topped with a sea of blue lights. Two IRVs sat on the side of the road, one more down a side street next to an ambulance. Kett spotted Clare's Mercedes parked behind them. The house they were surrounding was detached, and it boasted an enormous garden that stretched halfway down the hill. A *Let By* sign was almost lost behind the neatly clipped hedge. Kett bumped them onto a spare patch of kerb, then got out, taking a welcome breath of fresh air.

"It's an old police house," Savage said as she joined him, keeping a respectful distance. "You can tell by the number of driveways."

"Student house now, by the look of it," Kett replied. He glanced behind him to see Porter's Mondeo approaching. The window was down, and through it Porter shrugged dramatically.

"Where am I supposed to park?" he said.

"Up the street," Kett replied. "Then walk back. It's not exactly a bloody marathon, Pete."

"Sir," Porter grumbled, driving off.

Savage opened the gate and let Kett through first. The forensic crew was already there, a young man on his knees as he dusted the front door for prints. There was no sign of blood, and no sign of forced entry. Kett waited for the technician to notice him.

"Sorry, sir," the man said, shuffling back. "You're fine to go in."

"Gloves and booties?" Kett asked.

"Not for this one."

Kett ducked through the door into the house's cool interior, seeing two more forensic technicians in the narrow hallway, including Cara Hay. She nodded to him and he nodded back.

"Not seeing a lot of clues here," Kett said, looking one way to a closed door that had to be the kitchen, then turning the other way to see a living room. "What's this all about?"

Cara opened her mouth to answer but was cut off by a shout from the kitchen.

"Kett? That you?"

The door opened and Colin Clare appeared, glowering like an angry bulldog. In the months since Toltham Lodge, the Superintendent had made an apparent effort to keep his ear hair trimmed, but for some reason he'd let his nose hair grow back out. And it had grown with a vengeance, halfway to becoming a weird little moustache. Kett found it difficult to look at anything else.

"What's going on, sir?" he said.

Clare waved them on, opening the door so they could edge past him.

"Tossing hell, what's that smell?" he barked as Savage entered the kitchen. "Christ, it's like somebody ate a bucket of shit and then threw up over their clothes."

"Uh, that would be me," said Savage, her eyes on the floor. "Sorry, sir. It was all the pigs."

"Right," said Clare. "Well good job my sense of smell isn't as good as it used to be."

Kett looked at the nose hairs again, suddenly jealous. Clare rubbed his stomach. He looked a little greyer and sweatier than usual.

"Last tossing thing I need at the moment," he said.

"You not feeling too good, sir?" Savage asked.

"It's a bug," he replied.

Kett turned to Savage, mouthing the word '*cake.*'

"I'm here," came a shout from outside. "Hold up."

Porter rushed through the door, everybody shuffling to one side so that there was room for him.

"Sorry, nowhere to bloody park. Ended up halfway up the street."

"So?" snapped Clare. "What's wrong with your legs, you lazy sod?"

"Uh..." said Porter, looking down as if there might actually be something wrong with him.

"Enough," Clare said, turning to the kitchen. "Let me tell you why you're here. Or better still, see if you can work it out."

The kitchen was big enough to house a small breakfast bar and Kett saw that it was littered with bottles. Dirty dishes were piled high in the sink and food wrappers sat on pretty much every surface, as well as a large cardboard box, its flaps open.

Past the bar was a small table, the chairs moved against the far wall. Something small sat on the floor in a hail of polystyrene packing chips, something Kett couldn't make sense of. There was a puddle of liquid around it, but it was too dark under the table for him to work out if it was blood.

"What is that?" Kett asked, nodding to the object.

"That, Detective, is a foot."

"A *what*?" said Savage, gently leaning past Kett.

"Not a *what*, Savage. A foot. Severed at the ankle and wrapped in cling film."

Kett actually felt the cold current flow through him, an army of goosebumps rising on his arms. He turned and met Savage's eye, her expression of shock mirroring his own.

"It was delivered to this house just over an hour ago, in that box," said Clare, pointing at the cardboard container on the worktop. "The label is handwritten. A name, Douglas Ireland, and this address. House number, street, postcode. Douglas is one of four students who live here. He's currently across the road with a couple of other people who were present when the foot was delivered. They were having some kind of end-of-term party."

"Some party," Porter said.

Kett had a quick look at the box, seeing the neat, distinctive text, all in capitals. There was no postage, and no packing slips anywhere to be seen. He took a couple of photographs of it on his phone.

"This wasn't sent by a courier," Kett said. "There would be shipping labels."

"Some local delivery companies wouldn't bother with them," Savage said. "Where was it left, sir? Surely if they were having a party, then somebody saw who delivered it."

"Apparently not," said Clare. "One of the students who lives here, uh..."

He looked at the ceiling and scratched his sweat-drenched forehead.

"Merletta, I think. Merletta Shaw. She claims she saw the parcel first, brought it in here to open it."

"Even though it was addressed to somebody else?" asked Savage.

"Quite. She opened it along with another woman, Jane Hewitt. They found the foot and called the police immediately."

"How did it end up on the floor?" Kett asked.

"My guess is that if you pull a severed human foot out of a cardboard box, you don't hang onto it for long," said Clare.

"You're sure it's real?" asked Porter. "I mean, it looks like a prop or something."

"Oh, thank toss for that," Clare said, feigning relief. "It's made of plastic, it's a Halloween prop. Why the hell didn't I think of that? You're a buffoon, Porter. Hay analysed it when she arrived. Hay?"

Cara Hay appeared in the doorway and stopped there, no room for her to walk inside.

"This obtuse tossmonkey wants to know if the foot is real," Clare said.

"It's real," she answered, her Trinidadian accent as strong as ever. "I..."

She sniffed.

"What's that awful smell? It's like somebody has been moisturising themselves with manure."

Savage put her hand up, muttering an apology.

"That is awful, Kate," Hay said. "I do not know what to say to you. I didn't unwrap the foot, but I did take a sample. It's the left foot of what appears to be an adult male, size ten. Whoever cut it off used something sharp and heavy. It seems to be a single blow."

"Holy shit," said Porter. "An axe?"

"Franklin will have more answers, but yes, that's my guess. An axe, or a machete. Maybe a spade."

Kett breathed slowly, the kitchen seeming to tighten around him like he, too, was being shrink-wrapped.

"Any idea who it belonged to?" he asked.

"There's nobody with a missing foot in any of the hospitals in the region," said Clare. "But we're still checking further afield. The foot has a tattoo across the heel, a piece of script. '*Never give up.*' Mean anything?"

"Sports?" said Porter with a shrug. "Sounds like a runner's mantra to me."

"Or it could be a mental health thing," said Savage. "However bad it gets, never give up."

"Good thinking," said Clare. "We'll need to run it past tattoo shops. We're checking DNA, obviously. It's surprisingly hard to identify a foot, but we will."

"Do you know if they were alive or dead when it was cut off?" Savage asked.

"Not yet," said Hay. "But there's a lot of blood inside the shrink wrap."

"What does Douglas have to say about it all?" Kett asked. "It was addressed to him, after all."

"He's not said much," Clare replied. "He's drunk and high, and he's also an arrogant prick. Won't talk to any of us unless he has a lawyer present."

"He does know he's not actually under arrest, right?" said Savage.

"Maybe it means he should be," said Porter.

"I'll need one of you to go and chat to him. I'd like you to interview Merletta, too, and Jane. They're over at Jane's house, across the street."

"Yes, sir," said Kett. He looked at Clare and saw the question there, and when nobody else asked it, he did so himself. "You're sure there was no note? It's not that long since the Sweet Briar Rose case. We all remember the severed fingers. You think this is connected?"

"I think sick people just like cutting off body parts," Clare replied, belching into his hand. He looked like he was close to throwing up, the sweat actually rolling off his head. "Maybe it is related, maybe it isn't. It's your tossing job to find out, Kett. Now hop to it."

There was a moment of silence while everybody studied the foot that lay beneath the table.

"You know what this reminds me of, right?" said Porter. "Sherlock Holmes."

"Sherlock Holmes?" said Clare, grimacing. "What the toss has he got to do with anything?"

"It's what he used to say, isn't it?" Porter said. "The case—"

"Don't do it, Pete," said Kett, reading the DI's mind. "Don't go there."

"Go where?" Clare said, his eyeballs bulging.

Porter grinned.

"The case is afoot!"

A wooden spoon lobbed from Clare's side of the kitchen chased them all from the room.

CHAPTER THREE

"Here we go again," said Savage as they walked out of the front door. "You okay, sir? You look a little peaky."

Kett nodded, grateful for the warm, late-afternoon air. There was no sign of the students now, just the swelling chorus of the birds from the garden. It was idyllic here, so much so that the idea of a severed foot being delivered seemed impossible.

And yet, here they were.

"Just thinking about what the Boss was saying," he said. "The Sweet Briar Rose case. Those poor women who lost their fingers. Hollenbeck was behind that. Bert was one of theirs."

"You think this is them, too?" Savage said, frowning. "I don't know. That whole case was because of some horrible accident. Bert only targeted those women because they found out what he was up to. And it was a... it was a joke to him, right? The fingers didn't mean anything, they were just him passing time, turning it into a game. Bert's dead, and this feels different."

"Maybe," said Kett. "Hopefully."

He pushed himself away from the house into a wild front garden that smelled of lavender and rosemary. There was a fig tree growing up the side of the shed, the fruit a while away from being ripe. Wasps still busied themselves there, dozens of them. There was probably a nest, he thought. He walked up the short path, opening the gate. There was a row of terraced houses opposite, but no sign of any police there.

"Which one is it?"

"Number four, sir," Savage replied, taking the lead.

"Wait up," Porter called out as he ran after them, his shoes click-clacking on the pavement like he was late for a tap class. "Three interviews, three of us. Bagsy not the douchebag."

"I second that bagsy," said Savage. Kett scowled at them both.

"This isn't a bloody democracy," he said.

As they approached the house the front door opened, a uniformed constable standing there. She smiled at them, nodding to Kett.

"Sirs, they're all inside," she said.

"Thanks," said Kett.

Ahead was the kitchen, which was deserted. The living room was to the right, another PC standing by the window. Kett walked through and saw the two women sitting on the sofa. One looked like she was trying to curl herself into oblivion, her legs pulled up to her chest, her arms wrapped around her knees. Her face was hidden but Kett could hear her sobs clearly enough. The other woman lay across almost the entire length of the sofa, drowning in an enormous dressing gown and lost in her phone. This one looked up, her expression unreadable.

"Sir," said the PC, tapping his fingers to his helmet in a salute. "This is Jane Hewitt and Marletta Shaw."

"It's *Merletta,*" said the woman who was lying down.

"Hi," said Kett, advancing into the room. "You're Merletta?"

"No, I'm Jane. *She's* Merletta."

The other woman peeked over the top of her knees, her eyes bloodshot. She said something that Kett didn't catch, then tried again a little louder.

"Merle. It's just Merle."

"Okay," said Kett. "I know it's been a traumatic day, and I know you might not want to talk about what's happened, but it's really important we speak to you now. Okay?"

Merletta nodded, but Jane turned her attention back to her phone. The way her thumb flicked up again and again made it pretty clear she was browsing something on social media. She didn't look fazed at all, but her eyes were puffy, and the longer Kett watched, the more he noticed the tremor in the hand that held the phone. He turned to the PC.

"There's another one, isn't there? A man?"

The constable rolled his eyes.

"You'll find him in the upstairs bathroom. He locked himself in."

"He locked himself in, as in he's using it?"

"Well, he might be, but if that's the case, then you should probably call a doctor because that's one serious case of constipation. He's been in there since we got here."

"Isn't that going on an hour?" said Savage.

"Oh, I've been checking on him," said the constable, sensing her worry. "He's not up to anything. He's just incredibly rude."

"I'll go see if he's ready to come out," said Savage.

"Thanks," said Kett. "Let's just start here then, shall we? Do you girls need a tea or anything?"

They both shook their heads, which was something of a mercy as Porter looked like he was about to head towards the kitchen. Kett perched on the arm of the chair across from the sofa, taking in the room. It was a typical student place, film posters Blu-Tacked at wonky angles on all four walls and empty cups everywhere. Dozens of DVDs had been released from their cases and scattered across the worn carpet. They captured the sun from the small window, glinting like shards of a broken mirror and leaving imprints in Kett's vision. The air smelled of fabric conditioner from the clothes that hung over the radiator.

"This is your place, right Jane?" he asked. Jane didn't answer, her eyes still locked on her phone. "Jane? This will be a whole lot easier and quicker if you put that away."

She sighed dramatically, dropping the phone onto the sofa beside her. Then she angled her body around so that she was sitting next to Merletta. Beneath the dressing gown, she looked like she was dressed for a party, her silver dress sparkling like a disco ball.

"What was the question?" she said in a tone of voice that instantly worked its way beneath Kett's skin.

"You live here?"

"Yeah."

"And you were over the road at Douglas' place?"

"Yeah."

"Because..."

"Because he was having a party," she said, as if Kett had asked the stupidest question in the world. She was acting like a child, but she definitely seemed older than the other woman.

"You're a student at the university?" he persisted.

"Yeah."

This time Kett didn't reply, the seconds ticking by like an unexploded bomb until Jane lifted her hands in disgust and carried on.

"International Affairs and Politics," she said. "I'm in my second year."

"You started late? How old are you?"

Jane took offence to this, looking to Merletta for support only to see that the other woman had disappeared behind her knees again.

"Twenty-five," she said. "Took me a while to work out which course I wanted to do. Why does any of this matter?"

"It doesn't," said Kett. "I'm just breaking the ice. So Douglas was having a party. What time did you arrive?"

"Like, just before five?" she said like she was asking another question. "I went with Mari, she lives up the road. We headed over just before five because Duggie wanted to start early and he had some..."

She looked nervously at Kett, then at Porter, who was still standing in the door.

"I don't care about the drugs," said Kett, reading her mind. "You were smoking some marijuana."

"Yeah, some *ma-ri-juw-arna*," she echoed sarcastically. "Is that what you call it when you're over forty? Weed, whatever. We've all finished our exams, Duggie wanted to celebrate, we—"

"I haven't," came a quiet voice from the other girl. She looked up, sniffing. Her hair was dark and it was stuck fast to the tears on her cheeks.

"You haven't finished?" Kett said.

"Haven't even started. First one is tomorrow. I don't know how I'm going to..."

"You're obviously not going to have to do it now," said Jane. "Like, they'll write you a note or something."

"Will you?" Merletta said, her eyes widening.

"Uh, sure," said Kett. "I'm pretty sure these count as extenuating circumstances."

There was almost a smile on Merletta's face, but it was only there for a second.

"You were the one who found the package?" Kett asked. Merletta nodded. "What time was this?"

"Five," she said.

"Exactly?"

"No, roughly. I've got a clock in my room, but it's a little wrong. It's fast. So..." She let her knees drop as she worked it out. "Yeah, I think it was probably four-forty, something like that."

"You were downstairs?"

"Yeah," she said, then she shook her head. "Actually, no, I was back upstairs when it arrived. I went down to talk to Duggie because the music was so loud and I didn't want people in the house. I was trying to revise. But he... he didn't listen."

"He's an arsehole," said Jane. "I mean, he's fun, and he throws good parties, but he's not a nice man."

"He said I was a loser," Merletta went on. "Told me to go back to my room. But before I could get there, somebody delivered the box."

"You saw them?"

"I..." She shook her head again. "I saw someone. The front door was open and I looked out as I was walking upstairs. I remember, because I was really angry that more people were coming to Duggie's stupid party. But I didn't really look. I just saw, you know, the *shape* of them."

"Can you be any more specific than that?" Porter asked. "Shape is a little vague."

Merletta shrugged.

"All I remember is that they were blue," she said.

"Blue?" asked Kett. "Their face or their clothes."

"It's not going to be their face, is it?" Jane said.

"No, their clothes," added Merletta. "I saw blue trousers and a blue shirt or jumper."

"Dark blue, light blue, different shades?"

"Um, same shade, I think. Like that."

She pointed to the cushion that was on Kett's chair, a light denim blue.

"Could you tell if it was a man or a woman?" he asked.

"No, sorry. I didn't look at them, I just kind of saw them out of the corner of my eye. Does that make sense? I was upset, I was crying, everything was kind of blurry. Sorry."

"Don't be," said Kett. "It all helps. So you heard them delivering the parcel, then?"

"Yeah," she said. "They knocked. It was loud, because I heard it over the music. When I went downstairs again, the box was right there."

"They knocked," said Kett. "Even though the door was open?"

"Yeah. Twice."

Kett looked at Porter, catching his eye.

"And nobody else was in the hall when you went back downstairs?" Kett went on when he'd turned back to her. "Nobody was looking out of the kitchen door, or the living room?"

"I don't think so."

"You didn't hear the knock?" Kett asked Jane.

"You kidding? Duggie had the music so loud I think my

eardrums burst. A bomb could have gone off and I wouldn't have noticed."

"You were in the living room?"

"I think so," Jane said. "I mean, I started in the kitchen, made a drink with Mari, walked through to the living room. Merle here was in there, all upset and everything. She almost knocked into me as she ran out. I gave it a few minutes and went after her. Felt bad. Duggie's a twat."

"So everyone keeps telling me," said Kett. "Okay, so by the time you were back in the kitchen, Jane, Merle had the package."

"Right," said both girls together.

"It was addressed to Douglas, his name was on the label. What made you pick it up, Merle?"

She squirmed in her seat, her hands laced together in her lap.

"You're not in any trouble," Kett said. "I promise. I just want to know what happened."

"I thought it was mine, to start with," she said so quietly that Kett had to lean towards her. "I ordered a book, for my exam. Hadn't come. I thought that was it, and then when I saw his name I... I was so mad at him I just thought I'd open it. You know? To get even."

"You were going to steal it?"

"No," she said. "Bin it, maybe. I don't know. I hadn't thought that far ahead."

"So you took it into the kitchen, put it on the counter."

"On the breakfast bar, yeah. And I started to open it, and then I stopped because Jane came in."

"You wanted to check on her?" Kett asked the other woman. Jane shrugged.

"Yeah, I guess. And I wanted a drink. Saw the parcel and was curious. We thought..."

He saw the girl's face fall, heard the noise she was making deep in her throat. The room fell silent, quiet enough that Kett could hear Clare's voice from across the street.

"When did you first realise what it was?" Kett asked.

Nobody wanted to answer. Nobody even wanted to look at him.

"Merle?"

"I didn't know," she said. "It was wrapped up like, like a gift. Tissue paper and this little sticker. It had these packing things, peanuts I think they're called. We couldn't figure out what it was because it was... it was all red and..."

She gagged, one hand slapping her lips.

"I got it out of the box," said Jane. "I thought it was some kind of sex thing."

"A *sex* thing?" said Kett.

"Like a... you know?" Jane made a circle with the fingers of one hand and slipped another finger through the middle of it. "Toy."

"A sex toy? Shaped like a foot?"

"You can get them," said Porter. Kett craned over his shoulder.

"Get what?"

"Foot dildos, for men."

"*What*?"

Porter shrugged.

"They're not called dildos, obviously. They're like the opposite of dildos."

"How do you even know this, Pete?" Kett said, and when Porter opened his mouth, Kett raised a hand to stop him. "Actually, don't answer that. What happened next?"

"I just pulled the fucking thing out of the box," said Jane, looking at her hands as if they had betrayed her. "Just like that. Pulled it out and then I realised what it was. It... It felt too light, you know? It felt too light to be real, but I knew it was real because..."

"Because what?" Kett prompted.

"Because it was still warm."

Kett's breath caught in his throat, the room seeming to tilt.

"Warm?" he said. "You're sure?"

"I'm really fucking sure," she said, still staring at her fingers. "I am never going to forget that feeling. It felt like a real person, you know? Like it was still attached."

"Pete," Kett said, standing up. "Get that info to Clare, right now."

"Yes, sir," said Porter, bounding out of the room.

"Think hard. Was there a note? Was there anything else in the box that might have fallen out, or you might have put in your pocket without thinking? Maybe not on paper, maybe a thumb drive, or a business card, or a... I don't know. Anything at all."

No answer, but he was pretty sure they weren't hiding anything. They both looked hollow, as if every truth had been pulled right out of them.

"Do either of you have any idea whose foot that is?" he said. "The tattoo. *Never give up*. Have you ever seen it before, or do you know anyone who uses that phrase a lot?"

Both women shook their heads.

"And can you think of any reason somebody would do this? Why would somebody send a foot to Douglas?"

Jane shrugged.

"Because he's an arsehole?"

"I know plenty of arseholes," said Kett. "But I've never wanted to send one a severed body part. This is something else. You both know Doug, so think. What does it mean?"

"He's on the football team," said Merletta, almost a whisper. "Foot? Football? Sorry, that's really stupid."

"No, it helps," Kett said. "Anything else?"

Nothing.

"Right," he said. "Thank you, both of you. Stay where we can find you, okay? And if you think of anything else, call us."

He eased himself up, his knees cracking. He'd made it halfway to the door before Jane called out to him.

"Why does it matter so much?" she asked. "Why does it matter that the foot was warm?"

Kett swallowed, running a hand over his dry lips.

"Because it means whoever's foot that was, they might still be alive."

CHAPTER FOUR

"You can't stay in there forever, you know."

Savage stood on the small landing, one ear against the bathroom door as she tried to figure out what was going on inside. She'd been up here for five minutes and the only response she'd had so far was a firm, "Fuck off, I'm busy!" This had been followed by a number of thumps and squeaks, plus a lot of running water. At first, she'd worried that the man inside the bathroom might have been trying to hurt himself, but for the last minute or so he'd been singing the theme tune to the Wombles with some gusto, so she was pretty sure he was okay.

She knocked again.

"Douglas, I mean it, you're going to have to come out sooner or later."

"Why?" said Douglas. "I'm in the right place for a siege, aren't I?"

"It's hardly a siege," Savage said. "We just want to talk with you."

"Not until my solicitor is here," he said. "He's on his way."

"From where?"

"Derby, it's my mother's solicitor. He's one of the best. He'll fuck you right up."

"Right," said Savage, checking her watch. "Well, that's going to be hours. You may as well talk to me until he gets here."

"Talk to yourself," Douglas replied. "You pig."

"Wow," said Savage. "You're a charmer."

"No," came the muffled reply. "Not because you're a police officer, because you smell like a pig."

Savage sniffed gently, testing the air.

"Oh. Right. Fair enough."

She looked down the stairs, hearing Kett's voice from the living room.

"Look, Douglas. Is it Douglas? Doug?"

"Mr Ireland," came the reply.

"Dougie? Duggie?"

"Fine, it's Duggie. Just go away."

"Duggie. You're not under any suspicion, okay? We just want to speak with you."

"You can—"

"But from my experience, do you know what sort of people ask to speak with their solicitors when they're not a suspect?"

Duggie didn't reply. Savage could hear him turning the tap on and off, on and off, over and over.

"Have a guess," she prompted.

"Guilty people, obviously," he replied after a moment. "But I'm innocent."

"I don't doubt it. You'd have to be pretty stupid to cut off somebody's foot, then mail it to yourself using your own name. You're not stupid, right?"

"No, of course I'm not," he said. "I'm about to get a First Class Honours Degree in Law."

"Good for you. Did you cover any case studies involving missing body parts?"

"No, I'm going into *corporate* law, obviously. That's where the money is."

"So show us you're on the right side of the law," Savage said, trying to keep a lid on her temper. "Tell us why somebody would send you a foot."

The tap sprayed then fell quiet, sprayed then fell quiet.

"It's probably not even real," Duggie said. "You ever think of that?"

"It's real."

"Then I have no idea," he said. "Some sicko, probably fancies me or something. This is his way of showing his affection."

"You think it's a man?"

"Uh, no," said Duggie. "I mean, how do I know? Men fancy me too; it's not just women."

Savage shook her head.

"It takes some ego to convince yourself somebody would send you a severed foot because they fancy you," she said. "Not to mention a slightly twisted understanding of human nature."

"Well, why do *you* think it happened?" he said. "If you're so smart, you tell me."

"Has anyone ever threatened you, Duggie?" she said. "Before this, has anyone ever threatened to hurt you?"

Silence, and when Duggie spoke again, he was right behind the door.

"You think that's what this is?" he said. "A threat?"

"Do you?"

"I mean, most people like me. But yeah, some guys are jealous, I'm not going to lie."

"Anyone in particular?" Savage asked.

Duggie sniffed.

"You know, ugly blokes, the ones who can't get the birds. Mainly them."

"Right," said Savage. She heard Kett's voice from outside the living room, then the creak of him coming up the stairs. She smiled at him. "Duggie, I'm going to have to warn you. You know the whole good cop bad cop thing? I'm the good cop, and if you have anything you need to tell us, then I'd do it now, because the next guy isn't going to ask so nicely."

"Fuck you," Duggie replied. "Nothing you can do to me."

"Everything okay?" Kett asked as he reached the landing.

"I'm using my inalienable human right to privacy," Duggie announced from behind the door. "And I can stay in here for as long as I like."

"You can," said Kett. "But only if there's a lock on the door. I can't see one."

"What do you mean?" Duggie said. "Of course there's a lock on the door, it's a—"

Kett lifted his boot and slammed it into the door, just beneath the handle. There may as well not have been a lock there, because the door opened with zero resistance.

Inside the bathroom, Duggie fell back and landed on the toilet, his mouth a perfect O of shock. He was wearing pink shorts and a yellow polo shirt, and he looked like he'd just fallen out of an Abercrombie and Fitch catalogue.

"Whoops," said Kett. "Sorry, I could have sworn there was no lock. My mistake."

"You..." stuttered Duggie, still sitting. "You can't do that! I was using the bathroom, I was going to the toilet, you..."

"I may be wrong, Duggie, but if you're going to take a shit it's best not to have your shorts pulled up. Shall we?"

"I did warn you," Savage said, trying not to smile. "He's the bad cop."

"My solicitor is on the way," Duggie said. "You can just wait—"

"No," said Kett. "We can't. The foot that got delivered to your house an hour ago was still warm, which means the person it came from might not be dead yet. We need to move fast. If you want to wait for your solicitor, then that's fine, but if that's your decision we *will* be arresting you. If you want to keep this chat civil, just answer some questions. Clear?"

Duggie licked his lips, eyeballing Kett with undiluted hatred. Savage could see that he wasn't a man who was used to losing.

"Whatever," he said. "But make it quick. I've got stuff I need to do."

"Yeah," said Kett, looking around the bathroom. "I can tell you're a busy guy. First, why would somebody send you a severed foot?"

Duggie gaped, squirming on his throne.

"I just said to *her*, it's probably somebody jealous of me."

"Why would anyone be jealous of you?"

"Because," Duggie started, then he gestured to himself as if the answer was right there.

"Trust me," said Savage. "You're not all that. What else can you think of?"

"Some people don't like me, okay?" he said. "I can't help that."

"No," said Kett. "Think harder. Has anyone made a threat against you? Is anyone blackmailing you? Is there any reason they would target you specifically? Something you've done, something you've said?"

There was a thump from below and Savage looked to see Porter coming through the front door. He charged up the stairs like a bull.

"You'll never guess who his mum is," he said when he'd got to the top. "Frances Ireland. Ex-MP, current mouthpiece for angry right-wing folk. Over in Derbyshire."

"Frances Ireland," Kett said, speaking to Duggie. "Your mum made any enemies lately?"

"Only the woke brigade," he replied. "The usual lot. Libtards."

"Watch your mouth," said Kett, pointing a finger at the man that made him snap his jaw shut with an audible *clack*. He turned to Porter."Call her, find out."

"Clare's already on it," the DI replied.

"What about anybody local?" Kett asked Duggie. "Anyone you've pissed off lately? Other than me, that is."

Duggie shrugged. The arrogance was slowly seeping out of him as the reality of the situation dawned. He still looked like an arsehole, Savage thought, but he didn't look particularly guilty.

"Look, Duggie," she said. "I think you're a victim here. Let us find whoever did this to you. If there's anything you're not saying, say it now."

Duggie sat back, staring at the ceiling.

"I don't know," he said. "I'm sorry. It feels like a joke, you know? Like a practical joke. That's the only thing I can think of. We play jokes all the time over at the club."

"Club?" asked Kett.

"Football," Savage said. "The UEA team?"

"No, we're a league team. Vikings. And yeah, we send each other stuff, embarrassing stuff, for a laugh."

"Yeah?" said Kett. "Like what?"

"Like, you know, dirty movies, blow-up sheep, I don't know. Anything to get a laugh."

He hesitated.

"What?" asked Savage.

"Like, we pushed a dead pigeon through Will's door last year, as a joke."

Kett met Savage's eye for a moment, and Duggie caught the look that passed between them.

"It's harmless, it's a joke. Maybe this was one of the lads? You're *sure* it's real, the foot?"

"We're sure. You train up at the uni, right?"

"Right."

"Any names stand out?" Savage asked.

"No. Like nobody would do this. But Spence is the one who's always doing stupid stuff. Ask him."

"Spence who?" Kett asked.

"Montgomery Spencer," Duggie said. "Posh twat. And Charles is just as bad. Charles Laird. He's the Vikings coach."

Savage filed the names away. Kett pulled a business card from his pocket and tossed it into the sink.

"You call me if you think of anything else, okay? Anything at all. And Duggie?"

Duggie looked up, utterly miserable.

"Don't leave town."

"Well where am I supposed to go?" he pleaded. "I'm not going back to that house."

"I'm sure you'll think of something."

Kett eyeballed the kid for a moment more, then squeezed past Savage and Porter, heading down the stairs. Savage waited a moment, until the young man lifted his eyes to meet hers.

"Next time, Duggie, just open the bloody door."

CHAPTER FIVE

Kett made his way back onto the street, waiting by the gate for Porter and Savage to catch up. The evening was full of the hum of low chatter as the Uniforms went door to door, but the loudest voice belonged to Superintendent Clare, who was on his phone in the front garden of the house opposite.

"What do you think, sir?" asked Savage as she walked up.

"I think all the reports were right, Douglas Ireland is a douchebag."

"But he doesn't seem stupid," Savage said, standing to one side so that Porter could escape. The DI was looking at something on his phone. "Doesn't seem like the kind of person who would mail evidence of a crime to himself."

"No, he doesn't," said Kett. "Who's his mum again? Frances Ireland? I know the name. She's on TV sometimes, isn't she?"

"I was just looking her up," said Porter. "She was an MP over a decade ago, pretty hard right. Started out a Tory then moved to UKIP, and she got booted by them after she made some comments about their immigration policy. She's a DJ now for some radio station in the Midlands. This is her."

Porter held his phone out, revealing a photograph that was too blurry to make sense of. Kett sighed, fishing his glasses from his pocket and slipping them on.

"Who invited Groucho Marx to the party?" said Porter with a grin.

"They're more Jarvis Cocker, I think," said Savage.

"Elton John?"

"Shut up, the pair of you," said Kett, taking Porter's phone. The woman on-screen looked like an older version of her son, her hair pulled back into a severe ponytail. It was a Wikipedia article and Kett scanned through the juicy bits. "Looks like she had a habit of making people angry. Has anyone got hold of her?"

"I think Clare's speaking to her now," said Porter as he took his phone back. "But she's a big target, makes sense that somebody was trying to send a message to her through her son."

"Maybe," said Kett.

He started across the road, the sun scorching his skin. By the time he'd walked through the front gate, Clare had hung up. He looked hot and bothered, and Kett wasn't sure it had anything to do with the weather.

"Like mother like son, apparently," he said. "Infuriating."

"Frances Ireland, sir?" Kett asked.

"You heard. Yes, and just as unpleasant as every newspaper would have you believe. She's not saying anything, but they've got the family solicitor on the way. Careful how you tread around her son, they're litigious."

"Sure..." Kett started, meeting Savage's eye and hoping she wouldn't mention the bathroom door. "I'll be careful.

He didn't have a lot to say for himself, but he said it might be a practical joke, somebody from the football club up at the university."

"A practical joke?" Clare echoed, almost choking. "Covering the urinal with cling film is a practical joke, cutting off somebody's foot is not."

"He told us he posted a dead bird through somebody's letterbox," Savage said. "Dead bird, dead foot."

"Worth a check," Kett said. "He named the coach specifically, Charles Laird, as well as another player, uh..."

"Montgomery Spencer," said Savage.

Clare nodded, checking his watch.

"Franklin should be here any minute. We need to know exactly when the foot was cut off. I've got PCs at every door on the street. Somebody must have seen something. Savage, while we wait, can you head up to the university? Talk to the football coach, see if he knows anything."

"Yes, sir," Savage said.

"Porter, I need you to coordinate things back at HQ. You're absolutely certain Jane Hewitt said the foot was warm?"

"She seemed fairly sure," Kett said.

"It doesn't mean the victim was still alive," Clare said. "It could have been heated up prior to delivery, might just have been a warm van or car. Pete, I need you to double-check every hospital, every morgue, and every cemetery too, just in case it's not as fresh as we think it is."

"Sir," said Porter. He turned to Savage. "I'll give you a lift, but you're riding in the back and I'm opening the windows."

They walked up the road, heading for Porter's car. Clare watched them go, then turned to Kett.

"Any alarm bells ring for you across the road?" he asked.

"No, sir. The two young women seem to be telling the truth. It's hard to fake that kind of shock. Jane's harder to read, but I didn't get the sense she was leading us on. Neither of them particularly like Douglas, especially Merletta, but my first impression is they're not responsible. Would be pretty weird for them to go to the trouble of sending a package then opening it themselves."

"Precisely," said Clare. "We'll need to interview the rest of the people at the party at some point. But our priority has to be identifying the person or persons who made the delivery."

"The label was addressed to Douglas Ireland, right?" Kett said. "At this address."

"It was," said Clare. "But I checked it against another piece of post and the postcode on the foot was wrong. It's for the next street over."

"That's weird," said Kett. "You had a look over there?"

"Sent a couple of Uniforms but there's no sign of anything. It's most likely a typo, but it's pretty careless given how much effort went into packaging the foot. It doesn't add up."

"I agree," said Kett. "It feels deliberate. It feels like they're trying to tell us something."

"But what?"

Kett didn't have an answer. He turned to the gate instead as a familiar voice rose from the road.

"There is absolutely bloody nowhere to park along here *at all.*"

Emily Franklin poked her head around the tall hedge, taking in the house, then the garden, then Kett. She was wearing a yellow summer dress with big green flowers, a rucksack and a pair of enormous pink sunglasses, and she looked far more like a student than a forensic pathologist.

"I thought students were supposed to be poor," she said. "They've all got about fifty cars. I had to park halfway to the university."

"You're young," said Clare. "You'll survive. It's inside."

"Your message was a little garbled," the young pathologist said as she walked down the path. "I blame the nose hair. There's a body in there?"

"Part of one," said Kett.

"Ooh," Franklin said, rubbing her hands together. "Which part? Actually no, I like surprises. Where?"

"Kett will show you," said Clare. "I need you to work fast, Franklin. The owner of this foot might still be alive."

"Dammit," said Franklin, pouting. "You just spoilt it."

"Go!" Clare roared.

"This way," Kett said, walking back into the house's cool interior. Cara Hay was still working inside the kitchen, scrutinising the cardboard box on the worktop. She looked up at them as they entered.

"Emily, I'm glad you're here."

"Hey, Cara," said Franklin. "I hear we've got a foot?"

"Under the table," said Kett, pointing.

"I have had a cursory look," said Hay. "Enough to know that it is real. I didn't want to move it."

Franklin dropped her bag on the floor, then joined it there, on her hands and knees.

"Well, it's definitely a foot," she said.

"Thank heavens you're here," said Kett with a little more sarcasm than he'd intended.

Franklin was too engrossed in the foot to respond, approaching it on all fours like a hungry dog. Kett thought she might even be *sniffing* it. After a few seconds she opened her rucksack and pulled out a set of gloves, a metal tray, and a small bag. She set the tray on the linoleum floor and opened the bag, then she pulled on her gloves.

"Let's have a closer look. You've got everything you need, Cara?"

"Certainly not everything I need," Hay replied, walking to Kett's side. "But everything I can get. No prints on the plastic wrap, no hair or skin. Whoever packaged it was wearing gloves."

"Cool," said Franklin. "Here we go."

She lifted the foot and dropped it onto the metal tray, then rocked back on her haunches. Reaching into her bag, she pulled out a small tape and took some quick measurements.

"Twenty-seven point nine centimetres, that's a size ten and a half, if I'm not mistaken. Above average for men, and way above average for a woman. But I think this belongs to a man."

"How can you be sure?" Kett said.

"Because his toenails are a mess," she replied. "Look at them. Absolutely no self-respect."

She looked back and raised an eyebrow.

"Joke, obvs. Although the nails *are* a mess. People assume women and men have the same feet, just scaled differently, but that's been proven wrong time and time again. The sexes differ significantly in several ways, most notably in the calf, ankle and foot shape variables. We don't have a calf here, and barely an ankle, we only have the foot. But looking at the arch, the lateral side of the foot, this first toe and..."

She turned the foot over.

"Yep, the ball here. I'd say with some certainty this is a man's foot. Ten and a half. You mind if I unwrap it?"

Kett looked at Hay, and she nodded.

"It's like Christmas!" Franklin said with genuine glee.

She picked gently at the cling film, the material coming loose with a disturbing series of squeaks and squelches. Hay stepped forward and collected it in an evidence bag, sealing it up tight. Franklin turned the foot in her hands—the severed limb so much worse now that it had been unwrapped—her tongue poking between her lips in a portrait of concentration.

"The foot was amputated at the base of the tibia, right where it meets the ankle joint. It's almost a perfectly clean cut through the joint, avoiding the main bone, but the angle is slightly off because the fibula has shattered. Posterior talofibular ligament is severed, as is the Achilles."

"Ouch," said Kett.

"No other signs of injury, although we've got two verrucas on the sole, nasty ones. Grim. Nails are a little crusty but in good health, no sign of a nutritional deficiency, no sign of low calcium or anaemia or hypothyroidism. The skin looks like it belongs to a younger person."

She turned the foot a few more times.

"Yep, I would say young, moderately healthy. A bit of a fungal infection here between the toes. Lovely."

She sat up straight, then gestured to the floor.

"Down you go, DCI Kett."

"Excuse me?" Kett said.

"Lie down, right there."

Kett looked at the floor, at the little puddles of spilled alcohol, the armies of crumbs and the trails of blood.

"On the floor?"

"Unless you can levitate, then yes," said Franklin. "Hurry up, please."

"Can it be over there?" Kett said, gesturing at the door.

"Whatever, just get your backside on the floor, please."

Kett walked to the door then lowered himself gently onto the linoleum, groaning as his muscles protested. It was cleaner back here, but it wasn't *clean*. He thought he could feel the layers of grease through his suit. He rested his head on the floor and looked up to see Franklin standing above him.

"Amputation was achieved by a single, powerful blow," she said. "DCI Kett, are you aware you're wearing odd socks?"

"I didn't think anyone would be looking at them too closely," he replied.

"That's no excuse. The blow came from above, but I don't think it came straight down. A machete maybe."

Franklin imitated a strike, using enough force for Kett to flinch.

"No, the angle is wrong," she said. "Even if the victim was raised on a table or something. Maybe an axe."

She performed the attack again, this time with two hands. Then she shook her head.

"I don't feel that this would have been powerful enough to splinter the fibula, but I might be wrong. It looks like a heavier blade, something weighted, like a... a guillotine, maybe?"

"A guillotine?" said Kett, pulling his legs up defensively. "You don't need to demonstrate that one, Emily."

"You're no fun at all," she replied, still staring at his ankle. "But that seems right, a mechanical device of some kind. There's no evidence of chopping, you know? If you're going at a bit of wood, or a joint of meat down at the butcher's, it's rare to get through in one go. There are slashes and half-marks. *Chop chop chop.* Even a hefty axe would struggle to get through a human leg with this much precision. This is so clean, and the angle is so straight that it was either a mechanical strike or somebody immensely, almost superhumanly strong."

Kett nodded, starting to get up.

"Wait a moment," said Franklin.

"Why?" he said, hesitating.

"No reason, you just look funny down there."

Kett grumbled his way back to his feet, using the breakfast bar to help him stand. Both Franklin and Hay were grinning at each other.

"Comedy gold," Kett muttered, glaring at the young pathologist. "I didn't mention this before because I wanted to wait until you'd seen it for yourself. But the woman who unpacked the foot claimed that it was still warm."

Franklin frowned, pursing her lips. She clambered back down to examine the foot again, turning it slowly in her hands like an archaeologist with a mysterious artefact.

"What kind of warm?" she asked.

"I, uh... just warm," Kett said with a shrug. "She said it felt like it was still attached to a living body."

"It's possible," Franklin said. "It takes twelve hours for a body to cool to the touch after death, but something this small will lose heat much more quickly post-amputation. I'd guess less than an hour. What was it packed in?"

"Polystyrene packing chips," said Hay. "A lot of them."

"Polystyrene is a good insulator, it may have kept the foot warm. I take it you don't know who delivered it, or what mode of transport they used?"

"Nope," said Kett, brushing crumbs from the back of his trousers.

"It's really impossible to say, then. It could have been sitting in a hot van for hours, days, and still be warm to the touch. Especially in this weather. It's hard to be sure about the time of amputation, to be honest, because the wound has been rubbed with salt."

Kett felt his stomach turn.

"Salt?" he said, his voice quiet.

"It's used as a preservative, obviously. Somebody went to great trouble to preserve the cut. When I get it back to my lab, I'll be able to tell you with a little more certainty when the event occurred, but right now, given the quality of the limb, I'd say it happened less than a day ago. There's something else you might want to consider as well."

"Yeah?"

"Yeah. Something this small could have been put in a fridge or freezer. The individual who lost this foot may have done so some time ago."

Kett swore beneath his breath. He hadn't even thought of that.

"There's one more reason I don't think we're looking at fresh goods," Franklin went on, holding the foot up. Kett saw the tattoo that ran along the outside edge, next to the cracked skin of the heel. "*Never give up*. It's an interesting choice of words, right? But good for a foot, I suppose. Never give up, keep going, keep moving."

"We wondered if he was a runner," Kett said. "I can't think why else he'd pick those words."

"Oh, I don't think he did pick them," Franklin said. "I think somebody else did. See the way the skin has reacted to the ink here, the lack of scar tissue? The tattoo is fresh, the ink is still seeping, because it was inked onto dead flesh."

"What?" said Kett. "*Dead*?"

"Yup," Franklin finished. "I can say with absolute certainty that whoever tattooed this jaunty little mantra did so either after their victim was dead, or after the foot had been cut off."

CHAPTER SIX

Kett left Franklin to bag up the foot, partly because he didn't think he could be of any more help, and partly because the small kitchen was starting to feel suffocating. The stench of vodka was as strong as paint stripper, but the stench that lay beneath it was a million times worse. Free of its cling film, and even with the salt, the foot was starting to smell like a butcher's shop. The summer heat would make short work of it, the flies already arriving.

In contrast, the evening air was warm and fresh, full of lavender and something else, something Kett didn't recognise. He took a moment to sniff the bush that was growing next to the front door, the white blossoms intoxicating.

"What are you doing, Kett?" barked Clare as he walked out from behind the shed.

"Nothing, sir," he replied, stepping back. "Just trying to get the smell of foot out of my nose."

"Jasmine," Clare said with a nod of approval.

"Franklin says—" Kett started, but Clare bustled past.

"Save it. I'm going to talk to her myself. I need you

working the doors. We need witnesses, anyone who might have seen the delivery take place. Go on, skoosh."

"*Skoosh*?" said Kett, but Clare had already disappeared.

Kett sniffed the bush again for good measure, then made his way through the gate. The street was busier now, crowds of students trying to peek past the PCs who blocked their way. A sleek grey press van was rumbling up the hill like a shark drawn by the smell of blood. Kett turned away from it, heading along the pavement. The coppers were knocking on doors further up the street, the sound muted by the warm air. He headed their way, making it halfway up the road before he heard somebody calling his name.

"DCI Kett, sir?"

A constable was standing by the front door of a long, low building that Kett had assumed was a retirement bungalow. When he checked the sign on the wall, though, almost entirely hidden by ivy, he saw that it was a community centre. Another man stood with him, this one in his late seventies and dressed in a black tracksuit and tartan slippers. What little was left of his hair was shaved almost to his scalp, and his cheeks were shot through with broken veins. His smile was warm enough, though, and he lifted a hand in welcome as Kett approached.

"Sir," said the copper. "This is Bernard Roman. He's the caretaker here."

"How do," said Roman in a strong local accent. "Busy today alright, boy."

"That it is," said Kett. He looked back the way he'd come to see that Duggie's house was perfectly visible from here. "You didn't happen to see anyone near that house this afternoon, did you? Between four forty-five and five fifteen? A car, a van, a bike or somebody on foot? Maybe carrying a large box wrapped with a pink ribbon?"

"Already told this young woman here, didn't see anything. Eyes aren't as good as they once were."

The distinctly male copper nodded in agreement.

"But Mr Roman says the centre has a CCTV system," he said.

"That is very welcome news," Kett said, scanning the front of the building and not seeing any cameras. "Facing the street?"

"No," said Roman. "Out the back. Neighbours don't like us to have cameras on this side, a breach of piracy."

"Privacy?" said Kett, and the man nodded.

"That's what I said. Piracy. But we have to have 'em out the back because kids are always hanging out there, getting up to all sorts."

"Hopefully not piracy," Kett muttered. "Mind if I have a look?"

The man smiled and nodded, walking out of the door and down the side of the building. It wasn't a big place and the passage behind it was just about wide enough for a bike shed and some bins. Roman stopped and pointed at a small, white CCTV camera mounted just beneath the guttering, pointed at the bins. There was no door into the building on this side.

"That's great," Kett said, swallowing his impatience. "But I meant could we take a look at the *footage*."

"Oh, right," the man said, clearing his throat. "That makes more sense."

He led them back, passing through the front door into a tiny lobby. A reception desk sat there and Roman lowered himself into the chair, staring at a computer monitor that looked older than he was. He clicked the mouse and then seemed to freeze, like he'd crashed.

"Mr Roman?" Kett prompted.

"Oh," said Roman, nodding. "What was it you needed to see again?"

"Do you mind if I have a look?" Kett said. "It will only take a second."

"Be my guest," said the man, gesturing at the screen. He made no attempt to get up so Kett had to squeeze in beside him, almost sitting on his lap as he reached for the mouse.

"Sorry."

He double-clicked on the security software, the ancient computer rattling beneath the desk. Mr Roman stared at him with rheumy eyes and an expression that suggested he'd already forgotten who Kett was. After what felt like forever, the screen loaded. Kett saw the back passage and the bins, and beyond them was the side road. The feed was disappointingly blurry until he remembered his glasses.

"Any good, sir?" asked the PC.

"I'm not sure," Kett replied, slipping them on. "It depends what route the courier took. Does this side road lead anywhere?"

"My nan wore glasses like that," said Roman.

"Lucky her," said Kett. "The side road, does it lead anywhere?"

"Sure," the PC replied. "Head up the hill and you can double back round to the shopping parade and the uni. Or you can cut through to the main street out of the city."

Kett clicked the rewind button, watching the footage slowly scroll back. He saw himself there for a blink of an eye, then Bernard Roman tottering down the path to put something in the bin. Kett watched the timestamp, backing up to 4:30 and letting it play.

"Hello," said Roman, smiling up at Kett.

"Hi," Kett replied, not taking his eyes off the screen.

Cars appeared for a fraction of a second, slowing down

as they approached the junction, their drivers barely more than smudges behind the window. A small red one drove into view at 4:31, then two silver estates, then a large blue van at 4:39. Kett paused it, seeing the Amazon Prime logo on the side. The footage just wasn't good enough to make any sense of the driver, and it didn't help that the passenger window was closed and drenched in sunlight. The camera was at the wrong angle for the registration plate, too. Still, Kett snapped a photo of the van on his phone before pressing play again.

"I like your suit," said Roman, running a hand up Kett's sleeve. "It's lovely and soft. My nan had one just like it."

"Thanks," said Kett.

On-screen, a group of students walked past, dressed for a night out. They were carrying open bottles, and even though the camera had no sound Kett swore he could hear them laughing and shouting. Another pedestrian appeared at 4:41, and here Kett paused the feed again because he was wearing a large rucksack. It was a man, dressed in jeans and a long, black coat, his dark hair short and greying. The bag was draped over one shoulder, but it looked too baggy to have held a box like the one they'd found in Duggie's kitchen. Kett let the footage roll, seeing the man disappear behind the wall of the community centre. Then he rewound it and let it play again.

"Four forty-one," he said.

"No," Roman answered, checking his watch. "It's quarter to ten."

Kett checked his own watch to see that it was coming up for half-past seven, but he didn't say anything. He took a photo of the man, then tapped the screen with his finger.

"You know this man?" he asked. "Is he local?"

"Yes," came the reply.

"Yes, to which part?"

Roman stared at the screen, the artificial light making his skin look yellow.

"Is he?" he asked after a moment.

"Is he what?" Kett asked.

"He is!" Roman said with a heartfelt laugh.

Kett took his glasses off for a moment, pinching the bridge of his nose and wondering if he'd stumbled into some kind of alternative universe. He slid them on and let the camera roll again. Less than a minute later, a white van rolled into sight. It was small, a Caddy or a Berlingo, maybe even a Transit, and the passenger window was down. Kett pressed pause as the van drew level with the camera, seeing a silhouette in the driver's seat.

He frowned. The driver's head looked too big.

Way too big.

It was almost perfectly circular, too. There were only three seconds of footage where the van was in sight before it rolled out of frame, and Kett rewound it, watching again. There was definitely something weird about the driver's head.

"Hey," he said to the PC. "What do you make of this?"

The constable rounded the desk, although there was no room for him at all. Kett shuffled to the side, and the PC squeezed in between him and the old caretaker.

"Hello," said Roman. "This is nice."

The PC smiled politely at the man, then ducked towards the screen. Kett pressed play and the van drove by.

"His head's massive," said the PC. "Like he's wearing a mask, maybe?"

"Or a helmet," said Kett, nodding. "A motorbike helmet."

"Yeah, could be," said the PC, extracting himself with no small amount of difficulty from the tiny space.

Kett snapped a couple of photos and let the video play on. Two more cars passed by, but by this time the stamp read 5:17 and if Merletta was to be believed, the foot had already been delivered. He scrubbed through until 5:50 just to make sure the van didn't return, then clicked stop.

"Mr Roman, do you mind if we take this with us?" he asked. "It will be extremely helpful."

"Yes," the man replied, shaking his head. "Hmm?"

"Thank you." Kett gave the old man's shoulder a gentle squeeze as he walked back around the desk. "Constable, can you get this back to HQ? Get it in front of digital forensics as a matter of urgency. It was a good find, well done."

"Yes, sir," the man replied.

Kett pushed through the door onto the road, nodding to a couple of constables who were walking back towards Duggie's house.

"Anything?" he asked.

"Nothing yet, sir," said one. "Not many doorbell cams around this way. Landlords don't seem to bother with them for student houses."

"Keep looking."

He paused for a moment, looking down the hill to see what looked like a huge strip of marshland edged with trees. The presence of the countryside just a street or so away took him by surprise, as if it had marched into the city without warning. He turned his back on it, retracing his steps towards Duggie's house.

If the driver of the van they'd seen in the community centre footage was their courier, then he'd have driven this way. The road was narrow and trees grew all the way down the verges, their crooked branches like a giant's fingers.

Every available space was taken up either by parked cars or by wheelie bins, and other than his Volvo and an IRV they weren't police cars. It meant that the driver would either have pulled onto the verge or left their van on the road while they dropped off the box.

It also meant that after they'd made the delivery, they would almost certainly have kept going. It would have been too hard to turn around here, especially if they were in a hurry. It wasn't a busy road, but it wasn't quiet either.

Kett walked past Duggie's house, seeing Clare in the garden shouting at his phone. He put his head down before the Super could see him, keeping it down to try to avoid the attention of the reporters who had pushed to the front of the crowd, much to the irritation of the growing assortment of students.

"DCI Kett!" shouted one, and then they were all calling him. "What's going on? Can you give us any information?"

He cupped his hand to his ear like he couldn't hear them, circumnavigating the scrum and breaking into a jog just in case anybody decided to follow him. It was too hot and he was too knackered for it to last, though, and after thirty seconds or so he stopped, clawing in lungfuls of hot air. He was standing at a crossroads halfway down the street, one side heading up towards the West Earlham shopping plaza, the other leading down another shallow hill lined with brick cottages.

A white van was parked right at the end of it.

Kett looked back up the hill, wondering if he should call for one of the PCs. But all it would have done was bring the entire pack of reporters down on his head. He walked alone into the welcome shade of the trees that guarded the narrow lane. The houses watched him with dark eyes, no sign of life here at all.

With every step, the van grew closer. It was parked with its nose pointing down the hill, and from here Kett could see the Renault logo. It was a 55 plate Kangoo, and it had seen some real wear and tear over the years, orange rust on the wheel arches and a large dent in the rear panel. There was another dent in the right-side wall, he saw as he reached it, and the driver's mirror had been completely torn away, the wires exposed.

He found the photo he'd taken of the van from the security feed, trying to compare it to this one. It was impossible to tell, the image was just too blurry. He put a hand on the Kangoo's bonnet, feeling for residual heat and not finding any. Then he slid his hand into the cuff of his jacket and tugged the door handle. It was locked. Cupping a hand to the glass of the driver's window, he tried to make sense of the dark interior.

"Oi, mate, is that yours?"

Kett stood straight so quickly a dagger of pain worked its way into his lower back. He turned to see a man standing in the open door of the last cottage on the lane, half-hidden in shadow. He was in his fifties and he was wearing a red flannel shirt and brown corduroys, his wiry hair almost reaching his shoulders. In one hand he held an open notepad, in the other a yellow pencil.

"Excuse me?" said Kett.

"The van. You're not allowed to park down here without a permit."

"It's not yours, then?" Kett asked.

"Why would I be asking if it was yours, if it was mine?" he replied, stepping out into the light. "If it's yours, you need to move it."

"Why would I be asking if it was *yours,* if it was *mine*?" Kett echoed.

The man took another step across his small garden, his pencil held out like a weapon. He'd got as far as his gate before Kett pulled out his warrant card, stopping him in his tracks.

"Police," he said.

"Oh, sorry mate. I didn't know."

"How long has the van been here?" Kett asked, putting the warrant card away.

"That thing, not long," said the man, shuffling his feet awkwardly in the gravel path. "But I get cars down here all the time, you know? Bloody students think they own this city, think they can leave their shit wherever they like. I make a note of them all and send it to the council, but they—"

"How long?" Kett said, more firmly now.

"Couple of hours, maybe?" the man replied with a shrug. "I was only asking because some idiot parked his bike here as well. I couldn't get out of my drive."

Kett checked the empty drive, and the man followed his line of sight.

"Don't have a car no more, but that's not the point. Couldn't get out of my drive if I *wanted* to."

"A motorbike?" Kett said.

"Yeah, parked right there for days."

"How many days?"

"Four," said the man. "Turned up on Saturday and just sat there. No permit or nothing. You know, I always thought I could be a policeman, I'm a stickler for the details, and for the—"

"When did it leave?"

"No idea," the man said, a little irritated to be cut off. "I was mowing the lawn out back. Came out and the bike was gone and *that* bloody thing had taken its place."

Kett glanced down the road to see that it narrowed into a dirt track a dozen yards ahead, the entrance gated. There was no way a car could get through there, but a motorbike would fit easily.

"What's down that way?" he asked.

"River, and there's a trail that goes all the way up to the university. Get students down here all the time causing a ruckus, leaving their bloody beer bottles in my garden. And worse, if you can believe it. Four decades I've lived here and that UEA lot get worse every year. Bloody animals."

Kett looked at the van again. It was a long shot, and they were *never* this lucky, but maybe this time would be different. He pulled out his phone and called Clare.

"Speak," the Super demanded when the call connected. "And make it quick, I'm about to descend onto the toilet."

"Uh, right, sir. I'm not sure, but I may have found our delivery vehicle. Head down the hill, first road on the right."

"Are you tossing me off?" Clare said.

"Uh..."

"Wait there."

The line went dead and Kett turned his attention back to the man.

"I don't suppose you got the make and model of that motorbike, did you?"

At this, the man held up his notebook and grinned.

CHAPTER SEVEN

"It's... really not... that bad..." said Porter as he drove them up the road, and Savage might have believed him if he hadn't been holding his nose with his free hand.

It *was* bad, the smell of pig manure seeming to get worse rather than better, but there wasn't a lot she could do about it right now. The university was one street over from Duggie's house, and Porter was already driving his Mondeo down the long, straight access road. To the left were the sports centre and swimming pool. To the right was Earlham Park, literally hundreds of students sitting on the grass or playing with footballs and Frisbees, the entire scene drenched in golden sunlight. There wasn't a single cloud in the vast, blue evening sky.

"It's a hard life, eh?" Porter said. He let go of his nose for a second, took a deep breath, then immediately replaced it. "Oh God, Savage, it's like Godzilla has taken a dump in the back of my car."

"Just let me off here, sir," Savage said.

Porter stamped on the brakes so hard the car skidded. A bus honked its horn behind them as it fought to stop in time.

"I would offer to come with you..." he said, then shrugged apologetically.

Savage threw him her middle finger as she climbed out of the car.

"I can still smell it!" Porter called out as he drove away.

Savage turned her attention to the Sportspark building, thinking that this would be as good a place as any to look for the football team. It was quiet inside, the reception desk abandoned and the café behind it all but empty. There was a small shop, Savage saw, and she made her way to it, picking up a pair of jogging trousers and a University of East Anglia hoodie. By the time she'd made her way back over to the desk, a young woman had appeared from the office. She was barely out of her teens, and the badge on her polo shirt read: *Patricia.* She flashed Savage a tired smile.

"Hey."

"Hey," Savage echoed. "Just these, please."

"They're cheaper over in the union," said Patricia. "Like, a *lot* cheaper."

"It's fine."

Savage looked out through the main doors at the park beyond. There were so many people it could have been a music festival.

"Busy out there."

"Yeah, it's silly season," said Patricia, scanning the hoodie and then the trousers. She sniffed the air. "God, sorry. I have *no* idea what that smell is. Must be the drains or something."

"Must be," Savage said, taking a step back.

"Everyone's finished their exams," Patricia went on. "Goes a bit mental here afterwards."

The young woman had to stifle a yawn with the back of her hand.

"Take it you were out partying last night, too?" Savage said.

"Just a little. Only at the LCR."

She yawned again, then laughed.

"Sorry. That'll be forty-two, please."

Savage tapped her card on the reader.

"Hey, you don't know where the UEA football team hangs out, do you?"

"Official club or the Vikings?"

"Vikings, I think."

There was no mistaking the look of disgust that creased Patricia's face.

"You're in the right place, although if I were you, I'd leave them well alone."

"Why?" Savage asked as she took the receipt and stuffed it into her pocket. Patricia glanced back then leaned over the desk.

"Just trust me, they're not nice people. And I'm only being diplomatic because I'm at work. Let me guess, they've asked you to come try out for the women's team? What year are you? First? They always go after the first years, get them to try out behind closed doors, if you know what I mean. They don't even have any say over the women's team. They just make all the girls run around while they take photos and stuff."

"Seriously?" Savage said. "How are they allowed to get away with that?"

Patricia shrugged like it was the easiest question in the world to answer.

"Because they're men."

Savage nodded, collecting her clothes.

"Don't say I said anything," Patricia whispered, checking over her shoulder again. "Mr Laird, he kind of runs a lot of stuff around here. He has a habit of making things disappear."

"Wait, what?" said Savage. "People?"

Patricia smiled, but it didn't last long.

"No, not people. Like, allegations and accusations and stuff. The uni's investigated him and that stupid club a hundred times and nothing ever sticks. Go figure."

"Thanks," said Savage. "And don't worry, this isn't for try-outs."

She pulled out her warrant card and the girl's eyes almost shot right out of her head.

"I'm just looking into a couple of things," she said as she tucked the warrant card away. "Do you know a student called Douglas Ireland?"

"Rings a bell," said Patricia. "He one of the Vikings?"

"Yeah."

"I'd know him if I saw him. He in trouble?"

"No," Savage said. "He mentioned that the team plays practical jokes on each other. Have you ever seen anything like that?"

The office door opened again and an older woman stepped out. Patricia's mouth snapped shut and she shook her head.

"The pitches are out the back," she said quietly. "Good luck. Give them hell."

"I will."

Savage made her way to the toilets, locking herself in a cubical and taking off her suit and her trousers. She balled them up as tight as she could before pulling on the jogging trousers and the hoodie. Her boots looked a little ridiculous with the new ensemble, but there wasn't much she could do about them.

She washed her hands before making her way back into

the lobby, following the signs down a wide central corridor until she found the door to the football pitches. There were too many of them to count, but only one was occupied—a dozen or so younger blokes in casual training gear taking turns kicking a football into an unmanned goal.

An older man stood at the back of the pitch, talking on his phone.

Savage dumped her old clothes under a tree before walking over. The men caught sight of her long before she reached the gate, welcoming her with wide grins and dark eyes. A couple of catcalls whistled their way up into the blue sky, followed by the thud and rattle of the football being kicked against the fence. One of the men bounded over and opened the gate for her, but she hesitated. She had the feeling she was walking into a tank full of sharks.

"You lost?" the guy at the gate said.

"No," Savage replied. She took a breath and walked onto the pitch. "I'm looking for Charles Laird."

More wolf whistles and whoops, the men laughing. The guy at the far end of the pitch glanced back, but his eyes were shadowed beneath the brim of his claret-coloured cap. He turned away again, continuing his conversation.

"Aw, you sure about that?" said another of the young men, approaching her with a swagger, his bottom lip extended in a dramatic pout. "You sure you're not here to see me?"

"What the fuck would she want with you?" said a third man. "It's *balls* she's after."

The man who'd approached her made an exaggerated show of looking Savage up and down, and she literally felt her skin crawl. He was in his very early twenties, his arms and legs boasting cords of muscle. He wore the exact same look of smug, predatory superiority that Duggie had back in the house, and even though Savage had dealt with far worse men than him, even though she'd been a copper for years now, she still felt intimidated by it.

"Hot day for all those clothes," he continued. "You want some help taking them off?"

"Spence, pack it in," came a voice from the back of the group. Savage peered past Spence's broad shoulders to see another of the men closer to the goal. He was standing on one foot and balancing the ball on the other. He was as fit as the other men, but his face held none of their contempt.

"Just a bit of fun, *William*," Spence said. "She's not going to say anything, are you?"

"That depends," Savage said, resisting the urge to pull out her warrant card.

"On what?" said Spence, taking a few steps towards her, close enough to touch. He was well over six foot and Savage had to crane her neck back to meet his eye.

"On whether or not you continue to be an arsehole."

Spence's smile dropped, and for a second Savage saw the anger underneath it, the entitlement, and the unmistakable promise of violence.

"Spencer, back off," came a louder voice with a strong cockney accent. "Now."

The young man eyeballed Savage for a moment longer, just to make his point, then he turned and strolled away like he didn't have a care in the world. The older guy had finished his call and was jogging over. He was as fit as the footballers, and something in his bearing made Savage think he was probably ex-military. He stopped some distance away, taking off his West Ham cap to reveal a widow's peak. The face beneath it belonged to a man in his late thirties, maybe early forties, clean-shaven and angular. His eyes were sharp, almost hawk-like, and they didn't even blink as he took her in.

"Can I help you?" he asked.

"You're Charles Laird?"

He nodded curtly.

"This is the Vikings football team?"

He looked back, taking a moment to think about his answer.

"Why do you want to know?"

The footballers stood quietly while their coach spoke, not so much as a whisper between them. There was respect there, Savage thought.

Or fear.

"Duggie isn't with you this evening?" she said, and Laird's face split into a sharp smile.

"Of course," he said with apparent disgust. "You're one of his. I know he'll have told you this already, and I'm sorry you weren't able to keep it inside that tiny head of yours, but girlfriends aren't allowed at training. Too much of a distraction."

A swell of anger rose in Savage and she took a step closer to the older man.

"That's one seriously unpleasant attitude you have," she said. "Is this how you treat all the women in your life?"

"Tell her to go away, sir," said one of the footballers, but Laird lifted a hand and silence fell once again. He studied her, seemed to see the way she was standing, the way her jaw was set.

"You're police," he said, catching Savage off guard. She pulled her warrant card out of her tracksuit trousers and held it up. Laird's smile reappeared. "Can always tell a copper. Served myself. RMP."

"Military police," Savage said as she returned the warrant card to her pocket. "Then you should know better."

"I call it as I see it," Laird said, tugging the cap back onto his head. "These guys are a pack of wolves. Show them a pretty thing and they lose their heads. Why are you here?"

"I'm here because of Duggie," she said. "I take it you all know him?"

"And nobody is the better for it," said Laird. "He's the reason there's bugger all people here tonight, him and his damned parties. What's he done now?"

"We're not sure," Savage said. "Maybe nothing. We're investigating an incident that took place inside his house this afternoon."

Laird rolled his eyes like he'd heard it all before.

"Where he sticks his diseased little cock is none of my concern," he said. "I don't know anything about it."

Savage's breath caught in her throat as she understood what the man was saying—and what he *wasn't.*

"No," she managed after a moment. "Nothing like that. Something was delivered to his house, a package addressed to Douglas Ireland."

"What was in it?" said the man with the ball.

"A foot," Savage replied. "A human foot."

She wasn't sure what the reaction would be to that, but she couldn't have guessed that half the men on the pitch would burst out laughing.

"Fucking hell," Spence called out, slapping another player on the back. "A *foot*?"

Savage's anger simmered just beneath the surface. Laird was angry too, because he shot a look back that stopped the laughter dead.

"Is this a joke?" he said to Savage.

"That's what I want to know. When I spoke to Duggie,

he told me you all enjoy playing pranks. You like to send each other things."

Laird's face tightened.

"He said that, did he?"

"So I guess the reason I'm here is to ask if any of you are responsible for it?"

Savage looked at each of the men in turn, and none of them met her eye.

"I don't need to tell you how serious this is," she said. "But talk to me now and you will save yourself a lot of grief."

"Nobody here killed somebody and cut off their foot," Laird said.

"I'm not saying they did," Savage replied. "There are other places you can find a body. A hospital, for one. A graveyard. Maybe even a university. What happened with the dead pigeon?"

Spence laughed again, like a braying donkey. The man with the ball lifted his head to the sky.

"They're talking about your *bird*, William," Spence said to him. "Crying shame, that. Was the only bit of action he got all year."

"Spencer, shut your mouth," said Laird in a tone of voice that made the other man clamp up immediately. "The pigeon incident was regrettable. A stupid stunt. That idiot over there, and the idiot you just referred to, picked up a dead pigeon from the street and posted it through William's letterbox. Disgusting, yes. A crime, no. We had words, they assured me it wouldn't happen again."

"And the other pranks? Sex toys? Pornographic magazines?"

A ripple of laughter crossed the pitch, and Laird smirked.

"It's a bit of fun. They're just trying to embarrass each other. One lad will send a magazine to another lad in the middle of class or have something rude delivered to their parents. Tiresome. But again, it's not a crime."

"It's a bit of a coincidence, don't you think?" Savage said. "I'd call that an escalating pattern of behaviour."

Laird shrugged.

"What can I say? If it's one of these muttonheads, their DNA will be all over it. When that happens, come back to me. Until then, we've got work to do. So if you don't mind..."

"I mind," Savage said. "What else can you tell me about Duggie? Is there anyone in particular who might have a grudge against him? Anyone who has threatened him?"

Laird checked his watch and groaned a sigh of impatience.

"He's a mouthy prick," he said. "But he's talented. Annoyingly so. He's probably the best midfielder I've seen at the university. He's halfway to getting signed already—not the big leagues, of course, he's not that good, but there was a Second Division team scouting here the other day and he's the one who got their attention."

Another ripple of noise, but there was no laughter now. If anything, the other footballers looked pissed off.

"So, is there anyone who might have a grudge against him?" Laird continued, shrugging. "Sure. Half the lads here probably hate his guts. I don't like him much myself. But you know the thing about men like Duggie, Officer?"

Savage waited, the smile back on Laird's face.

"They're blessed. It doesn't matter what they do in life, they'll win. They have it all. Money, family, connections. When they fuck up, they don't have to own it because somebody else will rescue them, but they'll take that as another victory because that's what they do. He's the proverbial

Golden Child. Nothing will ever go wrong for him. So if I were you, I'd forget all about this, because whatever it is, Duggie or his mum will make it blow away."

"Nobody's untouchable, Mr Laird," said Savage.

"If you believe that, you're an idiot," he replied. "Now look, we've got a match to prepare for and half a team missing, so please, do me a favour."

He gestured at the gate behind her with both hands, like he wanted to scoop her up and throw her out. Savage stood firm.

"Two things," she said. "One: if any of you think of anything else, if any of you know anything, then you contact the police urgently. Somebody's life may depend on it."

Nobody replied, everyone staring at her in a way that made her feel like she'd jumped into an icy lake.

"And two, know this: we are watching you. Next time there's even a whiff of inappropriate behaviour towards a female student then it won't be the university investigating, it will be us. Is that clear? I will come down on you like a hammer."

This, at least, knocked the smile from Laird's face.

Savage yanked open the heavy gate, counting ten steps before she heard the thump of the football being kicked, the scuff of feet on AstroTurf. She looked back as she approached the tree where she'd left her suit, seeing the young footballers throwing themselves back into their training.

Only Laird was still watching her, his eyes dark beneath his cap, his mouth a thin, grim line.

CHAPTER EIGHT

Porter pulled the Mondeo into an empty space and wound all four windows up. He sniffed, gagged, then wound them all immediately back down again and left them that way. He jogged across the car park into the ugly bulk of HQ, making his way straight to the Major Investigation Team's open-plan office. It was busier than it had been that morning as word of the severed foot had spread, detectives sitting at desks and talking on their phones. The hum of their chatter was strangely reassuring. As much as he detested the crime, he hated the quiet more.

He threw his jacket on the back of his chair, walking to Dunst's desk. The grizzled DI was looking at something on his screen, his chair rocked back on two feet. He had a pencil in his mouth and he was going at it like a beaver with a log.

"What's the latest?" Porter asked, perching on the edge of the desk.

"They found out who did it," Dunst replied without taking the pencil out of his mouth.

"What?" Porter said, not sure whether to be relieved or disappointed. "Who?"

"The mother, if you can believe it," Dunst said.

"The mother? Seriously?"

"Yeah." Dunst took the pencil out of his mouth and jammed the wet end unceremoniously into his ear, using it to scratch an itch. "She was drunk, apparently."

"But why?" Porter asked. "Why on earth would she do it?"

"Come on," Dunst said. "We've all been there. We get drunk, we slip up, do something stupid."

Porter didn't have the words to reply.

"I've done it myself," Dunst went on, putting the pencil back between his lips and holding it like it was a cigarette.

"You've cut off a human foot and left it on somebody's doorstep?"

Dunst looked at Porter like he was mad.

"No, I've forgotten to lock the front door," he said.

"Wait, which case are you talking about? The foot?"

"The *pigs*," Dunst said. "Farmer's mother was on the lash. She fed the pigs and forgot to lock the gate, which is why they all barrelled down onto the A47."

"Right," said Porter. "I was asking if there were any updates on the severed foot."

"Spalding's on that," Dunst said. "I just need to close this one and I'll be there to help."

"I can't wait," muttered Porter.

Spalding's desk was empty, but when Porter checked the Incident Room he found her there. She was tacking various photographs to the wall, that obscene foot right in the middle of it all.

"Alison," Porter said as he entered. "What do you make of this one, then?"

"It's gross," she replied without looking back. "I hate feet."

"All feet, or just the ones that aren't attached to a leg anymore?"

"All of them," she said, pinning a photograph of Douglas Ireland above the severed limb. "They think they found the delivery van, did you hear?"

"No," said Porter.

"White Renault Kangoo, left around the corner from the house. Kett just called. Ran the plates. It was last registered to a bakery in Norwich, but it's been SORN for the last three years. I spoke to the owners and they claim it was stolen."

"And they didn't report it?"

"They didn't notice. Apparently it's been sitting in a garage, nobody checks on it. They're... hang on."

She pinned up the last photo, this one of the van in question, then turned to face Porter.

"They're clean, the bakery people. No priors, no links at all to Douglas Ireland or anyone else in the house, and alibis for today as well. Forensics are on their way to check the garage, it's out near Postwick."

"So whoever delivered the foot used a stolen van to make the drop," Porter said. "That suggests a lot of planning."

"More than you'd think," said Spalding. "Kett said there was a motorbike parked on the same side road as the van. It was there for four days. Witness claims the bike disappeared as soon as the van arrived."

"Seriously?" said Porter.

Spalding tapped her finger on one of the photographs she'd just mounted.

"What do you make of this?"

He walked over, seeing a grainy snapshot of a CCTV feed. There was a white van in the middle of the picture, the passenger window down and the driver visible. They were just a silhouette, but there was definitely something wrong with their head.

"Is that *hair*?" Porter asked.

"Look closer, sir."

He did, and he saw it.

"It's a motorcycle helmet," he said. "Has to be."

Spalding nodded and Porter shook his head.

"We spoke to a witness, a woman who claims she saw the delivery driver right before they dropped off the package. She didn't mention a helmet. She mentioned blue clothes, maybe overalls."

"Weird," said Spalding.

"But she also said she wasn't really looking properly," Porter conceded. "It's something you'd pick up on, though, isn't it? You don't notice the colour of somebody's clothes without noticing that they're wearing a giant helmet."

Spalding shrugged.

"I get deliveries all the time, I couldn't tell you anything about any of the drivers. And I'm a copper."

A rare smile appeared on her face.

"Actually, I tell a lie. There's one guy who delivers for Amazon and he wears the tightest shorts you've ever seen in your life. I remember him."

"Not his face though, I bet," Porter said. He looked at the photograph again. "It makes sense that this is him, right? You're dropping off a human foot, there are people literally everywhere and there's an actual party taking place at the delivery address. The front door is *open*. He parks his van right outside, gets out. Nobody is going to notice the fact he's wearing a helmet once he's out of the van, because

Deliveroo folk never take their helmets off, there's no time, they just lob your food at you. He drops off the parcel, gets back in the van, drives around the corner, dumps the first vehicle and gets away on the bike."

"It's a lot of trouble to go to," Spalding said. "And a lot of premeditation."

"We've got plates for the bike?" Porter asked.

"We do, but they're fakes," she replied. "There's no such registration number."

"And that takes effort too," Porter said. "Who's working the bike?"

"I am, sir. But there's a bunch of *mispers* Clare wants us to look through, see if anyone might match the foot."

"I'll take them," Porter said. Spalding smiled.

"They're already on your desk."

Porter made his way back through to the bullpen, crashing into his chair and picking up the sheaf of documents that had been left on his desk. He flicked through them and two dozen people stared back, kids, teenagers, adults and old folk alike. All of them missing, all of them lost. He threw the pile back down and used his desk phone to call Kett's number.

"Sir," he said when the line connected. "Anything new?"

"Nothing yet," Kett replied, the sound of an engine almost drowning out his words. "We're on our way back. You at HQ?"

"I've got the *mispers,* just wanted to check what size the foot was."

"Franklin said it's almost certainly a male foot, size ten and a half. Not old, she said. She can't give us a time of death because it was preserved."

Porter's stomach clenched like a fist.

"That's... horrific," he said. "I'll go through the files now, pull out any matches. How long will you be? You want me to put the kettle on?"

Kett hung up.

"Bloody charming," said Porter. He dropped the phone back into its cradle and picked up the files again, pulling out the children first and moving them to one side. He did the same with the women, which made up the vast bulk of the collection. It broke his heart, seeing them there, and he had to turn the pile upside down in the end so that the guilt wouldn't gnaw him down to the bone.

There were five files left, all men. Two were elderly and recent—both within the last week—and both were labelled as having dementia. It wasn't uncommon for elderly folk to wander out of their homes and go for an adventure, but Franklin had said the foot belonged to a younger person, so Porter dropped these files on top of the others.

The next one was a man who'd been missing for some weeks, a homeless guy who'd been in and out of prison for most of his life. Porter knew him, he'd spoken with him a dozen times over the years, mainly looking for information. Nice fella, always polite. The last time anyone had seen him he was running out of a Tesco Metro with an armful of Cathedral Cheddar, which meant he was probably just lying low.

Beneath him was a younger man. Benedict Gilbert. Porter wasn't familiar with his case, and he scanned through the information. He was twenty-six, worked as a trainee gas engineer, and lived with his parents in a house just outside of Aylsham. No trouble with the police, but a slight history of depression. He'd gone missing—and here Porter felt the hairs on the back of his neck rise—last Tuesday evening after a five-a-side football match in the city.

"Shit," he said. He looked down at the information sheet to see that it had been DCI Pearson who had interviewed the parents, then he turned to Dunst's desk. "Keith, is Kate Pearson in?"

"Not today," Dunst said. "Why?"

Porter didn't answer, looking at the final *misper* report on his desk to see a man in his late thirties. Seamus Stafford. A rig worker who'd gone missing three weeks ago after a bender in Yarmouth. The photo didn't seem to match the record, the man there boasting white hair and a matching beard that made him look like an angry Santa. But the eyes were young, Porter saw. He'd just had a hard life.

Porter dropped Stafford's file and returned to Gilbert's, everything in his gut telling him that this was the lead to follow. There was a number there for the young man's parents and he called it, counting thirteen rings before the call died. There was no voicemail, so he dropped the receiver and picked up the file, pushing himself out of his chair. He was almost at the door before it swung open, Superintendent Clare marching through with all the urgency of a man whose arse was on fire.

"Porter!" he roared, before practically running past and disappearing into the corridor that led to the kitchen and the toilets. Kett followed a moment later, cleaning his glasses on his tie.

"What's up with him, sir?" Porter asked.

"Well, he claims it's a stomach bug, but we all know it's that bloody cake," Kett replied. "Please tell me you didn't eat any."

"I wouldn't have touched that thing if I hadn't eaten for a month," said Porter, grimacing.

Kett nodded, looking at the file in Porter's hand.

"Lead?"

"Maybe. Maybe not. Missing person. He's twenty-six and he disappeared last week after a football match."

"That's something," Kett said. "Who were they playing? If you tell me it was Douglas Ireland's team, I'll kiss you."

"Not sure if that's an incentive or not," said Porter. "But no, Duggie plays with a full squad, this guy was five-a-side. Still, it's a weird coincidence. Can't get through to his folks on the phone, so thought I'd take a ride over there. Wanna come?"

Kett nodded.

"Wouldn't miss it."

CHAPTER NINE

The roads out of the city were mobbed as people fought to get home from Norfolk's sunniest spots, and it was almost nine by the time Porter's Mondeo turned off the roundabout into the little town of Aylsham. Nobody had told the sun, though, which hung fierce and forgetful over the rooftops. Kett looked up from Benedict Gilbert's file, nodding to the first road on the right.

"It's down there."

Porter drove past an enormous water tower that looked more like a medieval castle, waited for a bus to rumble past, then swung right. A dozen hunched bungalows squatted proudly behind their manicured gardens, the flowers almost too bright to be real. It looked almost like something from the *Wizard of Oz*. Porter stopped halfway up the road, the tyres kissing the kerb as he slowed to a halt. He switched off the engine, the world so quiet Kett felt like he was on a plane, his ears about to pop.

"When was the last time anyone spoke to the parents?" he asked.

"Pearson was leading the case," said Porter. "She'll have been speaking to them every day, knowing her."

"Tread lightly," Kett said as he climbed out of the car. "They're going to be in a bad way."

Even speaking the words made it feel like a cold blade was sliding into his heart. For a second, he was right back there on the day that Billie had been taken, and on every day afterwards. Five months of not knowing, five months of fearing the worst.

Five months of hell.

"I wasn't planning on marching in like a one-man band," Porter said. "I always tread lightly."

The DI took the lead, crunching his way over a gravel drive and knocking on the door. This bungalow was well-maintained, just like the others on the street, but there were weeds springing through the gravel, and the hedge needed a trim. There was a pile of mail wedged in the letterbox and both front windows were blinded with heavy curtains.

This was a house where everything had stopped.

"Maybe they're not in," said Porter, knocking again. "Mr and Mrs Gilbert, it's the police. We just need a moment of your time."

Still nothing. Kett looked up and down the street, seeing the shadows behind the neighbours' net curtains, the half-open front doors. He walked to the side of the bungalow and saw a low gate that opened into a neat and tidy square of back garden. There were two more windows here, the curtains so thick they might have been made from stone. It looked more like a mausoleum than a house. He reached for the gate, pausing when he heard the sound of the front door being unlocked. By the time he'd walked back, it was open, a goblinesque face peeking through the gap.

"Thank you for answering," said Porter. "My name is

DI Pete Porter, and this is DCI Robert Kett. Before I start, I just want to say we don't have any more concrete information about your son. Not yet. We're just following some leads."

The face at the door didn't reply. It belonged to a short, skinny woman, her skin doughy, her eyes red raw like she hadn't stopped crying for a week. Most of her grey hair was pulled into a ponytail, but the rest hung in loose strands over her cheeks. She was wearing a knitted jumper covered in reindeer, and pink velour trousers that had been tied tight around her scrawny waist. Her feet were bare.

"Mrs Gilbert?" Kett said, approaching cautiously, afraid of startling her. "Sorry it's so late. May we come in for a moment?"

The woman peered up at him, blinking rapidly. It seemed to take an age before she turned and teetered into the darkness of the house.

"Was that a yes or a no?" Porter asked.

Kett used the tips of his fingers to gently nudge the door open, seeing a short corridor that led into a shadowy kitchen. There were no lights on at all in the house, just a trickle of sun from the front door, and Kett ran his hand down the woodchip wallpaper until he found a switch. It didn't make much of a difference, the bulb an older one that didn't want to wake up.

"Through here," came a soft, gruff voice that Kett was pretty sure didn't belong to the woman who'd let them in.

Kett followed it through the bungalow's shadowy interior, looking into a room that was so dark it was like the world ended right there on the threshold, then into another, which was somehow even darker. A third door was shut tight. The bulb blinked and struggled, the strobing yellow light making him feel like he was inside a carnival ride.

He passed a sideboard littered with framed photographs, most of which showed Benedict Gilbert in various stages of his life—a boy in a school uniform, a teenager in a football kit, a young man standing next to a van. It took him a moment to work out why the photographs made him uneasy.

Benedict wasn't smiling in a single one of them, his eyes dark, his mouth a straight, serious line.

Figurines filled the rest of the space, an assortment of china animals whose too-wide grins and bulging eyes followed Kett to the final door.

The kitchen was as dark as the rest of the house, a single lamp in the far corner throwing a soft, red light over a small dining table. The woman from the door was lowering herself gracelessly into one of two chairs. The other was occupied by a man, although Kett couldn't make much sense of him because the light was right behind his head, turning his face into a block of shadow. He gripped a cane in one hand, arthritic knuckles flexing. Kett could hear the sound of him swallowing over and over. It was the sound somebody made when they were drowning, and Kett had to take a deep breath of stale air to remind himself he could breathe.

"Is it okay for me to switch on the light?" he asked. "I'm having trouble seeing you."

"I'd rather you didn't," said the man, his voice made of dust. "My eyes. I have a sensitivity to bright light."

"Mr Gilbert?" Kett said, taking a step closer. "Mrs Gilbert?"

"Have you found him?" the man asked. "We've still not heard from him."

He made the same swallowing noise, a series of desperate gulps.

"I'm sorry, no," Kett said. "I know my colleague DCI Pearson has been keeping you updated. We're just here to follow a couple of leads. I apologise if we ask you some questions you've already answered, but we just want to make sure we have everything right."

"You do," said the man, and Kett wasn't sure if it was a question or an agreement. His eyes were adjusting to the dark, the man's face slowly emerging from the gloom—big cheeks and hollow pits where his eyes should have been. Mrs Gilbert sat opposite, but even so, the light seemed reluctant to find her. She had her hands pulled up to her chest, clamped together like she was praying.

"You last saw your son on Tuesday, is that right? Eight days ago?"

"In the morning," said Mr Gilbert. "Before work."

"He lived here?"

"He's always lived here. He has his room."

"And he's twenty-six?"

"He never wanted to leave us," Mr Gilbert said. "We're his family."

Something in the way he said it, the wet sound of that last word, made Kett shudder. He didn't know what it was about this place that was getting under his skin.

"He left for work," Kett said. "Then what?"

"Then we waited here for him, like we always do," Mr Gilbert said. "We waited for him to come home."

"And he was supposed to come home right after work?"

Mr Gilbert nodded, and his wife made a soft sound in her throat—not quite a word. The man nodded, tapping his cane softly on the floor.

"That's right, he had football," Mr Gilbert said.

"You remember what time?"

"Seven."

"Kick off or final whistle?" Porter asked.

Mr Gilbert swallowed.

"Kick off. He plays in the city, a place called Goals. He sometimes goes out for drinks after but we don't approve. Most of the time he comes right home. We look after our boy."

"He didn't go for drinks," Porter said. "It's in the notes. He showered at the club and there's CCTV footage of him getting in his car and driving off, alone. He makes it as far as the Holt Road roundabout, then we lose him."

"You know all this," Mr Gilbert said, tapping his cane on the floor again. "Why are you here?"

"Do you know if your son knew a man called Douglas Ireland?" said Kett.

Mr Gilbert shook his head. Mrs Gilbert stared at Kett like she didn't even understand the question.

"Okay, one more thing, if you don't mind. Can I ask what size shoe Benedict wore?"

"What does that have to do with anything?" Mr Gilbert asked.

"We're just ruling a few things out," Kett said. "No need to worry."

The man humphed and swallowed, his hand flexing on the handle of his cane. After a moment, he looked at his wife.

"He was an eleven," she said. "I always said he had big..."

And her voice trailed away as her husband clacked the cane on the floor again.

"You won't find him here," he said, coughing wetly. "Go and do your job."

"Thank you," said Kett, more than happy to make an exit. "You've been extremely helpful. We'll be in touch."

He turned to go, Porter standing to one side to let him out of the kitchen. Back in the corridor, Kett glanced into the first room. His eyes had adjusted to the dark and he saw a master bedroom there, a neatly made bed and a chest of drawers that was teeming with more china figurines. The door opposite was shut, and when Kett tried the handle he discovered it was locked.

"Benedict's room," Porter said, pointing to the top of the door. Kett had to squint to make out the phantom letters of his name there, just memories where the grain of the wood had been covered. He tried the door again, seeing the keyhole—as big as the one in the front door.

"That's a little weird, don't you think?" he said.

"It's the only door that has one," Porter replied, looking around.

Kett scanned the corridor, searching the top of the sideboard. A large, silver key sat in the outstretched hands of a porcelain cat, like it was being given as an offering. He looked back towards the kitchen to check that the Gilberts weren't on their way out, then took the key and gently inserted it into the lock. It turned easily, like it had been recently oiled.

"Watch my back," Kett whispered.

He pushed the handle down and the door opened inwards. This room, like the others, was unbearably dark, and when Kett clicked the switch on the wall nothing happened. He fired up the torch on his phone, sweeping it from right to left and seeing a single bed, bare walls, a small, open wardrobe. Two pairs of shoes sat beneath the bed, but that was the only sign that anyone used the room.

And there was certainly nobody in it.

"Heads up," Porter said, and Kett heard the clack of Mr Gilbert's cane.

He closed the door quietly, turning the key as gently as he could before dropping it into the cat's waiting hands. Porter was already opening the front door, a wave of evening light pouring in from outside. Mr Gilbert had reached the door and the daylight seemed to strike him as if he was a vampire, his free hand held up to his face.

"Careful," he said, retreating into the shadows.

"Sorry," Kett replied. "We're just leaving."

Porter had already bolted but Kett hesitated, wrestling the wad of mail from the letterbox and holding it up.

"I'll just bring these in," he said. "Best not to leave things in the door, people will think nobody's home."

Mr Gilbert waved his words away like he was under attack, sliding back into the shadows of the kitchen. Kett straightened the post, ready to drop the letters into a gap between the ornaments on the sideboard.

Something stopped him, a flash of red amongst the white envelopes. It was a postcard, he saw, A5 in size—a black spider sitting on a red background.

He turned it over, seeing that the back of the postcard was the same shade of red. Written there in black ink was Benedict Gilbert's name, followed by his address. Beneath that was a single line of carefully written text.

Thank you.

Kett walked into the light, checking the faint postmark on the stamp.

"Came today," he said, holding it up for Porter to see.

"What is it?" he replied.

"No idea. But does anything look familiar to you?"

Porter shook his head, then frowned.

"Wait, the handwriting. Right? It's similar to the writing we found on Duggie's package."

Kett sighed, hoping he'd been wrong. But there was no

denying it—the same square shapes, the same distinctive sharp angles.

"Shit," Kett said. "Bag?"

Porter patted his pockets, pulling a crinkled evidence bag out and opening it up. Kett dropped the postcard into it, then dropped the rest of the post onto the mat.

"You want to ask them about it?" Porter said.

"Not yet," he replied. "Let's be sure."

He stared into the darkness of the corridor, into the deeper darkness of the kitchen.

He couldn't be sure if somebody was looking back.

"We'll be in touch," he said, then he closed the door behind him like he was sealing a tomb.

CHAPTER TEN

Kett was still feeling uneasy an hour later when he walked into HQ, the chill of the Gilbert house clinging to him like a dead man's skin. It was past ten now but the day was hanging on by a thread. Dust particles busied themselves in the quiet shafts of light that cut through the high windows, looking like they were imitating the frantic movements of the people who worked below.

"I'll round everyone up," Porter said. "Meet you in the IR."

Kett nodded, stifling a yawn with the back of his hand. He made his way to the Incident Room, hearing the Superintendent's voice from half a corridor away. When he pushed through the door he saw Clare pacing back and forth at the front of the room, his skin as grey and damp as a Cornish pasty that had been left in the sink for a week. Savage sat two rows back dressed in what looked like gym clothes. PC Aaron Duke sat right behind her, so huge that his knees were touching the underside of the desk. He looked like a yeti who'd found himself in a primary school classroom.

"And that," said Clare, finishing a point with some gusto. "Is mathematical proof that my cake is not responsible for the spate of illnesses that have plagued HQ."

"Why do I feel like I've missed the best part of this story?" Kett asked.

Clare glowered at him.

"You would have heard it if you and Porter hadn't tossed off with each other," Clare said.

"We really didn't—"

"Oh, you're all in here," Porter said, peering around the door.

"Where did you expect us to be, Detective?" Clare snapped back. "In France? Up a chimney? In your grandmother's boudoir?"

"Uh..."

"Sit down, Porter. I am tired, and my arsehole feels like Niagara Falls during the rainy season."

A low groan rippled across the room. Porter took a seat on the other side of Duke and Kett sat behind them.

"While you two were gallivanting around doing who knows what, we've been working. Savage, fill them in."

"Hi, sirs," Savage said, craning back in her seat. "So Duggie's football team is as bad as we've heard. A couple of them are even worse than Duggie, if you can believe it. The coach isn't much better. Charles Laird, ex-military police. I got a weird vibe from him, I can't quite explain it. It's like..."

She chewed on it for a moment, her brow creased.

"It's like he was a father figure to them. But not a decent one. More like a cult leader or something. He didn't seem to have a problem at all with their behaviour, with the way they treated me or women in general. When I told him something had happened to Duggie, he seemed to think Duggie might have assaulted somebody, and he said it in a way that makes me think it's happened before and he couldn't have cared less. I don't know, there's a pretty horrible vibe there, and they admitted to posting a dead pigeon through somebody's letterbox. But is this them? I'm not sure. There's something missing, it doesn't quite fit."

"And while you two were pussyfooting around the countryside, we got a hit on the motorbike," Clare said. "The plates are fake but the witness knew enough to describe it, and he's since confirmed it. The bike is a Ducati Scrambler. Blue and white livery, which means it's brand new. This year. They're not common, and they're certainly not cheap. The good news is no Scramblers have been reported as stolen, which means there's a chance it belongs to our courier. We're checking showrooms and garages now, plus the DVLA, obviously."

"That's good," said Kett. "But the bike was there for four days. Whoever this is, they were planning this for a while."

"Exactly," said Clare. "But until we know whose foot that is, we don't know *why*."

"We might have a lead on that," said Kett.

He lifted the evidence bag containing the postcard they'd found at the Gilbert house, holding it out. Clare remained standing at the front of the room, glaring at Kett with undiluted irritation.

"I'll just walk over to you, shall I?" he barked after a few seconds had passed. "With my *Superintendent's* legs? Shall I?"

"Oh, sorry sir," said Kett.

He carried the bag to the front of the room and handed it over. He returned to his desk, earning a sympathetic look from Savage. Clare was holding the bag to his face, studying it intently.

"I know that handwriting," he said. "Where on earth did you find this?"

"Porter was checking missing persons reports," Kett said. "One stood out, a young man called Benedict Gilbert. Lives out in Aylsham. He went missing after a football match last week. He wears a size eleven shoe. He lives with his parents, and we spoke to them. It was... weird. I don't quite know how I'd describe it."

"I thought they were going to skin us alive and turn us into leather tea cosies or lampshades or something," said Porter.

"Yeah," said Kett. "It did have that vibe."

"Boil my liver and eat it," Porter added.

"They were older, in their late sixties, early seventies. The mum didn't say much, and the dad didn't seem to want to say much more. Benedict is twenty-six and he still lives at home."

"Nothing unusual there," said Clare. "My kids won't bloody leave. Everything's too expensive."

"But I'm pretty sure you don't lock your kids in their bedroom," Porter said.

"Benedict's room, or what I assume was his room, had a lock on the door," Kett went on. "I thought maybe *he* kept it locked, but the key's on a sideboard right outside, which makes me think it's only locked when somebody's inside."

He felt a sudden chill, one that made him shiver.

"Maybe Benedict was keeping someone else inside," Savage said, speaking his thoughts aloud.

"Maybe," said Kett. "But it's a built-up area, a lot of houses down that road, and there were no boards over the windows or anything. If somebody was a prisoner there then it would be easy enough to draw attention or to get out. This felt more like... I don't know. Like his parents locked him in his room."

He waved the thought away.

"I'm just guessing. It might be nothing."

Clare held up the postcard, suggesting it certainly was something.

"Right," said Kett. "The Gilberts had a bunch of mail in the letterbox, a few days' worth. That was stuck in the middle of them, postmarked yesterday and a first-class stamp, delivered this morning presumably. The handwriting does seem to be a match."

It was easy enough to tell, because somebody had pinned a photograph of the box on the board. Clare held the postcard up next to it and they all crowded around to get a better look—all except for Duke, who seemed to be having trouble extracting himself from beneath the desk. Kett put his glasses on, bracing himself.

"Somebody call security!" Porter said. "Sally Jessy Raphael has sneaked into the building!"

"Enough," Clare said. "I won't have any bullying in my workplace. It's not Kett's fault he looks like Woody Allen."

"What?" Kett spluttered.

"Remind me to give you the number for my friend Jeff," he went on. "He has a shop in the city. He can sort you out a pair of spectacles that don't make you look like a serial offender."

"*What*?"

"You do look like you should be on some sort of list," said Porter, gravely.

"Focus!" said the Superintendent. "What can you tell me?"

"The writing's exactly the same," said Porter. "The

square shape of the letters, and those weird angular peaks. It's unusual."

"It's almost deliberately unusual," Savage said, the end of the sentence morphing into a yawn.

"In what way?" asked Clare.

"I've never seen handwriting like that, have you, sir? It's like somebody has gone out of their way to make the letters blocky, but keep those angles at the top. Whoever wrote this was trying to make their writing unique."

"Right," Clare said. "My gut tells me this was the same person."

As if on cue, Clare's stomach gave a mighty rumble.

"See," he said, rubbing his tummy. "I'll get this to our handwriting guy immediately. We'll know for sure by the morning."

Kett nodded, yawning into his hand. Clare turned the postcard over to show the spider on the other side. It wasn't dissimilar to the *Spider-Man* logo, the spider's body bulbous and its legs short and crooked.

"What can anyone tell me about this?" Clare asked.

"It's a spider," said Duke, who had finally joined them.

"Give that boy a gold star," mumbled Porter.

"Actually," said Savage. "I'm not sure it is."

"It is," said Duke.

"It is," Clare echoed. "It has eight legs, count them."

"Duke can't count to six yet," Porter said. "That's in next week's lesson."

Duke growled.

"Spiders aren't the only things that have eight legs," Savage said. "It looks more like a tick to me. Spiders have an abdomen and a thorax. Ticks just have one large body section. I think it's called a scutum."

Everyone looked at her.

"What?" she said. "I like bugs."

"You're a regular encyclopaedia, Savage," said Porter.

"Thanks, sir."

"Not sure if it was a compliment," he replied with a smile. "So it's a tick, what does that mean?"

"Could be anything," said Duke. "Could be a flier for pest removal services."

"Except we know it's not," said Kett. "Because of the handwriting. That's just too much of a coincidence. It's the same person."

"And they want us to know that, right?" said Savage. "I mean, whoever delivered the foot could have printed the label with Duggie's name on it, and they could have printed an address onto this postcard. Or they could have used slightly different handwriting and we probably never would have picked up on it. They want us to know."

"And therefore the tick has a meaning," said Clare.

Kett took off his glasses so that he could pinch the bridge of his nose, another yawn working its way up from deep inside him. He clamped his teeth shut to conceal it as best he could.

"Spiders eat their prey," said Savage. "They paralyse it, wrap it up, then drain it."

"So?" said Clare.

"Ticks are simpler. They don't kill their prey, they just feed on it for a while. They take a little part of it, that's all."

"A little part of it," Kett said. "Like a foot?"

Savage shrugged.

"Big leap," Clare said. "But you're not wrong. What about this?"

He pointed to the words beneath the address.

"*Thank you*. What for?"

"A foot?" said Kett, and nobody disagreed with him.

"You think it's Gilbert's foot?"

"He wears size elevens," said Porter.

The DI yawned, and it spread to Savage and then Duke, whose mouth opened so wide and for so long somebody could have climbed inside. Clare watched them all with apparent horror.

"Have I strayed into an old people's home?" he said when Duke had finally closed his mouth. "Do you all need your cabbage soup and a lie-down? Christ!"

"Sorry sir," said Savage. "Long day."

Clare nodded, checking his watch.

"Okay," he said. "Our priority has to be finding Benedict Gilbert. I've got the night crew out looking for the bike, and we're still waiting for forensics to get back to us. I need everybody back on this tomorrow, but you may as well head off for the night, get some rest."

"Are you sure, sir?" Savage said.

"I'm sure. You need to be sharp, and right now, all I'm seeing is a bunch of slack-jawed old farts. I'll man the fort."

Clare's stomach rumbled again and he winced.

"That doesn't sound good, sir," said Kett.

"True coppers push through the pain, Detective. We have to be tough."

"There's only so much you can push through crippling diarrhoea," Kett said, earning a bug-eyed scowl. He held up his hands in surrender. "Okay, we'll go. But call us if anything happens, okay?"

"I will," Clare said. "Still plenty of cake left, by the way."

He backed towards the door with some urgency, his stomach sounding like a bad high school brass band.

"If Gilbert's our victim, with any luck this will be the

end of it," the Super said, breaking into a run and vanishing down the corridor.

"There's no way this is the end of it," Savage said, and Kett nodded.

"No way at all."

CHAPTER ELEVEN

It was finally dark by the time Kett parked the Volvo on his street, although the only empty space was so far away from his house it almost would have been better walking back from HQ. It was one of the many reasons they were so keen on moving, because the stress of trying to find somewhere to leave the car was sometimes the straw that broke the camel's back after a long day at work.

There were other reasons too, of course. Grinning men in black Peugeots, for one. Hollenbeck knew where he lived, and even though Kett would never be able to hide himself from them—they were far too powerful for that—the idea of moving to a new place, a more secure place, was infinitely reassuring.

He got out of the car, arching his back until he felt it pop. Even though the light had faded, the evening chorus was in full swing. Blackbirds hid in the trees that lined the street, invisible other than their voices. The sound of them made Kett's heart feel weirdly heavy, although not in a bad way. It was a sound that reminded him of his childhood, of long evening walks with his mum and dad through the city's cemetery, cocooned by summer. It felt too long ago to be real.

Every single light in the house was on, the way they always were. Kett didn't bother with his keys, because after the incident with the man in the Peugeot Billie had secured deadbolts on the front and back doors, and they were drawn as soon as the sun set. He knocked quietly, wary of waking the girls. In the end, though, it was a little voice that answered him.

"Who is it?" asked Evie.

"It's Daddy, sweetie. Let me in."

"How do I know it's really you?"

It broke his heart that some of Billie's fear and suspicion had spread to the girls—his own, too, of course. They'd been through so much already. They'd been all the way to hell, almost burning to death inside Bingo's house as the Pig Man tried to sacrifice them to the flames. Evie and Moira never spoke about it, and they were young enough that he wasn't entirely sure they remembered it as anything more than a nightmare. But Alice had been older, and he could see the scars of that night in so much of who she was now.

Fuckers, he thought, directing the word at the Pig Man, at Hollenbeck.

"It's me," he said. "I promise."

"Tell me the password," said Evie.

"Uh... unicorns?" he said.

"No."

"Mermaids?"

"Uh-uh. I don't think it is you, Dad, because you'd *know* the password."

He took a moment to think, then smiled.

"Is it farty butt cheese?"

"It *is* you!" Evie said, giggling. "But you can only come in if you do the farty butt cheese dance."

"I think that's enough," came Billie's voice. "Stand back a bit, Evie."

Kett heard the bolts being drawn, all four of them, then the key turning in the lock. The Yale was the last thing, the door creaking open. Billie stood there, a flash of worry on her face like she'd made a mistake, like she'd opened the house to a stranger wearing her husband's face.

Then a smile, *her* smile, one that made everything okay.

"Farty butt cheese," Kett said, holding his hand up like a Boy Scout. "May I come in?"

"Yeah!" said Evie, running to him.

He scooped her up, hugging her as tight as he dared while carrying her inside. The worry was back in Billie's face as she scanned the street, as she pushed the door shut so quickly it clipped his hip. She slid the bolts home, turned the key, then tested each one to make sure it was secure. Only then did she turn to him.

"Sorry," she said with a sad little shrug.

"Don't be. Don't ever be. Come here."

He hugged her, Evie sandwiched between them and groaning theatrically, like she was being squashed by a couple of hippos. They parted and Kett switched Evie to his other arm, the five-year-old ridiculously heavy.

"And how come you're still awake?" he asked, booping her on the nose.

"She couldn't sleep," said Billie. "Wanted to know you were okay."

"My bum hurts when you're not here," she said.

"Excuse me?"

"My bum," Evie said, rubbing her chest. Billie laughed quietly, shaking her head.

"Alice managed to convince her little sisters that their bottoms are where their hearts are, and vice versa."

"It happens when you get to my age," Evie said matter-of-factly. "Your bum and your heart change places."

"That's... I really don't know where to start with that, Evie."

"And my knees are now my elbows and my elbows have moved to my knees," she said.

"Just don't ask her where her kidneys are," Billie said.

"They're right up—"

"Everything's just where it needs to be," Kett said, cutting her off. "Don't listen to Alice, okay?"

Evie shrugged.

"Can I stay up all night?"

"No," said Kett. "I'll put you to bed."

"Yay!"

"And I'll get the tea on," said Billie. "You look like you need one."

"More than anything," said Kett. "Thank you."

He carried Evie upstairs, both of them yawning in tandem—his cut short when Evie stuck her entire hand in his mouth.

"I can see right down to your bum when you yawn like that," she said.

"You really can't," Kett said, pulling back her covers and lowering her into bed. He tucked her in, giving her a kiss on the forehead. She yawned again, her little face frowning.

"The bad men won't get in, will they, Dad?"

"No way," Kett replied, holding her hand in both of his. "Nobody can get into this house, not when me and your mum are here. I promise."

It didn't seem to do much to reassure her, but after a moment, she nodded.

"But we're getting a new house, aren't we?"

"Hopefully," he said. "You're okay with that?"

She shrugged beneath her blanket.

"I like this one. But I just want to be where you are."

"Me too," he said.

"I love you, Dad."

"Love you too, Evie. To the end of the universe and back."

He kissed her again then left, checking Moira on the other side of the room, and Alice, who had buried herself under half a dozen duvets and blankets like she always did, one bare leg poking out. On his way back down the stairs he kicked himself, realising that his answer to Evie's question should have been that she was perfectly safe in the house at all times because there were no bad men to break down the doors, no monsters lurking in the shadows.

He didn't think she'd have believed him, though. She knew better than most that monsters were real.

The smell of tea hit him as he was walking down the corridor, and he entered the kitchen to see Billie with three steaming cups in her hands.

"Figured you could use two," she said.

"Have I ever told you how much I love you?"

"Yes," she said. "But I'll never get tired of hearing it."

She put the cups on the table, where her laptop sat open in the middle of an ocean of fresh printouts. Then she walked to the back door and tested the bolts there. She would have done it a dozen times already, Kett knew, and she'd do it a dozen times more before bed. But it was okay. It was what she needed.

"Long day?" she asked as they both sat down.

"Long," he said. "New case. Somebody received a foot in the post."

"I saw," she said. "It was on the news. Well, they didn't mention the foot bit, but I saw you and they said there had been a 'grisly discovery' or something. A foot, though? What's that all about?"

"I have no idea," said Kett, rubbing his eyes. "Nothing good."

"Do you think you'll still be able to make it tomorrow?" she asked, spinning the laptop to face him. Right Move was open on the screen, a large, detached house surrounded by gardens. They'd already been to see it once, nestled back from the main road in the north of the city, and both he and Billie had fallen in love with it. Four bedrooms, a large kitchen diner, a home security system already built-in and, probably the most important thing for Billie, there was a satellite police station right across the road. If there was trouble, help was on the doorstep.

"I'll do my best," he said. "It's not until after school, right?"

"Two," said Billie. "They didn't have anything else until the weekend. I'll have to collect the girls early, but I really want them to see it."

"They'll love it," he said, resting his hand on hers. "It's the right thing to do."

But it hadn't been easy. The sale had just gone through on their London house, the beautiful three-bedroom semi beneath the railway arches in Stepney Green. That had been a gruelling ordeal in its own right, nothing to do with the sale itself and everything to do with the chaos of memories the house contained. Joy, because this was the first house he and Billie had bought together, the first house they'd decorated. It's where all the girls had been conceived, and where they'd all come home to after the hospital. It's where they had been a family for so long.

Until *he'd* found them.

The Pig Man.

And now that's all the house would ever be. It would be the moment Kett had looked back across the kitchen and seen his wife feeding Moira, somehow knowing that something was wrong and yet leaving for work anyway. It would be the moment he'd come home after Billie had been taken, with no idea that he wouldn't see her again for five endless months. It would be the place he'd taken the girls when they'd finally found out what had happened to Billie, and the place Bingo had snatched his daughters from when Kett had decided to go after her.

Those moments. Those awful moments. That's all the house was to him now.

It was time to move on.

It was time to *move.*

"It's the right thing to do," he said.

She nodded, so unsure.

"My heart hurts just thinking about it," she said, putting a hand to her chest.

"That's your bum," Kett said. "Didn't you pay any attention in biology?"

She laughed, the sound of it golden. Kett laughed too, taking a long sip of too-hot tea.

"Telly or bed?" Billie said, covering a yawn with the back of her hand.

"I'm going to fall asleep either way," Kett said. "So let's head up."

They did, taking their tea with them.

And only after checking the bolts, of course.

IT WAS A LIE, though, because Kett didn't fall asleep, not straightaway. They lay in bed together, Kett finishing his tea as he listened to Billie talk about their day, laughing with her, sharing her frustrations, feeling guilty, like he always did, that she had to do so much of it by herself.

Eventually, she drifted off with her head on his chest, at first peacefully and then plagued by the same dreams she'd had since she'd come home to them. He stroked her head as her body twitched, as the anger and fear caught in her throat in guttural, animal noises. He hushed her and hugged her until the nightmare passed, and he still didn't let go, even though he was numb from his shoulder to his fingertips.

He just held her.

It was long past midnight before he fell into a fitful sleep, his own dreams plagued by terrors. And in the end, he needn't have bothered, because it was just after two when his phone began to vibrate across the bedside table, the Super's name on the screen.

"Sir," Kett said, sitting up as slowly as he dared. "What's wrong?"

A stupid question, he knew. Because there could only be one answer to that.

"Sorry, Kett," Clare said, his voice heavy with exhaustion. "There's been another delivery."

CHAPTER TWELVE

Thursday

Kett drove through the night, the world fast asleep around him. He didn't see a single other car until he'd left the city, an ambulance passing him on the North Walsham road, its siren off but its lights painting the street blue. He followed it for a while, wondering if it was heading to the same place he was, but it turned off at a roundabout and he travelled onwards alone through winding streets and sleepy villages. The trees were almost invisible against the lightless sky, giants who crowded the side of the road like bouncers and silently watched him go. He wasn't welcome out here, in the dark heart of the night.

So it was with some relief that he pulled into the village of Coltishall and saw more blue lights ahead. Two IRVs were parked on the forecourt of a petrol station, another blocking a side road. Kett pulled the Volvo onto the kerb and switched off the engine, climbing out. The earth was cooling slowly after a day in the sun, the air still warm. There was no sign of anyone.

He didn't think the neighbours would appreciate him shouting, so he started walking down the road, listening for any sign of life. It was like the Mary Celeste, the streets abandoned, the only sound the crunch of his boots on the pavement. After a moment or two he pulled out his phone and called Colin Clare.

"Speak!" came the answer.

"I'm here," he said. "Where is everyone?"

"I'll send Duke for you," Clare replied, then hung up.

Kett stood where he was, his head cocked. A few seconds later, he heard the thunder of heavy feet and the giant PC appeared in a narrow alleyway that Kett hadn't even noticed.

"DCI Kett, sir," Duke said. "This way."

"You been awake all this time?" Kett asked.

"I don't sleep," Duke replied, fidgeting and blinking like he'd drunk a bathtub of Red Bull. "I'm a machine."

"Right."

The alley curved gently to the right, boxed in by tall hedges, opening into a sweeping gravel driveway. There was a huge house here, a three-storey regency brick property with sash windows and a yellow door guarded by lion statues as big as Labradors. More Leylandii hedges shielded the house from the road, thirty feet high in places, and a very new red Range Rover sat in the driveway, its number plate personalised. Most of the windows were dark, but puddles of yellow light spilled out from the ground floor and half a dozen coppers stood in them like they were sunning themselves. Most were in uniform, but Porter was there with his back to the driveway. He turned around at the sound of footsteps.

"Alright, sir," he said, offering a curt nod. "Bit late for all this."

"You mean early?" said Kett. "Have you been to bed yet?"

"Kind of," Porter said. "Neither of us has been getting much sleep these last few nights. Allie's got some kind of bug, I think. Keeps throwing up."

"Oh Christ, she didn't eat the cake, did she?"

Porter winced.

"Yeah, but only because Clare made me take a slice home," he said softly. "I was going to chuck it in the bin, but Allie found it first. I didn't stop her in time. She loves Bounties."

"And yet you still married her," said Kett.

"You get any sleep, sir?"

"Not really. Knackered."

"I didn't sleep," said Duke. "I'm a machine."

"You said that already," Kett told him.

"He's a machine alright," said Porter. "A mechanical dildo."

Kett laughed, and thankfully Duke's reply was cut off by a shout from inside.

"Kett? Is that you? You'd better not be lollygagging out there."

"Lollygagging?" Kett said to Porter, and the DI shrugged.

Kett made his way into the house, finding himself in a tall, wide entrance hall that felt like it was refrigerated. A sweeping staircase rose from the flagstones, splitting in the middle and extending to a huge galleried landing. A crystal chandelier hung above Kett's head, swinging gently in a breeze that he couldn't feel. Portraits lined the walls, stately men with pompous faces who glared at the police with apparent disapproval, alongside a tapestried map of old Norfolk. The air was thick with the scent of incense—or maybe burnt sage—pungent and unwelcome.

The voices were coming from the closest door of four and Kett followed them, finding an immaculately decorated sitting room. Five people stood in close proximity between the sofas, even though there was a *lot* of space in there. Colin Clare occupied the middle of the group, the tallest person here by some way. Savage stood next to him, catching Kett's eye and lifting her head in welcome. They both looked as tired as Kett felt.

"Kett," Clare said, spotting him in the door. "Finally."

The three other people in the room all turned to look his way. Two were in their late forties, dressed in matching tartan pyjamas and navy dressing gowns. They were both average height and skinny, her with thin, brown hair and him with barely any hair at all. Something in the narrow shape of their faces and the pale colour of their eyes made Kett think they were probably brother and sister.

The third person was an older, shorter woman dressed in black, her grey hair tied back. Her hands were clasped to her chest and her eyes flitted nervously between the other people in the room.

"Hi," Kett said. "Sorry, it took me a while to get here. What's happened?"

"You mean he doesn't know?" said the man, anger making his angular face even sharper. "What kind of shitty operation is this?"

Clare took a breath, his entire body vibrating like it was close to exploding.

"As I said to you, Mr Bower, it is very late. Please be patient."

"Patient?" the man spat back. "I've got a human hand lying on my parlour floor and you want me to be patient? Fuck you."

Kett's scalp tightened.

"A hand?" he said, and Clare nodded.

"We weren't sure, because the package was only partially opened when Mrs Bower notified us. But yes, it's a hand. It was delivered this morning, but only opened a couple of hours ago."

"In the middle of the night?" Kett said.

"What's wrong with that?" snapped the taller of the two women. She was wearing an assortment of silver necklaces, Kett saw, shards of amethyst and chunks of tiger's eye hanging in the folds of her dressing gown. "What I do at night is none of your business."

"You're right," Kett said. "Look, I think we're getting off on the wrong..." There was no way of avoiding it, so he committed. "Uh, *foot*. It's late, we're all tired, but time is crucial, so if you could just stay calm and answer some questions, we would be very grateful."

"More questions," said Mr Bower, scowling at the woman. "I told you we should have waited until the bloody morning."

He pointed a long finger at Kett.

"I've got a very important meeting in the city tomorrow, and this is going to fuck it right up."

"How about this, then?" Kett said, losing his patience. "Let's get you all in a police car and take you to Norwich. You can answer my questions in the comfort of an interview room and you'll be in the right place to get to your meeting in the morning. How does that sound?"

Mr Bower stewed silently.

"Now," said Kett. "Take a deep breath and tell me what happened."

"It's better if we show you," said Clare.

"I'm not going back in there," said Mrs Bower. "Not with that horrible thing on the floor. I'll talk, but I won't look at it again. No."

"Just talk, then," Kett said.

The woman sighed, staring at the floor like the hand was lying right in front of her.

"I often can't sleep. I've always had trouble with it, even with the Circadin. It's worse when I see people, and we have a book club on Tuesdays, usually here. It's frightfully boring. So quite often I'm up and about in the night, and I do jobs, I potter, you know?"

Kett nodded, watching Mr Bower as the woman spoke. His face flexed, his jaw bulging like he had some kind of tic. There was anger there, but there was fear too, just glimpses when he forgot to hide it.

"I often deal with the mail in the night," Mrs Bower went on, playing with the amethyst that hung from her neck. "Jeremy sleeps like a donkey, and he gets irritated when I shuffle around."

"You're in the same bed?" Kett asked.

"What kind of ridiculous question is that?" said the man. "Of course, we share a bed. Is that a crime?"

They both stared at him with their near-identical faces and Kett found that he didn't have an answer.

"Margarite here prepares the mail during the day, she leaves it in the parlour."

"Margarite," said Kett. "You're the..."

"Maid, yes," the older woman answered in a thick Spanish accent. "I work for Mr and Mrs Bower many years."

"Tell me what happened today," Kett said. "Start from the beginning."

The woman kneaded her hands together, swallowing noisily. She glanced at Mr Bower as if asking for permission to speak, and he gave her a curt nod.

"I arrive this morning, as I always do. Six forty-five. I take off my coat and hang it in the cupboard in the hall. I walk upstairs and knock on bedroom door to wake Mr and Mrs Bower. I make breakfast. Mrs Bower eat cereal and milk, Mr Bower enjoys kippers. I fry them, in a little oil with some capers, it's very delicious and—"

"Maybe don't start from the very beginning," Kett said. "Focus on the delivery."

"*Si*," she said, swallowing again. The woman was squirming, her forehead damp with sweat. "After Mr Bower goes to work, Mrs Bower goes back to bed for a little while."

"Because I don't sleep well in the night, like I said," the other woman added defensively.

"About ten-fifteen, mail arrives. I collect it from doormat and drop it on parlour table. Three letters today, all for Mr Bower. About half an hour after that, I hear *knock knock* on the door. Very loud. I walk to door, I open door, nobody there. I see box. Pretty box, pink ribbon."

"You're sure you didn't see anyone?" Kett asked. "Somebody walking away?"

"I see nobody. So I collect box and put it in parlour."

"How long did it take you to get to the door after you heard the knock?" Kett asked.

Margarite shrugged, another glance at Mr Bower. She looked like a mouse who'd spotted a hawk.

"I don't know. Usual time. I go straight away."

"From which room? It's a big house."

"From this room," she said, but her eyes had dropped to the floor.

"You're sure?" Kett pressed.

No answer. He didn't want to push it, not yet.

"You collected the box and put it on the parlour table," Kett said. "That's it?"

"I leave it there and shut door, same as always."

"And you're certain it was ten forty-five, yesterday morning?"

"I certain," she said. "Maybe ten fifty. I take my break at eleven every day, and this was very soon before that."

"Okay," Kett said. "Last thing, for now. Whose name was on the box?"

"Mr Bower," Margarite said.

"Let's turn to you then," Kett said to the man. "You came home from work at..."

"Seven on the dot," he said. "I believe in punctuality, unlike you."

"You work in Norwich?"

"Obviously," he said. "Do you think there's a thriving financial sector in Coltishall?"

"I wouldn't know," Kett said, meeting Clare's eye for a moment and seeing the exact same desire to throttle Mr Bower that he felt. "Tell me what happened when you came back."

"I walked in the door, I hung up my coat, I kicked off my shoes." The man knew exactly what he was doing, but Kett didn't give him the pleasure of reacting. "I walked to the kitchen and got a drink, I gave my wife a kiss on the cheek—not illegal, I can assure you—then I walked to the parlour and opened the door and picked up my mail. Three letters, like Margarite told you. A credit card statement, a letter from a friend and a response from my local MP about the dreadful traffic in the village."

"And the parcel?"

"I didn't even look at it," he said, puffing out his chest. "I never receive parcels, especially ones tied with ribbons. They're always for my wife. She has an Amazon addiction, mostly all the hippy shit she believes in. I assumed it was for her and left it."

"Okay," Kett said, turning to Mrs Bower. "And now we're back with you. What time did you get up?"

Mrs Bower shrugged.

"It was after midnight. I didn't check the time."

"So how did you know it was after midnight?"

"I don't appreciate your tone, Mr whatever your name is," Mr Bower said. "We are not under suspicion here."

I wouldn't be so sure about that, Kett almost replied.

"So how did you know it was after midnight?" he said again, his tone softer.

Mrs Bower shrugged.

"I just know. It's just a feeling. The night's familiar to me. I got myself a glass of water, then went into the parlour. There was no mail for me but I saw the parcel and opened it without thinking. I assumed it was mine."

"Were you expecting a delivery today?" Kett asked.

"No, not particularly, but I do order things some days."

Mr Bower scoffed, his eyes bulging, his jaw flexing.

"*Most* days," his wife admitted. "I collect things to keep the house pure, to keep the air clean. I opened the box and saw packing chips, lots of them. And crepe paper. I thought it was an ornament or something. It was all wrapped up..."

She stalled, looking like she was literally choking on the words.

"I know this is hard," Kett said. "But it's important."

"It was wrapped up, but I peeled off the sticker and opened it and saw... I saw it, and I knew what it was. I knew exactly what it was because of the... the fingernails. It... I dropped it, I couldn't stand it."

She looked at her hands as if they were contaminated, then scrubbed them down her dressing gown.

"Awful," she said. "Awful, awful, awful."

"That's about where we were when you came in," Clare said. "Thank you, Mrs Bower. I'd like for you all to stay in the house, if that's okay with you? Just until we finish."

"Where else are we going to go?" Mr Bower spat back, disgusted.

"What about me?" Margarite said, raising her hand like a child at school.

"You can go home," Clare said. "Sorry we had to get you out of bed."

"Do we get an apology, too?" Mr Bower demanded.

"No," said Clare, a little too bluntly. "With me, Kett, Savage."

The Super walked through the living room door without a backwards glance and Kett followed.

"He is *not* nice," Savage said as they made their way across the front hall. "And she's not much better."

"Siblings are often quite similar," Kett said, and Savage snorted a laugh into her hand.

"Right?" she said. "I mean, I know this is Norfolk and everything, but they are weirdly identical."

"Enough chitter-chatter," Clare said as he reached the door directly opposite the living room. It was closed, but when he pushed it open Kett saw another living room, this one much smaller. The walls were covered with woven dream catchers and antique, gilt-framed reliquaries depicting forgotten saints. Two armchairs sat against one wall, a large walnut desk beneath the window on the opposite side, with a high-backed wooden dining chair pulled out at an angle. Stacks of papers were piled on the desk, towers of them.

But it was what lay below it that caught Kett's eye.

He saw the brown cardboard box first, the exact same size and shape as the one that had been delivered to Douglas Ireland. It lay on its side like it was ill, the ribbon unspooled beside it, as pale as intestines. A vomit of pink packing chips gorged from its open mouth, a trail of them leading to a mound of tissue paper three feet away.

The object was still partially wrapped, but there was no mistaking the single finger that pointed towards the ceiling like it was trying to show them something.

"Shit," said Kett, just a breath.

"I don't want anyone touching it until forensics has been here, but feel free to go in for a closer look."

"Thanks, sir," said Kett with no small amount of sarcasm.

He walked to the table and dropped onto his haunches, getting close enough to the package that he could smell it—that awful first hint of meat on the turn. All the lights in the room were on, but the table held the hand in its shadow like it meant to hide it.

"You think this is our same victim?" he said.

Nobody answered, and when he fired up the torch on his phone, he saw why.

The hand was small, the fingers long and the bones delicate. Kett could see the letters of a tattoo disappearing into the tissue paper, a word that might have been 'stop' inked in the same style as the writing they'd found on the foot. He adjusted the light, looking at the finger again and seeing the nail, the bright red varnish that had chipped around the edge.

"Looks like a woman's hand," he said.

He sat up, seeing Clare nod, seeing Savage's down-turned mouth.

"Different victim," Clare said.

Kett sighed, and tried to rub the exhaustion from his eyes.

"Shit," he said again.

CHAPTER THIRTEEN

The dawn chorus was starting by the time Kett left the Bower house. Just one brave bird to begin with, battling the monstrous dark with its lone voice. More joined in, and before long, there was a swell of noise that sounded almost deafening after the quiet night. It seemed strange to hear them when the sun hadn't even started rising yet. It felt almost as though they'd started early, a keening song to honour the dead woman whose hand lay on the other side of the window.

Maybe not dead, Kett reminded himself, although that seemed too naïve a thought to be real.

It did belong to a woman, though. Emily Franklin had arrived a short while ago and she'd unwrapped the hand like it was Christmas morning. Although she hadn't given her full report yet, she'd been pretty sure. She was still in the little parlour, along with Cara Hay and her forensic team. Kett didn't think they'd find anything. This didn't feel like the work of somebody who made mistakes.

He heard footsteps and turned to see Porter walk out of the house. He was rubbing both of his eyes with his fists like a small boy and stumbled off the high stoop with a squawk. Kett grabbed his arm to steady him and Porter blinked in confusion, like for a moment he couldn't remember who Kett was.

"You should get home," Kett told him. "Get some sleep."

"Huh?" Porter said after a second or two.

"Sleep. When you put your head on the pillow and aren't awake."

"Right, sir," Porter said. "Yeah. I will. Soon as we're out of here."

"Go," said Kett. "You've been up all night. I'll call you if there are any developments."

Clare had left a little while ago, stomping angrily to his Mercedes. Half of the Uniforms had gone too thanks to a nasty RTC on the other side of the city.

Porter nodded.

"I should see how Allie's doing anyway. You sure?"

"Go."

Before he could leave, Duke appeared from the direction of the street, a giant can of energy drink clenched like a dumbbell in his hand. He was jittering hard.

"Duke," said Kett as the PC closed in.

"Sir," Duke replied, his teeth chattering. "We've been through the entire village, pretty much, very little in the way of CCTV, hardly any doorbell cams but the garage opposite has some cameras and they show the street but not the entrance to this place so I don't know how good they'll be and I couldn't see many other—"

"Slow down," Kett said as Duke's words started to run together. "How many of those have you had?"

Duke turned his red, bulging eyes to the can in his hand like he'd forgotten it was there. Then he took a massive sip.

"Six."

"Jesus Christ, Duke. That's enough caffeine to kill a giraffe."

Duke's eyes widened even more.

"Giraffes don't drink this stuff, sir."

"Amazing," said Porter, a grin breaking through the exhaustion. "You're buzzing your tits off."

"In short," Duke said, giving Porter a side-eye. "There's nothing in the village that can help us."

Kett sighed, checking his phone to see that it wasn't even half-past four yet.

"Go home, both of you," he said. "Get some rest. There's not much more we can do here."

"I'm not tired, sir," Duke said. "I'm a..."

He frowned.

"Machine?" Kett ventured.

"That's the one. I'm a machine, sir. Grr."

"Well, if he's not tired then neither am I," said Porter. "Grr."

"You look pretty tired, sir," Duke told Porter. "You should have a sit down."

"I'm much more awake than you, Duke. So much more. Ten times more."

"Yeah, well, how about now?"

Duke downed the rest of the energy drink in half a dozen enormous gulps, swaying wildly. He looked almost green in the muted light from the house.

"I think I need to sit down," he said, belching pure sugar.

"Yeah, you do," said Porter. "Weak."

"Porter, take him home."

Both men groaned.

"Now."

Duke wobbled off down the drive.

"He could probably fly home right now," Porter said.

"What's up with Duke?" Savage asked as she walked out of the house. Franklin was with her, both of them fresh-faced and perky. Kett wasn't sure how they did it.

"Too much Red Bull," he said. "He's got the mind of a teenager in the body of a woolly mammoth."

"But what a body," Franklin said, and both Kett and Savage looked at her in surprise. She shrugged. "Just saying, purely as a pathologist studying a specimen."

"Ahem," Porter said, clearing his throat and gesturing to himself.

"What?" Franklin said.

Porter rolled his eyes in disgust, then set off after Duke.

"Unbelievable," he muttered as he went.

"So," said Franklin, taking a deep breath. "We're definitely looking at a second victim. Skin tone is slightly darker, for one. The index and ring finger ratio is higher than average, meaning we're almost certainly looking at a female hand. It's a left hand. There's an indentation in the skin on the middle finger, I believe there was a ring there of some kind. The nail varnish is old and I found teeth marks in it, which means our victim was probably a nail biter. Good diet, lots of calcium. Healthy, and I'd say almost certainly young. Twenties or thirties. Not much in the way of damage to the skin, so not a manual labourer, but some green residue on the fingertips that I'd say came from vegetation."

"Different victim, same attacker?" Kett asked.

"Yes. I have absolutely no doubt. Wrist was severed in a single blow using a very heavy, very sharp blade. They knew what they were doing, because they managed to hit all the soft tissue between the arm bones and the wrist bones, just a slight nick on the scaphoid. Again, the force needed to do this, and the accuracy involved, makes me think the amputation was mechanical, performed while the victim was either asleep or dead. It's fresh, fresher than the foot. I'd say two days tops."

"And the hand was delivered first," Kett said, thinking aloud. "Just before eleven yesterday. The foot was delivered to the house in Norwich almost six hours later."

Savage nodded.

"The tattoo on the hand says '*Don't stop*,'" she said.

"Inked post-mortem," Franklin added. "Same script."

"A variation on the same message," Kett said. "Never give up, don't stop. It feels almost like the attacker is talking to himself."

"Or herself," Franklin and Savage said together.

"Sorry, I know. I'm being lazy, not jumping the gun."

"Wound was packed in salt, just like before," said Franklin. "But I analysed our foot yesterday and there's no evidence that it was frozen. Refrigerated, maybe. I'll check the hand as soon as I get back to the lab."

"We've sent the prints over too," said Savage. "If she's known to us, we'll have an ID shortly."

"Good work," Kett said. "Cara find anything?"

Savage shook her head.

"They were careful. No prints, no hair or fibre—on this one or on the foot. She's trying to find out where the packing chips came from, but I can't see it helping. You can buy them everywhere. Same with the tissue paper, the sticker and the box."

Kett scratched his cheek, feeling the stubble. He thought about his bed at home, he thought about the warmth of his wife as she slept next to him.

"This fucking job," he said, more to himself than to anyone else. "Okay. There's not much more we can do here.

Thanks, Emily. Kate, head home, get some rest while we wait for the results to come back. We're going to need to be sharp tomorrow."

He checked his watch.

"I mean today, obviously."

"Yes, sir," Savage said. "You should get some shut-eye, too."

"I had some," he said. "Well, kind of. I'll be okay. I'm a machine. Grr."

"Course you are, sir," said Savage. "You driving, Emily?"

"Yeah, I'll give you a lift."

"Call me as soon as you need me, sir," said Savage.

Kett nodded, watching them go. Mr and Mrs Bower had retreated upstairs an hour or so ago, but Kett didn't really want to head back to the city until the forensics team had finished. He made his way down the drive instead, reaching the street in time to see Savage and Franklin climb into a sleek, pastel blue TVR Tuscan. Its roof was down despite the ebbing dark, and both young women flashed Kett a smile as it purred down the road.

"You have got to be kidding me," Kett said, casting a look at the very uncool orange Volvo parked on the side of the road.

The garage wasn't open yet, a handful of Uniforms hanging out on the forecourt.

"Anything new?" Kett called to them, and they all shook their heads.

He made his way along the high street, passing quaint shops and small houses, their front doors opening up almost straight onto the road. The PCs hadn't been subtle in their search, and most of the windows were lit up, the village looking almost like a theatre set. There were no doors open, though. Nobody seemed to want to talk.

He kept going regardless, happy to be away from the house and its severed hand. Ahead was a fork in the road, watched over by a stately brick mansion, and Kett took the right-hand lane. The pavement here was ridiculously narrow, so he walked on the road, keeping an ear out for traffic and hearing nothing except the birds. The sun had finally woken, its sleepy light seeping over the horizon and catching the tops of the trees. He was happy to see it, because even though he'd never admit it to anyone, he hated the night.

Bad things tended to happen in the dark.

He was halfway up a shallow hill when he heard his phone ring, seeing Billie's name on the screen.

"Hey you," he said as he answered.

"Hey you," she replied, midway through a yawn. "You're up early."

"Sorry, I didn't want to wake you."

"Same case?" she asked.

"Yeah."

"Well, you be careful, Robbie, okay? Please. This one feels... I don't know. I'm getting a bad vibe from it."

"Me too," he said. "I'll be careful, I promise. Go back to sleep."

"I can't," she said. "Moira just came in, sat on my head and farted. In her sleep."

Kett laughed.

"She's got some serious talent, that girl."

He pulled the phone away from his ear, aware of a faint growl from nearby.

"I'd better go," he said.

"She's stirring anyway," Billie whispered. "I just wanted to make sure you're okay. Love you."

"Love you," he said, but she'd already hung up. He slid his phone back into his pocket, the growl growing in volume as he reached the crest of the hill. The road arced to the right here, the glow from a set of headlights splashed across the asphalt. An engine idled, and past that was a low voice. Kett rounded the corner, one hand up to shield his eyes from the glare.

A small, white van sat in a patch of scrubland to the side of the road.

Kett froze, trying to see anything through the dark windscreen. If there was anyone in the vehicle, they were invisible. He was disadvantaged here, he knew, lit up by the headlights like an actor on stage. He glanced back down the road, wondering whether to run and get help before investigating any further—or call control and get some of the PCs up here.

The voice rose again, coming from behind a dilapidated wooden fence. It was hard to make out over the sound of the engine, but there was definitely anger there.

Kett crept closer, keeping to the side of the road and what little cover the overhanging trees provided. There was still no movement from inside the van, so he chanced it, his breath locked in his lungs as he crossed in front of it.

No revving engine, no lurch of movement.

He cupped his hand to the driver's window and saw that the seats were empty. It was too dark in the back to make out anything at all. Kett glanced at the fence. Whoever was speaking was definitely arguing with somebody. But it was good, they were distracted.

As quietly as he could, Kett opened the door. He fired

up the torch on his phone, sweeping it into the back of the van.

"Shit."

Laid out there was an assortment of tools, including a spade—its sharpened head glinting. Paperwork littered the floor, a collection of maps, some old books.

And there, poking out from beneath the handle of the spade, what looked like an illustration of a tick.

"Shit," Kett said again, his heart drumming against his ribs loud enough surely for the entire village to hear it.

He clambered out of the van, using his phone to call Cara Hay.

"Kett," she said when she answered. "I'm almost done here, we—"

"Cara, sorry, this is about something else. I'm up the road, just north of the village. I've found a van, and there's somebody here. It might be our guy. Can you send the Uniforms up here? It's a minute away if they drive."

"Oh, yes, of course. One moment."

The line went quiet.

And so had the voice behind the fence.

Kett held his breath, listening for anything over the tick and rattle of the idling van.

Footsteps. The crack of a twig.

Kett reached into the van and switched off the engine, silence falling like a hammer. He tossed the keys onto the verge behind him, hearing that same voice hiss on the other side of the fence. In the sudden quiet, Kett could make out what it was saying.

"... catch me, they're going to catch me. Oh, God."

More footsteps, fading fast.

He was running.

Kett glanced down the road, no sign yet of the Uniforms.

"For fuck's sake," he said.

He broke into a jog, reaching the fence in seconds. It was eight foot high, no obvious place to cross it, but a little further down it became a chain-link fence. Kett struggled over it, the heel of his boot catching on the top. He fell hard, the wind knocked out of him, but he forced himself back to his feet.

The woods were thick on this side of the road and the night still ruled here. But only just. Brittle fingers of sunlight picked out a shape moving away from Kett at speed, weaving in and out of the trees.

"Oi!" Kett tried to yell, his winded lungs pushing out a whisper instead.

He picked up speed, crashing through branches, the dry, root-thick ground doing its best to trip him. The man he was chasing didn't look particularly fit, and he wasn't fast. Within a minute, Kett had almost caught up to him.

"Stop!" he roared. "Police!"

The man broke out of the trees, barrelling towards a low barn fifty yards ahead. He was making wet gasping noises as he struggled for breath.

"Last chance!" Kett yelled, making some pretty awful gasping noises himself.

The man didn't listen, halfway across the open waste-land. He was holding something small and dark in one hand, but his other was empty.

Kett put his head down and sprinted, ignoring the pain in his chest, the stitches in his side. The man was slowing, his arms wheeling. He looked like he was going to collapse all by himself.

Kett didn't give him that luxury.

He slammed into the back of him, the man grunting like a bear as he landed face-first in the dirt. The phone in his hand went flying, the battery sleeve pinging free as it hit a rock. Momentum almost pulled Kett right over the top of the guy, but he grabbed hold of a fistful of back fat, rooting himself in place. The man screamed, and there was almost something familiar about the noise.

"It's me balls!" he shrieked. "Balls!"

"I'm nowhere near them, mate," Kett said, settling himself on the man's back.

The guy bucked and wobbled, but the run seemed to have sapped the strength from him. Kett caught his breath, leaning in.

"Stop struggling. Who the hell are you?"

"It's me!" came the same reedy reply. "Don't hurt me."

The man twisted his head around, his forehead damp with sweat and streaked with dirt. A pair of wire glasses hung diagonally over his bulbous face, and his small eyes blinked up hopefully.

"It's me," the man said again.

Kett muttered a silent curse at the sky before pushing himself to his feet.

"Norman Balls," he said. "What on earth are you doing here?"

CHAPTER FOURTEEN

Norman Balls sat in the open back door of the little white van, a plastic cup of tea in his trembling hands. The internet conspiracy theory obsessive, owner of the *Balls Knows It Alls* website and undisputed thorn in Kett's side, had thrown a tartan blanket around his shoulders and had two plasters stuck to his forehead—*Paw Patrol* ones, although Kett hadn't asked why a man in his late thirties with no children would have bought them. Two more were wrapped around one arm of his glasses, which had snapped when Kett had tackled him to the ground. His nose was red and swollen and he had a wadge of tissue up one nostril.

All in all, he looked in a sorry state.

"You're sure he doesn't need an ambulance?" asked one of the uniformed coppers who stood next to the van. Four of them had piled into the woods minutes after Balls had hit the dirt, which had proved useful because according to the strange little man he'd stubbed his toe and couldn't walk. They'd practically had to carry him back up the hill.

"He doesn't," said Kett.

"I *do*," said Balls, sniffing.

"He *really* doesn't." Kett glared at Balls. "But the day is young."

The day *was* young, and it was going to be another scorcher. The sun was fully awake and even though it wasn't even half-past five, Kett could feel the kiss of its heat on his face. The birds were still singing their hearts out, but now it sounded more like laughter than anything else. He didn't blame them, every time he saw Balls, he wanted to laugh too.

"Norman, I'm going to ask you again," said Kett. "What's going on?"

Balls sniffed, taking a sip from his cup. It was the lid of a thermos, and even though Kett was certain the tea inside was probably mediocre at best, his mouth still watered at the smell of it.

"I'm not sure I want to talk to you, DCI Kett," he said, prodding a welt on his lip. "That was excessive force if ever I saw it."

"Technically, you *didn't* see it. You were too busy running away. Why?"

"Well, I didn't know it was you, did I?" said Balls. "You could have been anyone, you could have been a killer. I wasn't going to hang around and find out."

"I was shouting 'Police!' pretty loud."

"I have a medical condition," said Balls. "I go deaf when I run."

"You go deaf when you run?" Kett said, one eyebrow climbing towards his hairline.

"It's real, look it up. My body is so finely tuned that all my available resources go into moving my legs. The blood leaves my ears."

"Right," said Kett, nodding. "And, presumably, your brain."

Balls opened his mouth and left it open, but no words came out.

"Whose van is this?" Kett asked. "Because I know it's not yours. I ran the plates."

"It's Ron's," he said.

"And Ron is..."

"My mum's stupid boyfriend," he said. "It's his stupid van. My Rover's in the garage and Mum won't give me the money to fix it. She wants me to buy a new car, an electric car, because she's tired of forking out for it. Fat chance. A distinguished local author and celebrity personality such as myself can't be seen in a little electric golf cart. What will people think?"

"Ron knows you've got it?"

"He bloody does now," said Balls. "Thank you very much."

"And that's who you were on the phone to before you started running?" Kett asked. "Ron?"

"No. I'm not talking to Ron until Mum lets me have my car back. I have made a point of it."

"How old are you again?" Kett asked.

"Thirty-eight, but that's not the point. The point is Ron isn't my dad and he can't tell me what to do. I won't talk to him until I get my way."

"I'm sure Ron is crying himself to sleep every night at the thought of not speaking with you," Kett said. "You were talking to your mum, then?"

Balls nodded.

"You can see why I chased you, can't you?" Kett said, leaning on the side of the van. "I heard you say, and I quote, 'They're going to catch me.' You're driving a white van full of suspicious objects, and you're idling right next to the scene of a crime."

Again, the man's mouth flapped wordlessly.

"Balls, I have been up most of the night. I'm tired. I'm fast running out of patience. If you don't start talking, then I'm going to—"

"Going to what?" Balls said. "You can't arrest me. There's nothing to arrest me for."

"I'm going to drive you home," Kett finished. "And I'm going to have a word with your mum. *And* with Ron."

"Fine," Balls spat. "You win."

He took off his glasses, wiping them on his dirty shirt. When he put them back on they were wonkier than ever.

"I'll talk, but only if you do. I heard about the foot that was delivered to the house in Norwich."

"How?" said Kett. "We didn't release the specifics."

"I have my sources," Balls said. He tapped his nose and his glasses fell into his lap. He made no attempt to put them back on. "A foot is one thing, no big deal. I'm sure feet get delivered to places all the time."

"They really don't," said Kett.

"But when I heard you'd all been called out to another delivery, my interest was piqued. Let me guess. This time, it was something bigger. A whole leg. Or maybe an arm. Not a head, for sure. Not yet."

"Balls, where are you getting all this from?"

"Uh-uh," the man said. "Not until you confirm or deny what I've said."

"Okay. I confirm and deny it."

Kett gave him the same look he gave his girls when they were pushing their luck, and Balls swallowed noisily.

"Talk."

"Fine!" Balls said, balling his free hand in frustration and hitting himself gently on the leg. "You win. Again. I have a source, somebody who gives me a heads up when there's a call out. They're a fan."

"You have fans?"

"More than you could ever imagine," he said. "My blog has a hundred followers."

"You're right," said Kett, rubbing his temples. "I can't imagine why a hundred people would follow you."

"You're being very mean today, Robbie," Balls said, pouting.

"I know," he replied, taking a moment. "I'm tired. Sorry."

Balls seemed surprised at the apology, and he leaned forward, more relaxed now.

"I was planning to pass all of this on to you anyway, but I just wanted to be sure. This isn't the first time a bunch of body parts have been delivered in the mail."

"No?" said Kett.

"It happens quite a lot. Well, relatively speaking. A hand there, a foot here, some genitals once in a while. You'd be surprised. I wrote about it once, on my website, *ballsknowsitalls.net*. You're familiar with it, of course."

Kett nodded and Balls beamed.

"Have you read that one?"

"I, uh, I haven't read any of them," Kett said with an apologetic shrug. The man's smile dropped away like a shot bird.

"Well, if you *had* read it, you'd know that at least once every few years, somewhere around the country, somebody receives a piece of human flesh from an unknown delivery driver. A plain box, a severed limb wrapped in cling film and tissue paper, no note, no explanation."

Kett shook his head.

"That can't be right. We'd have records of it."

"Only if they went to the police," Balls said, wagging his finger at Kett like he'd solved the mystery already.

"Which they would obviously do, if they opened a box and found themselves looking at a severed hand or foot."

"Or genitals," said Balls. "Don't forget about the genitals."

"I'm *really* trying to forget about the genitals."

"That's a very typical police attitude, Robbie," Balls went on. "To assume that whenever something bad happens, a victim's first thought is to call law enforcement. Believe it or not, some folk come to people like me for help."

"Right," said Kett. "I can see that happening. Somebody wakes up in the night to a burglar and they call *Normal* Balls. Then what? You come waddling through the door with your underwear pulled over your trousers and that blanket flapping like a cape?"

He tried not to laugh at the idea of it, but he couldn't help himself. He was almost delirious with exhaustion, this entire episode feeling like a fever dream.

Balls was not amused.

"No," he said, speaking like Kett was a child. "Obviously not if there is a violent crime taking place that second. But strange occurrences, things like that. I know of four or five examples of limbs being neatly packaged and then delivered, and none of those people opted to let the police handle it."

"If that's true, I'm going to need names," Kett said.

"Well, I don't have names as such," Balls replied. "They're just facts that we pass amongst ourselves in the conspiracy community."

"Right. Facts, as in not really facts."

"I can tell you what I know, though," Balls said.

"That would be great. But not here, and not to me. I'll have somebody drive you to HQ and take your statement."

"I can drive myself!" Balls said.

"Not in Ron's van, you can't," Kett told him. "Unless you're telling me you have his permission, and you're insured."

Balls' lower jaw dangled for a moment.

"A ride would be lovely, thank you."

"But I would like you to answer one question for me," Kett said.

He leaned past Balls, pulling free the sketch he'd noticed earlier. It was definitely a tick, the same wide, flat body, the same tiny head. Unlike the image they'd found on the postcard at Benedict Gilbert's house, though, this tick had no legs.

"Tell me about this."

"Ah," said Balls, a sly grin. "So this *is* the same person. I knew it. You've seen that image before."

"Not exactly," said Kett. "But similar."

"It's a tick," Balls said. "That is the one I drew for my article, based on the account of somebody whose friend had seen a copy of the original which somebody else had seen first-hand."

"You've lost me," said Kett. "How many steps removed are we talking?"

"That's not the point," said Balls. "The point is that the original image was given to somebody alongside a human ear, back in 2008."

"You're sure?"

"I am. In the Highlands, this was. The ear was delivered in a cardboard box, wrapped in tissue paper. Pink tissue paper, I believe. But a few days earlier, somebody had posted this picture through the door."

"A picture like this? Hand-drawn?"

"No," said Balls. "It was a postcard. Black and red."

Despite the heat of the morning, Kett's arms crinkled into goosebumps. He shuddered, and Balls smiled.

"Yes, quite," the other man said. "It's good stuff."

"But you don't have any names? Exact dates? Precise locations?"

"I'm not a miracle worker, Robbie. I'm just a detective."

"You're not a detective, Balls."

Kett looked at the picture, trying to get his head around it.

"It doesn't make any sense that if somebody got an ear through the post, they wouldn't report it to the police," he said.

"People have their reasons."

Kett turned his eyes to the road, and it took his brain a moment to catch up, the world spinning like a top. He had to grip the van again to stop himself from falling over.

"Burning the candle at both ends?" Balls asked, picking up his cup.

"Something like that. Can you tell me anything else, Norman? Anything that might help?"

Balls clamped his mouth shut for a few seconds.

"Just tell me I'm right," he said when he opened it again. "Tell me you found a postcard. Tell me that one thing and I'll pass on something else, something important."

Kett didn't answer, he just gave Balls the same withering look he'd perfected on his children.

"Okay, fine!" Balls yelled, tea sloshing from his cup, his dangling legs kicking the air. "You win, goddammit! We have a theory about the tick."

"We?"

"Me and my internet friends."

"Not sure if you can really class them as friends," said Kett. "But go on."

"These postcards have been seen more than once. Always the same image, always black on red. A tick. I've done my research, and the tick in question is a species known as *Ixodes Scapularis*. To somebody like you, it's better known as the deer tick, or the black-legged tick."

"Someone like me," Kett said. "Thanks."

"Well, I don't expect you to know much about Latin names, Robbie. Although I may be wrong. *Scapularis*. Know what it means?"

"Uh..." Kett shrugged, wishing Savage was here because she was sure to have known the answer.

"*Uh* is wrong. It actually refers to the shoulder. The Scapula. It's your shoulder blade. It's because of the shape of the tick's body."

"Okay," said Kett, a yawn taking him by surprise. He tried to cover it with his hand, but it was just too big and too long. It seemed to go on forever.

"Rude," said Balls. "The use of the tick may be related to the fact that whoever this is, they extract a piece of their victim. A foot, a hand, occasionally their gen—"

"Please don't say genitals again."

"Well, whatever." Balls leaned forward, speaking quietly as if he was sharing a world-ending secret. "But some people have posited that the use of the term scapularis refers instead to another kind of scapular."

Kett groaned, wishing with all his heart that the strange little man would get to the point.

"It's a cloak," Balls said. "It's part of the Christian monastic dress. Very simple, just a bit down the back, then two strips that sit over the shoulders. You'd recognise it if you saw one."

"I'll take your word for it."

"People wear them as a sign of their devotion to their religion," Balls went on, undeterred. "Their commitment to a cause."

Kett was halfway into another yawn, but Balls' words chased it away.

"A cause?" he said. *Never give up. Don't stop.* "What kind of cause?"

"Whatever kind they believe in," Balls said. "But in this case, I'd guess it isn't anything particularly religious. But that's what people say, Robbie. That's the name they've given this person, whoever they are. Scapular, the monastic cloak."

Kett waited, Balls delivering his final line with a dramatic flourish.

"They call him the Monk."

CHAPTER FIFTEEN

Kett climbed out of the air-conditioned Volvo into the blistering heat of the Norfolk Constabulary's car park, sweating by the time he'd reached the main doors. He made a quick pit stop in the toilets, splashing cold water on his face to try to wake himself up a bit. He wasn't tired, as such, because the sunshine had acted like an injection of pure caffeine, but everything was definitely a little fuzzy around the edges.

The Major Investigation Team's office was quiet, a handful of detectives studying documents and computer screens at their desks and the smell of coffee filling the air. Kett hung his jacket on the back of his chair before making his way to the Investigation Room. Colin Clare sat on a desk at the front, staring murderously at a collection of photographs in his hands. DI Dunst was the only other officer present, although 'present' might not have been the best word to use because his legs were on the desk and he looked like he was fast asleep.

"Sir," Kett said as he walked in.

Clare looked up for long enough to shoot Kett a glare of

profound irritation, then returned to whatever he was studying. Kett walked to the wall, seeing a few new additions to the gruesome montage. Somebody had pinned a photograph of the severed hand on the far side of the board. It lay on its back like a dead spider, its fingers curled above it. The stump was marbled and rough with rubbed salt, layers of yellow fat and greasy bone visible like islands in a bloody sea. It was almost worse seeing it here than it had been looking at the real thing, and Kett belched, his empty stomach roiling.

He scanned the rest of the images, photos of Douglas Ireland and Merletta Shaw, and one of Mr and Mrs Bower looking about as miserable as they had in the middle of the night. Near the bottom of the wall was a shot of the UEA's football team, the coach front and centre and Duggie right behind him. Both men were grinning like sharks, and both had been circled in red pen—as had one other, near the back. There was a photo of Benedict Gilbert as well, a broad smile that didn't go anywhere near his eyes.

"Balls," barked Clare, loud enough to make Kett flinch.

"Sir?"

"Balls. I've looked into what he was telling you. There are a handful of cases of limbs being delivered to somebody's door, but it's hardly a deluge. The last case I can find on the system was two years ago, down in Dorset, and that turned out to be an unpleasant epilogue to a domestic. A husband dug up his late mother-in-law and mailed parts of her to his wife, just a joke apparently."

"So Balls was talking balls?" said Kett. "No surprise there. What about the Monk stuff?"

"There's no known criminal who goes by that name," Clare said. "Nobody on file anyway. Not a surname, not a nickname we've ever seen."

Clare sighed, resting the photographs on his lap.

"I'm not saying ignore it, because Balls has come through for us before. But for now, the direction of our investigation stays the same. We need to identify the owner of the foot, and the owner of the hand. If there's a link between them, then it's our best shot at finding them. If they're still alive, of course."

Kett nodded.

"Handwriting is a bust, no matches," Clare went on.

"Shame. Anything from the fingerprints?"

"No," said Clare. "But Franklin found a nasty break in the thumb, one that would have needed surgery. We're asking around. Dunst's following up some leads on the foot as well."

Dunst snorted in his sleep and they both turned to look at him.

"That lazy tosspole," Clare said, snatching a pen from the desk and lobbing it across the room. It was a good shot, striking the old DI right in the middle of the forehead. Dunst woke with a choking cough, then toppled backwards, legs akimbo.

"You okay, Keith?" Kett said.

Dunst stood up, his eyes wide with alarm.

"What happened?" he said.

"Absolutely nothing," Clare replied, firing a warning glance at Kett. "You just fell off your bloody chair. Must have been something you were dreaming about. The foot."

"What?" said Dunst, coughing into his sleeve.

"Foot."

"Foot?" Dunst looked down at his own feet.

"Give him a break, sir," Kett said. "We've all had a long night."

"Dunst went home at six," Clare said. "He got here just before you."

Dunst shrugged.

"Got about nine hours sleep," he said. "But I'll be okay."

"And the foot?" Clare said.

Dunst shook his head, then it finally clicked.

"Oh, *that* foot. Right. No, nothing yet. Sorry."

"Well, that's thirty seconds of my life I'll never get back," muttered Clare. "But there's good news on the bike front. Only two Ducati Scramblers of the model we're chasing have been sold in the county this year. One was to the owner of the showroom, and he's taken it for a tour around Europe. He's currently in Spain, I believe. The other's registered to a man called Armel Roux, a firefighter who lives over near Wisbech. I've had officers at his house this morning, but there's no sign of him."

"Any links to the case?"

"None so far, but there are still plenty of open windows for him to toss through."

"For him to *what*, sir?"

"Everyone's looking for him, so he won't get far."

"I'll look into it," said Kett, checking his watch. "Unless there's something else you need me for?"

"Not yet, but... hang on."

Clare pulled his vibrating phone out of his pocket and answered it.

"Speak."

Kett heard a voice on the other end, but he couldn't place it. Clare nodded a couple of times, then pushed his gangly frame off the desk.

"You'd better not be tossing me off, Spalding. Send me the address. Actually, no, send it to Kett."

He hung up.

"We've had a hit on the broken thumb. A woman called Alis Sayer was in the N&N two years ago with a broken metacarpal. She's local, *ish*. Find her. And take Porter with you."

"Porter only went home a couple of hours ago," Kett said. "I don't think he's back in yet."

"Savage, then."

"Same thing. Sorry, sir."

"Duke?"

Kett shrugged.

"Tossing hell," said Clare. "I need Spalding for something else."

As one, they both turned to Dunst. Clare clapped Kett on the shoulder.

"Just try to keep him awake."

'LOCAL' was pushing it. Alis Sayer's house was almost an hour's drive from the city, in a village called South Creake. Fortunately for Kett, Dunst was quite the conversationalist —for about five minutes, that was, until he fell fast asleep in the passenger seat. Kett let him rest, taking the busy A47 as far as he could before cutting north. The sun roasted the side of his face through the window, and even with the air conditioning back on and the windows open, he felt like his blood was boiling.

The village itself could have sat quite happily on a jigsaw puzzle, sleepy cottages with blankets of carnations pulled up to their chins and a wide green that boasted a towering weeping willow. Kett pulled over when the satnav told him to, seeing a church that looked far too big and far too grand for such a small place.

He looked at Dunst, at the dribble that hung from his bottom lip, and wasn't sure he had the heart to wake him. As soon as he opened his door, though, Dunst sat bolt upright in his chair with a noise like a startled moose.

"I'm on it," he said. "I'm doing it."

He stared at Kett for a moment, then crashed back in his seat.

"Nightmare?" Kett asked.

"About Clare," said Dunst. "It was horrible."

"We've all had them."

Dunst got out, pulling a pack of Marlborough Lights from his jacket pocket and sparking one up. He took a long drag and Kett had to look away, the cravings still there even after all these years. The smell of it reached him, though, and he took a deep breath through his nose, holding it in his lungs. It didn't count when they were somebody else's.

"Can you see any numbers?" Kett asked, looking at the line of little houses that backed up to the church. "We're looking for 14a."

Dunst shook his head, but he pointed his lit cigarette to a bulky brick annex that stuck out awkwardly from the last house on the right. Sure enough, there was a separate gate and a separate front door, and when Kett walked over he spotted the house number half hidden beneath a cloak of ivy. He knocked on the door while Dunst finished his smoke on the street.

No answer.

He knocked again, standing back to study the front of the house. The annex was so overgrown with ivy that he doubted the crumbling wooden windows would open even if somebody wanted them to.

"Mrs Sayer?" he shouted, knocking again, then flapping the letterbox. "It's the police. Can you open up, please?"

The house sat still and silent. Even from out here, Kett was certain there was nobody home. He tried the handle, but it was locked.

"Can you check the back, Keith?" he asked.

Dunst nodded, grinding out the cigarette beneath his heel before walking past the low front wall and down an empty driveway. Kett made his way to the front window, doing his best not to knock over the lavender and rosemary plants that grew in carefully tended pots on the gravel. He cupped his hand to the filthy glass and peered into a dark interior, seeing two sofas and a bookshelf.

"Hello?" yelled Dunst from the back of the house, followed by a hacking cough. "It's the police. If anyone's home, open the door."

The annex was connected to a much bigger house, and much older too—stately Victorian brick with enormous sash windows. Kett hopped over a low wooden fence and navigated a crooked path to the front door. An old-fashioned bell hung there, and he rang it as hard as he could.

It took less than two seconds for the door to open, as if the man who stood there had been expecting visitors. He was in his late sixties, his hair bright white and his moustache immaculately trimmed. He was wearing a white shirt, white trousers and white tennis shoes, the only splash of colour was from his purple braces and a matching cravat. He stuck his thumbs in his braces and rocked back and forth, a friendly smile on his face.

"Good morning!" he said.

"Hi," said Kett, pulling out his warrant card. "My name's DCI Robert Kett, I'm with Norfolk Police."

"Good for you!" said the man with some enthusiasm.

"You are?"

"Jasper Dinwiddie. Very pleased to meet you."

The man removed his hand from his braces long enough to tip an imaginary hat.

"The property next door, is it yours?"

"The annex, yes. 14a, as we call it. We're number 14." He pointed to the sign next to the door as though he thought Kett might accuse him of lying. "The 'a' stands for annex."

"Is there anybody living there now?"

"Oh yes," Dinwiddie replied with a sly wink. "A young maiden."

"Maiden?"

"Yes. A maiden. Young." He uttered an odd, purring noise that made Kett's stomach contract. "Her name is Alis."

He winked again, twice, like he was trying to pass on a secret message.

"Maybe the 'a' stands for Alis," he went on. "I don't know!"

By now, the smell of sweet rum had reached Kett, and he realised the man was drunk—a feat that was almost impressive, given that it wasn't yet nine.

"Have you seen Alis recently?" Kett asked. "In the last few days?"

Jasper shook his head.

"Alas, no. And not for lack of trying."

"What's that supposed to mean?"

Jasper grinned loosely, snapping his braces against his chest. His eyebrows wiggled.

"She's very lovely," he said eventually. "I only rent the house to the lovely ones."

"I'm sure," said Kett, suppressing a shudder. "When was the last time you saw her?"

"She was here at the weekend, she had a friend round. She was lovely too!"

He snorted a laugh through his nose like this was the funniest statement that had ever been uttered. He leaned in, one hand to the side of his mouth and whispered his next words.

"They sat in the garden, for hours."

"Right," said Kett.

He heard crunching footsteps and looked back towards the annex to see Dunst emerge. The old DI did a full circle, his eyes blinking.

"Kett?" he called out.

"Over here," Kett said.

Dunst did another circle, his arms shrugging.

"Here!" Kett shouted, louder now.

Dunst started walking in the other direction and Kett pinched his nose, taking a breath.

"Jesus Christ," he said quietly.

He turned back to Jasper.

"Alis isn't answering the door, and we're concerned about her. Can you let us in?"

Jasper leaned back so far he had to compensate for it with a few staggered steps. He propped himself up against the wall, then wagged a finger in the air.

"I'm afraid that just won't do. Not without a... a... one of those..."

"Warrants?" said Kett, and Jasper nodded.

Kett leaned towards the man.

"I'll make a deal with you," he said. "You open the door to the annex and I won't open an investigation into the hours you spent spying on Alis and her friend in the garden."

Jasper's mouth dropped open. He wagged his finger again, looking like he was about to argue. Instead, he shrugged and hiccupped.

"I suppose that's fair enough," he said. "Give me a minute."

He staggered up the hallway and Kett stepped onto the street to see Dunst still walking.

"Keith!" he yelled to deaf ears.

"Here we go," said Jasper as he reappeared, a set of keys in his hand. He jingled them at Kett like he was a baby, and when Kett reached for them he pulled them away, laughing. He walked out of his gate, then back through the annex's, dropping the keys on the mat as he tried to use them. Kett called to Dunst again, the DI now standing in the middle of the road like a lost child.

"Whoops," Jasper said as he dropped the keys again. "Slippery little buggers."

"Kett?" Dunst called. "Where did you go?"

"Unbelievable," Kett said.

Jasper finally succeeded in opening the door, standing back with a cry of triumph. He teetered for a moment like he was going to go down and Kett was half tempted to help him on his way.

"Keys," he said, clicking his fingers.

"I'll hang onto them for now if it's okay with—"

Kett pulled them from his fingers, his patience gone.

"Wait for me in your house."

Jasper shook his head.

"You're just looking for the woman?" he asked. "Nothing else?"

"What else is there?"

"Nothing," Jasper said with a belch. "Absolutely nothing."

The lie was written all over his face.

"Kett?" Dunst walked back into sight, sighing with relief

when he spotted Kett in the open door. “Where did you go?”

“Doesn’t matter,” Kett said. “You coming in?”

Dunst nodded, jogging down the path. Kett didn’t wait for him, he just shot Jasper a silent warning to stay back, then made his way into the dark.

CHAPTER SIXTEEN

THE ANNEX WAS A CONVERTED DOUBLE GARAGE, AND IT was bigger than it had looked from the outside. The front door opened into the large living room that Kett had seen through the window, nothing here other than the two sofas and the waist-high bookshelf. A handful of framed Art Deco prints hung on the walls, old theatre posters with glamorously illustrated women. The books were mostly fat science fiction novels, their spines bent and broken. There was no TV.

"Hello?" Kett called out, although he knew without a shadow of a doubt that the house was empty. The air was dead.

"Who in this day and age doesn't have a TV?" Dunst asked as he walked in after Kett. "Bloody weirdos, that's who."

There were two doors out of the room, and when Kett opened the first, he found a small cupboard. Three coats hung on pegs, as well as a couple of small rucksacks and a black handbag. Shoes littered the floor in no particular order, plenty of trainers. A hoover and an ironing board were the only other residents.

"No need to check the cupboards, is there?" Jasper called from outside. "She's not going to be hiding in there."

Kett ignored him, using his elbow to open the other door and finding himself in a short corridor. To the right was a bedroom, lit only by a lantern window in the flat roof. The plastic had turned yellow at the edges and green in the middle. A low double bed was hidden beneath a tie-dyed blanket, the bedside table cluttered by thick candles that had melted into each other to form a monstrous lump. More books lay spread-eagled on the bare wood of the floor.

He backed out of the bedroom and entered the bathroom opposite. It was brighter in here, partly because of the large window and partly because the light was on.

"You didn't switch this on, did you, Keith?"

"No, sir," Dunst said from the kitchen further down. "Haven't touched anything."

The bathroom was surprisingly large, a walk-in shower on one side next to a Victorian-style toilet and sink, and a boat-sized roll-top bath beneath a giant mirror.

The bath was full of water.

"Weird," said Kett.

He dipped the tips of his fingers into it, the water cold. There was no soap residue, no sign that it had been used. He stood straight, studying himself in the enormous mirror and seeing the exhaustion on his face. He looked more like his dad than ever.

Kett walked out of the bathroom. There was another door right next to it, but when he tried the handle, it was locked.

"Nothing in there," said Jasper. The man had crept into the living room like a fungus.

"There has to be something," said Kett.

"I use it for storage. There's not enough space in the old house. It's just boxes, rubbish, really."

"One of these open it?" Kett asked, looking at the keys in his hand.

"Nope."

Kett ignored the locked door and walked into the kitchen. It took up the entire back of the annex, long and thin, pine units at the business end and a long table at the other. There were plants everywhere, well-tended and healthy. Dunst was standing by the sink, one yellow finger aimed at a glass that had been left on the counter, some kind of liquor left inside. It was half empty—or half full, although Kett was starting to worry that there wasn't much to be optimistic about here. The bottle sat next to it, the cap off. It was some kind of alcohol-free liquor.

"Bath's full," he said. "It looks like Alis left in a hurry."

Dunst nodded, taking a handkerchief from his pocket and using it to open the oven. A tray of fish fingers sat there, uncooked and on the turn.

"Weird," he said.

Kett turned to the other side of the room, looking past the wall of greenery to the reconditioned church pew that ran the length of the table. More books were stacked at one end, and at the other was a sleek black iPad.

"You got gloves, Keith?" Kett asked.

Dunst patted his pockets and shook his head. Kett carefully picked up the iPad using its corners, lying it on the table. The screen was filthy, fingerprints visible everywhere. He double-tapped a clean area of the screen and it came to life—only just, though, the battery at three percent. The photo on the screen was of a little Jack Russell dog on a tiled floor, its eyes red from the camera flash.

Kett swiped the screen up and it asked him for a passcode. He tried six ones, then six zeroes, then he used 1, 2, 3, 4, 5, 6 and the iPad let him in. The same dog greeted him there, its tongue out.

He selected the messages app, but Alis evidently hadn't synced her iPad to her phone because it was empty. The same with her emails and FaceTime. There were precious few other apps, just a Kindle and a subscription to Apple News. He opened Photos, seeing line after line of the same little terrier.

"You see any dog stuff around here?" he asked Dunst.

"Nope," the DI replied, rummaging through some letters on the windowsill. "Definitely not a dog house, no smell."

Kett scrolled down the photographs, finally finding one of a young woman. She was in her late twenties, her dark hair dyed blonde and cropped under her chin. She had a silver stud in her nose and there was a tattoo visible across her collarbone, maybe flowers, although Kett couldn't tell because she was wearing a white shirt that was buttoned almost to the top. The photo was a selfie taken in the bathroom he'd just been in, the mirror behind her.

There was another photo next to it, a shot of herself in the mirror. Her face was hidden behind her phone, but Kett saw her hands—one wrapped in a bandage, the other bare. She was wearing red nail varnish.

Don't let it be this hand, he found himself thinking.

"Jasper, can you come in here for a second?" he said.

A few seconds later the landlord appeared, looking a lot more sober than he had when Kett had first met him.

"Is this Alis Sayer?" Kett asked, pointing to the screen.

Jasper took a closer look and nodded.

"Very pretty," he said. "She was my favourite."

"Was?" said Kett.

"Oh, uh," Jasper blinked wetly, one hand on the table like he was about to fall over. "You know, she *is* my favourite. I didn't mean anything by it."

Kett kept scrolling, seeing photos of the village, some of Norwich Castle and the cathedral too. There weren't many more of Alis until Kett got close to the end of the reel and found another selfie. The young woman stood in front of a silver plaque with a shy smile.

"Paradigm Investment," Kett read aloud. "Mean anything to either of you?"

"It's where she worked," said Dunst, holding up a sheet of paper. "Payslip from last month. Whoever they were, they paid her a pittance."

"She was an admin assistant," added Jasper. "Told me so on her application form."

"And how long ago was this?" Kett asked.

"Last year," said Jasper. "She's been a great tenant."

Kett tapped the photo. It had been taken in March, three months ago. He scrolled through the last few, then stopped dead.

"Holy shit," he said.

Towards the very end of the reel was a photo of Alis standing in an open-plan office next to a very grumpy, very familiar man.

"That's Jeremy Bower," said Kett, looking at Jasper. "You know him?"

Jasper shook his head.

"Bower as in where the... uh..." Dunst glanced at the other man. "*Thing* was delivered?"

"Yeah," said Kett.

They were the only two people in the photo, and they were standing closer together than they needed to be, their knuckles almost touching. Bower had the same expression of irritation he'd worn When Kett had met him, but Alis was smiling.

Kett pulled his phone out of his pocket.

"You can leave now," he said to Jasper.

The other man didn't move, squirming like an eel in a pot.

"I'd rather stay," he said.

Kett squared up to him, leaning in and speaking quietly.

"What are you hiding, Mr Dinwiddie?"

Jasper's mouth opened but nothing came out of it.

"Do you know what's happened to Alis?"

Jasper glanced to the side, in the direction of the corridor—only for a fraction of a second, but that was enough.

Kett pushed past him, picking through the man's keys as he walked. The door next to the bathroom was secured by a mortise deadlock and only two of the keys looked like they would fit. He tried one, hearing a whine of distress rise from the man who followed him.

"Don't! There's nothing in there, I promise."

Kett twisted the key but the lock didn't budge. He wrestled it out and inserted the other one, only for Jasper to grab hold of his arm. The man was surprisingly strong, yanking so hard that Kett almost lost his balance. In the sudden bright flare of anger that followed, Kett planted his hand on Jasper's chest and shoved him against the wall, hard. The other man grunted, his cravat hanging loose.

"Stay back," Kett growled. "Last warning."

"She's not in there," whined Jasper. "I know that's what you're thinking, but she's not in there, I swear on my life."

"Stay back."

Kett gave him another shove just to make his point clear.

Then Dunst stepped between them, giving Kett the space to try the second key. This time it turned, the lock releasing with what could have been a gunshot.

"There's nothing in there," Jasper wheezed.

Kett opened the door towards him, seeing a small cupboard.

A small, *empty* cupboard.

"See," said Jasper. "I told you."

"You told me you kept things in here," Kett said. "Where are they?"

Jasper's mouth opened and closed like a landed fish.

Kett walked into the cupboard, using the torch on his phone to illuminate the floor, then the ceiling, and finally the walls.

He almost missed it.

There was a small brass loop inserted at waist level in the wall opposite the door, and when Kett gave it a tug, the entire panel swung towards him.

He braced himself, half expecting to find a prisoner, or maybe even a body.

What he saw was almost as bad.

The hidden section of the cupboard was brighter than the one Kett was standing in, and this had everything to do with the light that seeped in through the window. Although window might not have been the right word, because through the glass Kett could see the bathroom next door, the bath itself right beneath him and the shower across the room.

A camera sat on a tripod in the middle of the cupboard, its red light blinking.

"You have got to be shitting me, Jasper," Kett said. He looked back to see the landlord standing in the open door of the cupboard, his hands over his face.

"It's not mine," he sobbed.

"You filthy old bastard," Dunst added as he peered inside.

"I didn't know that was there, I swear!" Jasper protested, his voice an octave higher.

Kett examined the camera as best he could in the small space. It wasn't a video camera, as he'd first assumed. It was a security camera, the kind designed to be mounted outside the house.

"Where can I see the feed?" he asked.

"I don't know," Jasper pleaded. "It's—"

Kett rounded on the older man with an expression on his face that promised nothing but violence. Jasper shrank back, his hands still held up in front of his face—not in shame this time, but in fear.

"Now," Kett said. "Or I swear to God I will lock you in that room and throw away the key."

"My place," Jasper said, his voice a low groan. "I have a computer."

"Of course you do. Keith, drag his sorry arse over to the house."

Kett walked out of the annex, vaulting the low fence again and making his way inside Jasper's residence. There was no sign of a computer in the living room, but when he checked the next room down the wide corridor, he found an office. A silver HP laptop sat open on an expensive desk, the screensaver full of popping bubbles. Kett sat on the chair and brought the laptop to life, quickly locating the security camera software. It loaded painfully slowly, as if it was as ashamed as Jasper had been.

On-screen, the live footage of the bathroom appeared. Kett ramped up the volume as high as it would go, scrolling back until he saw himself enter the room. He met his own eyes as he looked in the mirror, then scrolled back some more.

"I'm so sorry," said Jasper as he walked into the house. "You have to forgive me, I have a disease."

Kett ignored him, scrolling back some more until he saw Jasper on the screen. The clip was from yesterday, the man creeping into the bathroom and rummaging through Alis' laundry basket. He pulled out a bra, sniffing it, and Kett was glad he hadn't had any breakfast because it would have been all over the floor by now.

"Oh Lord," said Jasper as he appeared in the door, Dunst's hand gripping his arm. "That's not me. It's my brother. He looks just like me. I promise you, on my life, on my very soul."

On-screen, Jasper put the bra to his own chest and paraded around the bathroom. Then he dropped it back into the basket and walked to the sink, picking up the single toothbrush that sat there.

"No," said Kett as he watched Jasper's tongue flash out, touching the tip of the brush. "You did not just do that."

Jasper had given up, his hands covering his face again like he could magic himself into non-existence. Kett paused the footage, seeing that the bath was full of water.

"This was yesterday lunchtime," he said. "Why were you at her house?"

"It's *my* house, really," Jasper replied. "I knew she was out because I, er, I hadn't, you know, seen her in there all day."

"She hadn't used the toilet?"

"Right. And I knocked, but she didn't answer."

"So you let yourself in. You didn't notice the bath?"

"The bath?" Jasper said, appearing from behind his hands.

"It was full."

"Oh," the man said, taking a step closer and squinting at the screen. "I didn't see."

"Not hard to work out why," said Dunst.

On-screen, Jasper had pulled on a pair of Alis' pants and was wearing them like a ski mask.

"Did you see the glass on the counter? The open bottle?"

Jasper shook his head.

Kett rewound the feed some more, scrolling past yesterday morning to see no sign of her. It wasn't until Tuesday evening that Alis suddenly appeared in the bathroom. Kett let the video play, feeling uncomfortable as he watched the young woman. She was wearing a dressing gown, and she held her glass in one hand, spilling a little into the full bath as she leaned over to turn off the tap. He heard her mutter something, saw her rest the glass on the sink while she tried again.

Kett turned away while the young woman used the toilet, looking back again only when he heard the flush.

"I don't, you know," Jasper said. "I don't do it for *that*."

Kett didn't ask him what he meant. The anger was growing in him, and it was growing fast. It was taking every ounce of restraint he had not to pick up the laptop and insert it into Jasper's gaping mouth.

Alis washed her hands and then looked at herself in the mirror, her eyes meeting Kett's in a moment of connection that made the world seem to detach itself from reality—like he'd seen a ghost, not just a recording. His breath caught in his throat, his lungs frozen. Alis smiled, just for a fraction of a second, then she ran a hand through her hair and walked out of the room.

Kett forced himself to breathe, the room gyrating around him, fireworks blistering the corners of his vision.

Christ, he was tired.

"I'll delete it all," said Jasper. "I will, and I'll get rid of the camera. I'll never do—"

"Shut up," Kett growled. "Just shut up a moment."

He tried to turn the volume up a little more, but it was on its highest setting. He thought he'd heard something, and he rewound it a few seconds and pressed play.

Knock knock.

There it was, muffled but unmistakable.

"You hear that?" he asked Dunst. He rewound it again, pressed play.

Knock knock.

"Somebody's at the door," Dunst said.

Kett leaned in, holding his breath. A clunk, like a bottle hitting the kitchen counter. Footsteps, then Alis' muffled voice.

"Hang on." Or something very like it.

Knock knock.

Two solid bangs, like cannon shots.

A rattle of what might have been a key in a lock, then Alis again, although she was too far away now for the camera to pick up her words. She spoke for a moment and another voice answered her—deeper, maybe a man. Alis laughed, spoke again, and the door closed.

Nobody spoke, everybody waiting for what came next.

"... offer you much, I've got some Everleaf."

Alis' voice got louder as she walked past the bathroom door. More footsteps behind her, heavier, as if they were still wearing their shoes. Another laugh, this time echoed by that same deep voice.

Silence.

Then a dull thump and a heavy crash.

Kett's heart seemed to miss a beat, a shard of pain lancing through his chest. He put a hand to it like that might help, his ear practically against the screen as he fought to hear anything else.

A cough, another thump.

And another.

Kett heard a clatter that might have been the oven door opening, more footsteps that seemed to stop right outside the bathroom.

Come on, Kett thought. *Just one step. Just come into the light.*

Somebody was breathing, each one long and wet as if they were exhausted.

Come on.

The footsteps receded, then rose again, accompanied by a sound that could only have been something being dragged across the floor. Kett heard the front door being opened, slammed shut.

He heard the sound of the key in the lock.

Then nothing.

"Fuck," he said, sitting back. Alis had turned off her bath at twenty past nine, and the front door had closed eighteen minutes later.

He looked at Jasper.

"Do you have any other cameras? Inside or out? Anything at all."

"No, I—"

"You can't get in any more trouble than you are now, Mr Dinwiddie, unless you lie to me. You *do not* want to lie to me right now."

"I swear," Jasper said, his face so loose it looked ready to peel away. "It's just this one."

"Keith, call Clare," said Kett. "Tell him we need a full forensic team out here, and the digital unit as well."

"Sir," Dunst said, letting go of Jasper and reaching for his phone.

Jasper cleared his throat, his eyes wet with tears. He looked at Kett with what seemed to be a morsel of hope.

"So it was helpful, then?" he asked. "The camera. It was a good thing I put it there?"

"Yeah," Kett said, because there was no way of denying it.

"Oh, good," Jasper said, his body sagging with relief. "Does that mean—"

"Don't get too excited," said Kett. "You're still going to prison."

Jasper dropped to his knees, his hands grasping at his face, his cry like a kettle coming to boil. Kett left him there. Dunst ended the call.

"They're on their way," the DI said, looking at the screen. "This our guy?"

"This is our guy," Kett said, thinking of the photograph of the young woman with Jeremy Bower, thinking of her voice as she welcomed her guest. "And whoever did this to her, she knew them."

CHAPTER SEVENTEEN

Kett bumped the Volvo onto the same stretch of kerb where he'd parked it in the middle of the night, turning off the engine and getting out. The little village of Coltishall was quieter now, just a single IRV parked over the entrance to the Bower family's driveway. There was too much sun in the windscreen for Kett to see who was inside, but when the passenger door opened he was relieved to see Savage climb out.

"Kate," he said with a smile. "Can't keep you away."

"I can sleep when I'm dead," she said. "That's what Granddad always told me."

"Fair enough. Porter back?"

"Not yet, but Duke's right here, if that makes you feel any better."

"Not really."

"I heard that," came Duke's voice from the car.

"You were meant to," Kett replied. "Did Clare not leave a car here overnight?"

"He did," said Savage. "Couple of Uniforms. I sent them for coffee when we got here. They looked knackered. They said nobody came or went all night, other than us."

She glanced at the driveway, then spoke in a quieter voice.

"The boss called with an update. Jeremy Bower knows the owner of the hand?"

"Looks like it," said Kett. "Victim's name might be Alis Sayer. She's twenty-eight, works as an office administrator in Bower's investment firm, Paradigm. She broke her thumb in a car accident a few months back, the exact same fracture as our hand. There are too many links for it to be a coincidence."

"I hope she's okay," Savage said, although the expression on her face made it clear she didn't hold out *that* much hope.

"She was taken on Tuesday night, at nine thirty-four exactly. Her kidnapper knocked on the door and it sounds like she knew him. She invited him in, offered him a drink."

"Definitely a he?"

"Not definite, no," said Kett. "Sorry. Deep voice, though. My gut's telling me this is a man. It sounds like she was struck two or three times, and hard. Then she was dragged out of the house."

Savage shook her head, her eyes wet, her fists clenched.

"Digital forensics is analysing footage from a camera found in Alis' house," Kett went on. "They're amplifying the audio, might even have an image of Alis' abductor caught in a reflection, but they don't think it will be clear enough to help."

"That's not enough to bring in Mr Bower," said Savage. "You think it was him?"

"I don't know," said Kett. "Owner of Alis' rental place was a creep, but he's got an alibi. A good one. Dunst is taking him back to be interviewed. I don't want to arrest Bower yet. I just want to talk to him."

He made his way up the drive, Savage by his side. Kett heard the IRV's door opening, then heavy footsteps behind them.

"Wait for me," said PC Duke.

Kett looked back, doing a double-take when he saw the constable's face. Duke was green, like he'd stumbled right out of a horror movie. His eyes were small and dark and his hands were twitching.

"Jesus, Duke," he said.

"I'm fine, sir," he said.

"No, you're very clearly not."

"Looks like a zombie, doesn't he, sir?" said Savage.

"That's exactly what I was thinking."

"Brains..." Savage said.

"Not sure he'd know one of those if he saw one," Kett muttered. "I thought I told you to go home, Aaron. To get some sleep."

"I tried," Duke said. "I couldn't drop off."

"Something to do with the gallons of chemical horse-grade stimulants you were drinking?"

"I'm fine, sir, honest. Grr."

He pumped his bicep, then stopped and doubled over. Even from where he stood, Kett could hear his stomach grumble.

"Oh no," he said.

"There's a toilet in the petrol station," Kett said, and the giant PC trotted away.

"He didn't eat the cake, did he?" Savage asked before Kett had the chance to.

They rounded the corner to see the brand-new red

Range Rover still sunning itself on the driveway. There was no sign of life from inside.

"Do the honours, Kate," Kett said.

Savage rammed her fist against the door three times, making it tremble in its frame. They stood in silence as they waited, Kett closing his eyes for a moment and enjoying the warmth of the sun on the back of his neck.

A key turned in the lock, then the door opened. The Spanish maid, Margarite, stood there, and she performed an odd little curtsey.

"Good morning, officers," she said.

"Morning," said Kett. "Is Mr Bower home? We'd like a word."

"Mr Bower out," Margarite said with another awkward curtsey. "He go to work."

Kett looked at Savage and she shook her head.

"We've been watching the house," Kett told the maid. "Nobody left."

"He uses the back door," came another voice. Lydia Bower, still very much the doppelgänger of her husband, walked out of the living room. She wore a red dress that almost reached her narrow ankles, her feet bare. She looked about as happy to see them as Kett did to be there. "He always uses the back door when he goes to work. We have another driveway on that side."

"He works at Paradigm Investment, right?" Kett asked.

Lydia squeezed Margarite's shoulder and the maid retreated, as quiet as a mouse. She looked at Kett, the intensity of her gaze almost intimidating. Gone was the timid woman he'd met last night. This almost seemed like a different person entirely.

"We told you all of this last night," she said. "I'm in no mood to go over it again, DCI Kett."

"Then how about we change the subject," Kett said. He pulled out his phone, finding the photograph he'd taken of the image on Alis Sayer's iPad. When he held it up, the woman flinched—but only for a fraction of a second, her expression recovering so quickly Kett wasn't sure if he'd imagined it. "You know this woman?"

"No," she said. "Sorry. Who is she?"

"She works with your husband," Kett said.

"*For* him," corrected Mrs Bower. "Jeremy owns the company; they're all his employees. I don't know any of them. We don't associate with the staff."

"I'm sure they're heartbroken about that," said Kett. "Do all the staff hold hands with the boss like this?"

He held up the phone again, and Mrs Bower scoffed.

"They're not holding hands."

"They're not *not* holding hands," said Savage. "There's definitely contact."

"I could say the same about you two," she shot back. "You're standing next to each other. Very close, I might add. What should I read into this?"

"Fair enough," said Kett.

"I used to be a barrister, you know? Before Jeremy dragged us out into the arse end of Norfolk. I was one of the best. You won't get one up on me, I can assure you."

"I'm not trying to," said Kett. "You don't know this woman, then? Look closely."

She didn't look at all, her eyes not leaving Kett's.

"We have reason to believe that the hand delivered to your house yesterday belongs to this woman. Her name is Alis Sayer."

Mrs Bower flinched again, like she'd had a tiny electric shock.

"She was abducted from her house on Tuesday

evening," Kett went on. "Half nine. It's a bit of a coincidence that she's connected to you and your husband, don't you think?"

"Not to me," said Mrs Bower.

"I need you to really think. Have you seen her before?"

He held out the phone, and this time she looked.

"Maybe," she said. "At the work parties. I don't know. They all look the same."

"They?" asked Savage.

"The women my husband employs. Young, attractive. It's insufferably boring."

"Is his relationship with these women more than just professional?" Kett asked.

"What do you think?" Mrs Bower shot back, making no attempt to hide her reaction.

"And his relationship with Alis?"

"You'd have to ask him," she said. A small smile danced on her lips, gone in a heartbeat. "Or *her*."

"Where is your husband's office?" Kett asked. "We really need to speak with him."

Mrs Bower disappeared into the house, opening the chest of drawers next to the sweeping staircase. When she returned she was holding a business card.

"It's in the city," she said. "That's the number."

Savage took it, pulling out her phone as she walked away from the house.

"Where were you on Tuesday evening, Mrs Bower?" Kett said. "At nine thirty-eight pm?"

"Do I need to call some friends?" she replied, standing tall. "I can make your life very difficult, legally speaking."

"Maybe," Kett said, refusing to back down. "Or maybe you can just answer the question. Tuesday."

She chewed on it for a moment.

"I host a book club on Tuesday," she said. "As you already know. Eight through ten. You can check with anyone there."

"And your husband?"

She shrugged.

"Like I said, I was at book club. How the hell would I know?"

Savage crunched her way back over.

"He's not at work," she said. "Never came in this morning."

The first cold seed of fear sprouted inside Kett's spine, the day suddenly cold.

"Where is he, Mrs Bower?"

No answer. The woman stood in the doorway, her face seeming to subtly contort like she was trying not to cry.

Or trying not to smile.

"This isn't a game," said Kett. "Somebody's life may be in danger. If you know where he is, tell me."

"If he's not here, and he's not at work, he'll be in the Crow's Nest."

"Which is?"

"It's a property we own, just outside of the village. He goes there sometimes."

"Just him?" asked Savage. "Not you?"

"I have no interest in what goes on there," she said, her shifting expression settling on defiance. She folded her arms over her chest. "Take the road through the village and head for Belaugh Green. It's on the right, halfway up and just before the railway crossing. You can't miss it."

Kett looked past the woman into the quiet interior of the house. Something didn't feel right, but he couldn't put his finger on it, something in the silence of this place, in the way

Mrs Bower's flexing mouth seemed to shape voiceless, alien words.

"If your husband comes home, tell him we need to speak with him immediately," Kett said.

"Oh, he won't," came the reply as the woman sank back into the shadow of the door. "If he's in the Nest, he won't be back for hours."

Kett turned to go, only for Mrs Bower to call out.

"And whatever you do, DCI Kett, don't forget to knock."

CHAPTER EIGHTEEN

It took less than five minutes to find the Crow's Nest—which wasn't nearly as far away from Mrs Bower and her intense gaze as Kett would have liked.

"That has to be it," Savage said, stopping the IRV on the side of the road and nodding through the windscreen. Kett could see the top of a high building—not a house, but what might have been an old windmill.

There wasn't much room, so Savage left the lights on to warn traffic before opening her door. It hit the high verge and stopped there, so she shut it again.

"I'll have to get out your side, sir."

Kett climbed out, waiting for Savage to stand clear before slamming the door. They were right in the middle of the countryside here, a vast field of rapeseed looking like an ocean of sunlight stretching all the way down the hill. They'd only passed a handful of houses on this road, and most of them had looked neglected or abandoned. The only sound was a distant tractor and the ceaseless chatter of the crows in the trees.

"That was odd, wasn't it?" said Savage as they walked to

a narrow break in the verge that seemed the only way to access the building. "That whole conversation with Mrs Bower."

"People *are* odd," Kett said. "I realise that a little more with every new case. People are just odd."

"Present company excepted, of course," she said.

"Well, Duke's not here, so yes."

There had been no sign of the giant PC when they'd walked back to the street, so they'd decided to leave him. In truth, though, Kett would have felt better with the big fella here, dodgy tummy or not. Duke wasn't the brightest spark, but they could always count on him in a fight.

And he had a feeling that's exactly what they were about to get.

The Crow's Nest was worthy of its name. When they passed the hedge, Kett saw that it had definitely once been a windmill, the sails long gone but the body sticking out of the land like a pepper pot. There was no sign of an extension, and the few windows that pocked the curved sides of the building looked like they'd been there for decades. There was no driveway, no garden, just scrubland stretching in one direction to the tall fence that marked the neighbour's land, and in the other down to a marsh.

"Door must be on the other side," Kett said.

Savage nodded, following him over the uneven ground. "You smell that, sir?"

Kett's nose twitched, something acrid in the air.

"Smoke," he said, and he broke into a jog.

They rounded the base of the windmill to see that a small fire had been lit in a circle of cinderblocks. It was struggling, more smoke than flame, and small enough for Kett to kill with a couple of good stamps. He bent down, using a twig to poke through the ashes and seeing half-burned documents next to the blackened crusts of photographs. There was something else there too, a sculpture made of thin wire and scraps of cloth.

"What is that?" he asked.

"A bra," Savage said.

"Why is somebody burning bras?"

"Was all the rage once upon a time," Savage replied.

There was nothing much else to see, so Kett turned to the windmill. The low door was open, leading into a throat of darkness.

"Why do you think Mrs Bower told us to knock?" Savage asked.

"I dread to think."

Kett knocked twice, then cleared his throat.

"Mr Bower? Are you in there? It's the police."

No answer. He knocked again.

"Door's open, so we're coming in."

Kett poked his head beneath the lintel, his eyes slowly adjusting to make out a wide, circular room. The mechanical guts of the building were still intact, the bulky cob grinder serving as a crude dining table. A single cup sat on it, along with a hardback book. Kett walked closer to get a look at the title.

"*Children of Dune*," he said.

"Frank Herbert," Savage replied, walking to the foot of a narrow staircase that spiralled up to the next level.

"You read it?"

"I'm more of a crime fiction fan, sir," Savage said.

"Alis Sayer's house was full of sci-fi books," Kett said. "Coincidence?"

He took the lead again, walking up three creaking, groaning steps before shouting into the darkness overhead.

"If you're here, Mr Bower, let us know. And please don't do anything stupid."

He was answered by the dull thump of something falling, hard enough to rain a shower of dust from the rafters. Kett paused, popping his lips and wondering whether they should call for help. He looked at Savage and saw the same question on her face.

"Your decision, sir," she said after a moment. "But he might be hurt up there. The fire outside, it feels like he's cleaning house. If he's got something to hide, then the next step might be, you know..."

She looped a hand around her neck, sticking out her tongue. Kett nodded, starting up the stairs again.

"Mr Bower?"

The level above was significantly smaller, a single bed sitting awkwardly against the curved wall and an old armchair next to it, its stuffing hanging out. More books sat on a crude shelf made from cinderblocks and timber, an almost empty bottle of vodka propped next to them, and a fully empty one on its back. A wall of boxes had been piled on the far side of the space, dozens of them, towering over Kett's head in places. A ladder disappeared through an open hatch in the ceiling more than twelve feet overhead.

"Nope," Kett said, more to himself than anyone else. "Do not make me go up there."

Two more thumps echoed from the loft, then a soft warble that might have been a voice.

"I can do it, sir," Savage said, making for the ladder.

"It's fine, Kate. I'll go. Can you check the boxes?"

"Do you think you'll even get up there?" Savage asked, looking at him like he was ninety years old.

"I have climbed a ladder before," he replied.

He regretted it instantly, though, the ladder so old that

the rungs seemed to bend and creak beneath his boots. It obviously wasn't secured to anything at the top because it wobbled all over the place as he eased his way up, and every time he looked down, his stomach buckled.

There was no way he was asking for help, though.

He reached the hatch, his heart drumming against his tonsils as he pushed his head into the loft. It wasn't as dark up here as he'd feared, huge chunks of the ceiling missing and daylight streaming in. More half-rotted boxes occupied the space, looking like they hadn't been moved for a long time. Half a dozen pigeons cooed and chuckled, their flapping wings like firecrackers. They didn't seem scared of him at all, the big bull pigeons puffing out their chests as they harassed the females. One jumped onto a length of wood that rocked gently.

Thump.

"Nobody up here," he said. "Just a whole lot of pigeon shit."

"Boxes are full of old clothes," said Savage. "Something's been nesting in them, I think. They're—"

Thump.

Something big shifted downstairs and Savage cried out. Kett almost fell off the ladder in shock, looking past his feet to see Savage reel back like she'd been shoved. Her foot hit the bed, and she fell onto it, a cloud of dust exploding from the ancient mattress.

"What the hell, Kate? Are you—"

Somebody ran across the room, a dark shape moving fast. It kicked the bottom of the ladder and it spun out from beneath Kett. He grabbed the edge of the hatch just in time, the ladder clattering against the wall and leaving him hanging there.

"Stop!" yelled Savage, struggling off the bed. "Police!"

The shape was bounding down the stairs.

"It's Jeremy Bower," Savage said.

She grabbed the ladder, starting to hoist it back into place.

"Forget it," Kett yelled, scrabbling for purchase on the filthy floor above. "Just catch him."

Savage dropped the ladder and thundered down the stairs, almost missing one. Kett heard the sound of her voice fading as she chased Mr Bower outside.

"Shit," he hissed.

His fingers were slipping, nothing there to grip. The floor was a good eight-foot drop from where his feet kicked and swung—not far enough to do serious damage, but far enough to really hurt him if he landed wrong. He jerked his hands a little deeper into the hatch, trying to pull himself up. But it was hopeless. He just wasn't fit enough.

Above him, a beady-eyed pigeon strutted into view, twisting its head back and forth as it tried to make sense of what it had found. Another one joined it, both of them standing on the very lip of the hatch. A third hopped onto Kett's hand, its feet like needles.

"You can fuck right off," he told them, sweat rolling down his forehead, stinging his eyes.

The pigeons had no intention of going anywhere. The first one turned around, its backside hanging right over Kett's face.

"Don't you dare," he said in his best DCI's growl. "Don't you fu—"

The third pigeon flapped from his hand and dropped onto his face in a tornado of feathers and claws. Kett screamed, letting go of the hatch, his stomach rising into his throat as he fell. He managed to land on his feet but he punched right through the rotting boards, dropping into the bottom room. The dining table caught him in a fist of stone, knocking every scrap of air from his lungs.

He lay there for a moment, staring up through the clouds of dust, through the hole he'd made in the ceiling, seeing the pigeons flapping around like they were absolutely shitting themselves with laughter. He opened his mouth to speak, but all that came out was a low, awful groan.

He settled for his middle finger instead, then rolled off the stone table and forced a couple of breaths in. He could hear Savage outside, and when he ducked through the tiny door and rounded the building he saw her wrestling with Bower near the road.

"Oi!" Kett tried to yell, producing a dusty whisper.

Bower gave Savage another shove, catching her off guard and sending her sprawling into the dirt. He began running back towards the windmill, making it halfway before he spotted Kett.

"Stop!" Kett coughed, a little louder now. "Last warning."

The man spun on his heels, dancing on the spot as he tried to stop himself from falling over. Then he was heading towards the road again, his arms cartwheeling. This time, Savage was ready for him. She crouched low, launching herself at Bower as he passed her and wrapping her arms around the tall man's waist. She twisted her body, and he fell hard, faceplanting into the dirt. Even then he was struggling, Savage just not heavy enough to keep him on the ground.

Kett dropped next to her, bracing his knee in Mr Bower's lower back to pin him. He squawked like a chicken.

"That's enough," Kett said. "What the hell do you think you're doing?"

"Get off me!" Bower shrieked, his words slurred. It was

no wonder, Kett could smell the alcohol on his breath. He was as pissed as a fart.

He was strong, too, surprisingly so given his wiry frame and his spindly arms. Kett wasn't sure even the two of them would be able to keep him down for long.

"Cuff him," he said, using his body weight to hold Bower there while Savage pulled a set of handcuffs from her jacket. She snapped them on Bower's wrists and the man shrieked again, his words so full of fury that Kett couldn't make any sense of them. Savage sat on his legs, scrubbing the sweat and the dust from her face.

"You okay?" Kett asked.

"Yeah, sir, but are *you*?"

He glanced at his suit to see the dirt there, the green and white crust of pigeon shit, and a twelve-inch gash up the leg of his trousers. Only now did he notice the stinging sensation there, and he peeled open the torn material to see a nasty scratch along his shin. Blood leaked from it, meandering towards his shoe.

"I'm fine," he said. "But the ceiling isn't. And I'm not sure those pigeons will ever recover."

Savage frowned at him.

"Never mind," he said. "Can you let Clare know?"

She nodded, jumping up to make the call.

"You going to stay still?" he asked Bower.

The man grunted what seemed to be a yes and Kett got off him, still trying to suck enough air in. His back was screaming from the fall, the pain running from his backside all the way to his neck. He felt nauseated with it, too.

True to his word, Bower had stopped struggling, and was whispering muttered curses into the dry ground.

"You mind telling me what all that was all about?" Kett asked him.

"None of your fucking business," Bower said, the words blowing up puffs of dust.

"That's where you're wrong," Kett said, sitting back. "I know about Alis Sayer."

Bower's bloodshot eyes slid up to find Kett, and even though he didn't say anything, the fear there was obvious.

"She works for you," Kett went on. "At Paradigm. We visited her house this morning, and she's not there. Where is she?"

Bower tried to roll onto his back but Kett put a foot on his shoulder to stop him.

"No," he said. "Not until you talk."

"I'm not saying anything until my solicitor arrives," Bower said. "I'm sick of this bullshit. We're the victims here, we're the ones who had to look at that *thing*. This is unacceptable."

"Alis Sayer," Kett said, the pain in his back fuelling his anger. "I'm not going to ask again."

"Fine," the other man spat. "I know her. Of course I do. But I don't know where she is."

"How well did you know her?" Kett said.

"As well as all my staff," he said. "No more, no less."

"You bring all your staff out here to the Crow's Nest?"

Bower craned his head around again, his eyes bulging.

"What are you talking about?" he said. "I never bring anyone here. This is my place, I enjoy it alone."

"That's not Alis' copy of *Dune* on the table, then?"

"How—" he started, and even though he'd stopped himself the rest of the sentence was easy enough to read.

"Because we're not stupid," Kett said. "This is your chance to talk, so talk. She's been here?"

"Yes," Bower said, speaking to the dirt. "Once or twice."

"Why?"

"Because we share the same interests. We like to read. That's what this place is, a sanctuary. No electricity, no TV, no internet. I come here to read, by daylight or candlelight."

"Read and drink," Kett said.

"Alis didn't drink, just me. And it's not a crime."

"We're getting to the crime bit," said Kett. Savage was walking this way and he pointed at the Crow's Nest. She nodded, walking towards the windmill's door and disappearing inside. "How many times has Alis been out here?"

"Three or four."

"Which is it? Three or four?"

"Four," the man said. "I wanted to show her. She came out here and... read."

"She came all the way out here to read her book?" Kett said. "And drink?"

"A little bit, yes," Bower said.

"And..." Kett prompted.

"Nothing else."

That was a lie, clear as day.

"Whose underwear are you burning over there, Jeremy?"

He looked like he was going to try to push himself up, but Kett planted his boot on the man's shoulder again, just firmly enough to keep him there.

"I'm not saying."

"Because if it's Alis Sayer's then it will be easy enough to tell. Underwire doesn't burn."

"You don't understand," Bower growled. "You'll get the wrong idea."

"So it *is* hers?"

A crow dropped into the garden from a nearby tree, utterly fearless as it hopped towards the extinguished fire. It studied them with its dark eyes, and Kett couldn't help but see the unkind omen there.

"Yes, it's hers," said Bower. "But it's not what you think. She dropped some papers off for me the other day at the house and we got talking. I brought her out here and we got caught in that bloody storm. She was soaking wet, so I offered her some clothes."

"Whose clothes?"

"My wife's, if you must know. We keep some of our old things here, those boxes are full of clothes. I gave Alis a dress, a jumper, that's all. Kept her old clothes here, so they'd dry out."

"When was this?"

"Last Thursday," he said. "A week ago today."

"And you just drank vodka and read your books?"

"Yes," he replied, weakly. "Alis didn't drink, just me."

"That was the last time she was here?" Kett asked.

The crow called out in its hoarse voice, as if warning Bower not to answer—or Kett not to listen. It hopped into the ashes of the fire and Kett waved his arms at it, shooing it away with a hiss. It beat its way back into the tree, continuing to watch them.

"Yes. I haven't seen her since then."

"You didn't bring her here this Tuesday? Two days ago?"

Bower shook his head.

"Because she was taken from her home, by force, and by somebody she knew."

He peered up at Kett again, his expression unreadable.

"I'm sure she knows lots of people," he said.

"Where were you Tuesday evening, Mr Bower?"

The man pressed his face into the ground, sighing in a way that made the answer perfectly clear.

"You were here?"

"Yes. Alone."

"You see how this is starting to look, don't you?" Kett said. "You're in a relationship with—"

"It's *not* a relationship," he shot back.

"Your wife told us you've done this before, young women from the office."

"She... she would say that. She's jealous."

"You're in a relationship with Alis Sayer," Kett pressed on. "You bring her to this... whatever this place is. You have some of her possessions here, her underwear. You have no alibi for the night that Alis was abducted. And now you're burning evidence and attacking the police."

"I wasn't—"

"The only thing I don't understand, Jeremy, is why you'd cut off her hand and send it to yourself."

"No, I didn't, I *couldn't*."

"Because it was almost certainly Alis' hand that was left on your doormat, and I'm wondering how you didn't know that when you saw it. The nail varnish. You must have recognised it."

"No!"

"So why abduct her, and why mutilate her?" Kett went on, thinking aloud. "Unless she was going to tell? Unless she was going to let your wife know what was going on. Is that it?"

"Then maybe *Lydia* is responsible?" Bower said, his mouth twisted into a gruesome smile. "Maybe she did find out, and this is all her? You ever think of that?"

Kett didn't answer, happy to let the man stew. Savage had reappeared, wiping the sweat from her forehead with the back of a gloved hand.

"It's going to take a while to get through it all," she said. "But there's hair and fibre everywhere, and I found blood."

"Blood?" snapped Bower. "That's a lie. There's no blood in there."

"Might be yours though, sir," Savage said, nodding to his leg. "What are we going to do with him?"

"Not sure," Kett said. "Watch him for a moment, would you?"

Savage took his place and Kett walked to the fire, ducking down beside it. They'd got here too late, most of the documents burned beyond recognition. Kett saw the Paradigm Investment logo on a couple of pieces of paper, and a Barclay's header too.

"What were you burning?" he asked. "Apart from the bra?"

"Nothing," Bower said. "Just work stuff."

"Why?"

"Because it's better than a shredder," he shot back. "I do it all the time."

"No," Kett said. "I don't buy it. You're a big company, you don't just destroy records like this. You're very close to the edge of the cliff, Jeremy. If I were you, I'd start telling the truth."

"Jesus Christ," Bower said.

He took a deep, shuddering breath.

"Okay, you want the fucking truth? I'm broke. I'm fucking broke. It's all gone. My money, Lydia's money, I fucking lost it. But she can't know, okay? She can't know I've taken out mortgages on the house, she can't know about the loans. She cannot find out, is that clear?"

"That's why you're burning them?" Savage asked.

"She checks everything," Bower said. "She's a nosy cow,

always asking questions, always trying to peek at my accounts. But she can't do it if they're not here, can she?"

His eyes were almost out of their sockets, his wiry body squirming like a snake.

"Happy?" he said. "Happy now?"

Kett used the twig to poke around the ashes, seeing scraps of numbers, and at least one half-burned envelope with an angry red 'Final Warning' stamp.

"Do you know somebody called Douglas Ireland?" asked Kett.

"No?" said Bower. "Who's he?"

"What about Benedict Gilbert?"

"No!"

Kett probed some more, then stopped dead.

"Savage," he said. "Get over here."

"What is it, sir?" she asked, leaning over him. "Oh, shoot, is that what I think it is?"

It was. There was no doubt about it, even though only a chunk of the corner remained unburnt, any handwriting already burned away.

A postcard, red and black.

And a tick's head.

"What is it?" Bower cried out. "What have you found?"

"The last nail in your coffin, Jeremy," Kett said. "And it is my distinct pleasure to let you know that you are now under arrest."

CHAPTER NINETEEN

Porter woke in a bed made of golden sun.

He yawned, stretching like a cat and opening his eyes to see daylight pouring through the window, as thick as treacle. He was alone on the super-king bed, the black silk sheet pulled up to his chin, one leg hanging over the edge. He yawned again, sitting up and wondering why he felt so well-rested.

Then he checked the clock by his bed.

"Shit a brick!"

He tugged off the covers, almost tripping as he ran into the *en suite*. He cranked on the shower, brushing his teeth while he waited for the water to warm up. He washed as quickly as he could, grabbing a fresh suit from his side of the dressing room before running stark bollock naked back into the bedroom. He'd got one leg in his boxers before he noticed Mrs Dunbar standing in the upstairs window of the house across the road, her eyes wide and a grin plastered over her face.

"Shit a fucking brick!" Porter yelped.

He hopped towards the curtains but didn't quite make

it, betrayed by his own underwear. He fell with a yelp, crawling the rest of the way and yanking them closed. He pulled on his shirt, then his suit, peering through the curtains again to see Mrs Dunbar still in her window, the glass steamed up. He offered her a sheepish wave before grabbing his phone.

Three missed calls from the Super, and one from Kett.

"Shit on it," he said, calling the Superintendent back only for it to go straight to voicemail.

"I'm on my way, sir," he said.

He ran downstairs, barrelling into the kitchen so fast he almost collided with his wife. He clamped a hand to his heart, almost screaming.

"Jesus, Pete!" Allie yelled.

"What are you still doing here?" he said. "It's gone eleven."

"Still not feeling great," she replied, brushing a strand of platinum blonde hair away from her face. "Called in sick again."

She did look a little poorly, her skin paler than usual, darkest under the eyes.

"You've been sick again?" Porter asked, pulling her into his arms. He felt her nod against his chest and he held her tight, one hand stroking her hair—only for a second, though, then she pulled away.

"Sorry," she said, burping into her hand. "Need a little space this morning."

"Clare's been sick too," said Porter. "I thought he was going to shit himself yesterday. I wish you hadn't eaten his cake, I think it was poisonous."

Allie shrugged, something flashing across her face that Porter couldn't quite read. She didn't just look sick, he thought. She looked exhausted. It was no surprise, not really. They'd started preparing for IVF a few weeks back and it had been gruelling—the appointments, the questions, the endless, relentless pressure of what they were about to undertake. She'd tackled it like a trooper, the way she tackled everything. But it was taking its toll.

"Can I do anything to help?" he asked. "I can stay here, make you tea, massage your feet, whatever you want."

Allie smiled, but she shook her head.

"I'll be fine," she said. "Like you say, it's probably just that cake."

"I have no idea why he even thought Bounties were a responsible thing to bake with."

He checked his watch.

"I'd better run, then. Why didn't you wake me?"

"Because you crawled into bed at four, then spent the next three hours rolling around in your sleep groaning about crab cakes."

"*Crab cakes*?"

"I don't know, something like that. I couldn't make out a word you were saying. But you looked like you needed the rest."

She rose on her tiptoes and kissed him, tasting of peanut butter and leaving crumbs on his lips.

"Go on," she said as she wiped them away with her thumb. "I'll see you later."

Porter ran for the garage door, turning back.

"You need me for anything at all, you just call, okay?"

Allie nodded, giving him another look that he couldn't quite read.

"I love you," he said.

Just a nod.

He laced up his shoes, grabbed his keys, and ran to the car.

PORTER HAD ALMOST MADE it to HQ before Clare called him back.

"You out of bed yet, Pete?" he asked, his voice weirdly hollow, like he was standing at the bottom of a well.

"Yes, sir. Sorry. It was a late night."

"I'll forgive you when you do this one thing for me."

"Sir?"

Porter slowed down for some traffic lights, wondering for a second if the call had dropped because Clare didn't answer. There was a soft groan, a splash, then a sigh.

"Sir?"

"Douglas Ireland's mother is in town and she wants to speak with us. She refuses to come here, she wants us to go to her."

"I hope you told her to go to hell," Porter said.

"I..." Another groan, like Clare was trying to climb the well-shaft he'd fallen down. "I can't be tossed to fight with her. She can make life difficult for us if she wants to. Just go and see her. Probably just wants to give us a bollocking for not pandering to her toerag of a son."

"Sure thing," Porter said as he swung the Mondeo right. "Where is she?"

"Douglas' house," said Clare, his voice strained. "She was expecting you two hours ago."

"Sir," asked Porter. "Where are you?"

"Where do you think?" Clare replied, straining again. There was a thunderous echo, and the Super sighed.

"Oh no, sir," Porter said. "Please, no."

"It's called multitasking, you tosspuppet," Clare barked, the toilet flushing. "Now toss off."

Porter shuddered as the call ended, wondering if there

was a way of bleaching the images from his head. He focussed on the drive, heading back towards Norwich and making good time thanks to the quiet roads. He pulled onto Douglas' street fifteen minutes later, driving halfway up it before he found an empty patch of kerb. It was a short walk back, but the sun was so fierce he had to take off his jacket, slinging it over his shoulder as he entered through the gate and knocked on the door.

"Who is it?" came a voice from inside, muffled but familiar.

"Duggie, it's DI Pete Porter. Open up."

Somebody else spoke, an indecipherable conversation from inside. Porter waited patiently for most of a minute before he heard the rattle of a key in the lock. The door swung open to reveal a woman in her early fifties. She was immaculately dressed in a sharp crimson trouser suit, her hair bleached blonde and her nails as red as her lipstick. She was wearing a full face of makeup, like she was just about to go on TV. And that was why he recognised her, he realised, because he *had* seen her on TV.

"ID?" the woman said, snapping her fingers at Porter like he was her butler.

He pulled out his warrant card and she studied it, her serious blue eyes taking in his face. Eventually she nodded, standing back.

"I've been waiting all morning," she said as Porter stepped into the cool hallway. Her accent bore the slightest trace of the West Midlands. "What kind of amateur shit parade are you running here?"

Duggie stood in the kitchen door, his expression as smug as ever. He was wearing what looked like a brand new black and red Hugo Boss tracksuit, the hood pulled up. Next to him was a short, wide man in a cheap suit, his balding head gleaming with sweat and his round face ruddy from what Porter would guess was a lifetime of anger.

"My apologies," Porter said in the least apologetic tone of voice he could muster. "Mrs Ireland?"

"If you don't know that then the police in this part of the world must be shittier than I thought."

Smug Doug grinned at Porter, the kind of grin that he would happily have slapped off the young man's face if he could have got away with it. The shorter man cleared his throat in the way only a solicitor could. He was probably in his late forties, but something about his red face and serious eyes made it difficult to age him.

"I take it this is your brief, then," Porter said.

"Chris Shortle," the man said in a voice as cheap as his suit.

"You alone here?" Porter asked them. "Where's Merletta?"

"Gone," said Duggie. "I sent her packing, couldn't stand all the crying."

"Well?" said Frances.

"Well what?" Porter replied. "You asked to see us, not the other way around. Speaking to you is hardly a priority on this case."

Frances looked like she *had* been slapped, her mouth falling open.

"You do realise I'm going to file a complaint?" she said when she'd recovered. "Against your whole department."

"For..." Porter said, shrugging.

"For making my son feel like a criminal. That's unacceptable. He is the one who received that foul thing. He is the one who's being threatened. He is a victim here, and he will be treated as such."

"You think this is a threat?" Porter asked, making his

way into the living room. It was a mess in here, mostly the leftover detritus from last night's party. He lifted a bottle from the sofa and perched on the edge of the seat, draping his jacket over the cushion next to him.

"Comfortable?" asked Frances when she walked in after him, her brow creased with fury. Chris Shortle plodded after her like a donkey.

"Very," said Porter. "I asked if you thought this was a threat against your son."

"Well, what else could it be?" she replied, standing close enough to Porter to force him to sit back—a deliberate move to intimidate. "He certainly didn't order it from Amazon."

"You know of anyone who might want to hurt Douglas?" he asked.

"Plenty of people. People hate him because he's successful, because he's handsome."

It was easy to see where the kid got his arrogance from.

"And because he's related to you?" Porter added.

"What's that got to do with anything?"

"I've seen you on the telly, Mrs Ireland. Some breakfast show, I think, during the whole Brexit thing."

Frances folded her arms over her chest, looking smug.

"Personally, I thought you were full of..."

Porter stopped himself before it was too late, wiping his mouth like he was pulling the words to safety.

"Let's just say your politics and mine don't coincide."

"Which explains why you're not out there trying to find the person who did this," Frances said, her cheeks almost as scarlet as her suit. "My son is innocent; he's the victim in all this."

"It's funny how you keep saying that," said Porter. "Because I thought the victim in all this was whoever lost that foot. You have any idea who that might be?"

"My client is not prepared to answer that question," said Shortle.

"Well, maybe she should be," Porter said. "If you really want to help your son, then help us. Has anything like this ever happened to you before?"

"Of course not," said Frances. "I've had death threats, too many for you to count—although I'm guessing you can't count that high. You should read them, they're really fucking imaginative. The things people say they're going to do to you when you know that if they ever saw you face to face, they'd run off squirting piss down their thighs. They never have the balls to actually do anything."

"I would say this person has the balls," Porter said. "You think they're going through Duggie to get to you?"

Duggie had slunk to the doorway and was watching them beneath the shadow of his hood.

"My client is not prepared to answer that question," the solicitor said. "It's not relevant."

"It seems pretty relevant to me," said Porter. "Because I think this has nothing to do with you. I think this has everything to do with *him*."

He pointed to Duggie.

"Because what I'm hearing is that your son isn't particularly nice, and that whatever you claim, he might actually be a criminal."

"Go fuck yourself," said Frances.

"You'd better be very sure of yourself before you say anything more like that," said Shortle, suddenly a lot more confident.

Porter held up his hands in surrender.

"All I'm saying is that I'm hearing there have been a lot of complaints about his behaviour. Him and the other members of the football club."

"Bullshit," said Duggie.

"Bullshit," echoed his mother. "Girls will say anything these days to get a bit of attention. Look at him, Detective. You think any girl is really going to complain when they're under that?"

Porter actually felt the anger move through him like a forest fire. He stood up, Frances stumbling back to make room for him.

"You really think that's the way to bring up your son?" he said. "He has no more rights than the rest of us, no more entitlement. And if I find out any of these stories are true, I'll make sure he pays for it. You hear me?"

He looked at Duggie.

"Where were you on Tuesday, Douglas? At half nine?"

"He doesn't have to answer that," said Shortle.

"I say he does," said Porter. "Unless he wants to spend the rest of the day with me in an interview room."

"Footy training," Duggie said. "Ask the coach, check the cameras."

Porter sniffed, and Frances actually smiled, the exact same shit-eating grin as her son.

"You're nothing," she said. "Nobody. I don't give a rat's arse about you or your threats, and you know why?"

Porter didn't answer, but it didn't stop her.

"Because we're untouchable. You cannot touch us. You cannot even come near us."

"I wouldn't be so sure—"

"No," she interrupted, actually prodding Porter in the chest. "I'm telling you. This is how it is. We're protected. We're fucking blessed. There isn't a single thing you can do to hurt us."

There was something in her expression that was almost euphoric, like a preacher giving a sermon.

"My son will live his life the way I intend him to. He'll be the best at everything he does because I will make it that way. He'll get his little football team, he'll make his money, because I'll ensure it. Then you know what will happen? He'll go into politics, he'll become an MP just like I was. He'll fight for the good, hard-working *British* people of this country and one day he'll rule the whole fucking shebang. And you know what will happen then?"

Porter still didn't reply. He was grinding his teeth so hard he could hear it even over the shrill sound of her voice.

"Then every time you see him on the news, you'll know he won. You'll know that somewhere far, far down the chain, you pretty much work for him. And every time he walks into a room, you'll have to shake his hand and call him sir."

Duggie's grin was so big it looked like he had tenter-hooks in his mouth. Frances prodded Porter's chest again, leaning in.

"This is the way it will be, because I fucking say so. Clear?"

The inferno had spread to Porter's head, filling it with white noise. He wasn't sure what to say, even if he thought he could say it. Frances rocked back on her heels, the expression on her face smugger than ever.

"That's all," she said. "Now bugger off."

"Yeah," said Duggie from the door. "Bugger off."

"You heard them," added Shortle, squaring up to Porter in a way that made it clear he wasn't just a solicitor. There was muscle in his squat body, and a dull look in his eyes.

"I heard you," Porter said. "Loud and clear."

He could have brought them in, he knew. He could have slapped a pair of cuffs on Frances Ireland's wrists and thrown her into the back of his car, charged her with intimidation and harassment. But something in her face told him she probably wanted him to do exactly that. Frances was a woman who craved publicity, and anything that happened to her took precious attention away from the case.

And away from her son.

"Thanks for your time," Porter said, picking up his jacket. "You've been very helpful."

Some of the arrogance fell away from her face, and a little more followed when Porter gave her his best smile. He made for the exit, waiting patiently for Duggie to slope out of the way. The front door was still open and Porter stepped into the sun, squinting into the darkness of the house to see Frances appear from the living room.

"Enjoy the rest of your time in the city," Porter said.

He studied Duggie for a moment, frowning.

"What?" Frances asked. "What are you looking at?"

"It's nothing," said Porter. "It's just... he really isn't *that* good-looking."

He turned and made his way up the path, taking immense satisfaction from the crunch of the door as it slammed shut behind him.

CHAPTER TWENTY

Savage drove the IRV back towards Coltishall, Kett in the passenger seat and Jeremy Bower sitting in the back, his glum face smushed against the window. They'd hung on long enough for Cara Hay and her team to arrive, a flood of forensic technicians descending on the windmill and the extinguished fire. Kett knew for a fact they'd discover traces of Alis Sayer in the Crow's Nest, but what he didn't know was how much of the young woman would be left for them to find.

Whatever else he was guilty of, though, Jeremy Bower had attacked them both—not to mention murdering Kett's suit. He wasn't going anywhere for a while.

Duke was waiting by the entrance to the Bower's driveway, his grey face covered with a sheen of sweat. He seemed utterly relieved to see them pull up, smiling at Savage like a kid whose missing mum has come back to collect him.

"He does not look good," she said as she pulled the car up to the kerb and cut the engine. "You want me to book him?"

"For not looking good?"

"Book *Bower*," she said, gesturing to the man in the back.

"Oh, yeah," said Kett. "Take Duke with you in case he gets any funny ideas."

"Do I have to?" Savage said. "He looks like he's pooped his pants already, and what if it's contagious?"

"It's not contagious, it's that bloody cake," said Kett. He checked his watch, seeing that it was coming up for midday. "I'd better go, I've got an appointment."

"The house?" Savage said, and he nodded. "Exciting, sir."

"It is."

He glanced into the back, but Bower might as well have been comatose, his eyes closed. He didn't look like he was dangerous, but he was still cuffed just in case. Kett couldn't get a read on him, or his wife. But there were secrets there, he was sure of it.

He opened the door, enveloped by sweet-smelling sunshine, then by the distinctly *not* sweet-smelling Duke as he slouched over.

"Sir," the PC said. "Where do you want me?"

"There are so many answers to that question, Aaron," Kett said. "But for now, ride with Savage and keep an eye on him. Mrs Bower still home?"

"No," Duke said, massaging his stomach. "She left just after you."

"She say where she was going?"

"I didn't speak to her. I was over there." Duke nodded to the garage. "They asked me not to come back."

"Get home," said Kett. "Shitting yourself on the job isn't going to help anyone."

"Yes, sir."

Duke folded himself into the car, Savage taking a deep

breath and holding it, casting a desperate look at Kett as she pulled into traffic. Kett laughed quietly, making his way to the Volvo. He was halfway there when his phone rang, Superintendent Clare's name on the screen.

"Sir," Kett said.

"Where are you?"

"At the Bower place," he said. "We're bringing Jeremy Bower in. He attacked us. No alibi for Alis' abduction and he's burning evidence. Not looking good for him, but I'm not a hundred percent sold. Can you interview him, sir?"

"Yes," said Clare. "I need you on something else. Spalding was digging into Benedict Gilbert. She left a message with his GP and he's just called back, wants to talk. Spalding's doing something else, can you take it?"

Kett checked his watch again.

"In Aylsham?" he asked.

"Yes. Doctor Allister Colon."

"I'll have to make it quick, sir. We've... wait, did you say, Dr *Colon*?"

"I did. Why does it need to be quick?"

"We've got to view a house this afternoon."

"Why?" Clare snapped. "For the case?"

"No, because we're thinking of buying it," Kett said.

"Why?"

"To live in."

"*Why*, Kett?"

"Uh... I'm not sure I understand the question, sir."

"I don't care," Clare barked, then he hung up.

"Right," said Kett.

He drove the Volvo out of Coltishall, cutting north-west through country lanes clogged with lorries and tractors before arriving in Aylsham twenty minutes later. It took another twenty minutes to find the bloody surgery, and then ten more to wait for an ancient man to pull his ancient Ford Cortina out of a parking space. By the time he'd walked through the door, it was almost one.

The surgery had a large reception that was almost empty. Part of the reason for that had to be the awful pop music that was pouring from the wall-mounted speakers, a song that he half recognised as being by the Spice Girls. It seemed far too loud and far too jolly for a place full of poorly people.

"Hi," said Kett, laying his warrant card on the reception desk and drumming his hands. "I'm DCI Kett, with the police. I just need a word with Doctor Colon."

"He's with a patient," said the woman, without even glancing up. "Take a seat."

He did as he was told, sitting as far away from the man with the hacking cough and the woman with the seeping rash as was mathematically possible. His phone buzzed while he was there and he looked to see a message from Billie.

Don't be late!

He fired one back:

On my way.

By the time he'd put his phone back in his pocket, the surgery door had opened and a man walked out, heading for the car park. Seconds later, another man appeared, this one in his mid-fifties, his blue shirt open at the collar. He had an almost perfect circle of male pattern baldness in his greying hair and he put a hand to it like he was checking it was still there. He smiled warmly at the woman with the rash.

"Ms Cave, please come in."

"Hold up just one moment," said Kett, practically springing from his chair. "DCI Kett, Norfolk Police. You mind if I have a very quick word before you guys begin?"

Ms Cave looked like she very much did mind, but Kett didn't give the doctor any choice. He walked into the office, waiting for the other man to join him before closing the door.

"My apologies, Doctor, uh..."

"*Colón*," said the man. "You can say it, but make sure the emphasis is on the back end, so to speak."

Kett laughed.

"*Colón*. Got it."

"It's Spanish, originally," the doctor went on, gesturing to the two chairs beside his desk. "My father was Spanish, and the name is about all I inherited from him when he died, which is why I look about as olive-skinned as a digestive biscuit left in the bath. Some people think the name is related to Colin, which derives from the Greek Nicholas, which in turn stems from the words *nickan* and *laos*, or 'power to the people.'"

"Is that right?" Kett said, sitting down. "I know a Colin, I'll have to let him know he's a colon."

The doctor breathed out a laugh to let Kett know he'd heard it all before. He sat down in his office chair and steepled his fingers beneath his chin, studying Kett with serious blue eyes.

"I'm here because of Benedict Gilbert," Kett said when he realised the man was waiting for a prompt.

"Oh, gosh, yes," Dr Colón said, rocking back. "I completely forgot, I'm so sorry. Things are utterly bonkers today. It wasn't you who left a message, was it?"

"It was my colleague, DS Spalding."

"Right. That's right. She was asking if we could share any information about him. I didn't quite understand her message because it sounded almost like you found his *foot*."

Kett nodded, and the doctor's face fell.

"Gosh, right. I mean, do you know if he's okay? The rest of him, I mean."

"We don't," said Kett. He scrolled through the images on his phone, finding one of Benedict. "Just to check, this is him?"

The doctor nodded, running a hand over his bald scalp.

"And he was your patient?" Kett asked, sliding the phone away.

"Since he was a boy," said Dr Colón. "He must have been four or five when I first took up my practice here. Lovely young man, but a troubled childhood. You've met his parents?"

"I have," said Kett. "Weird vibe."

"They're not nice people. A whole history of suspected abuse, and social services has been involved many times."

"Violence?" Kett asked, and the doctor shook his head.

"No, not the kind you're talking about. I mean, I saw plenty of bruises on him when he was younger, but none of them couldn't be explained away as typical childhood bumps and scrapes. No broken bones. He was always healthy, but he was..."

He frowned at the ceiling, a large Adam's apple gulping.

"I think there was emotional abuse there, at quite a significant level. His parents were obsessive about his behaviour, they punished any perceived disobedience with emotional coldness. I'm speaking with plenty of conjecture here, you'll understand, because Benedict would not talk about it. But I saw it myself in the way his parents were with him during appointments. His father, especially. They had an incredibly unnerving power over him, wouldn't let him socialise, wouldn't even let him drink. He never did, as far as I know."

"He's still living with them," Kett said. "Even as an adult. There's a lock on his bedroom door, on the outside."

"Sadly, that doesn't surprise me," said Dr Colón. "That's exactly the kind of thing they did. It was ingrained in him that any misbehaviour would lead not to violence but neglect. It broke my heart, but there's only so much you can do."

"Did you ever speak to us about it?"

The doctor nodded.

"I worked with social services to find a solution, but to outward appearances Benedict was healthy, he achieved well at school, played football, from what I can remember. Physically, he was absolutely fine. Fit as a mule. You can't point out those emotional wounds so easily."

"No," said Kett. "You can't. Can I ask, when was the last time you saw him?"

"Recently, about town," the man replied, running a hand over his smooth head as if looking for the hair that had once grown there. "He always said hello. But for an appointment?"

He rocked forward in his chair and logged into his computer, clucking his tongue.

"It's been well over four years, and that was nothing serious, a dermatological thing. Nope, nothing since then. But like I said, he was healthy."

He dropped his hands into his lap, looking at Kett with genuine sympathy.

"A fine lad, a good heart. I hope he's okay."

"We're not sure yet if the foot belongs to Benedict," said Kett. "And there's only so much I can say right now. But do you think this is something his parents might have done to him? A punishment of some kind?"

"No," the doctor said without any hesitation. "I don't

think they would have resorted to anything physical, and certainly nothing this extreme. Not from my understanding of them. Besides, they're getting on a bit. I don't think they'd have it in them. Mrs Gilbert is quite deep into early-onset dementia and her husband is frail, he uses a stick. No, whatever this is, I don't think they're involved."

Kett checked his watch again, getting up.

"Thank you," he said. "If there's anything else, we'll be in touch."

The doctor stood too, rushing ahead to get the door. Before he could open it, Kett stopped him.

"Listen, as a doctor, have you ever seen anything like this before?"

"Missing limbs?" he replied. "I mean, sure. Amputations are surprisingly common, mainly in older people, and almost always related to diabetes. Feet are the most common thing to go, and it's relatively easy to see a foot lost to diabetic neuropathy. But in younger people, it's uncommon. Unheard of, to be honest. Although..."

He stopped, as if unsure whether to go on.

"There is a condition called Body Integrity Identity Disorder. Are you familiar with it?"

Kett shook his head.

"It's extremely rare, and not much is known about it. But essentially, a person with BIID desires to self-amputate healthy body parts."

"They *what*?" asked Kett.

"They want to cut off their limbs. Legs, arms, it could be anything. It's a neurological condition, we think. A brain disorder that produces a disruption of the body image, very similar to symptoms we sometimes see in stroke victims. Patients ask surgeons to remove limbs and will occasionally take matters into their own hands, so to speak."

"They'll cut them off themselves?" Kett said, the bile rising to the top of his throat.

"It has been known. I have read about cases where people lie on train tracks and let the train amputate a limb."

"No," said Kett, shaking his head.

"Yes. Or they'll produce some kind of device, a weighted blade or a guillotine."

"A machine?" said Kett. "For a clean cut?"

"Exactly."

Kett belched into his hand, and even the doctor looked queasy.

"I'm sorry," Dr Colón said. "It's not easy to hear. And I should reiterate that it's exceedingly rare. I've certainly never encountered a case, and neither has anybody I know. It's the kind of thing you read about in medical journals, that's all."

"Benedict never said anything to make you think he had BI... whatever it was?"

"BIID, no. Never. But like all these things, they manifest more easily in a brain damaged by trauma. It's not beyond the realm of possibility."

This time, it was the doctor who checked his watch.

"I'm so sorry, but I really must crack on. I finish at six tonight. I'm more than happy to talk to you further then."

He opened the door and Kett stepped out, walking gingerly around the woman with the rash who stood right outside. The music had changed, something equally upbeat and jolly.

"I like to think it cheers people up," said Doctor Colón with a futile shrug.

It didn't, but Kett nodded anyway.

"I sincerely hope he's okay," the doctor went on as he

ushered the woman into his office. "Can you let me know when you find him?"

"We will."

Kett made his way out of the surgery, twisting his head to the sun to try to burn away the horror of the conversation.

But even in the heat, he couldn't shake the cold that had settled in his bones.

CHAPTER TWENTY-ONE

"It's horrific," Savage said, her voice crackling down the line and filling the stationary Volvo. "I saw a documentary about it once, a young man who wanted the doctor to literally cut his spinal cord, paralyse him. But it's so rare, there's no chance that Benedict and Alis suddenly decided to cut off their limbs, is there?"

"That's what I was thinking," said Kett, glancing in the mirror to see the school gates, no sign yet of Billie and the girls. "And even if they did, why would they send them to people? There's nothing else connecting Benedict and Alis, is there?"

"Nothing yet," said Savage. "No shared friends on Facebook, no shared employment history, no medical connection, no common links at all. Oh, I meant to say, they found Benedict's van outside the Starbucks down by the river in Norwich. We're waiting for forensics to finish at the windmill before they head over there, but he'd just bought some verruca cream from Boots."

"Our foot had verrucas," said Kett. "That doesn't bode well. When was this?"

"Three days ago," said Savage, her voice fading for a moment. "Monday. Receipt was time-stamped eleven thirty-three am. Staff at Starbucks remember him coming in for an Americano ten minutes after that. They're sending us the CCTV. We're not sure where he went when he left, but it wasn't back to his van."

"Keep looking," said Kett.

"Also, they've matched the fingerprints of the hand to the prints from Alis' house. It's her."

He knew it already, but it didn't make it any easier.

A shrill scream of excitement rang out, and Kett checked the mirror again to see Alice run out of the gate. She'd had a growth spurt in the last six months and she ran over like a chimpanzee, her long arms flapping by her sides. Evie followed, her cheeks red and her legs like pistons as she fought to keep up with her big sister. Billie was next, Moira halfway out of her mum's grip as she made a bid for freedom.

"I'd better go," he said.

"Good luck," Savage replied. "I hope they all love it."

He ended the call, getting out of the car and taking Moira from Billie before she catapulted herself into the road.

"No, I want to run!" yelled the three-year-old, writhing like a baby bear. "I'm fastest!"

"You're slowest," said Alice, wrenching open the door and hurling herself inside. "I won."

"I won!" said Evie, huffing and puffing on the pavement.

"You all won," Kett said. "So stop arguing. We're going to look at a new house. It's going to be fun. Just get into your car seats."

Moira showed absolutely no sign that she was going to get into her car seat.

"If you're good you can get some Smarties on the way home."

"You've got to stop rewarding them with Smarties," Billie said as he clipped their youngest in. "They're going to end up with multicoloured, sugar-coated skin at this rate."

He gave his wife a hug, then a kiss on the forehead.

"You ready for this?" he asked.

"I've been ready for this for years."

He kissed her again, earning a round of puking noises from the girls inside the car.

"Then let's go find ourselves a new house."

THE HOUSE WAS as beautiful as he remembered it, sitting back from the main road out to Wroxham behind a towering laurel hedge that had all but swallowed the *For Sale* sign. Two magnolia trees straddled the driveway, and even though most of the petals had dropped, forming a blanket on the ground, they still looked magnificent. There was a compact black Audi on the drive but there was still plenty of room, and after a couple of buses had trundled past, he pulled the Volvo in next to it.

"This is amazing," said Billie, her voice raised. "You can't hear the road at all."

You couldn't hear *anything*, because the girls were singing a song in the back seat. It didn't seem to have any words, or a tune, but what it lacked in melody it made up for in volume. Kett switched off the engine and turned to them.

"If you carry on like that then the neighbours will ban us from moving in," he said, and the girls sang even louder.

"Let's leave them in the car," he said.

"Deal," replied Billie, and the song was instantly replaced with a round of protests.

Kett got out, looking past the trees to the police station that sat on the other side of the road. An IRV was pulling out and he lifted a couple of fingers to his forehead to salute them—not that either of the coppers inside noticed. Billie joined him, lacing her arm through his.

"It's not too close, is it?" she said. "I'd understand if you wanted to get away from the job a bit, but..."

She didn't say it, and she didn't need to.

"It makes me happy," he said. "It makes me feel safe."

Because if one of Hollenbeck's ghosts parked outside *this* house in a black Peugeot, if he fired the same psychotic grin through *this* front window, two dozen coppers would be at the door in less than ten seconds.

"You're not allowed to run over the road every time you hear a siren, though," Billie said, giving his arm a squeeze.

"Don't worry."

Behind them, the Volvo was rocking, a tornado of shouts and movement.

"I guess we'd better get them out," he said, walking to the car and opening the door. It was like the starting gate at a horse race, Moira already unbuckled and falling out face-first. Kett caught her, hefting her up.

"My house!" she yelled.

"It's mine!" Alice shouted back, pointing to the wheelie bin. "*That's* your house."

"No!"

"I'm not living in the bin," said Evie, running to her mum's side, her little face creased with anxiety. "I want to go back to our old house."

The front door opened as they walked towards it, a

sharply dressed young woman greeting them with a well-practised smile.

"Hi!" she said, the smile faltering a little as Evie and Alice raced towards her. "I was told you'd be bringing the kids."

"They're going to be on their best behaviour," Kett said. "Aren't you, girls?"

The estate agent stood to one side to let Evie in, then lurched the other way as Alice bundled past.

"We're just looking!" Kett called after them. "For God's sake, don't touch anything."

Moira flexed her body until Kett had no choice but to let go of her. She ran inside after her sisters, a hollow *thump* echoing out almost immediately.

"Was this a bad idea?" Billie asked quietly.

"Having those kids in the first place was a bad idea," Kett replied.

"This is your second viewing?" the woman asked as she ushered them into a wide, sun-drenched entrance hall.

"Yes," said Billie. "We wanted to give the girls a chance to see it."

"Three girls. Brave."

"Brave is one word," said Kett, who couldn't see any of his children anywhere. "Where are they?"

Another thump from upstairs, and a cry of anger.

"I'm not worried about them," said the woman, frowning in a way that made it very clear she *was* worried. "Are you okay to have a wander, or would you like the tour?"

"We can wander," said Billie, looking up. "Right?"

"Sounds good to me."

"I'll be right here if you need me."

Billie took the lead, her arm laced through Kett's again

and pulling him with some urgency. They walked through the house to the kitchen first, a large, open-plan extension with a pale, quartz-topped island and black and gold units. Bifold doors had been opened into the long garden, the summer curled up and fast asleep on the oak floor. From here he could just about see the little wooden cabin, complete with plumbing and electricity, that they'd already earmarked for Kett's mum—if she ever decided she could cope with living with them again, that was.

Billie's grip grew so tight it was almost painful.

"It's perfect," she said. "It's a proper family space, bigger than the one we had in London. We'll live in this room, I know it. And we can all be in here and not be on top of each other."

"We can," said Kett.

He could already picture them, the kids at the dining table, him and Billie cooking homemade pizzas. It was a proper family home, and it was what they deserved. For so long their family had been torn in half, for so long they'd done their best to repair it. But in this house, he knew, they could finally heal.

They made their way back down the corridor into the living room, the light here muted but the feel of it just as comfortable. Kett looked at the plush velvet sofa and found himself yawning. On the other side of the entrance hall was a formal dining room that could easily become a playroom.

"Somewhere to store all their stuff," said Billie.

"And them," he said, yawning again. "In a cage."

They were halfway upstairs when Moira appeared, a hat on her head.

"Moira, sweetie," said Kett. "Put that back, you can't wear other people's hats."

"Not a hat!" she shouted, running off.

"Not a hat?" said Kett as he reached the landing. "What does that mean?"

There were four bedrooms here, although one was little more than a box room. Moira had run into the master at the front of the house, and when Kett followed her in he saw Alice lying on the large bed looking like she was trying to make a snow angel on the immaculate duvet.

"Bagsy this room," she said.

"Uh, no," said Kett. "Sorry. Off the bed, please."

"Bagsy is the law," Alice went on, ignoring him. "You're a policeman, you should know that."

"It's really not. Off, now. Where's your sister?"

There was a giggle from the *en suite* and Kett pushed open the door to see Moira standing in the bath.

She was wearing a pair of pants on her head.

"Oh, no, Moira, take those off!"

"No!" she yelled, clambering out of the bath and diving past him. He made a grab for her but she was too fast, scuttling on all fours towards the bedroom door—passing Billie as she entered.

"Grab her," Kett said. "She's got somebody's pants on her head."

"Oh, God!"

Billie ran down the landing, Moira's peal of delighted laughter ringing like a bell as she vanished into another bedroom.

"Where's Evie?" Kett said, not sure he even wanted to know the answer.

"She needed a poo," said Alice, rolling on the bed.

"No," said Kett, following the smell to the family bathroom to see Evie standing arse-naked next to the toilet with a mountain of bog roll unspooled beside her. "Oh, Evie, hang on."

"I can do it," she said. "Go away."

"You're not allowed to poo on a house viewing," Kett said, helping her. "Couldn't it wait?"

"No," Evie said. "My poo needs a new house, too. Bye, poo."

Kett flushed the toilet, but there was so much paper it was blocked.

"Come on," he said, watching in horror as Evie's deposit floated to the top.

"My poo doesn't want to leave," she said. "Like me. It's a sign."

Moira's laughter rose up again and the three-year-old shot past the door. She still had the pants on her head, but the rest of her was stark naked.

"Moira! Enough!" Billie called as she chased her. "Do *not* go down those stairs."

Evie's eyes widened, full of mischief.

"Don't you dare," Kett said when it looked like she was going to kick her leggings all the way off.

She thought about it, then decided it wasn't worth it, pulling them up instead. Kett helped her wash her hands, then he tried the toilet again, praying to every God in the heavens that it would flush.

It didn't.

"Come on!" he pleaded.

"Is everything okay up there?" the estate agent called from below.

"Fine!" he yelled back, stepping out of the bathroom just in time to catch Moira as she flew down the landing. He pulled the underwear off her head—a pair of pink satin granny pants that were, thank God, clean—and clamped her naked body to his chest. "That's enough, Moo-moo. That's enough."

She slapped her hands on his shoulders with no real force, studying him with her enormous blue eyes.

"My room?" she asked.

"Give me one second," he said, walking back into the bathroom and using his elbow to flush the toilet a third time. He glared at the water the way he would have glared at a criminal who was resisting arrest, and it worked because this time the paper disappeared with a choked gurgle.

"My room?" Moira said again, looking towards the two rooms at the back of the house.

Kett carried her into the nearest one. It was being used as a study, a cosy armchair in the corner by the window, the garden laid out beyond, as picturesque as an oil painting.

"How about it?" he asked. "You like this one?"

Moira nodded, smiling.

"Can we share it?" asked Evie as she appeared at the door. "I don't want to be on my own."

"Yeah," said Moira.

"I don't want to sleep on a desk, though," Evie said, her face full of worry.

"I think they'll let you bring your beds," Kett said, reaching down to rest his hand on her head. She blinked up at him, so unsure, and he seemed to feel his heart detach itself from his chest and float upwards. She'd been through so much in the last few years. They all had. They deserved this. "You can bring whatever you like. It's your room."

She smiled, bounding off again to find her big sister. Billie took her place, holding Moira's clothes in one hand. She opened her arms and Kett passed his youngest daughter over.

"What do you think?" Billie asked, just as nervous as Evie had been.

"I think it's perfect," he said.

And her smile was golden.

He walked to the corner of the room, collapsing into the armchair. His thoughts were still full of severed limbs, of course, of torture and murder and mutilation. But when he closed his eyes, all he could hear were the birds outside, and the laughter of his children. The house felt so familiar and so comfortable that he might have lived here for a hundred years already.

So comfortable, in fact, that sleep ambushed him before he even knew it was coming. He fell hard, aware only faintly of the estate agent's voice.

"Oh, I'm not sure if... Should we wake him?"

And then Billie's.

"Leave him, just for a little while. It doesn't matter, does it? Because we're going to buy this house. Whatever it takes. It's ours. It's our home."

You're right, he thought as the quiet and the warmth swallowed him whole. *It is.*

CHAPTER TWENTY-TWO

"You fell asleep?" asked Porter, holding the door to the MIT's offices open for Kett.

"I did," Kett replied as they walked.

"During the viewing?"

"Yep."

"For half an hour? In a chair?"

"It was a very comfortable chair," Kett said.

Porter laughed, and Kett found himself smiling. Billie had only woken him because the estate agent had to lock up and leave for another appointment, but apparently she'd used the time he was asleep to make a formal offer.

"Whatever it takes," she'd told the estate agent again as they were leaving.

"So you think you'll get it?" Porter asked.

"Whatever it takes," Kett echoed.

"They're all in the Incident Room," said DS Spalding as they crossed the bullpen. "He's in a foul mood, so watch out."

"Does he come with any other moods?" Porter replied.

"I hear he's quite jolly when he's playing his flute," said Kett.

"Foul Clare, and Jolly Flute Clare," Porter said. "I'm not sure which one is scarier."

They were nearing the Incident Room when they heard the thunder of the Superintendent's voice.

"Foul Clare is scarier," said Kett. "No doubt."

Porter entered first, Kett following. The Incident Room was full of Detectives and Uniforms, although most of them had foregone the desks at the front and were clustered against the wall at the back. It was easy to see why. Colin Clare stood hunched and sweating in front of the display board, his face gurning like a Halloween troll. He pointed a long finger at Porter, then at Kett, then grumbled something that had very little resemblance to actual words.

"Sorry, sir?" Kett asked as he joined the people near the back. Savage was there, but Duke seemed to have obeyed his orders to go home.

"I said," Clare muttered. "Nice of you to bloody join us."

"You're welcome," said Kett.

Clare's eyes almost abandoned their sockets. His lips peeled back to reveal his teeth, and there was a slim possibility that he might have been growling. Kett stepped back from the precipice before it was too late, holding his hands up in surrender.

"Sorry, sir. How are you feeling?"

"Like somebody is using my sphincter as a rope swing," Clare said, belching loudly. "Dunst, you were saying?"

Dunst cleared his throat, reading from a sheet of paper in front of him.

"Digital forensics has analysed all the footage from Alis' abduction. The good news is there's definitely a shot of her attacker in the bathroom mirror, but the bad news is they're wearing a mask. Balaclava, by the look of it. The photo's on the board."

Kett couldn't see it past the Super.

"Uh, sir?" Dunst said. "Could you scooch up a bit?"

"No," said Clare.

As one, the crowd in the room moved a few paces to the right so they could see past the Superintendent's shoulders. The photograph was as bad as Dunst had made out, a vaguely human smudge framed at a bad angle in the dirty mirror.

"Are we sure that's a balaclava?" Kett asked. "And not a motorcycle helmet?"

"Could be," said Dunst, nodding. "No more CCTV on the premises—none that we could find, anyway. Couple of doorbell cams in the village, and the most useful of those showed what might have been the abductor's vehicle. It's... it's on the board, on the other side. Sir?"

"No," said Clare, and everyone shuffled back the way they'd come. Behind the Super's other shoulder was a grainy photograph of a white van, the registration plate too blurry to read. It looked very similar to the one they'd found close to Douglas Ireland's house, but Kett could see that it wasn't the same.

"Different van," he said.

"Yeah," said Dunst. "This is a Ford Transit Connect, spotted down the road from Alis' house five minutes before the attacker knocked on her door. This model is a couple of years old, they're everywhere. We're trying to trace where it came from, but no luck so far."

"It's a link," said Kett. "A small one, but not insignificant. We think our delivery driver used a white van to make the drop, makes sense they'd use one to abduct their victims."

"But if they're switching vans, it will make them very difficult to trace," said Savage. "They might have links to a hire company, or a showroom, a delivery company."

"We're looking into all of the above," Clare said. "So far, our strongest link is the bike. Armel Roux, the former firefighter who owned the Ducati, is still missing. Nobody has seen him since last Tuesday."

"The day Benedict went missing," said Kett, and Clare nodded.

"He has priors, including a violent assault against a copper during a charity football match."

"Shit, I remember that," said Porter, clicking his fingers. "Few years ago, wasn't it? He punched Bruce what's-his-name right in the snout because he kept saving his penalties. I didn't think he pressed charges, though?"

"He didn't," said Clare. "Not for the football match. But Roux went after Bruce again; nobody knows why. Knocked him out one night in the pub. Did four years for it and lost his job."

"Football," said Savage. "Might be a link to Douglas Ireland and to Benedict Gilbert, both of them play."

"Not to mention a pretty strong hatred of the police," said Clare. "If this is him, he might be trying to wind us up. But it's a big if. The bike didn't have plates, and for all we know Armel's not even in the county anymore. He could be anywhere."

"He could be a victim," said Kett.

Clare nodded.

"So in short, we know toss-all. But we're looking for him. He's forty-six, and he's got a face that isn't easy to hide, as you can all see."

With a collective sigh, the coppers in the room shuffled further to their left until the photo of Armel Roux appeared behind the Superintendent's stationary backside. He bore a striking resemblance to Mr Bean, Kett thought, but somehow even weirder, and much angrier.

"You wouldn't want him coming to save you, would you?" Porter said. "You'd just leap right back into the fire."

A low chuckle rippled across the room, cut short by a look from the Superintendent.

"We've allowed the press access to some of the details," he went on. "But only a handful. The crazy calls are already coming in thick and fast. We've had confirmation that the hand belongs to Alis Sayer, but nothing conclusive on the foot. I need proof that it belongs to Benedict Gilbert, and I need to know what connects them. Anything else?"

Spalding appeared in the door, a sheet of paper clasped in her hand.

"Digital forensics has just finished with Alis Sayer's iPad," she said. "Nothing much to report, but it seems she wasn't long out of a relationship with a man called Rob Sutton."

Clare shrugged.

"So?"

"There are a couple of older photos there, Rob rode a motorcycle. Well, a scooter."

"Find him," said Clare.

"On it," said Spalding, disappearing.

"Might be our suspect," said Porter.

"Might be," said Kett. "But it makes sense even if it isn't. If our attacker was wearing a motorcycle helmet when they arrived, Alis might have mistaken them for her ex. We know our suspect wore a helmet when they delivered the foot."

"But it doesn't help us at all," Clare said, jutting his chin out.

"I spoke with Bower on the way in," said Savage. "He clammed up, but he did say he didn't know anything about the postcard we found in his fire. It was only in there because it had been piled with all his other work stuff. All he could tell us was that it was dropped off a few days ago."

"That's a pattern," said Kett. "The postcard comes first, then a few days later the parcel arrives. Did we ever find a postcard at Douglas Ireland's house?"

"Nobody mentioned seeing it," said Clare. "And we didn't find one when we did the search. But the recycling had gone out on Monday, it might have been thrown away with all the other fliers."

"We know Benedict Gilbert got one," Kett went on. "Might be worth keeping an eye on the Gilbert house in case anything shows up."

"Gilbert's was different, though," said Porter. "It said 'thank you.'"

Kett nodded.

"So maybe he sends a postcard to his victim, as well as to whoever receives the delivery," said Savage. "Was there a postcard at Alis' house?"

"No," said Kett. "No mail at all, but I think Jasper, the landlord, might have taken some and disposed of it. He denies it, but he was well up in her business."

"Anything else?" said the Super.

"Yeah," said Porter. "We—"

"Nope, it'll have to wait," Clare said, clutching his stomach as he crossed the room. "And if it can't, you'll have to come with me."

"It can wait," said Porter, backing into the wall. "It can definitely wait."

Clare bolted from the room, followed by Dunst. The old DI was looking a little green around the gills as well.

"Not you too," said Kett.

"Feels like I've got live eels down there," Dunst said. "Hundreds of them. 'Scuse me."

He made it to the door before farting like an eager kid with a new trombone, the smell of it filling the Incident Room in under a second.

"Christ," Kett said, holding his nose. "Move, Porter, or I'm going to be sick."

There was a stampede of coppers towards the door, Kett making it into the corridor first and Porter tumbling out after him.

"That cake is going to take out the whole of Norfolk Constabulary," said Kett.

"It's still sitting there, if you can believe it," said Porter. "Right there on the counter. Nobody's brave enough to bin it."

Kett walked back into the bullpen, ready to head for the kitchen and put the kettle on. But Spalding flagged him down from her desk. She was on the phone, her face contorted with concentration.

"Yeah, it does," she said to whoever she was speaking to. She cupped the receiver. "Where's the Guv?"

"Toilet," said Kett. "Why?"

Spalding's frown tightened even more.

"Because I think our killer has just delivered another parcel."

THEY ARRIVED IN FORCE, three IRVs leading the way into the sun-baked city before dropping out into a suburb to the south. Kett followed in Porter's Mondeo, Savage and Dunst in the back. Clare was right behind them in his tank-like Mercedes, his face gurning over the steering wheel, his front bumper almost touching the back of the Ford.

They rumbled off the main road, following the sirens and the lights through a warren of streets named after characters from Robin Hood until the first IRV skidded to a halt. The second moved over to let the Mondeo and the Mercedes through, then pulled out again to block the road.

Porter and Savage were out in a heartbeat, Kett taking a little longer to ease his aching body from the seat. The day was hotter than ever, the heat not welcome anymore but somehow oppressive and intimidating. It was almost physical, a hand that seemed to want to push them away from whatever waited for them here.

Several of the tight-knit houses had their front doors open, people standing in the shadows with dark eyes. Nobody smiled, not even the kids who hung on their parents' hands or peeked from behind their legs. Kett had been here a few times since arriving in Norwich and he hadn't always had the warmest of welcomes.

"Which house is it?" Clare shouted.

"This one, sir," answered a Uniform.

He was standing outside one of the identical semi-detached brick properties that lined the street. The door was open, a man about Porter's age pacing back and forth through it, his hands clenched in his mousy hair. He was wearing grey jogging trousers and a bright yellow Norwich City shirt, his feet bare.

"It's in here," he shouted down the short path, removing one hand from his head to point through the door. "I don't know what it is. I just want it the fuck out of my house."

Clare took the lead, pushing into the house without a word. Kett followed, stopping to talk to the man.

"You are?" he asked.

"Ginge Skeldon," he said, his voice hoarse like he'd smoked a dozen packs of cigarettes already that day.

"Ginge?" Kett asked, looking at the man's brown hair.

"Ginger," he said. "Don't ask me, ask my fucking parents. You going in or what?"

"In a second," Kett said, standing to one side to let a couple of PCs past. Savage stopped by his side, her notepad out. "Can you tell us what happened?" Kett asked.

The man stepped over his threshold into the house. Then he stepped out again, every part of him moving. He was a bundle of restless energy, positively thrumming. Kett wondered if he'd taken something.

"Take a breath, Mr Skeldon," he said. "I need you to calm down."

"How can I fucking calm down when there's a *thing* in there?" he said, gesturing inside. "I've seen the news, mate. I know what's happening."

"You had a delivery?" Savage asked, her voice so soft that the man had to stop pacing. He leaned in, taking a deep breath and holding it for a few seconds.

"Yeah," he said. "Like, right before we called you. We was just sitting in the garden and we heard the door, proper knock, you know?"

He thumped the door frame: *knock knock*, then he pressed a thumb against the doorbell, an artificial chime echoing around the house.

"No idea why he didn't use the bell, you know? He just knocked. So my wife went to see who it was, came back into the house with a box but I saw it, I saw it through the window and I knew. Just knew it was like them others, the ones on the news. Same box."

"Did you see who delivered it?" Savage asked.

He shook his head, his left leg jiggling like he was trying to shake off an invisible insect.

"But I saw them other boxes on the news and this is just like it."

Kett pulled out his phone, finding the image of the postcard.

"Have you received anything like this in the last few days?" he asked. "A card, black and red, with an image of a tick."

Skeldon shook his head, looking at Kett like he'd gone mad.

"Kett, get in here," Clare yelled.

Kett squeezed past the man and walked into the house, a microscopic hallway branching out into three rooms and a staircase. Clare stood in the kitchen at the back, and when Kett went to join him he found there was barely any room to do so. It was a tiny room, most of the far wall taken up by a window and a door that was open onto a sizeable garden. There were two more people out there, a woman in her late thirties and a teenage girl in a wheelchair.

On the fake oak of the kitchen counter sat a box.

It was brown cardboard, just like the others, just like the millions of delivery boxes used across the country every day. But this one was bigger and squarer, and it was wrapped with brown parcel tape and a pink ribbon. From this angle, Kett couldn't see any writing or any labels. Clare handed him a pair of gloves and he fought to get them on.

"Go on," the Superintendent snapped.

Ginge Skeldon appeared in the door, moving up when Savage asked him to.

"It's him, isn't it?" he said. "Just like them others."

"I don't know," Kett told him. "It might not be."

Then he touched the corners of the box, gently turned it, and saw that the man was right.

Scrawled across one face of the box in large, even handwriting was a name.

"Charlie Skeldon," Kett said. "Who's that?"

"My daughter," he replied, his voice breaking up again. "Charlene, she's out there."

"And just to confirm, this is your exact address?"

Skeldon nodded.

Somebody knocked on the front door, Cara Hay's tuneful voice singing out.

"Where is everybody?"

"Back here," Kett said, everybody budging up to make room for her. Hay's forehead knitted itself into a frown when she saw the box.

"Ah," she said.

"I knew it," whined Skeldon. "I fucking knew it."

"You mind giving us a moment?" Kett asked him, and he shook his head.

"My fucking house," he said, pointing a finger at Kett. "And that's my daughter's fucking name. I'm not going anywhere."

Kett looked at Clare and the Super nodded.

"You might not like what you see," Kett told him. "It's all yours, Cara."

"Lucky me," she said, putting her bag on the floor and pulling on some gloves. "How much preamble do you want?"

"Just open the tossing box," said Clare.

"I thought you might say that."

She performed a cursory examination of the ribbon and the packing tape before dusting the tape with powder.

"No prints," she said.

She retrieved a sealed scalpel from her bag. Kett leaned in—*everyone* leaned in—as she delicately opened the box and peeled back the flaps.

Inside was a puddle of pink packing chips, a couple of them falling to the floor like petals.

"Shit," Kett said, too quiet for anyone to hear.

Hay pulled out a large evidence bag and began to scoop the packing chips into it, everyone holding their breath as they waited to see what they were hiding.

"Here we go," said Hay.

A slab of something red, something *meaty*.

"Is that part of a leg?" Savage asked.

Skeldon doubled up, groaning.

"Seriously, you don't want to be here for this," Kett said, and this time he nodded, retreating to the front garden.

"Not a leg," said Hay. "Unless my grasp of anatomy is very wrong. No central bone."

She continued to unpack it, switching to a new evidence bag when the first one was full. Whatever was inside, it was wrapped in the same cling film as the foot and the hand. This, too, belonged to somebody new.

"Skin's darker," Hay said. "And there's... what *is* that?"

They crowded in, shoulder to shoulder now. Despite the shrink wrap, Kett could smell the contents of the box, that sickeningly sweet stench of meat on the turn. He had to clamp his hand to his nose, taking slow, shallow breaths.

"Hair," said Savage. "It's hair."

Thick and dark, clustered around the base of a wide, round slab of flesh. Kett couldn't make any sense of it, it didn't look real.

Until he realised it was upside down.

"That's a neck," he said.

"I think so too," said Cara. "And this is a beard."

"Christ," said Clare, his voice tight.

Hay continued to unpack it, digging out packing chips like an archaeologist in the dirt. With every handful, the object inside grew more obvious, lips stitched together with wire, a nose compressed into one cheek from the tightness of the cling film. Hay stopped before she got to the eyes, standing back. Her whole body was trembling.

"I just need to take a minute," she said.

"Take all the time you need," Clare offered.

They took a collective breath, one that Savage released as a gentle sob.

"It's a head," she said, one hand to her mouth. "He sent them a head."

CHAPTER TWENTY-THREE

KETT WALKED INTO THE BACK GARDEN OF THE SKELDON family house, hoping beyond hope that the sun would sear away the memory of the severed head that still sat in their kitchen.

After a brief pause to collect herself, Cara Hay had unpacked the rest of the grim delivery, displaying it in all its horror on a steel tray on the worktop. Kett couldn't see it from where he stood now because Savage had possessed the good sense to pull the blinds down. He didn't think he'd ever *not* see it, though. The shrink-wrapped head with its slick, bloody hair and the salted nub of its neck had been etched into his brain with some fury. He would carry it with him for the rest of his days.

"Will they be much longer?" asked the woman who waited in the garden, more than a touch of cockney in her accent.

Like her husband, the woman was dressed in tracksuit trousers and a T-shirt, her feet bare. And like her husband, she was a ball of nervous tension, her hands flexing and unflexing, her toes scrunching the moss-thick grass. She wore a pair of old glasses whose thick lenses were so scratched and scuffed it was a wonder she could see anything at all.

Behind her, as close to the fence as she could get, the daughter sat in silence. She was probably eighteen, or close to it, and beneath her blanket, Kett thought she might have been missing a leg. He smiled at her as best he could, but she didn't smile back.

"I don't know," Kett said. "But yes, they probably will. Have you got anywhere else you can stay for the night?"

The woman shook her head.

"Can't afford a hotel neither," she said.

"I'll see what I can do. Mrs Skeldon, isn't it?"

"Pat," she said.

"You were the one who collected the box from the doorstep?"

"Yeah."

"And you didn't catch sight of the person who delivered it?"

She shook her head again, her eyes wide as she stared through the kitchen door.

"Can you talk me through what happened?" Kett asked, wiping the sweat from his face. "Exactly."

Pat took a big breath, like she was preparing for a sprint.

"We were just out here, enjoying the sun. Me and Ginge and Charlie over there."

Kett waved to the young woman in the wheelchair and again she ignored him.

"Had a couple of drinks, couple of beers. Ginge was clearing out the shed."

She nodded to a small shed in the far corner, the roof half rotted away. The door was open, a collection of deck chairs stacked against it.

"It's what you do, *innit*? Summer."

"And you heard the door?"

"Yeah. Thought it was me mum, she sometimes drops in, only lives on the other side of Tuckswood. Looked through the peeper and didn't see *nuffink* so I was going to leave it, then I thought I'd check anyway in case it was one of Charlie's mates. She's got a couple in wheelies like her and you don't always see them through the peeper."

She turned her head to the sky, her glasses flashing with sunlight.

"And I saw the box there, saw Charlie's name, and brought it in. *Nuffink* to do with me."

"You put it in the kitchen?" asked Kett.

"Yeah. Then Ginge came in and he was all panicked like, a right tizz. Started going on about this thing he'd seen on the news, like body parts getting delivered and shit. He told me to leave it, called you lot."

"That seems a little extreme, don't you think?" Kett asked. "Calling the police because of a box?"

"He saw the ribbon, showed me the web page thing from the news on me phone. Same ribbon, *innit*?"

"Yeah," said Kett. "It is."

"So what's in it, then?" Pat asked. "Don't tell me it's a part of somebody, I'll never go back in there as long as I live if you say it's some fella's foot or something."

Kett didn't want to lie, so he didn't answer the question.

"Have you had any other strange deliveries recently, Pat? Notes, fliers?" He pulled out his phone and showed her the postcard with the tick. "Anything like this, with Charlie's name on it?"

She shook her head, chewing her lip like she hadn't eaten in a month.

"Am I okay to speak with your daughter?"

"She's an adult," said Pat, her hands up. "Can't stop you. But go easy, she's had a shit time of it."

"I can see. Can I ask what happened?"

"Fucking drunk driver. Years ago now, he hit Charlie and her brother. She ended up in that, Josh ended up in a coffin."

The casual way she said it took Kett's breath away, like she'd physically punched him.

"Your son was killed?"

Pat shrugged, but he could see the pain in her face, there for a second before she managed to push it away.

"Life *innit*?" she said. "It's fucking shit."

Kett took another few steps across the garden towards the young woman. There was no shade here at all and he felt like he was broiling beneath an industrial grill. Charlie looked at him through a pair of cheap plastic sunglasses, the lenses pink. She was older than he'd first thought, maybe in her early twenties. She had a serious scar on her forearm, the kind you got when the bone had been pinned.

"Hi," Kett said. "Charlie, right?"

Charlie didn't respond other than to raise a hand to shield her face from the sun. She studied him intently for a few seconds.

"My name's DCI Robbie Kett, I'm with the police. You mind if I ask you a couple of questions?"

Still no reply.

"I'm just wondering if you recognised the handwriting on the box?" Kett persisted. "Or if you know why anybody would send it to you?"

Charlie continued to stare at him through the shadow of her hand.

"Has anybody threatened you recently? Has anyone made contact with you, somebody you don't know, somebody new? Any letters or postcards through the post, especially black and red ones with a tick image, like a spider?"

Nothing. Kett sighed, looking back to where Pat watched them, a smug look of satisfaction on her face.

"You could really help us out here," Kett said.

"I could," Charlie said. "But why would I?"

The question caught him off guard and it took him a moment to compose himself.

"Uh, because people's lives might be in danger. We might have a chance to save them."

"Like you saved Josh?" she asked. "Like you saved *me*?"

"The accident?" Kett said.

"Wasn't an accident, was it? Accidents are when something happens by mistake. Drinking and driving isn't a mistake. It's a choice."

"I'm sorry that happened," said Kett. "And I'm sorry about your brother."

Charlie shrugged.

"Shit happens. But like I said, I don't know shit about any box."

"It's got your name on it," Kett said.

"So does some graffiti at my old school," she said. "In the lads'. You think I wrote that too?"

"I'm just trying to understand what's happening," Kett said. "Because this isn't just about you. We—"

A sudden noise rose up from inside the house, one so loud and so alien that it didn't make any kind of sense out here in the day. It seemed to shatter Kett's heart, and he twisted around like he was under attack. Only when he saw Ginge Skeldon stagger into the frame of the open back door did he realise what he had heard—what he was *still* hearing. The man was screaming, a single, awful, endless cry that made Kett want to bury his head in the dirt and never come out.

"Dad?" Charlie shouted, her face crumpling. She started to wheel her chair across the grass, Pat already racing for her husband. Ginge stepped outside, his expression so scarred with grief that it didn't look real.

"No," he said. "No, stay away. Stay fucking back."

"What is it?" Pat shrieked. "What is it?"

Superintendent Clare stepped through the door, closing it behind him. He lifted one big hand in a plea for calm, then dropped it onto Skeldon's shoulder.

"Just take a—"

Skeldon twisted himself out of the Superintendent's grip, staggering into his wife's arms and looking at Clare like *he* was the one who'd dropped the head off at their front door.

"What's going on?" Kett asked.

"Get inside, Kett, now," Clare ordered.

"It's him," Skeldon was saying. "It's fucking him."

"Who?" asked Kett.

"Now," Clare said in a tone of voice that brooked no arguments.

Kett nodded, walking around Charlie and past her frantic parents to the kitchen door. He opened it and stepped into the unbearable heat of the kitchen, that dead smell more pungent than ever. Savage and Hay stood by the counter, thankfully shielding the head from view. Savage had her phone in her hand.

"What the hell just happened?" Kett asked.

"He knows him," Savage said. "The head, I mean. Mr Skeldon made an ID."

"You're kidding."

Outside, Pat's voice rose into a howl of what might have

been sorrow or what might have been laughter. The sound of it made Kett feel suddenly cold even as the sweat rolled down his neck and into his collar.

"His name's Andrew Donal," Savage went on, holding up the phone.

On the screen was a mugshot from the local newspaper of a man in his early thirties. And even though this man was very much alive, even though this man's head was still very much attached to his shoulders and hadn't yet sprouted a beard, Kett couldn't deny the similarity.

"Holy shit," he said, pulling his glasses from his jacket and putting them on. He took Savage's phone from her hand, reading the article. "'*Andrew Donal... Found guilty last night of death by dangerous driving. He was arrested in September after his VW Polo mounted the kerb on Exchange Street, killing Joshua Skeldon, 16, and injuring his sister, Charlene, 17. His car was travelling at sixty-two miles per hour when it came off the road, more than three times the speed limit. Donal admitted to driving while drunk, his blood alcohol...*'"

He looked at Savage.

"Holy shit," he said again. "It's him?"

Both women stood apart, the head appearing between them. Everything was distorted by the cling film. The man's eyes closed, the lids weirdly concave, the mouth almost lost beneath the beard, the nose crushed to one side.

"It's going to be impossible to say for sure until Emily does her thing," Savage said. "But it sure looks like him. He got off serious jail time because of a technicality and a good lawyer."

"Must have been more than just good," said Hay.

"This is big," said Kett. "It's huge. There's a connection. The head of the man who killed their son, who put their daughter in a wheelchair, ends up in a box at their front door."

"He's got a tattoo as well," said Savage. "Across the back of his neck, right below the hairline."

"Lift your head high," said Hay.

"That's what it says?" Kett asked, and they both nodded. "What the hell does that mean?"

He opened the back door, just a crack, to see the Skeldons in the middle of the garden, the daughter smothered in her parents' arms. The noise they were making still didn't sound human, it was almost the howling of wolves, and the goosebumps erupted on his arms as he listened to it. Clare stood next to them, one hand smoothing back his hair. He looked like he had absolutely no idea what to do with himself.

"What is going on here?" Kett asked, closing the door again.

"I don't know, sir," said Savage. "But there's something else."

"What?" asked Kett.

"Look in the box."

He really didn't want to, but it wasn't like he had a lot of choice. As slowly as he could, he made his way across the small kitchen to where the box sat on another one of Hay's steel trays. The flaps were open, and the box had been almost completely emptied out.

Almost.

Kett peered into it, seeing nothing but shadows and a flash of colour from the bottom, something red.

"Here," said Savage, shining her phone's torch into the base of the box.

Sitting there in a puddle of something that looked too

pale to be blood and too pink to be water was a postcard—black and red.

In the centre of it was an image of a fat, blood-packed tick.

"Holy shit," said Kett.

CHAPTER TWENTY-FOUR

Kett sat behind the wheel of Porter's Mondeo, the engine running and the air con going at full pelt. He'd stepped out of the Skeldon's house fifteen minutes ago looking for some fresh air, and when he hadn't found any in the sultry summer afternoon, he'd come here instead.

Through the windscreen the street was mobbed, Uniforms going door to door looking for witnesses and forensic technicians examining every square inch of the house. Emily Franklin had turned up a little while ago and kicked out everyone who wasn't essential, which had turned out to be everyone.

The Skeldons had packed their bags and left, a police transport van taking them to a hotel in the city and Savage riding along as an escort. This was partly to remove them from the ongoing investigation and partly so that the team could keep an eye on them.

Because the fact was that if anyone wanted Andrew Donal dead, it was them.

There was a knock on the window, and Kett looked to see Porter there.

"Can I come in, sir?" the DI asked over the grumble of the engine and the roar of the fans.

"It's your car, Pete," Kett replied.

Porter opened the door and dropped into the passenger seat, sighing with relief. He'd taken off his suit jacket and his shirt was damp with sweat. He'd loosened his tie and undone his top button, too.

"Christ, it is hot out there," he said, somewhat unnecessarily.

"Any joy?"

Porter shook his head.

"Nobody saw anything, and nobody's got cameras, which is weird for this part of the world. Neighbours all have good things to say about the Skeldons, though. They're tough, I guess they'd have to be after what happened to them, but they're good people. The dad's a plumber, helps out all the old folks on the street for free. Pat's a translator, believe it or not. Estonian. Helps us out sometimes, apparently."

"What about the daughter?" asked Kett.

"What about her? Andrew Donal's car took off her leg and damaged her spine. She doesn't work, somebody set up a *Just Giving* thing for her after the accident and it's still ticking over, barely. Gives her a couple of hundred a month, enough to live on."

"You think they had anything to do with this?" Kett asked.

Porter puffed out a couple of breaths.

"Hard to say, but if this is them, then why the hell would they leave the evidence on their own doorstep?"

"Because it's great cover," said Kett. "Somebody's dropping off body parts around the city, it's all over the news. Ginge or Pat, maybe even Charlie, they see their chance, they murder the man who killed Josh and pose the whole thing as another delivery killing. It gets lumped on whoever ends up taking the heat for this, and they get off scot-free."

"That would work," said Porter. "But Franklin's just told the Boss that the head's at least four days old, maybe more. So he was dead long before the foot arrived at Douglas Ireland's house."

"Could still be them," Kett said. "He might've already been dead."

Porter winced.

"We haven't released the information about the tick, though. The Monk. How would they know that?"

"The stuff about the Monk is out there," said Kett. "If Balls can find it, so can they. But yeah, it's some leap."

He paused for a moment as Dunst walked out of one of the neighbour's houses further down the street. The grizzled DI walked into the middle of the road, turned in a full circle, then scratched his head.

"What is he doing?" asked Kett.

Dunst turned in a full circle the other way, scratching his head again. He looked confused.

"You know that heartbreaking time in any dog owner's life when you have to take them to the vet for their final voyage?" Porter said.

"Yeah," Kett replied. "What about it?"

"I was just thinking about that for some reason."

Kett breathed a laugh through his nose, both of them watching Dunst as he checked his flies, cocked his leg for what was almost certainly a fart, then pulled out a cigarette.

"He's going to explode if he lights that," said Kett.

There was another knock, and they both turned to see Superintendent Clare's face peering through Porter's window. He seemed furious, even for him. Porter wound the window down and Clare pushed his head almost all the way in, looking like a hungry camel at a drive-through zoo.

"What are you two doing in here?" he spat."Because I can tell you what you're not doing. Working."

"We were just getting in the way over there," said Kett. "Franklin's doing her thing and the technicians wanted us off-site."

Clare pulled his head free and harrumphed.

"Two more dead ends," he said. "Armel Roux's in a rehab facility outside of Ipswich, staff have confirmed he's been there for more than two weeks. He doesn't know where his bike is, vaguely remembers leaving it somewhere during a bender."

"Shit," said Porter. "What's the other one?"

"Alis Sayer's ex-boyfriend, Rob Sutton, has been out of town too. He's got an alibi for the night she disappeared."

"A good one?"

Clare nodded.

"So, what are your plans?" he asked them. "Just chillaxing for a bit?"

"We're just waiting for orders, sir," said Porter.

"In that case, you're on Andrew Donal," he said. "He lived out near Eccles. I'll have somebody text you the address. I want to know how his head got in that box."

"Both of us, sir?" Porter asked.

"Why the hell not?" Clare said, his sweaty face looming back in. "Go on, *skoosh*. You can toss off together."

"Nope," said Kett as the Super marched away.

"We're definitely not doing that," said Porter. "Want me to drive?"

"Yeah," said Kett, getting out and walking to the other side of the car. Porter took the easy route over the gearstick. Kett was about to get back in when he saw PC Aaron Duke climb out of an IRV at the top of the street, talking to the Superintendent. Clare pointed at Porter's Mondeo, and Duke started to chug over like an angry rhino.

"Move it, Pete," Kett said as he got back in, slamming the door.

Duke lifted a hand as he ran, waving to them. Kett pretended not to see it. Porter stuck the Mondeo in reverse, the car whining as it barrelled backwards down the street. Duke was calling out to them.

"Don't look him in the eye," said Kett. "He'll give up in a minute."

They were running out of road, Porter easing the brakes on as they neared the junction. He twisted the wheel and the car spun neatly into somebody's driveway, but by the time he'd put it in first, Duke had reached them. He thumped into the car, trying the handle.

"Hello?" he yelled.

Porter pulled out of the drive, whistling innocently.

"Wait!" Duke cried out. "It's me, Duke!"

He tried the door again, the handle flapping. Then, as Porter was about to pull down the street, he hurled himself onto the bonnet.

"Keep going, sir?" Porter asked as the big PC thrashed around on the front of the car.

Kett sighed, unlocking the doors.

"We'd better let him in."

Duke wiggled himself off the bonnet and climbed into the back.

"Sorry mate," Porter said. "Didn't see you there."

"You should have shouted or something," said Kett.

Duke glowered at them.

"Super asked me to come with you, sir," he said.

"Let's go then," Kett replied, and Porter floored it.

THEY WERE on the right side of the city for the A11, and made good time. It was less than half an hour later that Porter pulled the Mondeo across the driveway of a house just outside of the village of Eccles, everyone craning through the window to get a better look at it. It was a large yellow cottage with a thatched roof that badly needed some repair work, standing alone in the middle of the countryside. An orange VW camper sat further down the driveway, its wheels and its doors missing.

"Use gloves," Kett said as he exited into the brutal heat. "We don't know what happened here."

The day was quiet, but Kett could hear the whine of a distant engine, like somebody was tearing hell for leather around the country lanes.

"Snetterton," said Porter. "The race track. It's right over that hill."

"Andrew Donal used to work there," said Duke as he unfolded his enormous bulk from the back of the car. "Before the accident."

"How do you know that?" Kett asked him.

"It's in his notes."

"Notes?" Kett said, looking at Porter. The DI shrugged.

"From Clare," said Duke.

"No idea," Kett said. "Anything else we need to know?"

"Not really," Duke said.

Kett led the way down the long driveway, the house watching them with dead eyes. It had been painted recently, but even so, Kett could still make out giant letters on the wall which had bled through—the kind of letters that never really went away.

"Does that say 'killer'?" he asked.

"Yeah," said Porter. "Looks like somebody wanted to make sure the world knew who Donal was. *That* might help."

Porter pointed to a security camera mounted above the door.

"Check the back, will you, Pete?" Kett asked.

"Will do. You got gloves?"

Kett patted his pockets hopelessly and Porter pulled some out, handing them over.

"Can I have some, sir?" Duke asked. Porter rolled his eyes, passing another set to the PC.

"Not sure they'll fit on those bunches of bananas you call hands, though."

Porter disappeared down the side of the house. Kett reached the front door, knocking hard.

"Why are you knocking, sir?" Duke asked as he fumbled with the gloves. "He's dead."

"Because there might be somebody else at home, *obviously*," Kett said, giving the PC a look.

"I doubt it. Donal lived alone, no wife, no kids."

"How—"

"In his notes, sir."

"Right."

Kett pulled on the gloves, trying the handle.

The door was open.

"Stay sharp," he said.

The hall was wide and airy, the floor made up of terracotta flagstones and an oak staircase leading up to the first floor. Kett took a step and then stopped when he heard movement from deeper in the house.

"You hear that?"

"No," Duke said.

"Porter," Kett called. "That you?"

A feeble cry, something scratching.

"Baton," Kett said.

"I've got my Taser too, sir," he said.

"Baton will be fine. I don't fancy being shot in the arse."

Duke pulled his weapon from his belt and snapped it out.

"This is the police," said Kett. "We're inside the house. Identify yourself."

Another desperate, high-pitched cry.

"Sir?" called Porter. "You in? Back door was open."

"Yeah, we're in. There's somebody else here."

Kett walked into the large kitchen to see Porter standing by the open back door. He was looking towards another door across the room. It was shut, and there was a sturdy bolt drawn across it.

Somebody was scratching their fingernails against the wood, an exhausted whimper for help.

"Who's there?" Kett demanded.

No answer.

He moved to the door, Porter on his left and Duke taking up position on the right, his baton raised. Kett looked at them both to make sure they were ready, then he slid the bolt back.

"It's the police," he said again. "You don't have to be afraid. I'm coming in, okay?"

That whimper again, breathless.

Kett turned the handle, the door opening into a small utility room.

"Shit," said Kett.

A golden retriever lay in its basket on the far side of the room, its body limp. It barely had enough strength to lift its head, and the cry that dropped from its mouth broke Kett's heart.

"Oh, yeah," said Duke. "The notes mentioned Donal has a dog."

Kett resisted the urge to slap the big PC around the back of his head. Instead, he walked over, dropping onto his haunches and letting the old dog sniff his hand. Then he ruffled the back of its neck.

"Hey," he said. "You're okay."

Despite its weakness, the dog's tail thumped up and down, its big eyes full of kindness and full of relief. Its food and water bowls were empty and it was roasting in here, unbearably so.

"Pete, get him some water, will you?"

Porter already had the tap on, filling the dog's bowl and lowering it gently in front of its sandpaper-dry nose. The dog heaved its old body over the edge of the bed, its tongue splashing in the bowl. More of it went on the floor than down its throat, but after a few seconds it managed to get to its feet, drinking deeply. Kett rummaged in a cupboard and found some tins of dog food, opening one up and shaking the contents out into the other bowl.

"What happened to you, eh?" he asked the dog.

It looked up at him as it ate, its tail sweeping dust from the floor. He ruffled the back of its neck again, then gave its flank a gentle pat.

"Duke, stay with the dog," he said. "Don't let it out."

Duke pulled a face, but he didn't complain. He compacted his baton and slid it into his belt, crouching next to the dog while it ate. A throbbing growl rose in the dog's throat.

"Don't eat his lunch," Kett said to Duke. "Pete, with me."

They made their way back into the kitchen, Kett closing the utility door behind him.

"I'll take upstairs," Porter said, bounding off.

Kett did a cursory sweep of the kitchen, finding nothing but neatly stacked dishes and sparse cupboards. From the look of it, Andrew Donal had survived on a diet of Pot Noodles, Pop-Tarts and, judging by the overflowing ashtrays and empty boxes, Marlborough Reds. There was nothing in the living room either, except for an entire shelf of DVDs, most of them classic comedies from the 1980s.

Kett wandered across the hall, entering a small study. A desk sat against the window, an Apple laptop open on it. The screensaver swirled around, oblivious.

"Come on," Kett willed, sliding on his glasses. "Be good to us."

He used his hip to move the chair out of the way, running a finger along the trackpad. The screensaver vanished, the login screen appearing over a backdrop of a bearded Andrew Donal and his dog. It waited patiently for a password. Kett opened the desk drawer on the left to see a clutter of pens and paper. The one on the right contained an Apple Watch and some AirPods. The watch was dead and Kett looked for a cable, not seeing one.

"Upstairs is clear," Porter said. "Looks like there might have been a struggle, though. Chair in the master bedroom was knocked over and there's a broken mug by the nightstand."

"We'll leave it for forensics," Kett said. "They're going to be busy in the Skeldon house for a while."

"You need a password, sir?" Porter said as he walked over.

"Yeah."

They looked at the image on the screen, then at each other.

"The dog," they said at the same time.

Porter disappeared, Kett popping his lips until the DI returned.

"Name on the collar is Mr Nipples."

"Mr Nipples?" Kett said. "Who the hell calls their dog that?"

He typed *mrnipples* into the password bar only for it to shake irately. He tried again with a 1 instead of an *I* but this didn't work either.

"It definitely said Mr Nipples?" Kett asked. "You saw that for yourself."

"No, Duke told me."

"It didn't say Mr *Nibbles*?"

Porter cocked his head, thinking about it.

"That does make more sense."

Kett tried it in the password bar, going through a couple of iterations before the home screen appeared. It took every ounce of restraint he had not to throw a fist into the air and whoop.

"You beauty," he said.

He opened Donal's emails, seeing nothing but spam. He tried his messages next, scrolling through texts from his mum, his sister, a couple of friends. The last message Donal sent was to his sister, just a smiley face.

"Saturday," Kett said. "Nearly midnight. He hasn't texted anyone since then."

"Try WhatsApp, sir," Porter said, and Kett loaded it up.

More messages from friends, barbeques and gym sessions, and a couple of women that he seemed to be dating at the same time. He'd sent photos of himself to both of them, shirtless and grinning. This didn't seem to be the life of somebody who'd killed one young person and paralysed another. Kett thought about Charlie Skeldon in her wheelchair, about the photos he'd seen of her brother, and the anger burned through him on their behalf.

Then he thought about Donal's severed head sitting on the kitchen counter, and the anger turned to nausea.

Nobody deserved that. Not even him.

"Go back to the other woman," Porter said, poking the screen hard enough to tilt it back. Kett righted it, clicking on one of the women that Donal had been talking to.

"Miriam," Kett said, studying her photo. It looked like it had been clipped from a lingerie catalogue. He scrolled through the messages, seeing that they'd only started messaging a couple of weeks ago. Miriam had initiated the conversation with a heart, and it had deteriorated quickly into some pretty heavy flirtation.

"There," said Porter. He looked like he was going to prod the screen again, and Kett slapped his hand away. "Ouch. Look, they were going to meet."

"On Sunday," Kett said. "He gave her this address."

"Idiot. There's no way that photo is the person sending these messages. He's been catfished."

The last message from Donal was at midday on Sunday.

'*See you later. Dress like your photo yeah?*'

Then the reply.

'*CU@10*.'

Kett closed the app and searched the computer for the feed from the security camera outside. There was a Google Nest app, and when he opened it up the password form filled automatically.

"Thank you very much," he told it as the footage loaded.

There was the driveway, baked in sun. He skipped back twenty-four hours, seeing nothing but hearing an endless chorus of barks from inside the house.

"Poor thing," he said. "Must have been desperate."

"And just when he thought it couldn't get any worse, Duke shows up."

Kett scrolled back, seeing nothing until Sunday night. It was after ten, but still light enough to see the woman who walked to the front door. She was wearing a figure-hugging summer dress, her face concealed beneath a wide, floral hat. Kett's breath was locked in his lungs as he watched her pound a fist on the door.

Knock knock.

Five seconds later, it opened. The angle of the camera meant that Kett couldn't see who stood in the doorway, but a muffled man's voice spoke out.

"*Hey. Miriam?*"

The hat rocked as the woman nodded, still no sign of her face.

"*You don't look much like your picture.*"

The woman turned and walked off-screen. Donal stepped into the space she'd just vacated, his phone in one hand and his keys in the other. He was wearing a black shirt and jeans, his hair gelled and his beard brushed.

"*Wait, it's a good thing. You're gorgeous.*"

He closed the door without bothering to lock it, running after the woman with one last muttered word.

"*Fuck.*"

Kett scrolled through the last of the day, then doubled back to Saturday, finding nothing else of any use.

"It's a woman," Porter said as Kett returned the feed to Sunday night and froze it. The woman's hat was so wide you couldn't even see her shoulders, just a slim waist and long legs. She was wearing chunky brown boots with buckles instead of laces.

Motorcycle boots.

"He knew her," Kett said. "Kind of. Same as Alis Sayer. She knew the person who came to her door."

He leaned in.

"You don't think that could be Mrs Bower, do you?"

"She's slim, holds herself well." Porter shrugged. "Maybe. I wouldn't exactly describe Mrs Bower as gorgeous, but then horses for courses, right?"

"Okay," said Kett, sitting back. "Let's make that job number one. Find out if there's any connection between Andrew Donal and Lydia Bower. And let's see if we can ID Miriam."

"On it," said Porter as Kett moved out of the way. The DI tilted the laptop towards him, closing the screen.

"Hang on," he said. "Tags."

"Tags?"

Porter pointed to a sticky white circle fastened to the lid of the computer, an Apple logo emblazoned on it.

"What are tags?" Kett asked. "Tell me they're something good."

"You haven't heard of tags?" Porter said, frowning with disgust. "How old are you?"

"Like four years older than you," Kett shot back. "I'm not old."

"Sure," said Porter, looking at Kett's chunky glasses. "Whatever you need to tell yourself to get through the day."

"I'm not old!"

"AirTags are tracking chips," Porter said. "They're fairly new. You stick them on whatever and use your phone to find them. You do know what a phone is, don't you?"

Kett glowered at him.

"You can get stickers like this, and you can get fobs too for your bags and stuff."

"Or your keys," said Kett, opening the lid of the laptop.

He clicked play on the security camera feed, finding the moment Donal stepped out of his door. The footage wasn't clear enough to make out the individual keys, but Kett could see a big brown fob attached to them.

"How do you find them?" he asked.

"The app," Porter said, nudging Kett out of the way and opening it up. A map appeared on-screen along with various items clustered around the house they were in at the moment.

"His bike," said Kett. "His laptop, his dog. Zoom out."

Porter did as he was told, an image of a set of keys appearing to the north.

"No way," said Kett. "It's that easy?"

"It's that easy," said Porter, jabbing the screen again. "His keys are five miles away, right there."

CHAPTER TWENTY-FIVE

"Here we go."

Savage opened the door of the hotel room, then stood back, allowing Charlie Skeldon to make her way inside. It was on the ground floor of the Premier Inn by the train station, right in the middle of the city, and even from inside the building Savage could hear nothing but car horns and rumbling engines.

She'd already shown Pat and Ginge into the room next door. They'd been in a state of shock, their faces slack, their bodies bent and bowed. They hadn't said a single word to her as they'd slammed the door behind them, and she wasn't expecting much from Charlie, either.

"If you need anything else, just call me," Savage said, pulling out a card and leaving it on the desk. "And there will be an officer right down the hall all night if you need him."

Charlie manoeuvred her wheelchair to the window, looking up.

"I supposed you need to go?"

"No," said Savage. "Not at all. You want me to stay for a little while?"

Charlie nodded, and Savage gently closed the door. She perched on the edge of the low bed, taking in the young woman who sat across from her, drenched in the diffused light that swam through the net curtain. She couldn't imagine what she'd been through, what she was *still* going through every single day. There was something in her eyes that made her look far older than she really was.

Charlie ran a finger down the scar on her arm, deep in thought.

"I can pop the kettle on, if you like?" Savage said.

"No," she replied. "Too hot for tea."

"Water?"

"I'm fine," she said. "Can look after myself."

Savage held up her hands in apology.

"It's really him?" Charlie asked, looking up. "Andrew?"

"We can't confirm it just yet, Charlie, sorry."

"It is him," she said. "Dad wouldn't've cried out like that if it were anyone else."

"I don't know," Savage said, struggling to find the right words. "How would you feel if it was?"

Charlie shrugged, the stump of her leg twitching beneath her blanket. She massaged it with both hands, wincing.

"Still hurts, you know? My leg. The bit I don't have anymore. How weird is that? How can it hurt when it's not there?"

"It's a nerve thing," said Savage. "Must be difficult."

"I know what it is," she said. "I feel sad, you know."

"About your leg?"

"About the man, about Andrew."

Savage frowned.

"You feel sad about the man who did this to you?"

"Nobody deserves that," she said. "Not that I haven't

thought it, you know? Back when it happened, I'd have given anything to see his head in a box. But now?"

She turned to the window, lost in the soft light.

"There's so much death in the world, I hate it. I told her I didn't want no more death."

"Her?" said Savage.

"You can't say nothing," Charlie said. "Promise?"

Savage didn't answer, but it didn't make a difference.

"My ex," Charlie said. "Happy."

Savage thought it was a question and she shook her head.

"Happy? I'm not—"

"That's her name, Happy. Stupid, right? She changed it by deed poll. It's supposed to be ironic. Happy Heptinstall."

"She was your girlfriend?"

Charlie shrugged again.

"For a bit. Wasn't serious. We met at one of those stupid support groups. She lost her mum a few years back. Cancer. I didn't want to go, but..."

She took a breath, obviously exhausted.

"Doesn't matter now, does it?"

"When did your relationship end?" Savage asked, if only to fill the awkward silence.

"Few months ago," Charlie said. "Was getting too intense, living with her and shit."

"I thought it wasn't serious?"

"It wasn't. You try living with *Pat* and *Ginge*." She spat her parents' names like she was choking on a bug. "But Happy's worse, she's so intense. She said she wanted to help me move on, but all she ever talked about was the car crash, my brother and my leg. It's like every time I forgot about it all, she wanted to remind me, because she wanted me to be sad, you know? It's like... I don't know, it's like if I wasn't sad, then I wasn't any use to her."

"I get that," Savage said. "Some people find meaning in grief. It's how they make sense of the world. You told Happy you didn't want anything bad to happen to Andrew Donal?"

Charlie's shoulders lurched up and down again, her answer to everything.

"She was always talking about what she'd do to him. She had this vendetta against him, and against the doctor who told her mum she didn't have cancer—told her like six times before it was too late to do anything about it. She had all these scenarios she'd talk about."

"Like what?" Savage asked.

Like cutting off his head and sticking it in a box?

"Nothing violent," Charlie said, reading Savage's mind. "Not like *that*, anyway. Happy isn't much of a physical person, but she's a geek, right? She spends her life online. She thought she was a bit of a superhero, because she'd find bad people and out them, spread their names about, their addresses."

"Doxxing?" Savage asked.

"Yeah, she'd doxx the hell out of them, spill their secrets into the public realm on Facebook and shit."

"What did she want to get out of that?"

"Revenge," Charlie said, as if it was the most obvious thing in the world. "But she didn't do the hard part. She'd just leave all those details out there and let other people finish the job."

"Hang on," said Savage, leaning forward. "Finish the job in what sense?"

"Not offing them, if that's what you're thinking. *Outing* them. There are loads of groups out there who go after shitty people. Paedos and conmen and crooks and all of them. There are sites on the web where you can find out all about what somebody's been up to, all their secrets—that's where Happy uploaded all the stuff she found. These groups pick their target and..."

"And what?" Savage asked.

"Mess 'em up, I guess," said Charlie. "I don't know. I never got involved."

"Happy wanted to send these people after Andrew?"

"Yeah, but I didn't let her. I didn't want any more violence or blood. He's a... there's no word for what he is. I hate him, and if that's really him, then I'm glad he's dead. But I don't want no part of it. I'm broken enough."

She sighed, massaging her leg beneath the blanket.

"I saw what happened to that doctor when Happy doxxed him," she said quietly. "They put him in a coma."

"*Really*?" said Savage. "Do you think these people might have gone after Donal too?"

"No," said Charlie. "No way, because I told Happy not to post his details. I said I'd leave her if she did."

"You left her anyway," said Savage. "She might have done it."

"She wouldn't. I know her. She loved me. Still does."

"Can you tell me where to find her posts online?" Savage said.

"No. It's all on the Dark Web. You have to know exactly where to look. She never told me shit about it."

Somebody laughed in the corridor outside, the sound so alien that it took Savage a moment to recognise it. She waited for a set of footsteps to fade before continuing.

"Charlie, where does Happy live? I think it's really important we speak with her."

"Just round the corner from me," she said. "Next street

over, opposite the school. Number 14. But I don't know if she's there because I haven't heard from her for a while."

"That's unusual?"

Charlie shrugged, then she nodded.

"I'm worried she's done something stupid."

"Like what, Charlie?"

The young woman sniffed.

"I don't know."

Savage stood up, brushing her hands down the front of her trousers. She felt her phone buzz, but she left it in her pocket.

"I'd better go," she said. "But this is really helpful, thank you."

"Don't do anything bad to Happy," said Charlie. "She's broken too, but she's not a bad person."

"I won't. You sure you'll be okay?"

"What do you think?" Charlie said, lifting her arms in one final shrug.

Savage opened the door, hesitating. Then she stepped into the corridor, closing it behind her and resting a hand against the warm wood for a second. She pulled out her phone, seeing a text message waiting for her from a withheld number.

She had to read it twice to make sure it was real, her pulse hammering in the back of her throat.

I know why the foot was delivered to Douglas' house. I can tell you everything, but only you. Earlham Park, the back path to uni. 11 pm. Don't tell anyone, and COME ALONE OR I DISAPPEAR AND YOU NEVER SEE ME AGAIN.

Savage checked the time, licked her lips.

Then made her way out of the hotel.

CHAPTER TWENTY-SIX

PORTER RODE FAST AND HARD, TAKING THE COUNTRY roads like he was tearing around Snetterton. Kett sat in the front seat, one hand gripping the strap above the door, the other holding his phone to his ear. Duke and Mr Nibbles occupied the back of the Mondeo, as shaggy as each other and both of them protesting the speed of the drive with a chorus of howls.

"Yeah, we're on the way now," Kett said. "Looks like an industrial site on the map, a farm maybe, but I'll update you when we get there."

"Be careful," Clare replied. "I just want you to observe. Don't move in until I get some more coppers out to you."

"Sure thing, sir," Kett said.

He hung up, holding his breath as Porter overtook a slow-moving Fiat. The driver leaned on the horn, the sound of it lost as Porter picked up speed. Kett had to close his eyes as they took the corner. The memory of his near-death experience during the Jaw Breaker case was still painfully vivid, and every time the car wobbled he thought they were going to topple over the edge of the road and roll down a slope in a hurricane of compacting metal and glass. The Mondeo hit a bump and his stomach clenched, bile rising up his throat.

"Pete," he said.

"I know," Porter replied, touching the brake. "Sorry, sir."

Kett opened his eyes to see they were coming up to a junction. He checked the photo he'd taken of the map on Donal's laptop, then pointed a finger to the right.

"It's up there."

The car shuddered to a halt, slipping on loose gravel. Porter tapped the wheel impatiently as he waited for three cars to whip past, then he pulled out. They were still in the middle of the countryside here, open fields stretching out to the horizon in all directions. Kett had the weird notion that they were on a boat in a wide, green sea, and that any minute now they'd plunge beneath the surface.

"There," he said, seeing a road to the right. "It's that one."

Porter pulled into it, the car rocking as it navigated the deep potholes. In the back, Mr Nibbles howled.

"Quiet back there, Duke," said Porter.

"That wasn't me, sir."

The road curved gently to the left, the high crops hiding the building that lay ahead until they were almost on it. It was a low, wide barn, its walls and roof made of corrugated iron. There were no windows, but the large double door was partially open, nothing but darkness inside.

Porter bumped the Mondeo over the rough ground and then cut the engine, everyone sitting in silence. The only sound was the gentle tick of the cooling engine and the crows, dozens of them circling overhead.

And a fearful whimper from the back seat.

"No need to whine, Duke," Porter said.

"That's not me!" the PC protested. "It was the dog!"

Mr Nibbles barked loud enough to make Kett's ears ring. He turned, ruffling the dog's shaggy neck. It nuzzled him, its big tongue sliding across his face, its dog food breath making him gag.

"Gross," Kett said. "Kiss Duke, not me."

"I wouldn't," said Porter. "Don't know where Duke's been."

"Been with your mother," came an angry mutter from the back. Porter spun around.

"What did you say, *Constable*?"

"Nothing, *sir*."

"Enough," said Kett, before the pair of them started trading blows. "Pack it in, both of you. Porter, you're with me. Duke, stay in the car. If there's any trouble, we'll call."

"Might be better to take the dog?" Duke said. "He'll know his master's smell."

"That's actually a good point," Kett said. "But stay here until the coast is clear. The last thing we need is a big dog charging into a possible crime scene."

Kett climbed out and arched his back, which had grown stiff with tension from the drive. It felt like somebody was sliding knives between his ribs and he winced, putting both hands on the car as he waited for the pain to subside.

Porter glanced at him as he passed.

"I'm not bloody old," Kett said before he could comment. "I'm pretty much the same age as you!"

"I never said anything," Porter replied.

"I could see you thinking it."

Porter took the lead, ducking low as he jogged across the overgrown path that led to the barn door. The crows wheeled above them, their hoarse song so loud it was almost alien. More of the birds sat on the crest of the roof and pecked for scraps in the guttering, studying them with pitch-black eyes. They flapped their powerful wings, their claws tapping out a tune on the metal as they hopped and danced.

"You don't believe in omens, do you, Pete?" Kett asked quietly.

"Only the good ones," he replied.

Porter reached the barn first, peering through the partially open doors. Kett caught up to him, studying the darkness while he waited for his sun-bleached eyes to adjust. The barn was one giant, open space, the ceiling propped up with a forest of narrow columns, and from the trickle of light through the knackered roof it was clear that it was empty.

"That's disappointing," said Porter.

Kett walked inside, inhaling the unmistakable smell of animal dung and mouldering bedding. Piles of straw and manure had been pushed to one side, but the far end of the barn looked relatively clean. Trickles of golden sunlight dripped from the ceiling, forming puddles on the floor, but the corners remained stubbornly dark.

He heard a click and turned to see Porter holding a torch, sweeping it along the base of the wall beside them, then freezing.

"Blood," he said, just as Kett was about to say the same thing.

It was, no mistake. A puddle of dark blood the size of a dinner plate, caked with straw.

"There's another one," Kett said as Porter moved the light.

This one was bigger, and the one past that was bigger still. Smaller drops connected the bigger splashes, as if something had been moving while the blood dripped out of it.

"An animal?" Porter asked.

"No," said Kett. "I don't think so."

They'd reached the far end of the barn now, and sitting in the corner was a large, black binbag. The top had been tied, and it was very, very full.

"Want to wait for forensics?" Porter asked.

"They'll be busy in the city," Kett replied. "Let's just take a look. Gloves?"

"One set left," Porter said.

"You do it."

Porter pulled on a fresh set of gloves and ducked down next to the binbag. He picked gently at the knot until it came undone, then pried open the mouth of the bag. Together, they leaned over to have a look.

"Shit," said Kett.

The bag was full of clothes, a black shirt sitting on a pair of jeans, all neatly folded.

"That's what Andrew Donal was wearing on Sunday when he left the house," said Porter.

And if there was any doubt at all that these were his, it died when Porter pushed the T-shirt to one side to reveal a set of keys beneath, next to a wallet and a phone. The keys were the same ones they'd seen on the security feed, the brown leather fob big enough to conceal the AirTag inside it. Porter carefully pulled the wallet free and opened it up. There was no driving license, but Donal's name was on every card.

Porter replaced the wallet and tapped the phone.

"Dead," he said.

He pushed the jeans to one side and Kett saw what might have been sheets underneath, drenched with blood.

"This is not looking good," Porter said.

"We already knew it wasn't good," Kett replied. "He had his head cut off."

"Yeah, fair point."

They stepped back from the bag, Porter sweeping the torch up the wall.

"Look," he said.

There was more blood there, a large circular stain about six feet above the ground. This one looked more deliberate than those on the floor, made more so by the fact that somebody had drawn eight little bloody streaks poking out of the circle, four on each side.

"It's a tick," Kett said.

"Who *is* this?" said Porter, searching the rest of the wall and finding nothing but cobwebs.

"More to the point, if this is where Donal lost his head, where's the rest of him?"

Kett walked to the smaller rear door of the barn, using his boot to shunt it open. A decade's worth of dust and metal flakes rained down on him and he smudged them out of his eyes to see more scrubland ahead, disappearing into trees maybe thirty yards away. He scanned the ground but couldn't see any more blood.

"We should get the dog out," he said. "Duke is right. He'll know Donal's scent. If they dumped the rest of his body in the woods, we might be able to find him."

"You do realise we have our own dogs for that, sir?" Porter asked as he stepped out after him.

"Not here, we don't. Go take a look, I'll let Duke know."

Porter set off and Kett walked back to the car, taking the route around the side of the barn so he wouldn't have to see those puddles of blood, that awful image of the tick. Mr Nibbles was barking his head off inside the Mondeo, but the noise stopped as Kett reached it. Duke wound his window down, looking miserable.

"I don't think he likes me, sir," he said as Kett opened the door.

Duke started to get out, but Mr Nibbles beat him to it, vaulting the PC's legs and almost leaping into Kett's arms. The dog licked his face, and he laughed before he could stop himself.

"You're a good lad, aren't you?" he said, taking hold of his lead. "Good boy."

He passed the lead to Duke, who took it like somebody had offered him a live snake.

"Go around the barn," Kett said. "Not through, there's evidence. Porter's in the woods out back, see if this guy can find anything."

"You want me to—"

The dog was off, jerking Duke after it. Kett watched him wrestle Mr Nibbles away from the barn doors and down the side of the building, the crows taking flight at the sight of the dog. Then he pulled out his phone and called Clare.

"Speak!" roared the Super when he answered.

"I think we've found the place where Donal was killed, sir," said Kett. He glanced up, blinded by the violent sun. "His clothes are here, as well as his keys, wallet, and phone. And a lot of blood. Somebody's painted a tick on the wall as well, the same as our fliers. In blood."

"I thought I told you to hang back," Clare said.

"We are," he lied, blinking sunspots from his vision. "We're waiting for forensics, but we'll have a search for the rest of..."

Kett stopped, cocking his head as the sound of an engine rose nearby.

"The rest of what?" Clare snapped. "Your sentence?"

The engine dulled, and Kett was on the verge of speaking again when it grew louder. He moved away from the Mondeo, staring down the track to where it curved into the crops.

Something was coming.

"Did you send somebody out to us, sir?" he asked.

"Yes, I did. They'll be with you in the next twenty minutes or so."

A throbbing growl, something powerful.

It sounded like a motorbike.

Kett's heart revved, just as hard.

"What's going on?" Clare said.

"I don't know, sir," he replied, lowering the phone to his chest as he watched the road, as he listened to that engine grow louder and louder.

A bike cruised around the corner, sleek and black, its gold forks seeming to flash in the sun. The rider was hunched over the handlebars, dressed in blue overalls and a black helmet. Kett couldn't see anything of their face behind the dark visor. He stepped back into the shade of the tree, lifting the phone to his ear.

"We've got company, sir. Black Ducati, one rider, coming this way."

"Jesus Tossing Christ, Kett, that's him!"

The rider hadn't spotted him yet, their head down as they steered carefully around the craters.

"Do not engage, is that clear?" Clare shouted. "We're dealing with a professional killer here. It's not worth it."

"Just get here as fast as you can," said Kett.

He hung up, calling Porter, trying to stay as still as humanly possible.

The bike reached the end of the road and the rider looked up.

Looked right at Kett.

Fuck.

"Police!" Kett shouted. "Do not move!"

The rider tugged on the accelerator, twisting the handlebars. The bike's back wheel kicked up a fan of dirt as the engine roared, the Ducati spinning in a tight 180 before gunning back up the track.

Kett swore, looking back at the barn to see no sign of Porter or Duke.

There was no time to wait for them.

He climbed into the Mondeo and started the engine, throwing the phone into the passenger seat as he steered the car in a wide, clumsy circle. He could hear Porter's voice on the phone and he yelled back to him.

"Pete, they were just here, a bike. I'm going after them."

He accelerated down the path, the potholes nearly ripping away the Mondeo's undercarriage. He couldn't see the motorbike anymore, but he could hear the whine of its engine as it hit the main road. The Mondeo was fast, but compared to the Ducati it might as well have been a donkey with a cart.

He reached the road and wound all four windows down, listening for the bike. Then he pulled out.

"He's going east," he shouted to Porter, hoping the DI would be able to hear him. "We're on Broad Way."

He pushed his foot down, the Mondeo hitting sixty in a heartbeat. He had to pump the brake almost immediately as he reached a crossroads. The bike had gone, but the sound of its engine still drifted back from Kett's left.

"North," he shouted, pulling out. He looked for a road sign but couldn't see anything, just vast fields and wild trees.

The road was long and straight and he hit sixty again, oncoming cars whumping past him with blaring horns, the wind battering his ears. He couldn't hear the bike at all now.

He'd lost him.

"Come on," he said, checking the sparse driveways as they flashed past, knowing the bike could be hiding in any one of them. "Where are you?"

The road curved gently to the right, fields giving way to woodland, the world suddenly dark out of the glare of the sun. Kett eased off the pedal and the engine quietened. He waited, cocking his head and holding his breath.

There, faint but still audible.

He punched it again, chasing the ghostly cry of the bike. He passed two more houses before the trees gave way to fields again, and there he spotted movement over the top of the low hedges that hugged the road.

The Ducati whipped down a track to the left, the rider standing like a jockey to counter the bumps.

"Got you," said Kett.

He slammed a foot on the brake and skidded clumsily onto a concrete track. Something scraped down the Mondeo's flank with a squeal as he thumped past a gatepost, but he ignored it. There was no sign of the bike amongst the collection of squat, ugly buildings that clustered up ahead.

"I'm heading towards a farm," he said, the car slow enough now for him to pick up the phone. "About two kilometres past the junction, just out of the woods. On the left. Can't see a name."

"Okay, sir," said Porter, and Kett heard him relaying the information down another line—probably Duke's radio.

Kett kept his speed low, listening for any sign of the bike. He thought he could hear it, but he couldn't be sure, the whine of an engine seeming to come from his left and his right at the same time.

"The boss says no further, sir," Porter said. "It's not worth it."

"I won't get out of the car," he said. "I promise. He's on a bike, he's not going to try anything."

"Famous last words," said Porter. "Just be careful, okay?"

"When am I anything else?"

The Mondeo crawled into the shadow of the first building, a barn not unlike the one they'd just been in. It was shut tight, giant chains snaked around the door. On the other side of the track was a concrete silo, then another barn, this one just three walls and a roof. There was nothing inside but rusted equipment. Even with the windows down, Kett couldn't hear the bike anymore.

He kept going, the Mondeo purring into a sun-drenched courtyard between the buildings.

The Ducati was right there.

It sat directly opposite Kett on the far side of the courtyard, facing this way. The engine throbbed, the rider's hand gripping the throttle and twisting it gently. Their face was a blank mask behind the visor, but Kett had no doubt at all that they were looking right at him.

"Okay," he said to nobody in particular.

"What's going on?" Porter asked.

Kett didn't answer. He dropped the phone onto the passenger seat and popped his lips, considering his choices. The rider was giving nothing away, their only movement the twitch of their hand on the throttle. The engine revved gently each time, a deep pulse of sound that Kett swore he could feel as well as hear.

"What are you doing?" Kett asked.

He put the car in neutral, one hand on the door. His heart was thumping like a piece of machinery, his head pounding. He licked his lips, aware of how thirsty he was.

He pulled the handle, the car door opening.

The rider didn't move, the Ducati throbbing.

Kett pushed the door open fully, hesitating again. Nothing about this felt right.

The motorbike revved hard, although the rider still wasn't moving. The whine of the engine seemed to change pitch, rising to Kett's left.

It was a *different* bike.

Kett looked into the long shadow of the concrete silo, seeing another motorbike crawl into sight. This rider, too, wore blue overalls, their shielded visor a fly's eye, utterly emotionless. This rider sat on a different kind of bike, but it looked just as powerful and just as fast.

On their feet they wore brown boots, the buckles gleaming.

"Shit," said Kett, drawing his leg back into the car.

A rising whine, then a third bike rode out from behind a barn to Kett's right, coming to a stop on the edge of the courtyard.

The three riders sat there, all of them perfectly still apart from the movement of their right hand on the throttle. The combined sound of their bikes was thunder.

"There's three of them," Kett said, hoping Porter would be able to hear him. "Three people dressed in blue overalls, black helmets, all on bikes. No plates."

Nobody moved, but the pressure of their gaze was almost unbearable.

"Right," Kett said, flexing his hands on the wheel.

It was his move, he knew. They were waiting for him.

He opened the door again, hot air flooding in. Then he

hauled himself out into the day. His head was a fizzing chaos of noise, his body weak from adrenaline, but he stood as tall as he could, looking at each of the riders in turn.

"I'm police," he yelled, surprised at the strength of his own voice. It echoed back to him from the surrounding barns. "Get off the bikes and—"

As one, all three riders reached behind their back and pulled out a long, lethal machete. The blades caught the light, full of blinding fire.

"Last chance," Kett said, holding his ground and pointing to the rider in the middle.

This time, his voice didn't carry at all.

The rider on the right accelerated, the roar of the bike deafening. Then they were all tearing across the courtyard, converging on the Mondeo.

Kett swore, dropping back into his seat and slamming the door shut an instant before the first bike reached him. The rider swung their blade low and the car lurched as the tyre exploded. The second bike thumped past on the other side, the car wobbling again as they slashed at that wheel. Both bikes burned past him, heading for the road.

The third stopped in front of the Mondeo, the rider pointing the machete through the windscreen, right at Kett's face. The message was a clear echo of Kett's own.

Last chance.

Then they twisted the throttle and skidded past, the engine fading into the heat of the day.

Kett put a hand to his chest to calm his heart, then he picked up his phone.

"Pete, you there?"

"Yeah, you okay?"

"They're heading for the road, three bikes. They're armed, machetes. God knows what else."

"What? You hurt?"

"No, but they took out your tyres."

"*What?*"

Kett opened his door again, but his legs felt too rubbery to carry him out. He wiped the sweat from his face with a trembling hand.

"You sure you're okay?" Porter asked.

"Yeah," said Kett, closing his eyes. "But I think I might have eaten a piece of Clare's cake after all, because I'm pretty sure I just shat myself."

CHAPTER TWENTY-SEVEN

Kett held the hot cup of tea in both hands, and even then it was a struggle not to spill it. Everything was shaking after his encounter with the bikes and their machete-wielding riders. Part of the reason for that was how close he'd come to getting in serious trouble.

And part of it was that this case had suddenly become a lot more complicated.

He looked up as Porter walked over, two Diet Cokes in his hands. Duke was right behind him, still wrestling with the dog, who was determined to sniff everything in sight. They were sitting in a large courtyard café that was part of a garden centre, less than a mile from the farm where he'd encountered the three riders. It was relatively busy given that they were well into late afternoon now, the dozen tables fully occupied and everyone glancing warily at the giant PC with the shaggy dog.

"Don't know how you can drink tea on a day like this," said Porter, sitting opposite.

"I could drink tea anywhere," Kett said. "As long as it's not one of yours."

The barb went unnoticed as Superintendent Clare bellowed something from the entrance to the café. Everyone turned to look at him, the hum of chatter quietening. It was no surprise. Clare looked like he'd been lost in the desert for a month, his face red and sweaty, his suit rumpled, his eyes wild. He must have still been having tummy trouble, because he clamped a hand to his stomach as he walked towards them, his body hunched. He grunted like a mule with every step.

"Can we just pretend we don't know him?" said Porter. He turned to Kett. "I can't believe you totalled my car, by the way. Two tyres and a massive scratch on the side. I don't know how they even did that."

"Very sharp machetes," said Kett, clearing his throat and trying not to think about how he'd scraped the Mondeo against the gatepost. "And you trashed my old Volvo, remember?"

"Yeah, I guess this makes us even."

Clare lurched towards the table, still bellowing.

"I said did you get me some water?"

"I got you a Coke, sir," said Porter, holding it up.

"Do I look like I fill my body with that poison?"

"You've been filling your body with *literal* poison all week, sir," said Kett. "That cake."

Clare grunted. Porter's chair scraped back, and he sighed loudly as he walked to the café. The Super took his place, running the back of his hand over his sweaty brow.

"Well?" he demanded.

"Sorry, sir," said Kett. He took a sip of the tea, his tongue turning instantly fuzzy. "Just needed to settle my nerves."

"I don't give a turtle's tosspole about that," Clare said. "There's no sign of your three motorcycle riders, not even a glimpse of them on any road from King's Lynn to Norwich."

"They know the area, I think," said Kett. "Both the farms they were using seemed to be empty."

"They were," Clare said. "Barn with the blood is part of an old estate that's currently unoccupied. We're combing the grounds as we speak. The farm where you almost got sliced and diced has been sold recently, it's vacant. Was owned by a conglomerate, no indication at all of any involvement in this. But we need to find out how the riders knew it was empty."

"There's no way that was a coincidence," Kett said.

"They didn't say anything?"

"No," said Kett, holding his tea to his chest, the smell of it doing a fair bit to settle him. "But one of them sent me a pretty clear message. They were pissed off that we found them."

"I'll bet they were," Clare said. "Almost as pissed off as I am that we let them go. If you'd just waited, we could have sprung a trap."

"If I'd waited, we'd have lost them," Kett said. "And now we know it's not just one person. There's three of them."

"At least," said Clare, a fat bead of sweat rolling down his cheek.

From the other side of the courtyard came a chorus of barks, and Kett looked to see Duke trying to pull Mr Nibbles away from a yappy little Pomeranian. The PC looked about as flustered as the Super did.

"What the hell is he doing?" Clare asked.

"Dog was Donal's," Kett explained. "Poor thing was locked in the utility since Sunday, no food or water. I'm surprised he made it. Somebody will need to drop him off at the vet's for a check-up, but he seems fine."

"I saw the security footage," Clare said. "Donal was contacted by a woman, she lured him out of his house on Sunday. Could she have been one of our riders?"

"I think so, sir," Kett said. "They were wearing blue overalls, but one of them had boots just like the woman in the video. They had helmets with shielded visors, so there's no way of knowing for sure. I thought it might be Lydia Bower at first, but I'm not convinced."

"I've got a tail on Mrs Bower," said Clare. "She's been nowhere near this part of the county all day. But the clothes you found in the binbag definitely belong to Andrew Donal. Franklin's there now and she's pretty sure it's his blood. We'll be able to match it to the head. The sheets are saturated. She thinks Donal was lying on them when he was decapitated. But there's no body in the woods, no murder weapon either. Just the blood on the floor and that picture on the wall."

"No!" shouted Duke. "Bad dog!"

Mr Nibbles was standing on his hind legs next to a table, living up to his name as he tried to get hold of an iced bun. The owner of the bun, a well-dressed woman in her sixties, was trying to bat the dog away with her bag. After a couple of swipes she started to swat Duke instead.

Kett took pity on the PC, whistling across the courtyard. Mr Nibbles dropped down onto all fours and bounded away from Duke so fast the leash slipped free from his hand. The dog ran to Kett and planted his front paws on his lap, a goofy grin on his face.

"You're a dope," Kett said, taking a sip of his tea before the dog could get his tongue in the cup.

Duke ran over, evidently not built for the heat. He put his hands on the back of a chair, breathing hard.

"He doesn't do a single thing I ask him to," he said.

"Welcome to my world," said Clare, licking his dry lips. "Where's my mothertossing water?"

Porter was just emerging from the café, a bottle in his hand. He dropped it in front of the Super, who looked at it like Porter had just given him a bottle full of piss.

"What is this?" he said.

"Water, sir," said Porter.

"*Sparkling*?" fumed the Boss. "What kind of monster are you?"

"Oh, uh..." Porter flailed. He reached for the bottle but Clare slapped his hand away.

"Leave it. I'll be dead from old age by the time you manage to get a drink right."

He unscrewed the cap like a man possessed, sticking the entire top into his mouth and suckling it like a baby with a bottle. Kett watched, mainly because he couldn't turn away. Eventually, Clare stopped drinking, his eyes watering from the bubbles. He patted himself on the chest and unleashed a thunderous belch, one that turned every single head in the courtyard.

"Better," he squeaked, clearing his throat. "I'm going to need a full rundown of everything that happened when we get back to HQ, but given all the moving pieces in this case, that might not be for a while. For now, we need to focus on the links between the victims and the people who received their body parts. In the Skeldon and Donal case, it's easy. The Bower and Sayer case, too, because she worked for him and they were having an affair. There must be a connection with the other one."

Mr Nibbles lurched away from the table towards a man with a ham sandwich. Kett held the leash firm, tugging him back.

"Sit," he said.

Duke plopped into a chair, and the dog dropped onto its haunches.

"Good boys," said Kett. "I'll handle the links, sir."

"Good. But if there's anything else you can think of, now's the time to say. I have to confess, this case is a nightmare. I'll be damned if I can wrap my head around it, especially in this heat."

Kett patted the dog's head, scratching his ear.

"The one link in all this is the tick," he said. "Balls told me it's the symbol used by the man known as the Monk. We've got a black and red postcard with a tick insignia at Benedict Gilbert's house, another one being burned at Mr Bower's windmill, and a third in the box with Donal's head. Then there's the image that was left for us in the barn where Donal was probably killed."

"Yes," said Clare, belching again. "But what does it mean?"

Kett tested his tea to make sure it was cool, then chugged the whole mug back.

"I don't know," he said, wiping his mouth. "But I do know the right person to ask."

BY THE TIME Kett had been dropped off to collect his Volvo, then driven out to Dereham, it was getting late. The city still felt like it was under a grill, the roads shimmering and kids out in force with water pistols and hoses. There was a familiar white van in the driveway of the little box of a house where Norman Balls lived, and Kett parked his car in front of it. He allowed himself another ten seconds of blissful air-conditioned chill before turning off the engine and throwing himself into the oppressive evening heat. He knocked on the door, the echo of it rattling down the quiet street.

Knock knock.

There was a muffled shout from deeper in the house and Kett leaned in, hearing the shuffle of feet. The peephole grew dark, somebody watching him, and he pulled out his warrant card and held it up.

"DCI Kett, Norfolk Police," he said. "I'm here to see Norman."

A bolt slid back, then another, then the tumble of a key in the lock and the rattle of a security chain. The door opened, and at first, Kett thought the short man who stood in the relative darkness of the entrance hall was Norman Balls. Even as he was opening his mouth to greet him, though, he noticed the grey hair and the pure white moustache that grew on his top lip. He frowned, hazarding a guess.

"Ron?"

"Oh, yes," said Ron, offering his hand. "How did you know?"

"A little bird told me," Kett replied, shaking the other man's hand. "Is Norman home?"

"Is he ever *not* home?" Ron said, standing to one side. Kett walked into the house, closing the door behind him. Now that his eyes had adjusted to the dim light, he was amazed at how similar the older man was to Norman. He wasn't entirely sure that it *wasn't* him in disguise. "He's in the garage."

"The command centre, I think you mean," said Kett. Ron laughed.

"Don't you bloody start."

They walked down the corridor together, past several pieces of A4 paper Blu-Tacked to the walls. They were all covered in large print, and Kett read them aloud as they went.

"*Ron stole my stapler and he won't give it back. Ron ate the last cupcake. Ron leaves his socks in the living room.* What's all that about?"

"He's annoyed that me and his mum are together," Ron said with a sigh. "He's not shy of letting me know."

"*Ron drinks milk like a toothless goat,*" Kett said, reading another note.

Ron shrugged.

"Step-kids are sometimes hard."

"He's in his thirties," Kett said. "His *late* thirties."

Ron stopped outside the garage door. It was the same as Kett remembered it, covered in warnings to stay away. The only thing that was new was a sheet of paper stuck beneath the other signs that said '*Especially Ron*!!'

"Good luck," said Ron.

Kett didn't bother knocking, he just turned the handle and let himself in. Balls' command centre was as impressive as it had been the last time Kett had visited, way back after Hollenbeck had sent its ghosts to kill him. On one side of the room was a table groaning beneath the weight of a mountain of books and files. On the other was a collection of desks and computers, the screens almost as bright as the sun outside. Norman Balls sat at one of the desks with his back to Kett, his hands balled into fists on the armrests.

"Oh my God, Ron!" he shrieked. "I told you I'd bring my own laundry through when I'm ready! You can't keep coming in, because this is *my* command centre. Can you even hear what I'm saying?"

He spun his chair around, his mouth dropping open when he spotted Kett there.

"Oh!" he said.

"Oh," Kett replied. "You busy?"

"Yes," snapped Balls. "I thought you were him. I thought you were—"

He raised his voice.

"That *donkey* who keeps coming in *uninvited*!"

"Why don't you lock the door?" Kett asked.

"Because Mum won't let me anymore, she took the locks off. She and Ron think I'm... you know..."

Kett shook his head and Balls leant in.

"Looking at *things* on my computer. Rude things."

"Right," said Kett. "I'm sure that never happens."

"Never," said Balls. "So Ron can *suck it*!"

He cleared his throat, studying Kett.

"Why are you here?"

"I need some help," Kett said, which seemed to cheer the man up no end.

"And how can I be of service? My detective skills are unmatched."

"You're not a detective. But I need to know more about what you were telling me earlier. That tick drawing you had, and the man you referred to."

"Ah," said Balls, sliding his chair over to another desk. "The Monk. I knew you'd be back to ask me about him. There's been another delivery, hasn't there? Was it genitals? Please tell me it was genitals."

"It wasn't genitals," said Kett. "And I can't tell you anything else."

"Please?"

"No."

"Fine!" he growled.

Kett stared over Balls' shoulder as he logged into his computer. The man navigated through a series of files until he found the one he wanted, double-clicking to open it. He put a hand to the screen to hide whatever had emerged there.

"I'll help you, but you have to tell me something, something juicy. That's the only way this is going to work."

"No," said Kett.

"Fine, damn it!"

Balls huffed in his chair, moving his hand out of the way.

"I've spent the day going over what I know," he said. "Because I knew you'd come calling. I had a fairly extensive catalogue in the first place, but I also sent out a couple of tentative feelers to people I know and trust."

He looked up.

"I cannot reveal my sources, I'm afraid, but they are people like me."

"I'm sorry to hear that," said Kett, although Balls seemed to miss the remark entirely.

"I trust them. And they've come back with something very interesting."

Kett sighed, wondering if he'd been out of his mind coming here for help. The entire command centre smelled of arse, and when he happened to glance beneath the desk he realised Balls wasn't wearing any trousers.

"Christ," he muttered.

"Okay, let's start here," Balls said, positively quivering with excitement. He opened up a document, which appeared to be a transcription of some kind. "This is a conversation I had with another detective I know, called ArgleBargle."

"Not a name," said Kett. "And not a detective."

"It's not his real name, obviously. He's a specialist in Dark Web conspiracies. Do you know about the Dark Web, Robbie?"

"Not much," he admitted.

"It's where all the really good stuff is," said Balls. "But all the dangerous stuff, too. You don't ever go there unless you know what you're doing, because if you take a wrong step, then something very bad will get its hooks into you. But for every villain out there, there's somebody like me, and like ArgleBargle, who tries to unmask the bad guys and uncover the traps."

He scrolled through the document on the screen.

"Look, here. I'll read it. '*ArgleBargle: Seems to be a honeytrap algorithm, searching for keywords. Examples include need, help, sad, angry, broken, wish, genie, anything, shortcut, pay, life force. Redirects from ad to HT, then into encrypted message. No way I'm getting into that.*'"

"Right..." said Kett, the words making no sense at all.

"So I say, '*If you open the hole I'll jam it in,*' then—"

"I'm sorry, you say *what*?" said Kett.

"A hole in the HTML, obviously," Balls said. "I'll jam a tracker code in so we can see where it goes. What else could that mean?"

"Absolutely nothing," Kett said. "Look, Balls, this is all great, but dumb it down for me. Assume I know nothing."

"I assumed that a long time ago," he said, scrolling down a little more. "Here's the meat of it. ArgleBargle is obsessed with the Monk. He has endless theories about who he is and what he does. See, everyone on the DW is either selling something, or buying something. But they're the kinds of things you can't just sell or buy in your everyday village market. Guns, drugs, people, services. Everything. It's entirely anonymous, even the financial transactions use crypto, so they can't be traced. But people still need a trademark, as such, to advertise their wares. Or nobody will know where to look."

"Right," said Kett. "So this guy, the Monk, his trademark is the tick?"

"It's a whole package. His name, his image, and his spiel."

"Spiel?"

"Yeah," said Balls, scrolling down the document a little more. "Here's what ArgleBargle sent me this morning after I'd spoken with you. I'll perform it, it's more dramatic that way. '*The Monk seems to offer...*'"

Kett took hold of Balls' chair and wheeled him out of the way, giving him a gentle shove across the room.

"Hey! You can't grab another man's command chair!"

"Quiet," he said, putting on his glasses and leaning closer to the screen. He read in silence.

The Monk seems to offer a lifestyle service unlike any I've ever seen. The keywords he homes in on are from people who search terms like 'I need help to turn my life around' or 'my life force is low, what can I do?' These people are desperate, they want change, but they want to invoke it in a way that's not natural.

"Not natural," said Balls as he squeaked his way back over on the chair. "Have you got to that bit yet?"

"What does he mean?" Kett asked.

"Well, what's the opposite of natural?"

"Unnatural?"

"No," Balls said, rolling his eyes. "The other one."

"Supernatural?" said Kett. Balls grinned.

"Precisely. That's precisely what he's saying. When people access the Dark Web and ask for help to change their life, they find the Monk—or he finds them—and he offers them a service. He offers them a way to turn things around."

"You're losing me," Kett said.

"It's right there," Balls said, pointing at the screen. "Scroll down."

Kett did as he was told, seeing more information from ArgleBargle.

"This bit," Balls said. "AB put out a query last night, pretending to be a loser who needed help to turn his life around."

"Pretending?" Kett said.

"He got a reply almost immediately. Just two lines. The first is a data string with payment information and an untraceable crypto wallet for full payment, 2.6 bitcoin. The second—"

Behind them, the command centre door opened and Ron poked his head through.

"Norman, your mum's asking if you and your friend would like milk and cookies."

"Jesus Christ, Ron!" Balls screeched, thumping the arms of his chair. "Go away!"

Ron muttered his way back through the door.

"He's such an arsehole," said Balls.

"Yeah, a real tyrant," Kett said. "Go on."

"Right, so the second line was this. It's a disclaimer of sorts. '*Understand that your gain can only come from somebody else's loss. Your success is somebody else's failure. Your life is somebody else's death. What is given is first stolen. There is no going back.*'"

Balls sat back in his chair like he'd solved the case single-handedly. Kett scrolled a little further down the screen to see that all talk of the Monk stopped and what looked like an argument about *Star Trek* phasers began. He went back to the last paragraph, reading it again.

"What is this, Balls?" he asked. "You're telling me the Monk is offering to steal somebody's life force? Bullshit."

"I know it's bullshit, and you know it's bullshit. But people believe all kinds of things, Robbie. You don't need me to tell you that. People hinge their whole life on their beliefs, whether those beliefs are true or not."

"Your friend, Arse Baguette, did—"

"ArgleBargle," said Balls.

"Yeah, him, did he make payment? Did he find out anything else?"

Balls spat out a laugh.

"Did he make payment?" he said. "Did I not just show you the line? If you want the Monk to work for you, you pay him 2.6 bitcoin. That's a shade over £40,000."

"*What?*"

"Yeah," said Balls. "Ultimately, that's how I know this is real. Because the cheap stuff on the DW, that's always fake, always a way to scam people out of a couple of grand here and there. But something like this? Forty big ones? No, that's real."

Kett took off his glasses to massage the bridge of his nose.

"We could be brothers, you know," said Balls. "Now that we both wear spectacles."

"But how do you know?" Kett asked, ignoring the comment. "There's nothing there, no testimonials or anything. No names, no proof."

"AB told me he found somebody who was willing to talk to him," Balls said. "Wouldn't give me a name, but this person claimed they hired the Monk to turn their life around, and it worked. They paid the fee and went from zero to hero, new wife, new job, new house. The Monk gave them everything they wanted, but he also gave them something else."

"A body part," said Kett.

"Right, from their victim. Proof, I guess. Or maybe a way to make them complicit in the crime."

"A way to keep them quiet," said Kett. "If they really paid this man to... I still don't know what he does, to be honest, but if they paid him to kill somebody, and he sends them a foot, they can't go to the police. It's a guarantee."

He shook his head.

"But it doesn't make any sense, because they could bin it, burn it, bury it, whatever. Everyone in this case has come forward. They've reported the body parts."

"You sure?" Balls said, wearing a sly smile. "Everyone?"

"Just the ones we know about," said Kett. "Shit."

He perched on the edge of the desk, trying to get his head around what he was hearing.

"I don't believe a word of it," he said. "It's insane, and the only shred of not-proof you have is one internet weirdo who talked to another one, anonymously. But say you're right, say you and Anal Blister have stumbled onto something real. Is there any way we can get the Monk to do something for us? Maybe we can hire him, trap him?"

"You got a spare forty grand?" Balls asked.

Kett shook his head.

"Me neither," said Balls. "Mother doesn't even let me have my own bank account. No, this guy has been operating for years. Decades. He knows what he's doing. Even if you had the money to throw at him, he'll never let himself be caught."

Kett sighed, pushing himself up.

"So," said Balls, rubbing his hands together. "Ready to make me part of the team? I told you, I can be a great detective."

"You're not a detective," Kett said as he walked towards the door. "But I'm not going to lie, that was useful."

"Really?" said Balls with a fist-pump.

"Yeah. Can you email all that to me?"

"Yes," he said gleefully. "With pleasure."

Kett opened the door, looking back.

"You're sure this guy is for real? You believe it?"

Balls nodded, the smile sliding from his face.

"He's real, Robbie. I believe it, but you know what's worse? I think he believes it too. You've got a man out there who thinks he's... I don't know, God, I guess. He thinks he can steal somebody's life, their success, their energy, whatever, and pass it on to somebody else. And I don't think he's going to stop anytime soon."

CHAPTER TWENTY-EIGHT

Kett was flagging by the time he made the journey back to HQ, the stress of the case and the heat draining him so relentlessly he wasn't even sure he'd survive the walk across the car park.

Inside, though, the air con was working at full steam, reviving him a little as he walked into the bullpen. Five minutes later he'd brewed the kettle and made a tea, which made him feel infinitely better. He carried it to his desk only for Clare to stick his head around the corner and bellow across the room.

"Meeting, now!"

"Sir," Kett said, following the Super down the corridor.

Clare didn't hold the Incident Room door open for him, and Kett spilled half his tea as he shouldered his way through—most of it scalding his thigh. He limped to the nearest table and sat down before he lost any more. The room was busy, Detectives and Uniforms filling the space with mumbled conversations. There was no sign of Savage, and Duke had been tasked with taking Mr Nibbles to the emergency vet for a checkup.

"Okay," said Clare from the front. "You've all been updated on the case. We're currently looking for three people, might be men, might be women, but all of them on motorbikes. It's toss-all to go on, so who can give me something else?"

Kett put his hand up and Clare shot him a filthy look.

"Do you need to use the bathroom, DCI Kett?"

"Uh, no, sir. I had something I wanted to share."

"So share it. You don't have to put your tossing hand up."

"It's not my *tossing* hand," Kett said, pushing himself up from the desk. He nodded to the room. "What I'm about to say needs to be taken with a hefty amount of salt. It comes from a semi-reliable source, who got it from somebody else."

"Balls," barked Clare, although Kett wasn't sure if he was saying a name or making a statement. Either way, he nodded.

"The source believes that the image of the tick is used by a man who calls himself the Monk. The tick in the picture has the Latin name *scapulus*, which relates to the cloak worn by some monks."

"Big leap," said Porter.

"That's not even a leap," said Clare. "It's just walking off the edge of a cliff, like a lemming."

"Hang on," said Kett. "Apparently, the Monk offers a service via the Dark Web. It's... it's hard to explain, because it doesn't make a lot of sense, but bear with me."

He took a sip of tea, every pair of eyes in the room staring at him.

"If you're having a tough time in life, if you're broke or sick or whatever, then you can pay the Monk to fix things."

"Fix things?" said Clare.

"Yeah, that's what he does. He fixes your life."

"How?" asked Porter.

Kett took another sip of tea, wincing as it burned its way down his throat.

"He fixes your life by stealing somebody else's."

Nobody said a word, and Kett felt the heat rising in his cheeks.

"I'm not saying I believe it," he said. "But I saw a message supposedly from the Monk, a warning to whoever might want to use his services. Here."

He pulled out his phone and found an email waiting from Norman Balls. It took him a moment to find the right bit.

"'*Understand that your gain can only come from somebody else's loss. Your success is somebody else's failure. Your life is somebody else's death. What is given is first stolen. There is no going back.*'"

Clare lifted a hand like he needed to use the bathroom, but Kett didn't comment.

"I'm going to stop you there," he said. "Because this is nonsense. Some internet rumour? What does this have to do with our body parts and our missing people?"

"Maybe nothing, sir," Kett admitted. "But maybe everything. According to our source, one of the ways the Monk makes his customers complicit in the act is to send them a piece of their victim. Not a souvenir, but a... I don't know."

"A receipt?" said Porter.

"Yeah, maybe. A receipt, proof that the transaction has gone through, that the Monk has kept his word. But it's also a way of stopping the customer from going to the police, right? Because ultimately it could come back on them. Balls told me that this happens more than we'd think, which doesn't make any sense because we'd have a record of it. Or at least that's what I thought at first."

"Except the people who receive the body part wouldn't want to contact the police, because it would implicate them as well," said Porter.

"Right," said Kett. "Only in this case, they all contacted the police, which makes me think either the source has it completely wrong, or this *is* the Monk and something has changed."

Clare gurned at him for a moment, deep in thought.

"There might be a way of finding out," Kett went on. "The Monk isn't cheap. He charges £40,000 or so to do whatever it is he does. It's crypto, but that amount of money should be easy enough to spot leaving anyone's account."

Clare continued to gurn.

"But that doesn't make any sense," said Porter. "You're saying the Monk fixes your life by stealing somebody else's? Somebody more successful, right?"

"Maybe," said Kett with a shrug.

"But we're already looking at successful people. Douglas Ireland's a top student, a semi-professional footballer from a wealthy, influential family. He already thinks his life is perfect, so what would he have to gain from all this?"

"That's the bit I'm not sure about," said Kett.

"The foot that got delivered to him belonged to a man who barely had anything," said Porter. "Benedict Gilbert lived at home, he was a trainee with no steady job, didn't seem to be successful in any way, shape or form."

"True."

"And the Bowers, too," Porter went on. "They're rich. They have everything they could ever want. They don't need some magical fix, especially from a woman like Alis Sayer, who worked for them at a little over minimum wage."

"Except they're broke," Kett said. "When Savage and I

found Jeremy Bower at his windmill, he confessed they were penniless, they don't have anything left. He was doing his best to hide it from his wife, I'm not sure how much she knew."

"There's a massive step from being a few quid overdrawn to contacting an online sorcerer who will kill somebody and mail you their luck or life force or whatever. And a foot."

"Hand," said Kett.

"And nobody would be stupid enough to ask the Monk to kill somebody they know," Porter went on. "Somebody they're tied to, like Jeremy Bower and Alis Sayer, or the Skeldons and Andrew Donal. You're making yourself the prime suspect."

Kett nodded, a flicker of something flashing across his vision for a moment before disappearing. He sat back in his chair and took another sip of tea.

"Yeah, it's nuts," he said. "It doesn't hold together."

They turned to Clare, who was red-faced and straining at the front of the room.

"Sir?" said Kett.

"I think you've broken him," Porter whispered.

"I agree," the Super suddenly shouted, making the entire room jump. "It's ridiculous. I doubt the Skeldons would have that kind of cash, and going by what forensics dug out of Jeremy Bower's firepit, he didn't have two pennies to toss over. Douglas is a student. All students are broke."

"Yeah, but his mum isn't," said Kett, sitting straight. "His mum's loaded."

"Right," said Porter. "And she's insane. She made it very clear..."

The DI slapped a hand to his forehead.

"Holy shit, she actually said it to me. She told me her son will live his life the way she wanted him to, and that he'll be the best at everything he does because she will make it that way. She said they were blessed."

"Blessed?" Clare said. "Interesting choice of word, given the context."

"Very," said Kett. "You want us to bring her in?"

Clare scoffed.

"Do I want to bring in an ex-MP and current world-famous, big-mouthed bigot because we have a vague theory that she may have hired an internet troll to kill a man and bless her son with his ghostly juju?"

Everybody waited, the seconds ticking by on the clock.

"Of course I tossing do," Clare said. "But this is *not* an arrest. Skoosh!"

KETT PULLED the Volvo to the side of the road and cut the engine. He looked past Porter's broad shoulders to see a large wall and a set of cast-iron gates—thankfully open, although blocked by a Bentley—then an impressive Edwardian house at the end of the drive. He whistled.

"Did you say this is Frances Ireland's *weekend* place?"

"Yeah," said Porter. "She bought it when Dougie started uni, so she'd have a place to live in when she came to visit."

"Alright for some," said Kett, opening his door. "Why on earth wasn't Duggie living here instead of that student house?"

"Maybe he just didn't want to live with his mum."

The late afternoon had lurched into evening like a sweaty drunk, everything stifled and uncomfortable. Kett wiped the sweat from his brow with the back of his sleeve.

"I can't bloody wait to get out of these clothes and jump in a cold shower," he said.

"Please wait," Porter replied. "For my sake, and for Frances Ireland's, please wait."

Kett breathed out a laugh as they made their way down the immaculate brick weave, the borders bursting with summer colours and spewing out scents that made him feel light-headed. The house was on one of the most expensive streets in the city and its enormous sash windows looked down on them as they approached the front door.

"Just a chat," said Kett.

"Right, sir," Porter replied. "But honestly, I'm not sure she's going to want to."

Kett raised his hand to knock, but Porter caught his arm.

"I get the feeling that she likes publicity," he said quietly. "She likes the drama, and she likes making people do things they don't want to do so she can bust their balls for it later. She's a wind-up, so don't let her get to you."

"Thanks," said Kett, ready to knock again before Porter caught him.

"And she travels with a solicitor, Chris Shortle. But something about him makes me think he hasn't always been a brief, you know? He was doing his best to intimidate me earlier."

"How'd that go?"

"About as well as you'd expect."

"Noted," said Kett. He lifted his hand and held it there, waiting. "Anything else?"

"No."

Kett pounded on the door—*knock knock*—and stood back. They were in the shade of the house, old-growth trees towering on all sides and the birds going nuts. He listened to their evening chorus as he counted to thirty, then knocked again.

This time, he heard the sound of a key in the lock, and the door creaked open to reveal Frances Ireland. Kett had seen her on the TV before, mainly during the whole Brexit debate thing where she'd seemed to float into public view every other day like an unflushable turd. But now, out of the thick makeup she wore on-screen and dressed in a baggy coral velvet leisure suit, she seemed twenty years older. She was holding a glass of white wine and she took a sip as she looked at Kett, then sneered at Porter.

"Mrs Ireland," said Kett, holding up his warrant card. "Sorry to bother you, my name is—"

Frances kicked the door with a bare foot and it slammed shut.

"Right," said Kett. "Nice."

"She's *really* nice," said Porter, taking a turn to knock on the door. "Mrs Ireland, it's really important we have a quick word with you. It's about your son."

"My son is fine," she said, her voice muffled by the door. "So kindly fuck off."

"We need to ask you a few questions," said Kett.

"Actually, don't *kindly* fuck off," she said. "I don't want there to be anything *kind* about it. I want you to fuck off while ramming a red-hot poker down the end of your cock."

"Pretty sure it wouldn't fit," said Kett.

"Speak for yourself, sir," Porter replied. "Frances, we're going to keep knocking until you open the door, so just do yourself a favour, yeah?"

Kett hesitated, wondering how far to go.

"It's about the Monk," he said.

He heard the unmistakable sound of a glass breaking. Frances didn't reply.

"Mrs Ireland?" Kett said, trying the handle and finding it locked. "Open the door, now."

He looked at Porter and Porter broke away, heading for the back of the building. Kett knocked for a final time.

"Last chance," he said. "Open the door."

The handle turned, the door opening a crack and then stopping.

"Pete," Kett called.

He pushed the door open all the way, seeing a broken glass on the oiled parquet floor, a puddle of wine. The smell of it made him feel nauseous.

There was nobody in sight.

"Hello?" he called out, stepping over the threshold. Porter followed him in, his face knotted with worry.

"I'm in here," came Frances' voice from deeper in the house.

Kett followed it past a living room and a study that were almost empty of furniture, before walking into a large country kitchen that was equally as sparse. Frances Ireland stood with her back to them at the counter, the fridge open beside her. She twisted the lid off a new bottle of wine, filling the largest glass Kett had ever seen.

"Mrs Ireland," said Kett. "I—"

"You don't need to do a fucking thing," came a voice from the other side of the room. A short, wide man stood in the darkness of an archway that looked as if it led into a pantry or utility room. He, too, was wearing a velvet leisure suit, although his was forest green. He didn't have much hair on his head, but what was missing up there seemed to have grown on his feet—so thick and so dark it looked like a pair of socks. There was a bottle of red in one of his big hands, and he was holding it by the neck like a weapon.

"Mr Short?" Kett asked.

"That's Shortle," he replied with a growl.

"Right. If you're a solicitor, feel free to join in this conversation. Mrs Ireland, have we got your attention?"

The woman didn't turn around, she just chugged wine from the glass until, with a choking breath, she slammed it back down. She'd polished off most of it. Kett was almost impressed.

"I just need to ask you a couple of questions," he said. "Then we'll go."

"Is my client under arrest?" Shortle asked, walking into the room.

"No," said Kett. "But she can be if she wants. My advice, just answer the questions."

"Ignore them," said Shortle, placing his bottle on the large island but not letting go. He was wobbling a little, his eyelids heavy and his voice slurred. "They're here without pretext and without cause. Tell them to fuck off."

"I already did," Frances said.

"Tell them again."

Frances turned around, her hands on the worktop behind her. Her jaw was clenched, her eyes wide.

"You know exactly who I'm talking about, don't you?" Kett said. "The Monk."

"Tell him to—" Shortle started, and Kett jabbed a finger at him.

"Say it one more time," he said. "I dare you."

Shortle swallowed hard, like he was literally eating the words. His bottom jaw jutted out, his teeth small and yellow. He let go of the bottle and moved around the island so that there was nothing in between them, flexing his neck. He had the gait of somebody who'd been in the military, and Kett had no doubt of the man's strength.

"Whatever's going through that little head of yours, get

rid of it," Porter told him, taking a step in front of Kett. "I can promise you it won't end well."

"No," said Shortle, his smile blunt, his eyes dead. "But it will be great fun."

"This isn't exactly convincing me of your innocence, Mrs Ireland," Kett said.

"I don't know what you're talking about," she replied. "You come in here spitting bullshit about some priest or something, and what? What exactly do you want from me?"

She let go of the counter, taking a wobbly step towards him.

"You know what I think happened? You were desperate, you came barging in here, made me drop my wine glass, you initiated a physical confrontation with my solicitor, who was only trying to help me. Then..."

She turned to the sink, then lunged towards it and picked up a paring knife. With literally no hesitation, she drew the blade over the heel of her hand.

"What the hell are you doing?" Kett said, watching the blood patter to the floor.

"Then you attacked me, tried to make me confess. I didn't know what was happening. I tried to stop you. But you were relentless. Robert Kett, yes? I've read about you. Robert Kett, the man who'll do anything to catch the bad guy, whoever might get trampled in the process."

"You're insane," said Kett.

"No," said replied through a smile. "I'm not. I'm smarter than you, any day of the week. I have a mouthpiece, a voice, and people believe me. Nobody will listen to you even when you plead innocence. Kiss your job goodbye, and everything else, too. I'm going to win."

"And like I said," Shortle added. "Fuck. Off."

Kett looked at Porter, who shrugged.

"Your choice, sir," he said.

Kett sighed.

"Frances Ireland, you are under arrest for—"

Frances opened her mouth and loosed a scream that made Kett's blood run cold. She lobbed the knife at him, missing by some way, then turned and ran from the room—grabbing her almost empty glass as she went.

Kett started after her, making it all of three feet before Shortle's squat, heavy body thumped into him. It was a proper tackle, stealing the air from Kett's lungs and slamming him against the cabinets.

"Shit!" he said, just a wheeze.

Shortle still had his arms wrapped around Kett's waist, and with a warrior's cry, he twisted himself sharply. Pain flared through Kett's shoulder as his feet left the floor, and before he knew what was going on, he was airborne, flipping over Shortle's shoulder and landing hard on the other side.

"Judo flip!" Shortle bellowed, the sound of his voice barely audible over the ringing in Kett's ears.

He looked up, seeing Porter on the offensive. Shortle braced himself like a troll, his hairy feet wide, his arms out. He moved faster than should have been possible as Porter lunged for him, grabbing the DI's right arm and bending it outwards. For all his size and strength, Porter flopped earthwards like a rag doll, his leg kicking the island so hard the bottle of wine rolled onto the floor.

"Is that the best you've got?" Shortle said, laughing like a hyena.

"Christ," Kett groaned, using the cabinets to pull himself to his feet. "What the fuck is wrong with you? We're police."

"Not in this house, you're not," Shortle said, his words

slurred. He extended his hand, beckoning Kett. "Come on, old man."

"Old man?" Kett said.

He took his time, approaching Shortle slowly. The little guy was unzipping his top, revealing a broad chest that was as furry as his feet. With a graceful flourish, he pulled it off and threw it onto Porter's head as the DI tried to stand.

"Nobody can outmatch the judoka," he said.

Kett glanced to the other side of the room to see that Frances was long gone.

"Don't turn away from me," said Shortle. "Do not do me that dishonour."

Porter was back on his feet now, evidently dazed. He put one hand to his temple, wincing.

"How did you do that?" he asked.

"Through years of training and self-sacrifice," Shortle replied. "I don't expect you to understand. Now, who's first, fatty bollocks or his granddad?"

"Fatty bollocks?" Porter said.

"Good answer." Shortle moved towards Porter. "Prepare to eat the floor. Again."

"Fuck this," Kett said, running at Shortle.

The solicitor turned at the last minute, his arms flexing, but Kett didn't give him the chance to react. He gave him a mighty shove, his dense body resisting far more than it should have done but still flying. Shortle's foot landed on the wine bottle and he cartwheeled, almost a full circle, his head crunching into the cabinet behind him. He dropped to the floor and stayed there, groaning gently.

"How'd you do *that*?" Porter asked.

"The Force," said Kett, massaging his bruised neck. "It outperforms Judo any day of the week. You got him?"

"Nothing much to get," Porter said. "But yeah, go get her."

Kett ran through the door at the back of the kitchen, everything aching. The corridor there was empty, as were the two storage rooms. He kept going, seeing another door at the end of the corridor and hearing a key rattling.

Somebody was trying to lock it.

He didn't give them the chance, raising his foot as he reached the door and slamming his size eleven boot into the lock plate. It crunched open, Frances crying out as she fell backwards. The room was so big and so bright that Kett had to shield his eyes from the glare as he stumbled in, but there was no mistaking the splash he heard. He peeked through his fingers to see Frances flailing in the deep end of an impressive swimming pool, still holding onto her wine glass.

He walked up to her, ducking onto his haunches.

"Hi," he said. "Ready to try this again?"

Frances would have probably replied if her head hadn't been underwater. Kett reached in and grabbed her hair, hauling her up. She grabbed the edge of the pool, retching and spitting. Blood fanned out from the cut on her hand.

"You're..." she tried, fighting for breath. "You're trying to drown me."

Kett shrugged.

"If you say so, then it must be true. Who's the Monk?"

"Never heard... of... him," Frances gurgled, furiously treading water.

"I can wait here all day," said Kett.

Frances struggled some more, then seemed to remember she was holding onto the edge. She calmed down, staring at Kett through knots of wet hair. If looks could kill, he thought, he'd be at the bottom of the pool in seconds.

"You think you've got me, but you don't," she said. "You

think you know everything but you know nothing. You'll never be able to pin this on me because you'll never be able to find him."

Kett's heart, already thrashing, seemed to miss a couple of beats, clattering back into its rhythm like a faulty engine.

"So he's real?" he said.

"Not to the police he isn't," said Frances. "But to me he is. And you know something?"

"What?"

"Very soon, he's going to be real to you, too. Very fucking real. You don't go after the Monk, not if you want to stay alive. Because he doesn't just have the power to bless you, he can curse you, too. He can make your life rot away like the skin of a dead cat."

She grinned, looking like a Halloween decoration as the flickering reflections from the water lit up her face.

"You're fucked, Robert Kett."

CHAPTER TWENTY-NINE

Kett closed the door of the interview room behind him, rubbing his eyes and feeling like he'd quite happily curl up right here in the corridor, like a cat, and sleep for a week. Superintendent Clare had walked out before him and now leaned against the wall, his forehead pressed to the plaster like he was on a pilgrimage. He looked as tired as Kett felt, his skin waxy and his eyes bloodshot.

"Well that got us a big, fat toss load of nothing," he said.

"As expected," said Kett.

He and Clare had spent the last thirty minutes stuck in the little room with Frances Ireland and a brand-new solicitor—a bulldog of a woman from the talent agency who represented her—asking her every question under the sun. She'd had the same answer for every single one, spoken through the same smug smile.

"No comment."

"You're sure she confessed to you?" said Clare.

"In the pool, yeah," he said. "She knows who the Monk is, she hired him. She wanted me to know, because at the end of the day it's my word against hers. And let's face it, in this case my word is meaningless. Nobody will believe it."

Clare scratched his nose, his eyes lost to a thousand-yard stare.

"We've confiscated everything we can find in the house. Digital forensics is looking through her phone records, bank, laptop. But this isn't her main residence so we're waiting for Derbyshire Constabulary to catch up. There's a problem there too, though, because she's got friends in high places."

"*She* has friends?"

"Hard to believe, I know. Friends, enemies, they're all the same thing to somebody like that. People to use."

"True enough, sir," said Kett.

"If there's a link to the Monk, we'll find it," the Super said. "But I'm guessing there won't be. If this man of yours is as good as he thinks he is then there won't be a single trace. Nothing will connect him to Frances Ireland or to any of the others."

Kett opened his mouth to argue, then realised there was no point. Clare was right.

The door at the end of the corridor opened and Dunst appeared, looking even greyer than he usually did.

"There you are, sir," he said. "I'm done. Shortle didn't have anything to say for himself."

"Consider me shocked," said Clare.

"Oh, wait, he did say one thing," Dunst said, looking at Kett. "He said he was going to sue your arse off."

"For making him slip on his own bottle of wine?" said Kett. "Good luck with that."

"I didn't think he'd roll over on her," Dunst said. "Husbands rarely do."

"Husband?" said Kett. "He was her solicitor, Keith."

Dunst frowned at the ceiling.

"Oh," he said after a moment. "That would explain several moments of confusion."

"Jesus Christ!" Clare said, stomping off. "Give me tossing strength! Kett, Jeremy Bower is in Interview Room Three, go find out what he has to say about all this."

"Yes, sir," said Kett.

Clare opened the door so hard it almost came off its hinges, looking back.

"By the way, the bank statements we recovered from Bower's fire showed a £30,000 loan taken out three weeks ago, transferred out again almost immediately. We're trying to uncover where it went."

Clare disappeared, and Kett turned to Dunst.

"Are you okay, Keith? You haven't seemed yourself lately."

Dunst looked at him, something heavy passing over his thoughts. He lifted a hand, looking at the stump of the finger he'd lost to Hollenbeck's ghost. With a big sigh, he shrugged.

"I'm okay, sir. Just got a lot on my plate. You want some help with the Bowers?"

"No, thanks. Go home, come back tomorrow with a clear head."

Dunst nodded, coughing wetly.

"You should get home too, sir," he said. "Spend some time with those kids."

Kett nodded.

"You sure you're okay?"

Dunst waved the question away, chasing Clare through the door. Kett walked the other way, rounding the corner to see Savage heading towards him.

"Kate," he said, smiling. "I was beginning to forget what you look like."

"No great loss there, sir," she said. "Sorry, I was talking to Charlie Skeldon over at the hotel, then I had a couple of things to check out."

"How's Charlie doing?"

"Not good, as you can imagine. But she's a fighter."

"Did you ask her about the Monk?"

"It came through on the system too late," Savage said. "I didn't get the chance. I was just catching up on everything. This Monk, you think he's real? You honestly think people would do that?"

"Pay to have somebody killed?" said Kett. "Been happening for as long as we've been walking on two legs."

"Yeah, but assassinations are one thing. This is something new. This idea that you can take somebody else's life force or luck or whatever. I've never seen anything like it. It's so..."

"Extreme," Kett offered, and she nodded.

"Extreme. Yeah. But I haven't seen anything in Charlie's life, or her parents' lives, for that matter, that could explain a £40,000 payment. They're dirt poor, sir. Even Charlie's JustGiving was struggling by, less than a grand a month even at its height, and barely a tenth of that for the last year or so. That bit just doesn't add up. But..."

She paused, biting her lip.

"What is it, Kate?"

"Maybe nothing, and I don't want to cast a shadow on her or her family. I didn't see much there in the way of guilt over Andrew Donal's death. They didn't seem like they were responsible for it."

"But..."

"But when I was talking to Charlie she mentioned her girlfriend. I think they've split now, but she's still very much in her life. Happy Heptinstall."

"That's her name?"

"Yeah. She's a few years older than Charlie, and she's the one who set up the JustGiving page. She's not rich, not that I can see anyway, lives on the same estate. But she's a tech-head. Charlie said something to me that seemed relevant, and now all this Monk stuff has come up it makes even more sense."

"What did she say?"

"She said Happy had offered to find Donal's address and doxx him."

"Doxx?" asked Kett.

"Share his information. She said the internet is full of vigilantes who search for people who committed a crime but for some reason didn't get the punishment they deserve. People list their names and addresses and their crimes on special sites and these groups pick the ones they want to suffer and go after them. Happy wanted to do it, Charlie said no."

"She said no?"

"Don't get me wrong, she hates Andrew Donal for what he took from her, but she's a good girl, a kind girl. There's not a violent bone in her body. I think she just wanted it to end. She just wanted to move on."

"These Doxy sites," Kett started.

"Doxxing," said Savage.

"Doxxing, whatever. You can just find them online?"

"No, sir," said Savage. "That's the thing, you have to know where to look. That's what Happy does, apparently. Like I said, a tech-head."

"They're on the Dark Web?" Kett asked.

"That's what Charlie told me, yeah," said Savage.

"You know where she is?"

"Looked, but she's not home. No family in the area, none of the neighbours really know her. Sorry, sir."

"You've passed this on to the Boss?"

"Yeah."

"Okay." Kett checked his watch. "Keep looking for Happy. You want in on this with me? Jeremy Bower?"

"Oh, sure," Savage said. "We're old friends. Lead the way."

Kett walked to the interview room door and opened it, seeing Jeremy Bower sitting patiently at the table. Next to him was his wife, the pair of them looking more like brother and sister than ever.

"Whoa," said Kett. "Mrs Bower, you really cannot be in here."

"I can," she said. "I'm his representation."

"You're acting as his solicitor?" Kett said.

"As your department is already aware," she said. "And I must say, this is disgusting. My husband was arrested nearly twelve hours ago, and we have been waiting in this room for over three hours. It is far too late for any kind of interview."

"It's been a busy day," said Kett, letting Savage through the door before closing it.

"Now that you're here, I expect you to make this quick. My husband is guilty of nothing except defending himself."

"Didn't look like defence," said Kett. He sat at the table, waiting for Savage to get the tape rolling and do the introductions. "No, it almost certainly wasn't defence when you kicked that ladder out from under my feet, Mr Bower. Or when you attacked DC Savage here."

Bower stared at the table, his bottom lip pouting, his eyes wet. He was one of the sorriest-looking men Kett had seen in a long time.

"My client makes no comment," said Lydia.

"That's up to him to say," Savage said. "Mr Bower?"

The man wiped his nose on his sleeve, still staring at the table.

"Okay, let's forget about that for a moment," said Kett. "Forget about the assault charges, forget about the burning of evidence, forget about the affairs and the kidnapping. I only have one question to ask you right now, Mr Bower."

He paused for dramatic effect, the silence in the room almost unbearable.

"What can you tell me about the Monk?"

If anything, the quiet grew heavier still. It took a few seconds for Bower's forehead to crinkle into a frown. He looked up, first at Savage and then at Kett.

"What monk?"

"Don't play games with me, Jeremy," said Kett. "I am way too tired. We have reason to believe you hired somebody to murder a woman. I need to know who he is."

"What?" Bower spat, looking at his wife. "This is insane. I haven't done anything of the sort. It's ludicrous."

"These allegations are baseless," said Lydia. "Unless you've got some proof, I demand that this farce ends here."

"Is it true, Mr Bower, that you're broke?"

Lydia spat out a laugh of disbelief.

"These questions are out of order," she said. "My client's finances are nothing to do with anything."

"I disagree," Kett said. "I think they're the key to this whole thing. Your husband's broke, he's up to his ears in debt, he's borrowed from loan sharks too, because we found the slips in the fire pit. You've got maybe a month left before they take the windmill, and the house, and the car, and the business. There's nobody left to borrow from, there's nothing you can do to get above water. Unless—"

"This is absurd," Lydia said. "How can we be broke?

You've seen our house, you've seen my husband's business. We've got all the money in the world. Tell them, Jeremy."

Jeremy Bower lowered his head to the table like he was planning on having a nap. His wife looked at him with growing horror.

"Jer, tell them."

"You know what else we found in the fire?" said Savage, leaning across the table. "Your gambling slips."

Bower covered his head with his hands.

"Jeremy?" said Lydia. "What's going on?"

"They're right," he said, his voice muffled. "We've got nothing left. I fucked it all."

Kett had never seen a better example of the blood draining from somebody's face. Mrs Bower looked like a ghost.

"What?" she said, her voice quiet and dangerous.

"It was an accident," the man went on. "I swear. Just a flutter."

"You fluttered away our house?" she said. "Your fucking business? What the fuck is wrong with you?"

She slapped her husband hard on the back, the sound of it like a pistol shot.

"You fucking bastard!" she screamed. "As if the affairs weren't bad enough, that endless line of fucking women, you do this to me as well?"

She slapped him again, harder, and Savage leaped out of her seat to take her arm.

"Hey, that's enough," she said.

Lydia shook herself free and stood, retreating to the back of the room where she paced like a tiger. Her expression was murderous.

"Enough," said Savage, standing between the couple.

"So now that the truth is out," Kett said. "We might as

well have all of it. You found the Monk, didn't you, Jeremy? You heard about him, sought him out, and paid for his services with the last of your cash."

The man lifted his head from the table like a corpse crawling out of his grave.

"I don't know what you're talking about. Just leave me alone. Leave us alone."

"You did a shitty job of burning evidence," Kett went on. "There was enough left of your bank statements for us to see the loan. £30,000. Want to tell me what that was for?"

Lydia shook her head, still pacing.

"Unbelievable," she said.

"I don't know," groaned her husband. "I... I don't even remember. There were so many, I was using them to pay back the ones that I took out before. It's endless, relentless, I couldn't get a break. I... £30,000? You're sure?"

"I'm sure," said Kett. "You used it to pay the Monk, didn't you?"

"No," he whined. "I swear, I don't even know who that is."

"You used it to pay some prick on the internet?" Lydia spat. "What the fuck is wrong with you, you monster?"

She lunged again and Savage stopped her.

"I've had it," she screamed. "You can deal with this yourself."

She shoved Savage out of the way and walked to the door, escaping into the corridor. Her scream of anger echoed back as she walked away.

"What I don't understand," Kett went on, getting out of his seat to close the door. "Is where Alis Sayer comes into it? Because what we know so far is that the Monk has to murder somebody in order to pass their luck or life force or whatever onto whoever paid the fee."

"*What*?" said Bower.

"So why Alis? Did you have a say in that? Were you the one who collected her from her house on Tuesday night?"

"No," he said. "I swear. Whatever you think this is, it's not. It's *not*."

Kett pulled out his phone, finding the photograph he'd taken of the tick postcard in Bower's campfire. He turned it to face him.

"Why were you burning this?" Kett asked. He frowned at it.

"I wasn't," he said. "I've never seen that before."

Kett flicked back through the photos, finding the one he'd taken of the postcard at Benedict Gilbert's place.

"Try this," he said.

Bower shook his head.

"I swear, I've never seen it."

Kett sat down again, leaning back in his chair with a sigh of frustration.

"You're really not making this easy on yourself," he said. "The thing you need to remember, Jeremy, is that we're not after you. We're after him. This man called the Monk. If you can help us find him, you might have a shot at getting out of this without too much pain. So just start by telling us about the postcard you were burning."

"I don't know," he said. "Please. I didn't see it. I was just getting rid of everything. I needed to do it fast because Lydia was there and I couldn't risk her seeing it. I—"

"Your wife was at the Crow's Nest?" Kett asked.

"Yeah, right before you lot showed up. Half an hour or so. She came to find me but I hid in the boxes, same place I hid from you. I thought maybe she'd found out, because the fire looked different, like she'd taken stuff out of it, but she'd gone so I just carried on with it."

"Looked different, like she'd taken stuff out of it?" said Kett. "Or like she'd *added* something?"

"I..." Bower shrugged. "I guess so."

Kett met Savage's eye, seeing the realisation dawning there.

"It's *Lydia*," she said.

She bolted for the door, and Kett stood up so fast the chair toppled over behind him.

"She knew, didn't she?" he asked. "Your wife knew about the money."

Bower shrugged, his head collapsing back onto the table.

"I tried so hard to keep it from her," he said. "But she's so fucking nosy."

"Shit," Kett said, running for the door, looking back for a second to point a finger at Jeremy Bower. "Do not leave that fucking chair."

CHAPTER THIRTY

Savage crashed through the double doors into the reception of Norfolk Constabulary HQ, scanning the busy waiting area.

Lydia Bower was nowhere to be seen.

She swore, seeing Dunst about to walk through the exit.

"Sir," she called out. "Has Lydia Bower been this way?"

Dunst wheeled around.

"Jeremy Bower's solicitor?" he asked.

"His wife."

"I'm so confused," Dunst said. "But no, I haven't seen her. Sorry."

Savage pushed past him, running into the dwindling heat of the car park. It was late enough now that the lights had come on, fighting with the vanishing sun to be the one to illuminate the half-dozen people who were walking to and from their cars.

Lydia Bower wasn't there.

"Come on," Savage said, bolting for the exit gate.

She was halfway there when she saw the bright red Range Rover pulling out of a parking space. The windscreen was dark, no clue as to who was behind the wheel. But it wasn't like anyone else would have the registration plate JER 113.

"Hey!" Savage shouted, running into the middle of the road and waving her arms. "Mrs Bower, we need to have a word with you."

The Range Rover stopped twenty yards away, the engine purring. Savage took a step towards it, her hands still raised like she was approaching an angry bull.

"Mrs Bower, can you turn off the engine, please?"

The car revved, and Savage took another step.

"You're in the middle of a police station," she said. "There's nowhere to go."

The car lurched forward then braked. Savage tensed her body, ready to leap out of the way if she needed to. She still couldn't see a thing through the windscreen. She took another step, the car just half a dozen yards away now.

"Right now, we're not interested in you," Savage said. "We want him. We want the Monk. If you can help us find him then you can stop anyone else from dying. You can do something good. It's not too late, Lydia. I know you're not a murderer."

The Range Rover revved again, then the horn blared so loud Savage thought her skull might shatter.

"I know you don't want to hurt anyone," she said when it had stopped. "Just get out of the car."

The car lunged, the engine roaring. There wasn't even time for Savage to scream, let alone move.

Then Mrs Bower hit the brakes and it lurched to a halt, the bumper kissing Savage's chest. Savage put a hand to the car, more to keep herself standing in a sudden wave of vertigo than to try to stop it from getting any closer.

The engine died with a rattle, and Savage took a breath.

"Out you come," she said.

"Kate?"

She looked back to see Kett running across the car park, a tail of Uniforms behind him. Savage moved her hand from the Range Rover, a gentle wave.

"I'm okay," she said. "She's getting out."

The Range Rover's door opened and Lydia almost fell out of it. She looked like a different person, her body hunched over, her arms wrapped around her stomach. She was shaking her head wildly from side to side.

"Thank you," Savage said to her.

"How did you know I wouldn't do it?" Lydia said, her voice hoarse.

"Like I said, I don't think you're a murderer. I don't think you wanted to hurt anyone."

Kett and the officers clattered over and Savage motioned for them to stay back. Lydia leaned against the bonnet of the Range Rover, staring into the darkening sky.

"I am, though," she said. "Aren't I? There's no difference between him and me."

"The Monk?" said Savage. "Who is he? How do we find him?"

"You don't," Lydia said. "He finds you. You post a message on a forum and wait, and if he wants to help you he sends you a link for an encrypted message."

"What does it say?"

"It's a warning," Lydia said, still staring upwards, barely even blinking. "It tells you what will happen."

"That somebody will lose their life in order for yours to get better?"

Lydia laughed, but there was no joy there.

"It sounds crazy when you say it like that," she said. "But... but I honestly thought..."

She swallowed hard, looking at Savage with eyes that were haunted by guilt.

"You don't understand how much I hated him, Jeremy, for making me do this. He's a piece of shit, he's useless. His business? Mine. I fucking paid for it with the money I saved working endless days and nights as a barrister. This car? Mine. The house? It's mine. It was my mother's, and it costs us more money than a leaky fucking boat, everything's dropping off it, but he wanted to keep it because it made us look like millionaires."

She hauled in a wet, desperate breath.

"It's all mine, and he just wasted it. He wouldn't stop spending, wouldn't stop fucking it all away. Gifts for his stupid fucking whores, watches, rings, holidays. He gave them my fucking money, and when I didn't have any left, he borrowed it. He thought I didn't know."

Another furious laugh.

"He couldn't keep his mouth shut, boasting to friends, to colleagues, to strangers in the street. He thought I didn't know? That useless prick. I knew everything."

"That's why the hand was sent to Jeremy," said Savage. "You told the Monk you were your husband, right?"

She nodded.

"It was *his* mess, why wouldn't I use *his* name?"

"What happened next?"

"I paid him. I took out the loan in Jeremy's name and paid him the money. Just over £30,000, but I had some cash put away so I used that too. I bought bitcoin then transferred it to the Monk's account."

"And then?"

"Nothing," she said. "For days. I thought I'd been scammed. Then..."

She put her hands to her face, hiding behind her long fingers.

"Then?" Savage coaxed.

"I got another message. A list of names."

"Names?"

"First names," she went on. "There were eight of them, I think. Some men, some women. He asked me to pick one."

"The Monk asked you to pick a name? The person who would become his victim, right?"

"No," said Lydia, still hiding. "Yes. I don't know."

"Was Alis on that list?" Savage asked.

"No," the woman said again.

"Lydia, you've come this far. Tell us the truth."

"Fine," she spat, slapping her hands to her sides. "Yes, I saw her name there and it could have been somebody else but I picked it anyway, because fuck her, right? She was sleeping with my husband, she deserved it. I saw her name and I chose her. I chose her to..."

The truth seemed to hit her like a sledgehammer and she bent double, groaning.

"I picked her to die. Oh God, I picked her to die."

Savage glanced at Kett, his face full of grief.

"And what happened next?" Savage said.

"Nothing," Lydia replied. "I didn't hear anything. Then the package arrived at the house on Wednesday and I opened it and I... I saw her hand. I knew it was her hand. I knew it."

"You haven't had any contact with the Monk since that second message?"

She shook her head.

"And you definitely weren't the one who went to Alis' house on Tuesday?" Savage asked. "Because we think she recognised the person who took her. She knew them."

"I don't know who it was," she said. "It wasn't me. I'm sorry."

"Lydia," said Kett. "How did you even know how to contact him? How did you know about the Dark Web?"

"I've known for years," she said. "You'd be amazed how many people know about him, about all the monsters you can find when you know how to look. I spent years as a barrister in London, I heard all the stories. You wouldn't believe me if I told you."

Savage looked at Kett again. He'd taken a set of handcuffs from one of the Uniforms and he walked to Lydia. She didn't respond as he clipped them around her wrists.

"Lydia Bower, I'm arresting you for the murder of Alis Sayer. You do not have to say anything, but anything you do say may be used against you in a court of law. Do you understand?"

No reply.

"Can you tell us anything else?" Savage asked. "Anything at all that might help us find him? That might help us end this?"

"End it?" Lydia said, looking at Savage like she didn't understand the question. "But it's already over. *My* life is over. Why the fuck would I care about anything else?"

"Get her out of here," Kett said, passing the woman to one of the constables.

Savage watched her go, a heaviness in her heart that felt big enough to drag her down into the asphalt, down into the rock below, into the darkness and the silence that waited there.

"We're not going to find him, are we, sir?" she said.

"Don't give up," Kett said. "He's human. Sooner or later, he'll make a mistake."

But Savage wasn't so sure.

"You can take the interview, if you like," Kett said to her. "You did good bringing her in. Wasn't sure if she was going to flatten you."

"I wasn't sure either," she said. She checked her watch. "But no, I've got something else I need to take care of."

"Okay," Kett said. "Then get some rest. It's been a long day."

"Yes, sir," she said.

But the day wasn't over yet. She checked her watch again as Kett walked back to the main doors of HQ.

It was nearly time.

Earlham Park, the back path to uni. 11 pm.

Patting her pockets to make sure her keys were there, she made her way to her car.

And before she climbed into it, she sent a text.

SHE WAS RUNNING LATE by the time she pulled into the little car park on the edge of Earlham Park, right across the road from where she'd spoken to the football team yesterday. The sun had finally given in and she didn't blame it, it had pushed itself to its limits today and the air still felt tropical.

She locked the door, looking across the dark road to where the football courts sat empty, illuminated by the glare of the spotlights. Then she set off down the hill, the trees opening up onto the large green. As she walked, she checked her phone again, reading the message.

I know why the foot was delivered to Douglas' house. I can tell you everything, but only you. Earlham Park, the back path to uni. 11 pm. Don't tell anyone, and COME ALONE OR I DISAPPEAR AND YOU NEVER SEE ME AGAIN.

She'd tried to find out where the text had come from, of course, but no luck. It had been sent from a computer, not a phone, and through a piece of anonymising software. Impossible to trace. It was dodgy as all hell, but they were grasping at straws in this case, and if this really was somebody who knew about the Monk, then it was worth checking out. Any sign of trouble and she'd leave.

If she *could* leave, of course.

Because anyone who operated on the Dark Web would find it all too easy to send a text like that.

The park was bigger than she remembered, even though she'd brought Colin the Dog here countless times. There weren't many lights, but what few there were seemed desperate to compensate for the sun. A couple of people were still splashing in the river at the bottom of the slope, their drunken laughter carrying in the warm air, but other than them this side of the park was empty. There was no denying the fact that it had been full of students earlier in the day, though, because they'd left their rubbish everywhere.

She followed the river, reaching the woods a little after quarter to eleven. Night stalked the branches, crept between the gnarled trunks.

And it wasn't alone.

She'd barely passed the first tree when she saw a man ahead, sitting on a log. He was almost invisible in the gloom because of his black hoodie and black tracksuit trousers.

And his balaclava.

Savage stopped dead, a branch cracking beneath her foot.

The man looked up, then propelled himself from the log.

"She's here!" he yelled.

A whoop from her left. Savage turned to see two more men walk out from behind a cluster of bushes, lit by tendrils of light from further up the hill. They were wearing balaclavas too, although they were obviously homemade—just hats with holes cut in them for the eyes. Both of them were holding small bats, the kind that kids played rounders with at school.

More footsteps behind her, two more men jogging down the dark hill, boxing her in.

Savage held her ground, forcing herself to take a long, deep breath.

"I can't believe you came, you stupid bitch," said the man who'd been sitting on the log. He walked a little closer, adjusting the balaclava. His eyes were dark, his swagger slightly drunken.

"You said you had information," Savage said, keeping her voice as steady as she could. "So let's have it."

The man laughed, looking at his friends like he couldn't believe what he was hearing.

"She's so stupid," he said, turning to her again. "You're so fucking thick."

"That right?" Savage said, studying each of the men in turn. "Because I'm pretty sure I'm not the stupidest one here. I'm not the one about to go away for a few years for attacking a police officer. Right, Spence?"

The man fell still, his tongue crossing his lips beneath the mask. Savage held up her hands in an apology.

"Oh, you're supposed to be anonymous. Sorry!"

"Just do it, mate," said one of the other men, checking over his shoulder. "Hurry up."

Spence started walking towards her again, faster this time. He didn't have a weapon but his fists were bunched and he had the look of somebody who was all too keen to throw a punch.

"Doesn't matter," he said. "Know my rights. If we all attack you, there's no way of knowing who did it. You can't pin it on any one of us so we'll all go free."

"Hate to break it to you, Spencer," Savage said, bouncing on the balls of her feet. "But that's not the way it works. You take a shot, you go to prison."

She flexed her fists.

"But only if you land it."

Spence hesitated, looking to his friends.

"Come on," he urged them. "She's just a little bitch, let's do her."

"*Do* her?" Savage said. "I don't even know what that means."

Two of the other men were closing in, but they were unsure. Savage retreated carefully, keeping as many of them in her sight line as she could. Somebody else was approaching, somebody big.

She found it hard to keep the smile off her face.

"Evening, Kate," said Duke from the edge of the woods. "How's it going?"

Duke had taken off his copper's uniform and was dressed in a pair of combat trousers and a crisp white T-shirt that looked ready to split. His arms were bigger than half the trees in the woods, bulging as he folded them over his bear's chest.

"Evening, Aaron," she said. "Thanks for coming. Going alright, mate. You?"

"Better for seeing this bunch of twats," he said, advancing. "Haven't had a good scrap in ages."

One of the footballers—because Savage had no doubts at all that half the team was here—turned and bolted.

Another followed, tripping on a branch and faceplanting in the dirt. A third helped him up, and they scampered away together without looking back.

That left two.

Spence's eyes darted between Savage and Duke, his fists twitching. The other man was slowly backing away.

"Come on, Spence," he said. "It's not worth it. We'll get her another time."

"Yeah," Savage said. "Doesn't your coach know you're out past your bedtime?"

"He does," said Spence. "Whose idea do you think this was?"

Savage held out her arms, goading him. Her anger was a raging fire, impossible to ignore.

"Come on then," she said. "Have a go. Just me, he won't get involved. Right, Aaron?"

"Whatever you say," Duke replied.

"Bitch," said Spence. "Fucking brought this on yourself."

He ran towards her, surprisingly clumsy for a footballer. He wheeled his arm back, then threw it forward with some strength. Savage saw it coming from a mile off, stepping neatly to the side. Spence's momentum pulled him off balance and he stumbled past her like an angry bull past a nimble matador, almost falling.

"Missed me," said Savage, dancing on her feet.

Spence wheeled around with a roar, throwing another punch. This one was faster and harder, and even though she dodged to the side it clipped her ear. The pain burned in the side of her head, cold and bright.

Enough.

The man threw a third punch, and she twisted her head out of the way, throwing a strike of her own into his stomach. There was a lot of muscle there but it hit home, a belch of breath exploding out of his mouth as he doubled over. Savage drove her foot into the side of his knee, feeling something pop. Then, when he fell into her, she swung her fist into the meat of his jaw.

His teeth clacked together like a bear trap and he dropped hard, his lights out.

Savage crouched beside him, opening one eye to make sure he wasn't dead. Her blood pulsed through her ears like a roaring ocean, the adrenaline almost too much to bear. Duke was talking to her and she couldn't hear a word he was saying. He put a gentle hand on her shoulder, his voice filtering through.

"Kate? You okay?"

She put her hand on top of his, then pushed herself to her feet. There was a sharp pain in her right hand, the knuckles already swelling. Glancing back, she saw that the other guy had fled, leaving Spence alone.

"Yeah," she said. "I'm okay."

"Idiot," Duke said, looking at the man on the ground. "Can't believe he even tried that."

"I can," she said. "Monsters, all of them. The only thing they understand is force."

"He'll understand that, right enough," said Duke. "Want me to call an ambulance?"

"No," Savage said. Spence was groaning, his arms flapping like a dying pigeon, his hands reaching for her. She kicked one away. "He'll be fine."

"Are *you* fine, though?" Duke asked her. "Because this... I mean, this isn't really what we do."

He was right, and now that the anger was draining out of her, carried away by the adrenaline run-off, the only thing she felt was sick. She braced her hands on her knees, doubling over and spitting acid into the dirt. She was grateful to the night for hiding her shame.

"You knew it was them, didn't you?" Duke said.

"Had an idea," she replied.

Duke laughed quietly, but there was a sadness there.

"Guess you're learning more from DCI Kett than you thought," he said.

And standing there in the night, with Spence dribbling blood at her feet, Savage couldn't decide if that was a good thing or not.

CHAPTER THIRTY-ONE

"You sure you don't want to go home, sir?" asked Porter. "It's late, and you look knackered."

Kett followed the big DI through the front door of Happy Heptinstall's house, ducking beneath a low-hanging wind chime that Porter had already set off. Its delicate tinkle filled a small entrance hall that had been plastered with fairy memorabilia, dozens of porcelain figurines sitting on a shelf above the radiator and clinging to the woodchip wallpaper. They all bore different hairstyles and multi-coloured wings, but none of them were smiling. They looked, for want of a better word, evil.

He *was* knackered, there was no doubt about it. It was gone eleven, the bastard heat finally fading. They were back on the Tuckswood estate, the next street over from the Skeldon's house, and Kett was praying they'd find answers in this little two-bedroom house.

Because right now, they didn't have much at all.

"I'm fine," Kett said, realising Porter was waiting for a reply. "Maybe *you* should go home and get some rest."

"I don't rest," Porter said. "I'm young and fit."

He looked Kett up and down, tutting.

"Young and fit," he said again. "And handsome."

Kett scowled at him, realising too late that it made him look like an angry grandfather.

"No sign of Happy yet?" he asked.

"Guv says they've tried every known associate, nobody knows where she is. Charlie Skeldon's tried to text and call her and there's been no reply."

"They're not together anymore though, right?"

"Yeah, but that wasn't Happy's decision, apparently. She took it hard, and she's still infatuated with Charlie. Charlie says she *never* doesn't text back."

Kett finished working the gloves over his fingers as he walked into a small living room—although it had been kitted out like a bedroom. A double bed sat against the wall opposite a small TV. More fairies watched him from their resting places, their faces twisted with malice. He was so tired that the sight of them felt almost like a hallucination.

"Creepy, right?" Porter said. "Who fills their house with scary fairies?"

He laughed.

"*Scary fairies*, that rhymes."

"You should write a book," Kett told him. "Who's been in here already?"

"Nobody," Porter said. "We're the first."

Kett walked to a framed photograph on the wall, seeing Charlie Skeldon in her wheelchair next to a woman in her twenties. The woman was wearing a flowing dress and a flower tiara in her short hair, and her smile was enormous.

"This is Happy?" Kett asked.

"Yeah," said Porter. "She's twenty-six. She met Charlie after the accident, in a support group. They became friends, then more than friends. Happy's the one who set up the charity page."

"Savage told me," Kett replied, looking at another photo of the two women—a selfie taken in the room where they stood, the fairies visible in the background. "She works?"

"Nothing we can find," said Porter as he left the room. "Used to have a job over at Marsh Insurance, but she left a few months back. Tax returns say she's self-employed as an algorithm consultant, whatever that is."

"Tech stuff," said Kett.

"Probably. But she's not rich, not even *close* to rich. This place is rented and her landlord says she's always late and often short."

There were three rooms at the back of the house, the nearest of which was a small, perfectly kept kitchen. Next to that was a toilet that had been adapted for a wheelchair user. The last room, which was a converted garage, looked like a NASA control centre.

"Holy shit," said Porter as they walked inside.

Three of the four walls boasted huge metal desks, and on all three sat a trio of widescreen monitors—nine in all. LED lights had been fitted around the joint between the wall and the ceiling, colours flowing like something from a science fiction spaceship. More glowed in the ceiling.

"Hasn't your mate Normal Balls got something like this?" Porter asked.

"Norman Balls would shit himself if he saw this," said Kett. "And he's not my mate."

"He's your *best* mate," Porter said. "Your *soul*mate."

"I'll tell you who's *not* my mate right now," said Kett. "You."

Porter clasped a hand to his chest like he'd been mortally wounded. Kett ignored him, approaching the nearest desk. A framed cross-stitch took pride of place next to the keyboard, another scowling fairy on a bed of flowery text. It was the only decoration in the entire room.

"*All you need is faith and trust and a bit of fairy dust,*" he read.

"True enough, sir," said Porter.

Kett nudged the mouse of the nearest computer and watched the three screens blink to life. There was no password box, just an almost completely clear desktop. Porter had clicked the keyboard of the next screen over.

"No security," he said. "Weird."

Kett put on his glasses, leaning over and finding the email app. When he clicked it, it asked him for a password. He tried to open the Chrome browser and the same thing happened.

"Every app is individually protected," he said. "This will take forever."

"Yep," said Porter.

"ProtonMail," Kett said, reading the name of an app near the top of the screen. "What's that?"

"Encrypted email, sir."

"What about Tor?" he said, reading another.

"The Onion Router," said Porter. "It's a browser, like Internet Explorer only for the Dark Web."

"So you use it to what?" Kett said, feeling massively out of his depth. "Look for illegal stuff? Like Bad Google?"

"Yeah, *Granddad*," Porter said. "*Bad Google*. It lets you access stuff in the hidden part of the internet. There's a lot there, more than people think. The stuff you access with your regular browser is like the surface of the sea, the Dark Web is everything underneath. Tor's like a submarine, I guess. But it's not all illegal stuff, just stuff people don't necessarily want you to see."

Kett clicked it again, the password box appearing.

"Dammit," he said. "But at least we know Happy was accessing the Dark Web. There's a chance that she was the one who contacted the Monk."

He hesitated, frowning.

"Maybe a chance that she *is* the Monk," he added. "Although it sounds like the Monk has been operating longer than Happy's even been alive."

"We know she was trying to doxx Andrew Donal," said Porter. "She was trying to put his name out in public hoping a vigilante group would find him and give him the punishment she felt he deserved."

"Only Charlie wouldn't let her," said Kett. "She didn't want anyone else to get hurt. But then Happy hears about the Monk, and that's different, right?"

"Different how?" asked Porter, his mouse clicking.

"It's not just about hurting somebody. The Monk kills his victims and passes on their energy and luck to the person who pays him. It's not just an act of violence, or retribution, it's an act of healing."

"I guess so," said Porter. "If you believe it."

"Faith and trust and a bit of fairy dust," said Kett, looking at the cross-stitch. "I think she believes it."

"But it doesn't matter what she believes," Porter said. "Because I still don't think she had £40,000 to give him. So where did the money come from?"

Kett didn't have an answer. He clicked on another app, hoping that at least one of them might bear fruit, and all three screens suddenly went black—all except for a single line of text in the middle monitor, and a ticking clock.

"Enter master password," he read. "It's counting down, what does that mean?"

"It means you fucked it," Porter said. "I'm guessing if we don't give it what it wants, the whole drive will be wiped."

Kett swore, ducking beneath the desk and seeing the PC tower.

"What do I do?" he asked. "Turn it off and on again?"

He thought he could hear Porter rolling his eyes.

"Turning it off might not be a bad idea," Porter said. "Cut the power, and hurry, twenty seconds."

Kett tipped the PC towards him, seeing a whole bunch of cables.

"Fifteen."

He pulled out one, then another.

"Is it off?"

"No, ten seconds, sir."

"Jesus." He tried to wrench out another one, but it was stuck. He grabbed the last one and yanked it hard.

"Five, four."

He tried again, and the stubborn cable pinged loose so fast he cracked his knuckles on the metal leg of the desk.

"Good job, sir," said Porter. "It's off."

"Doesn't help us much, though," Kett said, struggling to his feet. He looked at the other computers. "They'll all be the same."

"Digital forensics are on their way," Porter said. "If there's something here, they'll find it. As long as you didn't fry the whole lot just now."

There was nothing else in the room, no books or papers or shelves or drawers, so Kett made his way back into the front hall and climbed a narrow staircase to the top floor. Happy had obviously converted the living room to the bedroom so that Charlie could use it, and the two bedrooms up here looked like they were being used for nothing but storage. Boxes and binbags filled almost every conceivable space, covered in a skin of dust. Nothing had been touched for weeks.

He made his way back down again, walking into the bedroom.

"Where are you, Happy?" he asked.

Happy was a tech-head, everything was locked down, everything in its place. Nothing was left to chance, especially the security of her computers.

But did that extend to her own security as well?

He checked beneath the bed, lifting the pillows. There was nothing there, and nothing in the little cabinet that held the TV. The kitchen was empty too, although there were plenty more photographs of Happy and Charlie in here. Kett wondered if Happy had even got the message that they'd split up.

"What are you looking for, sir?" Porter said when Kett walked back into the converted garage.

"I don't know," he replied. "Something doesn't feel right. Why would she vanish?"

"The Monk might have taken her," said Porter. "Same as he did Alis and Benedict."

Kett nodded, but still something needled at him.

"But why would he take *her*?" he asked. "If Happy was the one who hired the Monk, who somehow paid him, then she should have been safe, right? Let's say she found him on the Dark Web, contacted him, asked him to bless Charlie and help her recover. She obviously loves Charlie, it's not out of the realm of possibility that she'd do that. The Monk sends her a list of names, the same way he did to Lydia Bower, and asks her to pick one. But maybe she asks for somebody else? Maybe she asks the Monk to kill Andrew Donal instead. A life for a life."

"Maybe," said Porter, leaning on the desk and folding

his arms. "But he doesn't strike me as the kind of person who would risk breaking his own rules, especially for somebody who doesn't have a lot of cash. Unless they know each other, maybe?"

"Maybe," said Kett.

He searched the bare walls of the room, the almost-empty desks, the computers.

"Breaking rules," said Kett. "Shit, maybe that's it? Maybe it was *Happy* who broke the rules?"

"How so?"

"She's got no money, but she's clever. Clever enough to find the Monk, to hire him, to convince him to kill Andrew Donal instead of whoever else he had on his list. So maybe she's clever enough to trick him, too."

"Not following, sir," said Porter.

"What if she didn't make payment? Or what if she somehow spoofed it, pretended to pay? It's crypto, right? It's not like a bank transfer."

"Pretty similar," said Porter. "Hard to fake."

"But not impossible," said Kett. "Or, I don't know..."

Something clicked in his head, just like that.

"Or she found out who he is," he said. "She hacked him, got inside his operation. She made contact with him, maybe she knew enough to uncover his identity, or find out where he lives? What did Savage tell us? That Charlie was worried Happy had done something stupid. That's pretty stupid."

Porter pushed himself off the desk.

"Right," he said. "That makes sense. And the Monk comes for her."

"No," said Kett. "I don't think so. No break-in, no sign of a struggle. I think this is something else. I think maybe she was trying to blackmail him."

"That's a mighty big assumption, sir."

"No," he said again. "It fits. The Monk's MO seems to be to send the postcard ahead of the limb, right? Lydia Bower already had hers. But the postcard was sent *inside* the box with Andrew Donal's head. It's different, something changed."

"He was rushed," said Porter, and Kett nodded.

"He had to move fast because he knew he was being blackmailed."

Kett looked at the desk again, at the only thing in the room that wasn't a piece of machinery.

"If you were Happy, and you were blackmailing a man who's a master of the Dark Web, a tech wizard or whatever, you wouldn't leave any electronic evidence for him to find, right?"

"Right," said Porter. "You'd probably leave a note. A real one."

Kett picked up the cross-stitch, turning it around and undoing the catch on the back of the frame. He eased it off and pulled out a sheet of folded paper from inside.

"Holy shit," said Porter. "How the hell did you figure that out?"

"Faith and trust and fairy dust," he said as he opened it.

There were several lines of neat, small handwriting on the paper, in sparkly pink ink.

Charlie,

I know you warned me not to do it, but this is for you, and without you, I have nothing left.

He wants to meet me. I'm going tonight, Wednesday. If something happens to me, there's a thumb drive in the post with everything I have on him. I'm meeting him at the old ferry. It's where everything leads.

Wish me luck. I did all of this for you. Forgive me if you want, but promise you'll never stop loving me.

Happy

"She was going to meet him," Kett said, running for the door and pulling out his phone. "Move!"

CHAPTER THIRTY-TWO

"OLD FERRY," KETT SAID, THE VOLVO GROWLING through the night. "Any ideas?"

"Hundreds of boats in Norfolk, sir," Porter said. "Thousands. How many of them are ferries?"

The city was gripped in a fist of darkness. The roads were almost empty, as if everyone had fled the night. Kett was taking them towards the river, but only because he didn't have any better ideas. Through the hands-free, Superintendent Clare cleared his throat.

"There's Pull's Ferry," he said. "Down by the cathedral."

"Makes sense," said Kett. "Monks, cathedrals."

"And Thorpe Ferry too, further up the Yare. That one's not old, though."

It could be anything, Kett knew. A house, a park, a *pub*.

"Hey, is there a pub with that name anywhere in the city?"

"I'm not sure," Clare said. "Rings a bell. Hang on, Savage just walked through the door."

Kett heard him ask the question, then Savage's voice rattled from the speakers.

"There used to be," she said. "Place called the Ferry Boat, down on King Street. Right by the river. Been out of commission for a few years now. Grandad took me to a couple of gigs there when I was little."

"The old ferry," Kett said. "Worth a try. King Street?"

He punched the pedal, tearing through the dark.

"Do not enter," Clare said. "And I mean it this time, Kett. You could have been sliced into ribbons by those bikers, and we don't know what we might find there. Tactical is primed, they can be there in ten. Let them clear the place before you go in."

"Okay, but—"

"I have no interest in your but, Kett. That's an order."

Clare hung up.

"No interest in my butt," said Kett. "Not quite sure how to take that."

He braked hard as the traffic lights turned red, but when he saw the road was clear he pulled through them anyway. They were on the right side of town for the river, and in less than five minutes he pulled the car over, cutting the engine and the lights.

Directly over the steering wheel was a large yellow building that hunkered in the gloom, its walls defaced with graffiti. The windows and doors were professionally shuttered in a way that made it look more like a fortress than a pub. It was surrounded by squat blocks of flats, but the river was a dark, almost invisible presence behind it.

"Why on earth would Happy agree to meet a self-confessed serial killer here?" Porter asked. "Looks like every single haunted house I've ever seen on the TV."

"Did Happy drive a car?" Kett asked.

"No. I doubt she could have afforded to run one. Bike."

"Like that one?" Kett asked.

Further up the hill, a purple sit-up-and-beg bike with a wide basket had been chained to the railings along the side of the road.

"Could be," said Porter. "Not sure."

Kett turned back to the building. There were no lights on, no sign that anyone had been there recently. Impatience gnawed at him and he opened his door, only for Porter to give him a look.

"What, Pete?" he asked.

"I'm not saying anything, sir."

Kett climbed out of the car, leaning on it and shivering despite the warm air. He felt like an engine rattling through the last vapours in the fuel tank, utterly drained. Porter got out too, staring at the old pub, then checking his watch.

"We should probably wait in the car, sir," he said. "We look like a couple of coppers."

He glanced at Kett.

"Actually, maybe not. More like somebody taking his confused granddad back to the nursing home."

If Kett had something to throw at Porter, he would have happily done so. There was no time, though, because the other end of the street was turning blue, like there was another river rushing this way. The tactical team had their sirens off, but the sound of their vans filled the night like thunder.

"Here we go," said Porter. "You okay?"

Kett nodded, rubbing his chest and the fragment of bullet that still sat there. He barely noticed it anymore, but every time he saw a firearms officer with their weapon raised he felt like he was being shot all over again.

He walked into the middle of the road and raised his

hand, and the first van ground to a halt in front of him. A second followed, two IRVs close behind. Sergeant Julia Gorski was the first one out, dressed in full tactical gear with a rifle slung over her shoulder. She nodded at Kett.

"I should have known it would be you, sir," she said.

"Sergeant," Kett replied. "How's things?"

"Are they ever anything other than awful?"

She looked up at the building.

"I take it we're going into this shithole?"

"Yeah."

"Why do you never take me anywhere nice?"

She wheeled around to talk to the rest of the unit, who had assembled on the road behind her. People were starting to take notice, faces in the windows of the flats opposite and a couple of lads out on the town stopping to stare at all the guns. The Uniforms from the IRVs were fanning out, moving them on.

"Super says we've got three possible armed suspects inside," said Gorski. "That right?"

Kett looked at the building again, at the utter stillness of the place.

"I'm not sure there's anyone in there at all," he said. "But yeah. We're chasing three people. Maybe more."

Gorski nodded, pulling down her visor.

"Wait here," she said, pointing at the ground like he was a dog.

She moved away, the team following close behind, almost completely silent as they approached the front door. Gorski gave the order and two of the unit dug their crowbars into the metal grille, wrenching it loose—two more catching it before it could hit the pavement. A fifth approached with an enforcing ram and in seconds the door was open. They moved inside with battle cries loud enough to wake up the whole city.

"You have to admit it," said Porter as he watched them go. "They do look pretty cool."

Kett nodded. There wasn't much he could do until the building was clear, so he walked a little way up the hill to where the purple bike was chained. He fired up the torch on his phone and swept the light over the basket, then the frame, and finally the saddle. There was no name, but somebody had stuck a sticker showing a big, yellow smiley face on the seat.

"What does that look like to you?" he asked as Porter wandered over.

"Happy," he said.

"Right."

He looked back at the pub, at the railing that ran right outside its front door.

"If you were meeting somebody down there, why wouldn't you leave your bike outside the front door? Why chain it all the way up here?"

Porter shrugged his big shoulders. Kett angled the light towards the flats. They were side on to them from here, not many windows. But there was a narrow alleyway running down the middle of them, shrouded in darkness. Something glinted down there, a red light that seemed to blink every time he shifted the torch on his phone.

"Give me a second," he said.

He made his way down the path to the alleyway, the shadows parting a little with every step. A hulking shape peeled itself from the gloom, the reflector on the back wheel glinting.

It was a motorbike.

"Shit," Kett hissed. "Porter, get back here."

He beamed the light down the walls of the ground-floor flat, its back door shut tight and the blinds drawn. Porter ran over, his feet drumming the path.

"Shit," he echoed. "Is that one of ours? No plates."

Kett wasn't sure. He'd been so busy studying the bikers that he hadn't paid much attention to their rides. He glanced back down the alleyway, a clear view of the bicycle.

"If somebody was waiting for Happy, they could have flagged her from here," he said. "That's why she didn't chain her bike outside the pub."

He reached for the handle of the door.

"Sir," warned Porter. "There's literally a firearms team right across the street."

He tried the handle, and the door opened.

"*Sir*," Porter said.

"Go get them," said Kett. Porter muttered something, then ran back to the road.

Kett pushed the door open, the hinges squealing. He aimed his torch inside to see a tiny kitchen, everything spotless and white. Holding his breath, he listened to the air, feeling those minuscule currents.

Somebody was here.

He crossed the kitchen in two steps, reaching another door. It was closed but a faint light curled underneath it, as yellow as old fingernails. Kett put his ear to the wood, trapping the air in his lungs as he tried to make sense of what he heard.

Something wet, and past that a sound that might have been quiet singing.

He glanced over his shoulder, no sign of Porter or the tactical team. But the back door was open, he could bolt if he needed to.

He pushed the handle down, the kitchen door opening

softly and flooding the room with light from the corridor beyond. The wet sound was louder, the singing too—a woman's voice. Kett took a breath, ready to shout a warning.

Then stopped, because something clawed its way down his throat, something that burned.

Bleach.

He took another couple of steps, seeing an open door to his right, a bathroom mirror hanging above a sink. There was movement in the mirror, the back of somebody's head, their long hair tied in a bun and what looked like a denim shirt. A pair of oversized headphones were clamped over their ears and they sang along to whatever they were listening to in a voice that was soft and tuneful. Kett couldn't make any sense of the woman's movements, she looked like she was pushing something, and each time she did so it made a splashing sound.

Come on, Porter, he willed, looking back. Where the hell was he?

He lifted his leg, torn between taking another step and holding back. The woman continued to sing, continued moving, the smell of bleach heavy in the air.

She's cleaning, he realised, his tired brain finally catching up.

That did it. He walked to the door, peering through the crack.

The woman stood by a small bath, a mop in her hands. The taps were running, the bath almost completely clean.

But there were streaks and smudges of blood up the walls.

It wasn't a shirt she was wearing, it was overalls. Blue ones. And there was blood on these too. They were saturated with it.

Kett stepped back, the floor creaking beneath him.

Fuck.

The movement inside the bathroom stopped, the music growing louder as the woman pulled off her headphones. He could still just about discern the outline of her through the crack. She was looking right at him.

"Hello?" she said.

Fuck.

There was nothing else for it. Kett braced himself, then pushed the bathroom door open with enough force to crack it into the wall.

"Police!" he shouted.

The woman screamed, a noise of utter fury. He had time to see that she was young, in her twenties, then she hurled the mop at him. He ducked, feeling it thump off the side of his head, warm liquid sloshing in his face. When he looked again he saw her running right for him, a knee driving up towards his crotch. He staggered back, avoiding the knee but receiving a shoulder to his chest as she bouldered past him.

He crunched into the wall, falling onto his backside. The woman ran towards the front of the house, spinning through the door into the living room.

"Hey!" he wheezed, clambering up. "Stop!"

"Sir?" a voice from the back.

"In here," Kett yelled, racing towards the living room then stopping dead when the woman reappeared.

She was holding a gun, a slim, black pistol, and she aimed it right at his face.

"Easy," Kett said, his voice suddenly far away. He lifted his hands slowly. "Easy."

The woman stared at him, her big eyes full of fear. She was tall and slim, and on her feet she wore a pair of brown boots, the brass buckles gleaming.

"How did you find me?" she said, taking a step towards the front door. Her voice was heavy with an accent that Kett couldn't quite place, something European, maybe even Russian.

A clatter of footsteps and Porter rushed out of the kitchen.

"Gun!" Kett yelled as the woman swept the pistol past Kett's head and aimed it at Porter.

"Shit!" yelped Porter, falling back through the door. "Gun!"

Kett heard the word relayed around the back of the building, then onto the street in front. The woman heard it too, her face falling.

"There's nowhere to go," Kett said. "Just put the gun down and come with me. It's the only way you're getting out of here."

"No," she said.

"You're the Monk?" asked Kett, and she spat out a laugh.

"Me?" She shook her head, moving towards the front door. "You have no idea, do you? He'll kill me if I go with you."

"We can keep you safe."

"No, you can't. And even if you could, who would keep my sister safe? My mother?"

She reached for the handle.

"Don't," said Kett. "If you go out there, they'll shoot you."

The woman licked her lips, unsure.

"Just tell me your name," he said. "I'm Robbie. Robbie Kett. I just want to talk with you, that's all. Put the gun down and we'll just talk."

The woman seemed to hear him, lowering the gun a

little. It looked too light in her hand, and when Kett studied it, he realised why.

"It's not real, is it?" he said.

"No," said the woman. "But everything else is. You have no idea, Robbie Kett. You have no idea how bad he is."

She pulled the catch and opened the door, running into the night.

"Wait!" Kett shouted, racing after her. "It's fake, it's a replica!"

But his voice was drowned out by a dozen others, all of them shouting the same thing.

"Gun!"

Two shots cracked the night in two, as bright as fireworks. The woman spun almost like she was dancing, her arms out to her side.

"Stop!" Kett almost screamed as he ran onto the path, the derelict pub directly opposite him and the street full of armed police. "It's a replica!"

It was too late. The woman dropped onto the stone steps that led to the pavement, her body frozen.

"Shit," Kett said, running to her.

Gorski beat him to it, kicking the gun out of the woman's hand and kneeling beside her, one hand to her neck.

"Is she dead?" Kett said.

"No," Gorski answered, thumbing her radio. "Control, I need an ambulance immediately. King Street, the Friendship Bridge end. Female, gunshot wounds." She ended the call. "Help me get her off the stairs, she'll bleed out like that."

She grabbed the woman under the arms and Kett took her legs, Porter running up and grabbing her around the middle. Together they lifted her onto the pavement, turning her onto her back. She was utterly still, her eyes closed. There was a neat puncture wound in her chest, just to the right of her heart, and Kett felt like he was the one who'd been shot all over again.

One of the tactical team ran up with a medical kit, pressing a bandage onto the wound.

"Hold that," said Gorski, and Kett did as he was told, pushing down to stem the blood. There wasn't as much of it as he'd expected, but it felt as hot as boiling water. Gorski pulled out a knife and cut a flap in the woman's overalls, revealing another bullet wound in her flank, this one bleeding more heavily. "Stupid," Gorski said. "What did she think was going to happen?"

"I think she knew exactly what would happen," said Kett. "I don't think she thought she had any choice."

Gorski pushed another wad of bandage onto the second wound, then cupped the girl's forehead tenderly in her gloved hand. Now that she was on her back, Kett could see the gentle movement of her chest, he could feel the rise and fall of each laboured breath beneath his hands.

"Hang on," Gorski told her. "Just hang on."

The sound of a siren was rising from the quiet night like an air raid warning. Kett kept all his weight on the bandage, repeating the message inside his head.

Hang on, just don't die.

"Shall I check her, sir?" Porter asked.

"Yeah," he said. "Carefully."

Porter searched her pockets, shaking his head.

"Empty."

"Try the flat," Kett said. "We've got to find out who she is. And tell Clare."

"Sir."

Porter jogged away, his phone to his ear. At the other

end of the street the ambulance rumbled into view, weaving past the parked police vehicles. It parked as close to them as it could, the paramedics running out.

"Hurry!" Gorski shouted.

Kett stepped back to let them in, his heel hitting the bottom step and exhaustion bringing him down quicker than a bullet. He sat on the stairs, watching the paramedics as they went to work. Gorski studied him, her expression unreadable.

"You've got her blood on your hands," she said after a moment.

He looked at his hands and saw that she was right, his fingers slick with blood.

He wasn't sure that's what she meant, though.

He wasn't sure at all.

CHAPTER THIRTY-THREE

Kett wasn't sure how much later it was that he walked back through the door of the little flat. He'd waited with Gorski and the young woman until the ambulance had driven away, and in that time Cara Hay and another forensic technician had arrived, both of them looking absolutely frazzled. He could hear them talking now from where they'd set up in the bathroom.

He'd done his best to wash his hands using a bottle of water that one of the constables had grabbed for him, but they were still sticky, especially beneath the latex skin of his gloves. There was bloody mop water on his face and in his hair, too. It was the worst feeling in the world. His whole body seemed to itch.

It's not the worst feeling in the world, he had to remind himself. *Being shot in the chest is the worst feeling in the world.*

"Right," he said, rubbing the scar beneath his shirt and feeling the young woman's pain.

"Huh?" came a voice from the living room. Porter poked his head out of the door. "Oh, sir, it's you. You okay?"

"No, Pete," said Kett. "I'm not. Anything?"

"Nothing," Porter said. "The flat belongs to a woman called Irene Curry, she was moved into a care home last month and nobody's lived here since. I spoke to Irene's daughter, they just left the flat as-is in case she ever wanted to come home. Nobody's been here. They have no clue at all who that woman was."

"Is," said Kett. "They think she'll pull through."

"*Is*. Sorry. No wallet, no phone, no ID of any kind. All I found was a set of keys, one's for the bike, the other looks like a house key."

He nodded to the sideboard where a pair of keys sat in an evidence bag. There was no fob, just a ring.

"And there's a Discman in the bathroom. Whoever she is, she travelled light."

"A Discman?"

"Yeah, old school. Annoying, because if it was an iPod we'd be able to ID her."

"Nothing on the motorbike?" Kett asked.

"Nope. VIN is scratched off and there are a couple of these on the stolen motorbike database, so it's probably one of them. I don't think it will help."

"Prints?"

"Some good ones, I think," said Porter. "We'll find out who she is, sir. Don't worry."

They needed to, because right now the young woman was the only link they had to the Monk.

"Kett, is that you?" came a tuneful voice from the bathroom.

"Yeah," he said.

He peeked around the door to see Cara in a full forensic suit, kneeling in front of the bath. The panel had been removed, and the drain unscrewed, its contents dripping into a bucket. The aroma of bleach was stronger than ever and Kett could smell something far worse behind it. He tried to hold his breath, but he felt breathless enough as it was, the room reeling in a sudden attack of vertigo.

"Our friend was very close to getting rid of the evidence," she said, her voice muffled by a facemask. "But I can say with some certainty there was a body in this bath. There's hair in the drain, too much of it to have come from everyday use. And there are chunks."

"Chunks?" said Kett.

"Flesh, yes. It's been quite severely ground, like mince. There is residue in the toilet as well as the bath."

Kett's stomach heaved and he belched acid into the back of his hand.

"Have you seen the bedroom?" Hay asked.

"No."

"Well, nothing I say is going to prepare you, so I won't say anything. But I have no doubt somebody was either murdered in that room, or dismembered, and your young woman was disposing of their remains in here. I've got more than enough for a DNA run. We might get lucky."

"Run it against the results from Benedict Gilbert's foot and Alis Sayer's hand," he said. "Oh, and the head, too, obviously."

"Quite a collection," Hay said, returning to the drain. "I'm fairly sure it's not the head, though. This hair is a light brown, verging on blonde, and it's short."

"Benedict Gilbert," said Kett, remembering the photos he'd seen of the young man.

"Sir?" said Porter from the corridor. "Have you seen the bedroom yet?"

"No. I'm not sure I want to, either."

He followed Porter towards the back of the flat, and the DI stopped by the door opposite the kitchen.

"It's nasty," he said. "No other word for it."

"So I've heard."

Kett took a moment to centre himself before walking into the room. It had obviously belonged to an old lady, the carpet patterned, the quilted curtains decorated with bright orange roses. The mahogany single bed and the small wardrobe had been shunted against the far wall to make room for an enormous sheet of thick, clear plastic that stretched from the door to the window. Rivulets of blood had formed intricate patterns across its entire length and breadth, scraps of meat and hair and what might have been bone scattered in between—a Rorschach test Kett had absolutely no desire to read into.

"Jesus," he said, his stomach churning again.

The wall nearest to him had been covered with sheeting as well, although this looked relatively clean. A hook had been fixed into the ceiling, two more in the walls.

"I think she probably ran a wire between them," Porter said, following Kett's eyeline. "More sheeting, like a curtain."

"To contain the mess," said Kett, his voice feeble. "She was cutting her victim up?"

"I think so," said Porter. "But there are no tools, no saw, no meat grinder. Making a human body small enough to wash down the drain takes a lot of effort. I don't know how she was doing it."

There was a familiar angry shout from the door.

"Who's here? Kett? Porter?"

"In the bedroom, sir," Kett shouted back.

A few seconds later Colin Clare stuck his head through the door, staring first at Kett and then at the bloodied floor and then back again, as if he couldn't decide which of them disgusted him more.

"What. The. Toss?" he said, enunciating each word.

"Uh, we're still trying to figure that out, sir," said Kett. "But it seems like the woman we found here was disposing of a body."

"Down the drain?" came another voice, and Savage poked her head past the Super's shoulder. She looked different. Older somehow, her eyes dark. Kett smiled at her, but she didn't return it.

"Hey, Kate," he said. "How's it going?"

"I couldn't care less how she's going," Clare answered for her. "What have we got on the woman?"

"Nothing, sir," said Porter. "But we're working on an ID."

"You think she's the Monk?"

"No," said Kett. "But I don't know for sure. I think she was one of the riders, and either the three of them are working together and calling themselves the Monk or they're working for somebody else who goes by that name. I get the feeling she's taking orders from the Monk, cleaning up after him. The rider at the farm the other day, maybe they were going to clean up the last of the evidence, the stuff in the bags. This woman was trying to get rid of a body. The Monk must be earning a fortune, enough to pay a small army of people to tidy up his mess, right?"

"Not the kind of job you find advertised in the paper, though," said Clare. "Is it?"

"But it *is* the kind you find advertised on the Dark Web," said Savage.

Porter nodded, but Kett wasn't so sure.

"She seemed scared of the Monk," he said. "She said that if he found out we'd arrested her, he'd kill her, and he'd threaten her family too. She mentioned a mother, a sister. There's a chance she was being coerced into this."

"Either that or the Monk is the kind of person who punishes failure," said Porter.

"Christ," Clare said. "Well, I'm going to make her public. Her face is going to be all over the news tomorrow. Somebody must know who she is."

"I'm not sure that's a good idea, sir," said Kett.

"Shut it, Kett. That's what's happening. If we can ID her, then we're one step closer to the Monk. But this is good work. We've taken out one cog in whatever shitty little machine this turns out to be. Keep working."

Clare turned, then swung back so aggressively Kett thought he was going to punch him.

"Not you, Kett," he said. "You look like an old man who's been robbing graves in search of some kind of elixir of youth."

"That's, uh, a weirdly specific insult, sir," said Kett.

"Go home, get some sleep. We're not going to know much more until forensics gets back to us, so use this time to rest. You too, Porter, even though you look like a spring chicken."

Porter grinned.

"Spring chicken," he said. "I'll take that."

"I'll stay, sir," Savage said. "Feel wired."

Clare nodded, walking towards the bathroom. Savage fired a look back at Kett, one that was full of something he couldn't read. Before he could ask her, she moved away.

"Kate seem okay to you?" he asked Porter.

"Probably just the case," the DI replied.

"Probably."

Porter stepped into the corridor.

"Come on, sir," he said. "You can give me a ride back. Be good to get some sleep."

Kett nodded. Then he looked at the blood-slick sheeting on the floor, he thought about the chunks of flesh and matted hair in the drain, he imagined the flush of the toilet as the remains of a man—or a woman—slowly disappeared.

He wasn't sure he'd ever sleep again.

HE DIDN'T GO STRAIGHT HOME after dropping Porter in Wymondham. Instead, he stopped off at HQ, using the showers in the gym to get rid of the blood and the grime. He would have taken the entire top layer of skin off if he'd been able to. He dried himself, changing back into his old clothes before heading to the car.

It was almost one by the time he got home, the house lit up like a Christmas tree on the dark street. Billie must have taken pity on him because when he turned his key in the lock the door opened, the deadbolts drawn back. He walked in as quietly as he could, but he needn't have bothered because when he made his way upstairs he saw that everyone was comatose, Moira in his bed, her legs resting over Billie's face. He left them to it, heading down and filling the kettle.

While he waited for it to boil, he pulled out a chair and sat at their little dining table. Something felt different, the house strange and unfamiliar, as if it was already preparing to let them go. He'd only been here for a couple of years, but it felt like forever. That first day he'd arrived with the girls, still no word about Billie, could have been a lifetime ago.

He'd had to kick the door in because they'd given him the wrong key. It was as if it had happened to somebody else, not him.

He almost didn't have the energy to get back up again, but the lure of tea was more powerful than his exhaustion. He made two cups to save himself the bother of a second trip, then carried both into the living room. He closed his eyes while he waited for the tea to cool, trying to get on top of the case, trying to work out what the hell was going on.

Three victims, Benedict Gilbert, Alis Sayer and Andrew Donal. Three body parts delivered to different addresses, and two of those with some kind of connection. A serial killer who promised to drain the life force of his victims and pass it on to anyone who had a spare £40,000 to spend. Three riders on motorbikes armed with machetes and fake pistols, flushing human remains down the drain of an empty flat. And one missing woman who may or may not have tried to blackmail the Monk.

There was no doubt anymore that the Monk existed. Lydia Bower had confessed to hiring him, and so had Frances Ireland—off the record, of course, and while waterboarding herself in her own swimming pool. Happy Heptinstall had been perfectly positioned to contract the hit on Andrew Donal as well. Motive, means and opportunity were in good supply.

But was that all that connected the victims? That they were chosen by the Monk because they had a certain life force he wanted to steal? Lydia Bower had told him she was surprised to see Alis' name on the list. Had it been a coincidence? Happy might have asked the Monk to target Andrew Donal, and if she'd been blackmailing him then he might not have had a choice.

As for Benedict Gilbert, there didn't seem to be any

connection at all between him and Douglas Ireland, other than the fact they were both young and fit and played football. Had Benedict's name simply been one of many on a list sent to Frances Ireland after she'd paid the Monk? And what was the significance of the tattoos and the postcards? A message, a distraction?

There was one connection, of course. They were all local. Balls had claimed that the Monk struck his victims all around the country, but in clusters of three or four in any one location. Did he move around to make it harder for the police to trace him?

The problem lay with the riders, Kett thought. Because if they had been contracted out by the Monk to secure the victims and clean up the mess, then even if one agreed to talk, then they might not know anything. One of them—possibly the woman shot that evening—might have been the person who lured Andrew Donal out of his house. They could have trapped Benedict Gilbert the same way, or hired him to do a job before abducting and murdering him.

Alis Sayer had seemed to know her abductor, she'd offered them a drink, but if the riders had done their research and knew she used to date a man who rode motorbikes, then it might not have been hard to fool her into opening the door.

There was a chance, Kett thought with some dread, that the person who called himself the Monk never even had contact with his victims. He could orchestrate the entire thing from the other side of the world as long as he had the right people to help him.

It's impossible, he thought, exhaustion like a weighted blanket thrown over his head. *We're never going to catch him.*

For a moment, he looked across the room and thought

he saw the Monk standing right there, his face covered by a tick-shaped mask. Then the face changed, becoming a pig's head. Kett's entire body jolted, and he reached for his tea.

Only in his dream, though, because sleep had taken him.

CHAPTER THIRTY-FOUR

Friday

Kett woke to the sensation of being suffocated.

He opened his eyes to darkness, a heavy weight over his nose and mouth. His lungs were empty, his body rigid with panic. He tried to sit, but whoever was holding him down was too strong.

It's them, he thought, the last remnants of sleep blasted from his mind by the realisation that one of Hollenbeck's ghosts had broken into the house, had found him on the sofa and was choking him to death—all while giggling like a little girl.

Giggling?

Kett reached up, feeling the squishy backside that was squatting on his face. He stretched his hands further to find a slim waist, then hefted it off him. Moira squealed with laughter as she tumbled onto the sofa cushions.

"Daddy checked my heart!" she said.

Evie was on the sofa as well, laughing so hard it looked like she, too, was having trouble breathing. Her cheeks blazed, her hands covering her mouth like she was trying to hold the laughter inside. They were both dressed in their pyjamas, their hair mussed from sleep. The light coming through the curtains looked hesitant. It was still early.

"Check it again," Evie said. "Check Moo-moo's heart."

Moira lifted her rear end and wiggled it at Kett.

"Does it look okay?"

"That's not your heart," Kett said, wiping what he hoped was sleep dribble—not Moira dribble—from his cheek. He gave the girl a gentle pat. "But it looks fine. What time is it?"

"Time for the doctor," Evie said. "Can you check my heart, Daddy?"

She lifted her bum in the air and for a moment he watched both of them as they wiggled in tandem, wondering how on earth they could be his children. Then Billie poked her head around the door, her hair wrapped in a towel.

"Girls! What did I tell you?" she said. "Leave Daddy alone. Sorry."

"It's okay," he said.

"Rude awakening?" she asked.

"Literally."

He pushed himself out of the sofa, checking his phone to see that it was after seven—not as early as he'd thought. He still felt exhausted, his head full of cotton wool, his lungs aching. He wondered how long Moira had been sitting on him. The two girls were now wrestling on the sofa, still chuckling like a couple of bleating lambs. He couldn't help but smile, and when he glanced at Billie, she was smiling too.

"What?" he asked her.

She walked over, wrapping her hands around his waist and resting her head on his chest.

"I wanted to tell you in person, but you got home too late. They accepted our offer on the house."

He took her shoulders gently, leaning back so that he could look her in the eye.

"They said yes?"

"They said yes," she said, her face brighter than he'd seen it in years. "It's ours."

"We're moving house!" Evie said. "We're moving, ow!"

Moira had whacked her sister hard on the leg, and in a heartbeat the playful fighting turned to a genuine battle—the sound of slaps like fireworks. Billie ducked out of Kett's arms and hoisted Moira from the sofa, holding her tight.

"That's enough," she said. "It's *way* too early for that."

"Can we leave them here when we move?" Kett asked, and Billie laughed.

"Never!" said Evie.

"This is good, though, isn't it?" Kett said.

"It's perfect," Billie said, letting go of the squirming child in her arms. "It's a chance to make everything right."

"And the bad men won't find us there, will they?" Evie said.

Billie's eyes dropped to the floor, full of guilt, and Kett pulled her into another hug, holding her gently—never too tight.

"They won't," he said.

He kissed his wife on the forehead.

"I'd better run," he said. "We're going to need all the help we can get with this one today."

"The foot?" Billie asked. Kett nodded.

"What foot?" said Evie.

"Nothing, sweetie," he said, letting go of Billie and scooping his middle daughter up. She wrapped her skinny arms around him.

"My feet are going to change places with my hands soon," she said. "That's what Alice told me. Just like my butt and my heart and my knees and my elbows."

"Don't listen to your sister, Evie," he said. "She's winding you up."

"No, Daddy. You don't understand. Alice told me you wouldn't understand and that she's right and you're wrong."

"She did, did she?"

Evie nodded. Kett felt his phone vibrate in his pocket, but he left it alone. Phones weren't allowed when you were hugging, those were Evie's rules.

"Daddy," she said, her forehead knitted into a frown. "Can I change them back?"

"Change what?"

"My butt and my heart? I don't want my butt to be up here and my heart to be down there. Can I take them out and change them back?"

Kett laughed, but she looked so serious and so worried it was short-lived. He placed a hand on her chest.

"Evie, your heart is right here, and it will always be here. Nobody can take it or swap it or..."

He stopped, something igniting at the back of his mind —just the smallest of sparks.

"Are you sure?" she asked. "Can anyone take my butt?"

"Nobody can take anything," he said, fighting to keep that little fire alight. He kissed her on the cheek, then let her down.

"What is it?" said Billie, her face as worried as her daughter's.

"I'm not sure," he said.

He made for the stairs, then stopped and spun back around, giving Billie another kiss—this time on the lips.

"Gross!" yelled Evie. "Mum and Dad are *smogging*!"

"I've got to go," he said. "I'm sorry. But this is good, it's really, really good. I love you. I love all of you."

Billie smiled at him as he pulled away, a smile that filled his vision like a bright light as he ran up the stairs to change.

THAT LITTLE SPARK kept nagging him as he drove, Evie's words circling his head like embers.

Can I take them out and change them back?

He couldn't work out why, though. That little flame of understanding sparked in and out of life in the darkness of his mind, nothing there to get the fire going.

Can I take them out?

He must have walked into the bullpen with a frown on his face, because Savage looked up from her desk and mirrored it.

"You okay, sir?"

"I think so," he replied, taking off his jacket and hanging it on the back of his chair. "Just thinking. How're you? What happened last night?"

"Forensics took the flat apart, top to bottom. There's a whole lot of dead person, but nothing else. No prints, no CCTV anywhere near there. Closest camera is up the hill on the main road and it's not good enough to see anything. Best guess is that our cleaner rode to the flat on her motorbike at about eight last night, but we're not sure."

Kett sat down at his desk, rubbing the sleep from his eyes.

"How's she doing?"

"Critical, but alive," said Savage. "Not awake yet."

"That could be worse news," he said. "So, Happy left home on Wednesday evening, right?"

"As far as we know, sir."

"She bikes to the Ferry Boat, but she's distracted before she goes in."

"Right. There's no sign of a break-in at the pub, no forced entry, no evidence of disturbance inside. Place has a layer of dust about an inch thick. I think the Monk, or whoever, flagged her down at the flat, lured her inside. It was already set up for a murder, the sheeting and everything. They knew they wouldn't be disturbed."

"Still, risky move," said Kett. "There are a lot of people around there, anyone could have heard them. And it can't just have been the woman we found there. You couldn't bring all that sheeting on a motorbike, and what about the equipment used to dismember her? Either the woman made more than one trip, or the other riders were helping her. Anything else?"

"No, sir."

He looked at her, noticing the same darkness he'd seen last night—in the hardness of her eyes, the tenseness of her body, the way she rubbed her knuckles. They were swollen, he realised, but that wasn't always unusual because Savage loved her heavy bag.

"Did something happen?" he asked.

"Sir?"

But she knew what he meant, because she averted her gaze, studying the top of her desk.

"Kate?"

She took a deep breath, scratching at an imaginary mark.

"I'm sorry, sir," she said. "I got a text from somebody

telling me they knew something about the foot, asked me to meet with them last night."

"You're kidding."

"They told me to come alone or they wouldn't hang about. I just went to check it out."

"Alone? Kate, come on, that's—"

"I took Duke with me," she said. "Had him hang back. I wasn't alone. I knew who it was, or had a good idea, anyway. Those footballers. Arrogant..." She bit back on the rest of the description. "There were five of them, all wearing masks. Spencer was the leader. They tried it, but Duke scared them off and I..."

He didn't interrupt when she paused, he just let her find her way.

"I beat Spence pretty bad," she confessed. "And I know it was wrong, but I... It's like I couldn't help myself. I was so *angry* at them, at the Monk, at all of it. It just happened."

Savage clenched both of her fists, but there wasn't anger in her face, just remorse.

"I shouldn't have done it. I shouldn't have..."

"Ketted it up," said Kett. "No, you shouldn't have. You could have got seriously hurt, Kate. What if it had been the Monk? It could be you in that bathtub..."

And he had to stop, because the bile rose in his throat at the thought of it.

"I just wanted to teach him a lesson, sir," Savage said. "All of them."

"There are better ways, Kate," Kett said. "And I know I'm the worst person to say this, but there are. These people, they do deserve to pay. But we have to play by our rules, not by theirs. If we play by their rules, we're no better than them."

He held up his hands.

"Like I said, I'm the worst person to say this, I know. We can bring them in, do it right."

"Yeah," said Savage. "The coach too, he was the one who sent them, apparently."

Kett nodded.

"I'll make sure it happens. Did they tell you anything about the Monk?"

"No, sir. I don't think they have anything to do with this. They're too stupid, for one."

He smiled at her.

"It's okay," he said. "Mark it down to experience, and whatever you do, don't tell Clare."

She looked like she was going to reply, but she was cut off by the sound of the door opening. Porter walked in, looking as fresh as a daisy. Superintendent Clare followed, wearing the same clothes he'd been in last night, his face so loose it looked like a mask about to slip off and drop to the floor. Kett actually grimaced.

"Where are we?" Clare boomed as he crossed the floor.

"Uh, HQ, sir," said Porter. "We literally just walked through—"

"On the *case*, Porter," Clare said. "Where are we on the case? I'm not that tossing tired."

Nobody answered, and Clare spat out a choked cry of frustration.

"Incident Room, now," he barked.

Kett pushed his chair back and got up, waiting until Clare had disappeared towards the kitchens before turning to Savage.

"Has he had any sleep?"

"He was still going when I left," she replied. "And that was after two."

From the kitchen came a noise like an injured, very

angry bear. Kett hot-footed it down the corridor and into the Incident Room, Porter and Savage darting after him. Somebody had added more photographs to the wall during the night, including a snapshot of the rider who had been shot outside the flat. She had her eyes closed, her mouth so slack that she might have been dead. There was no name next to her, no other photographs, just a big, red question mark.

Kett walked to the wall, studying the photographs of the body parts that had been delivered—Benedict's foot, Alis' hand and Andrew Donal's head. He thought again about what Evie had said to him that morning, about her heart.

Can I take them out and change them back?

"What is it, sir?" Savage asked from behind his shoulder. "What are you seeing?"

Her words dampened the fire again and Kett cursed beneath his breath.

"Right," said Clare as he walked into the room, his voice oddly muffled.

Kett looked back to see that he was holding a party plate, and on it sat a large slice of his birthday cake. He wasn't bothering with a fork, he just lowered his face to the plate and took a huge bite like a pig at a trough.

"Oh no, sir," Kett said. "Not the cake."

"Nothing wrong with it," said Clare, spraying a fountain of crumbs. "Perfectly fine."

"It's been days," said Porter. "And it was giving everyone the shits when it was *fresh*."

"It wasn't the cake," Clare said, chewing and gnashing with some fury. "The cake is fine. Nothing wrong with a few leftovers."

Porter groaned, holding his stomach.

"I can't watch," he said.

But something in Clare's words had thrown a bucket of

kerosene over the flame inside Kett's head. He turned to the board again, looking at the body parts.

"Leftovers," he said.

"What?" Clare said, swallowing noisily.

"Leftovers." Kett put his hands in his hair as if he could literally pull the idea out through his skull. "Wait, maybe that's it? We assumed there was something important about the body parts that were delivered, that the Monk attached some kind of meaning to them, and that's why he gave those specific things to his clients."

"Right," said Savage.

"But what if we were wrong? What if the only reason he delivered those parts was because he was getting rid of them, he didn't need them. They're *leftovers*."

"Leftover from what?" said Clare, his face covered with frosting.

Kett closed his eyes, his hands still clenched above his head.

"Why would they need to go to so much trouble disposing of the body?" he asked. "Why not bury it or burn it or fill the pockets with rocks and drop it in the sea?"

"Because they needed to hide something," said Savage.

"Right, they're hiding something."

"Something they did to the body?" Porter said.

"No," said Kett, opening his eyes and letting his hands drop. "Something they *took* from it. Our victims, they were all in good health, weren't they?"

"Yeah," said Savage. "Benedict was a footballer, Alis was a jogger, Andrew Donal looked after himself."

"It fits," Kett said, looking at the board. "The whole thing's a charade. It's not real. The Monk offers a service to pass on luck or life force or whatever. It's bullshit. He doesn't believe it. But he needs his clients to, because if they believe it, then they'll stay quiet. They won't call the police."

"Because they'll make themselves the prime suspect if they do," Savage said.

"Exactly. That's exactly right. I remember thinking that before, about somebody being a prime suspect, and I couldn't work out why it felt important. But the Monk isn't interested in life force, he isn't even interested in the money his clients pay him. He's interested in what's *inside* his victims."

Can I take them out and change them back? Evie had asked.

Can I take them out?

"Oh no," said Savage. "Organs?"

"This guy lives on the Dark Web. Pete, you told me people can buy and sell anything there. That includes organs, right?"

"Yeah," said Porter. "There's a massive black market for organs on the Dark Web. Anything you need, as long as you've got the money."

"Wait," said Clare, holding up his free hand. "You're saying all this is about organ harvesting?"

"Maybe," said Kett. "It would have worked, wouldn't it? Under normal circumstances, the client is complicit in the crime. They receive part of the body to shut them up so they never contact the police. But Douglas Ireland didn't hire the Monk, his mum did in his name and she probably paid for it from one of his trust funds, so he didn't know what to do with the foot when it arrived. Same with Lydia Bower and her husband. She took out the loan in Jeremy's name and pretended to be him. And we already know that Happy was trying to force the Monk's hand. She tricked him into killing Andrew Donal for Charlie. Maybe she didn't know the

Monk was going to deliver the head to the Skeldon house. Maybe none of them knew the delivery was going to be part of the deal."

"No eyes," said Savage. "Donal's head had no eyes."

"Because the Monk had taken them out," said Kett, his stomach roiling. "He needed them."

"Jesus Christ," said Clare, dropping his plate on the nearest table.

"That's why the Monk needs so much help," Savage said. "If you're right, if this is all about harvesting organs, then it's a huge operation. You need to transport them, keep them cold, move them fast."

"Fast, like motorbike fast," said Kett. Savage nodded.

"It might not just be those three riders working for him. He could have more."

"And it still doesn't solve our main problem," said Clare, belching. "We don't know who he is."

"No," said Kett. "But we're close. I can feel it. We're really close."

CHAPTER THIRTY-FIVE

They weren't as close as he'd hoped, though.

They worked in silence, everyone hunched over their desk as they pored through what little evidence they'd managed to get their hands on. The bullpen was quieter than Kett had ever known it, just the clack of keyboards and the scratch of pens on paper and the occasional soft voice of somebody on the phone—not to mention the groans that emanated from the Superintendent's office every now and again. Dunst and Spalding had arrived in the last twenty minutes and had joined the hunt.

Savage was the first one to speak in what had to be the better part of an hour, the sound of her voice making Kett jump.

"Alis was fighting fit," she said, leaning back in her chair. "Her medical history is almost completely clear. She had a few anxiety attacks when she was at uni, they weren't medicated. Few trips to her GP as an adult, mainly to talk about contraception. She's a member of the local park run, fit and active."

"Who's her GP?" Kett asked.

"Uh, she's registered in the city. Dr Peter Adams."

"Benedict Gilbert has a clear medical history too," said Dunst from across the room. "Broke his ankle when he was a teenager, but he's never suffered from any serious illness."

"Did we know that Donal was teetotal?" said Porter, chewing a pencil.

"I don't think so," said Kett.

"He quit drink when he was serving his reduced sentence, made a point of it. Just been speaking to a neighbour of his who says he regularly attended AA. Just checked as well, no booze found in his house."

"Jeremy Bower told us Alis never had a drink when she came to the Crow's Nest," said Savage. "And wasn't she drinking Everleaf at home, the alcohol-free stuff? Maybe Gilbert was teetotal too?"

"His GP mentioned that his folks never let him drink," said Kett. "Would make sense if you want somebody's liver. Kidneys too." He suppressed a shudder. "So the Monk is somebody who has access to medical records."

"Like a GP," said Savage. "You spoke to Gilbert's doctor, what was he like?"

"He seemed pretty normal," said Kett. "Older guy, had a thing for cheesy 90s pop music from what I can remember."

Savage frowned.

"What kind of music?" she asked.

"I have no idea," said Kett. "It was playing in his waiting room. Bubblegum pop or whatever you call it. Why?"

"I'm not sure," she said, pushing herself out of her desk. "Give me a second."

She ran through the door, heading for the Incident Room.

"None of them share a GP," Porter said, reading from his screen. "Donal isn't even registered to one here in the county, he's registered back in Birmingham. Doctor Sabel. But..."

He scrolled down the page, then started to laugh.

"What?" said Kett.

"Nothing," the DI replied. "He was just assessed as part of his prison medical."

"What's funny about that?" said Kett.

"Nothing, just the name of the guy who did it."

Kett felt his blood crawl to a halt, the room seeming to tilt.

"Doctor Colon," said Porter, giggling like a child. "I wonder if he's a bum doctor."

Kett wasn't laughing. He shot out of his chair, running to Porter's desk and peering over his shoulder.

"That's Gilbert's GP," he said. "Allister Colón."

"Oh, Co-*lon*," said Porter. "That kind of spoils it. Wait, he's *Gilbert's* doc? Seriously?"

"Yeah," said Kett. "But I visited him. He seemed harmless, and genuinely concerned about Gilbert's welfare. He's been his doctor for years. He contacted us, returned the call after Spalding had been in touch."

"You don't do that if you're guilty," said Porter.

"Not necessarily," said Kett. "He might just be trying to make himself look innocent. But he has links to two of our victims, that's hard to ignore. Any connection to Alis Sayer?"

No reply. Kett sighed.

"We can check him out, but I'm not holding my breath. I don't think this is him."

"It is," said Savage, running back in. "I knew it rang a bell, but I couldn't put my finger on it, not until you mentioned the music."

"What, Kate?" said Kett.

"The tattoos, the words. *Don't stop, Never give up, Lift your head high*. They're lyrics from an S Club Seven song."

"From a *what* song?" said Kett.

"The words don't mean anything," she said. "They're not a message. They were just to throw us off the scent. They were a *joke*. But it's him, isn't it?"

"I'm not sure," Kett said, grabbing his coat. "But it's the best lead we've got so far. Let's go, and somebody get Clare out of the toilet!"

THEY HEADED out of the city on a wave of light and noise, four IRVs blazing north and Clare's Mercedes right behind. Kett sat in the passenger seat of the Superintendent's car as the world turned into a blur through the windows. His stomach churned, partly due to the speed at which they were travelling and partly the smell of the car—the seven pine-scented air fresheners hanging from the mirror doing little to strip away the stench of teenage boys and their unwashed football gear.

Clare drove like a man possessed, his chin almost resting on the wheel and his eyeballs almost touching the windscreen. Porter and Savage sat in the back seat, surrounded by sweaty football shirts and muddy boots. They looked as miserable as Kett felt.

"You sure you don't want me to drive?" Kett said as they thumped past cars on the Cromer Road. "You still don't look a hundred percent, sir."

"I'm fine," Clare snapped back, wiping the sweat from his brow with the back of his hand. "Anything from the local police?"

Kett checked his phone, but there were no missed calls.

They'd radioed ahead, asking any units in the vicinity of Colón's surgery to make sure he didn't go anywhere.

"No, sir."

"You're sure he's there?"

"The receptionist at the surgery said he was in this morning, sir," said Savage, looking up from her phone. "Took me nearly half an hour to get through."

"You didn't say you were police?" Clare said.

"No, sir."

The brake lights of the car in front blazed and Clare slammed his foot down, the Mercedes lurching so hard Kett thought they were going to come off the road. Then they were accelerating again, fast enough for him to feel like his intestines were being dragged along the street behind them.

"We're not going to catch him if we're all dead, sir," he muttered.

"Colón trained up in Yorkshire," Savage said, reading from her phone. "Spent some time in North Wales, then Yorkshire and Cumbria, a spell down in Cornwall, a year in Edinburgh, then he came here. Did Balls tell you where these other cases happened? The ones said to be the Monk?"

"No," said Kett. "Hang on."

He found Balls' contact details and dialled him, listening to it ring.

"Bet he's got him listed as soulmate on his phone," Porter said from the back. "With a little heart emoji."

Kett opened his mouth to fire back a choice insult, but Balls answered before he had the chance.

"This is the Norman Balls Command Centre," he said. "How may I direct your call?"

"It's Kett," Kett replied. "I need to ask—"

"Let me just see if he's available," said Balls.

"I know it's you, Norman. Just answer this. Those other cases you were looking into, the body parts being delivered. Do you know where in the country it happened?"

"I know some," Balls said. "But... Hang on, why do I hear sirens?"

"No reason."

"You're going to arrest somebody, aren't you?"

"No," said Kett. "Locations, now."

"I'll tell you if you tell me where you're going," Balls said. "I can borrow Ron's van. I can meet you there."

"No."

"Well I'm not going to say anything until you let me join in," said Balls. "Nothing will shift my mind, sorry."

"Balls," growled Kett.

"Okay, fine! *Ugh*. Give me a minute."

The phone clunked onto what sounded like his desk and Kett heard clacking keys over the roar of Clare's engine. He checked his watch. Aylsham couldn't be far away now.

"ArgleBargle found two verified instances of the Monk's handiwork," Balls said, coming back online. "Severed arm and some severed genitals. Both had tattoos, self-help quotes by the sound of it. The arm was found back in 1992, in Corwen."

"Where's that?"

"Wales, obviously," said Balls.

"Was Colón in Corwen?" Kett asked, cupping the phone and craning back. "Early Nineties?"

"Uh, Bala," she said. "It's very close."

"The genitals were found in Scotland," said Balls.

"Edinburgh?"

"No, Kirkcaldy. 2001."

"Right over the Forth," said Kett. "Thanks, Norman. That's all of them?"

"I'm going to get the van now," Balls said. "I'll find—"

Kett hung up.

"Didn't even say goodbye," Porter said with a mock pout. "Your best friend will be sad."

"Can it, Porter!" said Clare. "What did he say?"

"Some, uh, genitals were delivered, severed and tattooed, in Kirkcaldy. 2001."

"Fits his timeline," said Savage. "He left Edinburgh in 2002, came to Norfolk to open his own practice."

"Gilbert would have been a kid," said Kett. "If this is Colón, he's had his eyes on him for nearly two decades."

"Grooming him," said Savage.

"No," said Kett with a shudder. "*Growing* him."

"Tossing hell," Clare said. "And you didn't have any clue at all that this guy was a monster when you met him?"

Kett shook his head. No clue at all, and if he'd missed something, if Colón slipped out of their reach and Happy Heptinstall paid the price, he'd never forgive himself.

He felt his phone vibrate and answered the unknown number.

"Kett."

"Hi, sir," came a familiar voice. "It's Duke. I'm in Aylsham, took the call. We're camped down the street from the doctor's surgery. You want us to move in?"

Kett cupped the phone, looking at Clare.

"You want them to make an arrest, sir?"

"How far out are we?" he replied.

"Ten minutes, sir," said Savage.

"Do it," Clare said. "Go get him."

"You hear that?" Kett asked into the phone.

"Yes, sir," said Duke. "We're going in."

The PC hung up and Kett dropped the phone into his

lap. They were moving slower now, stuck behind traffic as they approached the town. Too far away, Kett thought.

Come on.

"He's been doing this for decades," said Clare. "Why the hell hasn't he been caught?"

"Because he doesn't work alone," said Kett. "He hides in plain sight. He's the Monk, he's totally devoted to his calling. And he's smart."

"That's what worries me," said Clare.

Kett's phone vibrated again and he answered it.

"Duke?"

"Uh, he's not here, sir," the PC said.

"What do you mean he's not there?" Kett said.

Clare thumped the wheel, cursing.

"Reception staff told us he was in," said Duke. "He came in at nine and nobody saw him leave. He must have snuck out."

"Duke," said Kett. "It's a small building, how the hell does he just sneak out past a load of coppers?"

"It might have happened before we got here, sir."

"Right," said Kett. "Well, search the place, top to bottom. This is Colón's surgery, he built it, and he seems like the kind of man who would need a few extra hiding places. Clear?"

"Yes, sir," said Duke.

Kett hung up.

"Where does he live?" he said.

"Over in Burgh," Savage replied. "There's a turn coming up on the right."

"Let the Uniforms know," Kett said. "With any luck, we'll find him at home."

But they wouldn't, he knew.

The Monk was smart, after all, and he'd be long gone.

CHAPTER THIRTY-SIX

THEY REACHED ALLISTER COLÓN'S HOUSE SEVEN minutes later, Clare following an IRV onto a wide gravel driveway that led up towards an enormous red-brick Victorian house. He almost hit the brakes too late, coming within an inch or so of kissing the bumper of the car in front.

"Go!" he yelled.

Kett was already halfway out the door, the sun doing its best to take the top layer of skin off even though it wasn't even mid-morning. He spotted Duke amongst the tide of uniformed police who stormed towards the doors.

"Round the back," he shouted. "Make sure nobody gets out."

"Sir," Duke said.

"Watch yourself, Duke," Kett said. "This guy's dangerous. And he may have a hostage. Happy Heptinstall."

He wasn't sure if the PC had heard him over the thunder of so many boots on gravel, but he let it go. He turned to Clare.

"Tactical?"

The Super checked his watch and shook his head.

Savage reached the front door first, receiving a nod from Clare as he stomped after her. She balled her fist and thumped the door hard—*knock knock*—the sound of it like cannon fire.

"Doctor Colón," she shouted. "It's the police. Open up."

"Move, Kate," Kett said, trying the handle to find the doors locked. He knocked again, far less impressively. "Allister, we know it's you. We know you're the Monk. This is your last chance to come quietly. Open the door."

He put his ear to the immaculately varnished wood, then ducked down and opened the letterbox, peering inside to see a wide hallway with a sweeping staircase. It led through to a grand conservatory, and Kett saw PC Duke there at the back door.

It was open.

"Round the back," he said, at the same time a copper appeared from the side.

"Back door's unlocked," she said.

"Get in there," Clare roared, lumbering after her.

Kett overtook the Super, then Savage and Porter both overtook him. Duke was already inside by the time they got there.

"Sweep the ground floor," Kett told him. "And one of you stay here, guard the door."

"Sir," said the Uniforms all at once.

"And ready your batons," yelled Clare, sounding like a king before a battle charge. "He's dangerous."

They fanned out to the left and right, their batons extended. Kett ran back through the house, grabbing the newel post and swinging himself onto the stairs. He took them two at a time, out of breath by the time he reached the landing. Porter bustled past, heading for the bedroom on the right.

"Take your time, sir," he said.

"I don't need to take my bloody time, thank you," he replied, heading for the bedroom on the left before Savage beat him to it.

He walked down a stretch of corridor to find two more bedrooms and a giant bathroom, and a quick peek into each of them revealed absolutely nothing. By the time he'd opened a few drawers and wardrobes, Savage had appeared.

"Nothing," she said. "Master bedroom is just clothes and books."

"Nothing in the upstairs study either," said Porter. "Except he seems to have had an unusual appetite for bugs."

"Bugs?" asked Kett.

"Yeah. The six-legged ones. He looks like a proper, uh..."

"Entomologist," said Savage.

"Right. Birds too."

"Show me."

Porter led Kett back down the landing and took a left into the bedroom across from the master. It had been converted into a large office with a desk by the window and mahogany bookcases against the opposite wall. Mounted in between were dozens of framed collections of neatly presented insects, mostly beetles. The colour of them—reds and greens and golds—were almost too bright to be believed.

There were birds, too, stuffed and preserved and perching silently on the shelves, their black eyes watching with a frightening intensity.

"Creepy," Porter said.

"Yeah, but it's not illegal," Kett replied. "Check the desk. Savage, see if you can get into the attic."

He walked out to find Clare struggling up the stairs.

"Seems to be clear up here, sir. Anything down there?"

"Nothing," Clare wheezed, hanging onto the bannister like he was climbing Everest. "But they've found a basement door. Duke's gone to get the ram. Go make sure he doesn't demolish the entire house, will you?"

"Yes, sir," Kett said.

He ran back down the stairs, following the sound of voices through the large kitchen and into a well-stocked larder. Two uniformed officers had hauled a large cabinet out of the way to reveal a small door in the wall.

Not just a basement, then.

A *hidden* basement.

"Clear the way," came Duke's voice from the kitchen.

The giant PC squeezed into the larder, the enforcing ram looking like a toy in his hands. Kett stepped back as he swung it at the door. The wood was old, and it didn't stand a chance, the top hinges ripping out of the wall in an explosion of dust. Duke almost went straight through, staggering at the top of a set of stone steps until Kett grabbed the back of his uniform.

"Easy, Constable," he said.

He stepped past him, clicking the switch on the wall. A single bulb blinked to life, revealing a narrow stairwell that dropped steeply into the basement below. Every single inch of the brick walls was covered in cobwebs.

He felt Porter's hand on his shoulder as the DI craned to get a better look.

"Urgh," Porter said. "I do *not* fancy going down there."

"Tough," said Kett.

"Age before beauty," Porter said.

"I'll do it," Duke offered, handing the enforcing ram to one of the Uniforms behind him. "If you're too scared, sir."

"I'm not scared," said Porter, fighting to get past the PC.

They started down the stairs at the same time,

managing to get themselves wedged between the narrow walls. Porter won out in the end, clattering down the stairs with Duke right behind him. Kett followed, his heart in his throat as he reached a bend in the stairs and followed it around.

"Whoa," said Porter.

Kett entered a basement that was far bigger than he'd anticipated, lit up by bare, filthy bulbs. Vaulted arches of brick held up the ceiling, and in between them was what looked like a lifetime of belongings in bags and boxes. The spiders from the stairwell had made this their kingdom as well, everything covered in cobwebs so thick they might have been blankets.

"Nobody's been down here in years," said Duke.

"You sure about that?" said Kett.

He pointed to the floor, where a track of half-formed footsteps could be seen winding through the piles of junk. Kett made his way carefully along it, rounding one of the pillars to see it disappear into a wall that had been lined with unpainted plasterboard.

"Doctor Colón?" he yelled, loud enough for a yelp to escape Duke's mouth. The PC tried to cover it up with a cough. "If you're in there, now's the time to come out."

Nothing.

"Happy, if you're in there, let us know," he shouted.

The basement sat in complete stillness, quiet except for the creak and thud of the coppers overhead.

"Get it open," Kett said.

Porter walked to the wall, running his hands up and down the joints in the plasterboard until, with a grunt of effort, he shoved hard. There was a click and one of the panels opened.

Beyond was nothing but darkness.

Porter was halfway through the door, but Kett reached out and pulled him back.

"Careful," he said.

"Here."

Duke passed Kett his torch and he shone it through the hidden door, seeing another large section of the basement. Unlike the one they were standing in now, this was clinically neat, the floor made up of white tiles and the work surfaces gleaming chrome.

"Move," Kett told Porter.

He stepped through the door, seeing the bank of light switches on the wall and using his elbow to fire them all up. They were so bright that he had to cover his face for a moment, the memory of them burned into his retinas like glaring eyes. He thought they might have blinded him.

And when he finally looked, he half wished they had.

This room belonged to a collector, just like the study upstairs. But this collection was something from a nightmare.

Mounted to the whitewashed walls were what had to be twenty box frames, their contents slick and red. Kett didn't know what half of them were, but he thought he saw a heart, cleaned and preserved and presented against a pristine white background. Next to it was a set of lungs, looking like a deflated balloon, the open tube of the windpipe obscene. A single green eye stared back at him from a small frame opposite the door, its optical cord curled neatly around it like tinsel.

"Jesus Christ," he said, putting a hand to his stomach as if that might stop the sickness which grew there.

Duke retreated with a retching cry. Porter had closed his eyes, his breaths shallow. Kett made his way deeper into the room, walking like a man on the edge of a cliff. A steel autopsy table dominated the space, its drain leading to a gutter which disappeared into the floor. Across from it was a collection of scalpels and other surgical equipment, laid out with obsessive neatness. The air was heavy with the smell of bleach, not a single drop of colour anywhere other than those awful artworks which surrounded him.

Don't look at them, Kett told himself, swallowing a mouthful of bile as he walked around the table towards the desk that sat against the far wall. There were no drawers or cupboards in it, but there was a stack of paper on the surface. On the top sheet was a hand-drawn picture of a small, black tick with eight short legs.

"Shit," Kett said, clicking his fingers at the door. "Porter, gloves."

"Sir," Porter said, making his way carefully across the room and handing Kett a set of gloves. Kett didn't bother putting them on, he just used them to push the top sheet of paper to the side. Beneath that was an old photograph of a man in his thirties that Kett had never seen before.

"What's happening down here?" yelled Clare from the other side of the basement. "Kett?"

"In here, sir," Kett called back. "It's him, but he's gone. We were too slow."

He used the gloves to push the photograph to the top of the desk. Beneath that was a sheet of information.

"Allister Colón," Kett read, seeing the doctor's date of birth, seeing his education history and his places of employment, all of them matching the details that Savage had given him. He looked at the photograph again, but the man definitely wasn't the same person he'd spoken to in the doctor's surgery down the road, even considering the age difference.

"Christ," said Clare as he walked inside. "What the... What is this?"

There was one more sheet of paper at the bottom of the pile, and Kett used the glove to tease it out. Written there in bold, distinctive, familiar letters were five lines of text.

"'*So close, Detectives,*'" Kett read aloud. "'*Closer than anyone has got before. But that's the thing about ticks, isn't it? They feed, they drop away, they're never seen again. Don't bother looking for me. I've only been Doctor Colón for twenty years or so, and now I'll be somebody else.*'"

"Who is that?" said Clare, pointing to the photograph.

"I think that was Doctor Colón," said Kett. "And I'm just guessing, but I think when he moved over to Norfolk, the Monk killed him, took his place."

"That's preposterous," said Clare. "Somebody would have noticed."

"No wife, no kids," said Kett, pointing at the information sheet. "He's halfway across the country. Who would notice?"

The Super couldn't answer, his mouth gulping.

"We were too slow, sir," Kett said again.

He looked at the organs which glistened in their glass frames, at the table where God knows how many people had met their end. Then he turned and met Clare's eye.

"We've lost him."

CHAPTER THIRTY-SEVEN

THEY TOOK THE HOUSE APART WITH RELENTLESS precision, the same way the Monk unpicked his victims. Level by level, corridor by corridor, room by room, nothing was left unturned, the walls opened with axes, the floorboards lifted with crowbars. The attic was stripped, and the basement—where so many horrors had been waiting—was unpacked one box at a time.

And they found nothing.

In almost every respect the house was just a regular house, belonging to a regular man—a man who used Head and Shoulders shampoo, who ate Marks and Spencer's ready meals and drank a glass of port every night, a man who wore a matching tweed dressing gown and slippers while reading the Guardian on Saturdays. To anyone glancing through Allister Colón's paperwork, all they'd have seen was a man who paid his taxes on time, who donated to the RSPB and the RSPCA, who was still paying the mortgage on his house, and who had an impeccable record as a General Practitioner stretching back decades.

Only that basement room gave any clue to his real

nature, and his real identity. It festered beneath the ground like a cancer, its cruelty and its darkness contained by a flimsy plasterboard wall.

"I've never seen anything like it," said Emily Franklin as she studied the framed organs that decorated the walls. "Death, torture, disembowelling, severed limbs, sure. I've seen almost everything, just not this."

Kett watched her as she reached out, almost touching one of the displays before pulling her hand back.

"There's a reverence here for the human body," she said. "A profound respect."

"They're trophies, aren't they?" said Kett.

"Yeah, no doubt," she replied. "But I think it's more than that. The Monk appreciates the machinery inside us, the engine of flesh and blood that keeps us going. This doesn't feel to me like a celebration of death, it feels like a testament to life. You didn't find any more?"

"This not enough for you?" Kett asked. "No, no more organs, just these."

"Twenty-three," Franklin said. "And I can safely say they're from significantly more than one victim. There are three hearts, two sets of lungs, four kidneys, two pairs of eyes, a slice of brain, a kneecap, two livers—although the cut here makes me think it was one liver sliced in two—a section of spinal cord, a penis, a—"

Kett raised his hand, the sickness still churning inside him.

"I get it," he said. "But this makes me wonder if we were wrong about him selling organs, because if he's framing them here, then he's not making any money from them."

"It's a ravenous trade," said Franklin. "But it's a fickle one, too. If you butcher a body, you're always going to end up with more parts than you can get rid of."

"Leftovers," said Kett.

"Yeah. And if these are the remains of twenty-three people, then there are a *lot* of bits and pieces missing. Plenty of profit to be made there."

"You don't sound massively fazed by it all, Emily," Kett said, and she shrugged.

"I resigned myself to the realisation that the human race was sick and twisted a long time ago," she said, making her way out of the room. "Organ trafficking happens all over the world. It's happening right now. Kids are encouraged to sell their kidneys for iPads, mothers have sold them so they can buy food for their children. In some countries, the government will put you in prison and execute you just to make sure there's a fresh heart or liver to pack in ice and sell to a millionaire."

Kett opened his mouth to deny it, then realised it would be pointless. She was right.

"We do our best to help," she said. "But there's an ocean of cruelty out there. It's bigger than anything, and nothing will ever stop it. Only a fool thinks he can stop the tide. We're fucked."

She sighed, and looked up at Kett.

"I could murder a Maltesers McFlurry right now, do you want one?"

"Uh... no," said Kett. "What about the table?"

"That thing?" she replied, looking at the autopsy table. "Professional bit of kit, probably five or six years old. I've given it a quick look and there's no sign at all it's been used recently. No blood, no fluids, and barely any bleach residue. Drain has some matter in it, but it's so dry it must have been left there months ago. Years, maybe."

"Right," said Kett.

"I'll get these bagged up," she said. "See if I can get an

accurate body count. You got a location on this butthead yet?"

"Working on it," Kett said. "Thanks, Emily."

Kett made his way through the empty basement and up the stairs. The house was busier than ever, Uniforms and Detectives and forensic technicians fighting over the space. He heard his name and turned to see Savage weaving through the crowd towards him.

"Kate," he said. "Any updates?"

"Not from the house," she said. "It's clean. There isn't even a computer here. But the digital team has managed to get inside Happy Heptinstall's PC."

"The one I wiped?"

"No, the other one. She's been chasing the Monk for a long time. She's got a lot of information about him. She hadn't made the connection to Allister Colón, or whoever this guy is, but she'd done a pretty decent job of tracking his online behaviour."

"I thought things were untraceable on the Dark Web," said Kett.

"They can be," said Savage. "And the Monk knew what he was doing. They can't find anything traceable in terms of communications or transactions. But..."

She ducked as a forensic technician walked by, a stepladder on his shoulder.

"But Happy must have known the Monk wasn't working alone, because she's got a list of phone numbers, dozens of them."

"His phone numbers?" Kett asked, taking Savage's arm and steering her away from the noise and the madness towards the large, bright front hall.

"No," said Savage as they went. "They're mobile numbers, and they look like burners. Most of them are dead.

Happy's got a list of locations associated with each one, tracking pins that stretch all the way across Norfolk and beyond. And guess what?"

"What?" Kett said.

"Three of the phones are still active."

"Three phones," said Kett. "Three riders. You think they're being used by whoever is helping the Monk?"

"Could be," she said. "One of the pins is at the barn where we found Andrew Holden's belongings."

"Shit," said Kett. "Where are the others?"

"Everywhere. Clare's going through them now. He wants us all outside."

Savage walked out of the house and Kett followed, the heat of the day nearly knocking him back through the door. Superintendent Clare was leaning over the bonnet of his Mercedes, a map laid out before him. Dozens of little blue stickers had been fixed to it, all over the county. Porter was there too, speaking to somebody on his phone. A couple of Uniforms watched with grave looks on their faces.

"What's this place?" Clare said, pointing to one of the stickers on the map. "Another farm?"

He looked up when he heard Kett and Savage crunching over the gravel.

"Where have you two tosspots been?" he grunted. "Come on, I need your help."

"It's a farm, sir," said Savage, peering at the map. "Says it right there. *Hope Farm.*"

The Super checked his phone, moving his finger an inch to the right.

"A hill, by the looks of it," said Savage.

"It's impossible," Clare said. "There are hundreds of them."

"If these phones belong to the riders, then Happy could

have sourced tracking pins everywhere," said Savage. "At home, at the shops, petrol stations, walking the dog."

"Christ," said Clare.

"And I hate to be the one to point out the obvious," said Porter, hanging up his phone. "But even if we get lucky and one of these pins leads us to the riders, the Monk is still long gone."

"But he doesn't know we have this, does he?" said Kett. "As far as he's concerned, he's already disappeared. He doesn't think we stand a chance of rooting him out. And he's still got Happy to take care of."

"Right," said Savage. "Would he pass up on the opportunity to harvest some more organs? That's a lot of money down the drain."

She seemed to hear her words, putting a hand to her mouth.

"Sorry, I didn't mean *drain*. I just meant—"

"You're right," said Clare. "The Monk seems like a fastidious man. There's a chance he's going to finish the job before he vanishes completely. Although that's assuming he hasn't killed her already. But this house looks like it doubled as his workshop, so where are they?"

"Emily says this place hasn't been used for anything medical for a while," said Kett. "Maybe he didn't want to risk doing it so close to home. He might have another facility."

"It'll be somewhere with electricity," Savage said. "And running water."

"Easy access," said Porter. "Close to the main roads, because when he's got those organs out he'll need somebody to move them quickly."

Clare ran a hairy finger down the A47, stopping at each sticker.

"There's still too many options," he said. "Narrow it down."

"What did he drive?" Kett asked.

"There's no record of Colón having a car," said Savage. "No insurance documents, nothing. He went to work by bike, the pedal kind. Nobody at the surgery ever saw him drive."

"That helps," said Clare. "Bike. Or train."

"Or bus," came a shout from the front door. Everyone looked back to see Spalding emerge, something in her upheld hand. "Tickets," she said as she walked over. "All local. North Walsham, Cromer and Bacton. There are dozens and they go back months."

Clare moved the map so that only the northeast quadrant of the county was visible. He pointed to Aylsham, where they now stood, then worked north to Cromer. Four stickers waited for them there.

"Farms," he said. "That fits his MO. I'll take Cromer."

He moved his finger to North Walsham, where the pins were clustered tightly together.

"That feels too built up," said Savage. "Hard to kill somebody in the middle of a town."

"True," said Clare. "But I'll send Dunst to make sure, you too, Alison. That leaves Bacton."

"We'll take it," said Kett. "What have we got out there?"

"A village hall, by the look of it, a B&B. Another farm, too."

"Okay," said Kett. "Let's do it."

"I don't like us splitting up," said Clare. "This guy is dangerous. He wouldn't hesitate to kill if you stood between him and his way out. I'm calling Gorski; the tactical team will meet you out there."

"Yes, sir," said Kett, more than a little grateful.

"Be careful," said Clare. "But catch this tosser."

"We can take an IRV," said Porter as they walked to the road. "I'll drive."

"Savage can drive," said Kett.

"I'll drive," came a voice from the far end of the driveway. PC Duke stood there, holding up a set of keys like they were a trophy.

"He can drive?" Porter said as they jogged over. "Thought you needed a brain for that."

Duke walked to the nearest IRV and opened the driver's door, cramming his enormous frame into the seat with such effort that he dropped the keys in the process.

"Shit," he said, bending down to fish them out of the gutter.

"Move over," said Kett as they reached the car. "Savage is driving."

"I'll do it, sir," protested Duke. He was still trying to collect the keys, but his knees were jammed against the wheel and he didn't have enough room to manoeuvre.

"Move!" Kett ordered.

"I can't," said Duke. "Give me a second."

"Here," said Savage, running to the next car along. The door was open, the keys in the ignition. She jumped in and fired up the engine.

"Shotgun!" yelled Porter, but Kett beat him to the passenger seat and climbed in. The DI grumbled his way into the back.

"Shotgun rule is law, sir."

"Then arrest me," said Kett.

"Wait," shouted Duke, still trying to extricate himself from the other car. "Wait for me!"

"Just drive," said Porter.

"Sir?" Savage asked, looking at Kett.

"Wait," pleaded Duke. He pinged out of the seat, landing on the pavement, up again in a heartbeat.

"Let him come," said Kett, much to Porter's disgust.

Duke opened the back door and slid in next to Porter.

"Thought you were going to go without me for a minute there," he said.

"Wouldn't have dreamed of it," Porter replied.

Savage switched on the blue lights and floored it, pulling around the forensic van parked in front and accelerating hard down the country lane. Kett switched on the air con, turning it as low as it would go, and was rewarded with a blast of lukewarm air. His stomach still roiled from what they'd found inside Colón's house, that sick display of organs, a silent cry from so many dead.

And deep inside, he knew it was only going to get worse.

CHAPTER THIRTY-EIGHT

THEY MADE GOOD TIME WITH THE SIREN AND THE lights, the IRV tearing through the sun-bleached Norfolk countryside. It seemed utterly empty out here, occasional clusters of houses that clung desperately to the side of the road as if trying not to fall into the bleak fields beyond. They didn't pass a single other vehicle for fifteen minutes, and even as they closed in on Bacton a short while after that, the streets remained deserted.

"Don't know how people don't lose their minds out here," said Porter as he watched the fields and the woodlands flash by.

"Apparently they do," said Kett. "Where's the first pin?"

"Place just off the main road," said Savage. "Turning's coming up."

"Switch the siren off," said Kett. "Just in case. And Pete, check on tactical, will you?"

Porter pulled out his phone to make the call. The car was slowing, Savage pulling them off the main road and down a narrow track. The trees crowded over the IRV as if eager to see who was inside. But the shade was welcome, all four minutes of it before they rumbled back into the onslaught of the sun. The road ended ahead, and to the right was a bungalow that had seen much better days. All but one of the windows had been covered up with sheets of plyboard.

But the door was open.

"No sign of a bike," said Savage as she pulled the car onto a driveway that was more grass than gravel. "Motor or otherwise."

"No sign of anything," said Kett. "Pete?"

"On their way," said Porter. "They're coming from the city, so they're still twenty minutes out."

"Their loss," said Kett, opening his door.

He climbed out, breaking into a sweat almost immediately. Savage's door opened, then Porter's, then Duke's—the only sounds in the world, it seemed.

"Just a look," said Kett.

"You always say that, sir," replied Porter.

Kett ignored him, crossing the drive and reaching the bungalow's front door. He heard Duke extending his baton with a flick of his wrist. His Taser looked almost neon yellow in the sun.

"Want me to go first, sir?" asked the big PC.

"Sure," said Kett. "Why not."

Duke ducked beneath the lintel, vanishing into the gloom.

"Police!" he roared, loud enough to bring the whole building down. "Make yourself known!"

Kett followed Duke in, seeing a short corridor lined with doors. With the windows boarded, the heat in here was unbearable, and the rancid air was thick with flies.

Never a good sign.

He fired up his torch, checking the door on the right to

see an empty kitchen, and past that a toilet that looked like it hadn't been flushed since it had been installed. A mountain of human faeces rose above the rim of the seat, the smell of it enough to make Kett double up and spit bile.

"Nope," he groaned.

"Somebody's been using this place recently," said Savage, beaming her own torch past his head. "They look fresh."

"I'll take your word for it," he replied.

"Clear this end," said Duke. "Some clothes and bedding, though."

Kett followed the sound of his voice past a couple of bedrooms into the biggest room at the end of the building. The board on the window here had been removed, but the sun still seemed reluctant to enter. Kett didn't blame it. The smell was almost worse than in the bathroom.

Somebody had been sleeping here. A mattress sat in the far corner of the room, a duvet and pillow laid neatly over it. Several carrier bags surrounded the makeshift bed, plus a couple of water-damaged books—non-fiction stuff about gangsters and hard men, by the look of it.

"Check the garden, Duke," said Kett as he walked over.

"Sir," Duke replied, trotting off.

"Kate, did Happy's list show when the phones were traced to this location?"

"Yeah," she said, pulling out her phone. "Hang on. Uh, there are quite a few here, all from the same number, and various times over the last eight months. Last one was three days ago."

"You think this is Colón?" Porter asked.

Kett walked to the wall and clicked the switch, but the bulb in the ceiling stayed dark. He retreated to the bathroom, holding his breath as he turned on the tap.

"No water, no juice," he said as he walked back. "I can't see Colón dissecting bodies here, can you?"

"Maybe one of the riders?" asked Savage.

"Makes sense," said Kett. "But why would they live like this?"

"They deliver body parts for a serial killer," said Porter with a shrug. "They find the victims and then clean up the mess. I don't think these are normal people we're talking about."

"Fair point," said Kett. "But the Monk is paying them good money. He has to be, unless he's forcing them to do it. So why live out here in the middle of nowhere? Why shit in a broken toilet? Why sleep in *that*?"

Nobody answered. Kett was feeling lightheaded from the heat and the stench and he walked back the way he'd come, escaping into the fresh air.

"Where was the other pin out here?" he asked Savage when she appeared.

"Petrol station," she said. "Ten days ago."

Kett swore beneath his breath.

"Might be too far back for CCTV, but we can try."

He looked at the bungalow, at the empty fields that surrounded it. The only other living creatures he saw were the crows who hopped across the garden, who bickered on the roof. They seemed to be following him everywhere, waiting for orders.

"Hang on," he said. "If you're right and one of the Monk's riders is squatting out here, there has to be a reason."

"Yeah," said Savage. "But you saw Colón's secret room, it was spotless. I can't see him doing anything in this place."

"Agreed. So if you're a courier who's regularly

employed by the same guy, and you don't want to spend your life riding around the county..."

"You find a place close by," said Savage, her eyes widening.

"To wait for your orders. What else is in Bacton?"

"Uh..." Savage looked up at the sky. "Well, I know it quite well. My granddad's place was only down the coast in Hemsby. We came up here a fair bit, but I never liked Bacton beach, there was never enough of it, if you know what I mean?"

Kett wheeled his hand to hurry her up.

"There's the gas terminal," she said. "It's where most of the gas comes in from Europe."

"Doesn't help us."

Porter lurched out of the door, his eyes watering.

"Christ," he said. "That is so bad. There's nothing there, just rubbish and stains. So many stains."

"Blood?" asked Kett, and Porter shook his head.

"Poop."

"There's a bunch of caravan parks," said Savage, rubbing her forehead, deep in thought. "He might be using one of those. I don't think there's a church but..."

"What?" said Kett when she tailed off.

"Bacton," she said, clicking her fingers. "There *is* a church here. Well, the ruins of one. And actually, I don't think it was a church. I think it was a..."

She looked at him, something clicking.

"It was a monastery."

"You're kidding," said Kett. "Bacton Monastery?"

Savage was on her phone, her thumbs a blur. A minute or so later, she held it out. Kett saw photos of an impressive set of ruins.

"It's called Bromholm Priory," she said. "It's just down

the road. That's why I didn't think of it. It's a Cluniac monastery, famous for once possessing a piece of the True Cross. It was an important place of pilgrimage for centuries thanks to—"

"Alright, *Wikipedia Jones*," Porter said, making his way to the car. "Where is it?"

"Five minutes away," she said as she chased him.

"Duke!" Kett yelled. "We're leaving."

Kett ran to the car, climbing into the passenger seat as Duke came charging around the side of the house. Savage was driving before he was even in, the big PC risking life and limb as he tried to clamber into the back. He fell into Porter's lap, his hat flying, his door slamming shut as Savage turned the IRV in a tight circle and accelerated down the track.

"At least buy me dinner first, Duke," said Porter as he pushed the constable away.

They roared onto the main road, cars pulling over for them even though the siren and the lights were off. There was no sign of the sea from here, as if it had retreated from the land in fear of what might happen next. Kett had his phone to his ear, the line ringing.

"Speak!" grunted Clare when he answered.

"Bit of a long shot, sir," Kett said. "We've found a ruined monastery outside of Bacton. Bromholm Priory. There's evidence that one of the Monk's riders was living out here, close by. We're on the way to check it out."

"I'll have tactical meet you there," Clare said.

"No need," Kett told him, looking into the rear-view mirror to see the police van pulling up hard behind them. "Gorski's with us. Can you find out who owns this place?"

"I will," said Clare. "Be careful, Kett."

"Yes, sir."

He hung up, looking out of the window to see quaint flint and brick cottages and thatched pubs and small schools. Doubt filled his mind, because how could a place like this be home to somebody like the Monk? How could evil live here amongst the potted pansies and the cosy cafes?

Evil can be anywhere, he thought. *It can be right next door and you never even see it.*

"If he's using the monastery, why is there no pin?" Porter asked. "Surely one of the rider's phones would have pinged while they were there."

"I bet he didn't let them bring them," said Savage. "I bet he didn't let phones anywhere near that place."

"Makes sense," said Kett. "He calls them when he needs them, they know where to go so they leave their phones behind. Ensures nobody can trace them."

"Hang on," Savage said, braking hard. The tyres whistled as she swung right, gunning the IRV up a small access road. Ahead, past a row of houses, sat a huge stone arch that looked ready to crumble into dust. "That's it."

"Slow down," said Kett. "We have no idea what's waiting for us in there."

Savage slowed the car to a crawl as they drove under the arch, fields opening up on either side of them. Maize plants towered over the road and Kett was grateful for the shade they provided, and the cover too.

"Looks like a farm," said Porter, sticking his phone between the front seats. Kett saw a satellite image of the priory on Google Maps, a handful of buildings huddled together and surrounded by countryside.

They made their way slowly up the track, the ruins gradually lifting themselves from the fields to their left. It looked like a stone submarine rising out of the depths, Kett thought.

The tower was bigger than he'd expected it to be, and if the Monk was inside it now, then he'd have a front-row view of the police arriving—and plenty of options for escaping.

"You want me to keep going, sir?" Savage asked.

"Too late to turn back now," he said.

Porter was right, the place looked like a farm—although there wasn't a soul in sight. A large house sat to the side of the road, its windows dark. Hulking barns and squat outbuildings guarded it, looking disapprovingly at the IRV as it rumbled by.

"Stop here," said Kett.

Savage obeyed, and he climbed out, running to the house and hammering on the door. There was no answer, and when he opened the letterbox and peered through, he saw a mound of unopened post on the mat. The air was still and quiet, the house empty. He ducked down the side and then around the back, hearing nothing from the barns except that all too familiar cawing from the crows.

He walked to the tactical van, Gorski's window already down.

"Kett, sir," she said with a tight nod. "I would say it's good to see you again, but you know..."

She shrugged, her face deadly serious.

"What are you looking for?" she asked.

"Not sure yet," he replied. "But I have the feeling we'll know it when we see it. Keep your eyes open."

"They never close," she said.

"Nobody home," Kett said when he climbed back into the IRV. "No sign of a bike, either."

They crawled forward, everyone seeming to hold their breath. The road kinked to the left ahead, sloping downhill past the crumbling perimeter wall. Kett had a perfect view of the ruins from here and it was painfully obvious there was nowhere to hide.

"Shit," he said. "I don't think this is..."

The words died in his throat as they rounded another corner and saw two more buildings down the hill. The barn on the left was enormous. It looked big enough to be an aircraft hangar, two stories tall, its walls brick and its corrugated steel roof flashing in the sun like a beacon. Kett had to shield his eyes from the brightness of it, and only then did he notice the smudge of smoke rising towards the cloudless sky.

"What's that?" he said, pointing.

"Fire," said Savage, squinting through the windscreen.

"Why would anyone need to light a fire on a day like this?" said Kett.

The answer was obvious, but nobody said it.

"Get down there, Kate."

The car accelerated, crops swishing by the windows as they flew down the track. The big engine of the van behind them seemed to be the loudest thing in the world, Gorski a silhouette behind the sun-bleached window. The building grew bigger as they approached, puffing itself up like an angry dog. Only a handful of windows pocked its sides, the ones on the ground floor boarded tight and the upstairs ones gleaming. A smaller barn sat on the other side of the road, no windows and no door visible from the road.

"Van," said Porter.

Kett followed the DI's finger, seeing the bonnet of a white van poking past the far end of the first barn. It was too far away to work out the make and model.

But close enough that Kett could see it had no plates.

"Shit," he said, the adrenaline surging into his system, making his stomach feel ready to cramp. "This is it."

The IRV thumped its way over a couple of potholes and stopped, blocking the track that led along the side of the barn. Kett climbed out, reaching the tactical van just as it pulled to a halt. The driver's door opened and Gorski jumped out, dressed in full tactical gear, her rifle slung over her shoulder.

"I have no idea if this is the right place or not," said Kett. "But my gut's telling me it is. We're looking for a man in his fifties, slightly balding, fit, looks like your favourite granddad."

"I hated both my granddads," she said.

"Good, because you're going to hate this guy, too. He's been using the alias Allister Colón, but he's better known as the Monk. Extremely dangerous, and he won't hesitate to kill."

"Neither will I," Gorski said, hammering her hand on the side of the van. The back doors opened and five armed officers got out, filing into position.

"Colón has a couple of accomplices, and the fact there's a van parked over there makes me think at least one of them is here. They're armed with machetes and there might be firearms—fake, like the one last night, or real. I don't know."

Gorski's face tightened.

"And there's a chance we've got a civilian in there," Kett said. "A young woman called Happy Heptinstall. I have a feeling the Monk is going to kill her and harvest her organs. We may already be too late. He knows we're onto him, but he doesn't know we know about this place."

"This is Happy," said Porter, showing the team a photograph on his phone.

Kett looked up at the barn, which towered overhead.

"I hope we're not too late."

"Then let's not leave it any longer," said Gorski. "Wait here. Alpha team, on me."

She ran silently towards the barn door, her unit flowing behind her. Kett watched them go, then turned his attention to the smaller building to the right.

"Worth a check, sir?" Porter asked, following his line of sight.

"I don't know," he said, the panic swelling inside his chest. There were too many variables here, too many unknowns. He bit down on it—*literally*, digging his teeth into his bottom lip until the pain chased away some of the uncertainty.

"Okay," he said. "You and Duke, just a quick look through the doors, okay? But do not enter the building."

"Yes, sir," Porter said.

The DI jogged across the road, Duke close behind him.

"What about me, sir?" Savage asked.

He didn't answer. There was a crunch as an enforcing ram hit the barn door, Gorski and her team making entry. The quiet air exploded with their shouts, crows scattering from the fields and from the barn roof, a storm of darkness that Kett couldn't help but see as another omen.

Another *bad* omen.

He watched Porter and Duke walk along the side of the smaller barn, their shadows seeming to dance on the walls beside them. They disappeared around the back.

Seconds later, Duke started shouting.

Kett swore, making it halfway across the road before the air behind him erupted with a blast of gunfire.

CHAPTER THIRTY-NINE

"JESUS, DUKE, COULD YOU *BE* ANY NOISIER?"

Porter whispered the words over his shoulder as he made his way up the side of the smaller barn, the sun so hot it felt like a hammer striking them against the flint walls. Duke was right behind him, his big boots scuffing the ground and his breaths like an elephant giving birth.

"I feel like I'm being chased by King Kong," Porter said.

There was no entrance on this side of the building, or at the front, but when Porter poked his head around the corner he saw a large double door in the back of the barn, both sides open. The sun might have been blazing, but it had no authority here—the barn drenched in darkness.

"Door," he said quietly. "Be ready."

Porter stared back past Duke's enormous frame to see Kett and Savage on the road. The tactical unit had already moved into the other building, he could hear them shouting. That was good. It would provide a distraction if there happened to be anyone inside the smaller barn.

He looked at Duke, at the baton in his hand and the yellow Taser on his hip.

"Actually, mate, you go first."

"Thought you might say that, sir," Duke replied.

"Just because you're armed," Porter said. "Nothing to do with who's braver."

"Sure, sir."

"Because I'm braver."

Duke shouldered his way past Porter and stomped towards the door, his baton held up to the side of his head.

"Police," he yelled, the barn swallowing the word whole. "Make yourself known."

Porter stepped in after him, realising that it wasn't a barn at all, but a stable. Stalls lined both sides of the large interior, all of them empty of everything except for mounds of mouldering straw. The air was thick with heat and dust and the stench of animal shit.

"Police!" Duke said, louder this time. He'd almost reached the end of the stable, and it didn't seem like anyone was here.

Then Porter saw it, a dark shape rising from one of the stalls to the right, halfway between where he was standing and where the big PC was still advancing.

"Duke, watch out!"

The shape rushed out of his stall, a man dressed in blue overalls and a black motorbike helmet. Something flashed in his hand—a length of sharpened steel that could only be a machete.

"Knife!" Porter roared, charging towards him.

Duke spun around, lifting the baton instinctively. The machete cut through the air, but it clipped Duke's weapon, twisting. The flat of the blade slapped against Duke's shoulder, spinning free of the man's grip.

"Shit," came a voice, muffled by the helmet.

"Police!" shouted Porter. "Get on the floor!"

The man was having none of it, hurling himself into Duke. He was tiny compared to the giant PC and Duke wrapped his spare arm around his neck and yanked him into the air, flinging him away like he was a rag doll.

The man landed hard but his helmet saved him, cracking off the stone floor of the stable. He rolled onto his back, scrambling into the darkness of another stall.

"Here!" Duke said, tossing the baton to Porter while he fumbled with the Taser.

"Stay down," Porter commanded, approaching the stable door. "Do not fucking move."

There was no response from inside, and it was too dark to see anything. Porter stared over the low wall and saw nothing but shadows.

"Where is he?"

Noise from the stall to the left, the sound of somebody grunting.

"He's moving," Porter said, walking to the next stall and seeing a pair of legs slide beneath the wooden divider. "Stop fucking moving!"

"Police, armed with Taser!" Duke said, the weapon finally in his hands and looking about as threatening as a kid's water pistol. "Stay where you are!"

Porter walked on, his boot landing on the machete. He kicked it back towards the open doors, holding onto the baton with a hand that felt too clammy and too weak. His heart machine-gunned in his throat, sweat rolling into his eyes. It was too dark in here, they were sitting ducks, and they didn't even know if there was anyone else lurking in the shadows.

"Duke," he said. "Back off."

"Sir?"

Duke held his ground, the Taser pointed at the far end

of the stable. There were more noises down there now, metallic clanks, but Porter couldn't make any sense of them. He reached out and touched Duke's shoulder.

"Aaron, it's not worth it," he said. "He can't go anywhere. Let's box him in, then the tactical unit can sort him out."

As if on cue, the crack of gunfire ripped through the quiet day—a powerful boom that sounded almost like a cannon. Porter counted two more shots from across the road, then another three. He held his breath, his blood freezing despite the heat.

"Shit," he said. "Duke, come on."

This time Duke retreated, the Taser never dropping. Porter kept his hand on the other man's shoulder, guiding him back until they stepped out of the doors into the golden light.

"There's nowhere to go," Porter shouted to the man inside. "This is your last chance to take off that helmet, put your hands in the air, and come out. Hear those shots? Armed police, and they're not taking any prisoners."

Nothing, except for those same metallic noises.

"Like I said, mate. Last chance."

Another shot tore through the air, and now that he was outside, Porter could hear shouts—maybe even a scream of pain. What the hell was happening over there?

"He's not coming," said Duke.

"Fuck him," Porter replied. "He's not going anywhere."

Another whirring thud from inside the stable, and this time Porter realised what it was.

"Shit," he said as the sound of a motorbike engine thundered to life.

The bike appeared from the far stall, its headlight brighter than the sun as the rider sped towards them.

"Move!" Porter yelled, diving to the side.

Duke held his ground. The Taser aimed through the barn doors.

The engine roared, the bike already doing well over thirty miles an hour by the time it thumped its way through the barn doors.

Duke stood back at the last second, pulled the trigger.

The bike was moving fast, but from this distance he couldn't miss. The barbs slammed into the rider's flank and his whole body seemed to contract, his hands leaving the handlebars. For a second he kept his balance, the momentum of the bike ripping the Taser from Duke's grip. Then the man fell back, landing hard. The bike skidded across the dirt before disappearing into the tall crops of the field, its engine still rumbling.

"Stay down," said Porter, running to the man, the baton raised.

The rider was groaning his way to his feet, reaching for something in his pocket.

Screw this, Porter thought.

He swung the baton at the man's head as hard as he could. It cracked into the helmet with enough force to leave a dent and he toppled backwards, a slim knife falling from his fingers. Porter planted a knee in his stomach, lifted the baton again.

"Helmet isn't going to save you next time, mate," he said.

The man groped for the knife. Then, when he realised it was gone, he raised both arms in surrender. Porter lifted the visor with his free hand, seeing a face that might have belonged to a kid. A pair of sharp brown eyes stared up at him from a sweat-drenched face, a wispy moustache doing its best to cling to his quivering top lip. The smell coming off him was something else, and Porter didn't think it was because he'd been squatting in the stable. He couldn't have washed his body or his clothes in weeks.

"Who the fuck are you, then?" Porter asked him.

He honestly wasn't expecting a reply, but he got one.

"Jim," said the kid, as if Porter had found him doodling graffiti on a wall, not attacking coppers with a machete. "Jimmy."

"And what the hell are you doing out here?"

The kid shrugged.

"Budge up, sir," said Duke, a set of cuffs in his hand.

Porter stood back while the PC secured the boy's arms behind his back.

"You got anything sharp on you?" he asked. "Anything in your pockets?"

"Fuck yeah," said the kid.

Duke rolled him onto his back again.

"I'm going to ask you one more time," he said, leaning over. "What's going on out here?"

He was answered not by the boy, but by another shot from the bigger barn. The kid grinned, doing his best to shrug again, even with his hands cuffed.

"Just waiting for him to come and get me," he said. "Because none of you are getting out of this."

"No?" said Porter, managing a grim smile. "Why's that then?"

"Because the Monk doesn't let anyone live," he said, breaking into a childish laugh that made Porter's skin crawl. "You and the rest of them are already dead, you just don't know it yet."

CHAPTER FORTY

Kett broke into a run, his ears still whining from the barrage of gunshots—two, then three more. He reached the door of the larger barn, backing against the wall as he tried to make sense of the darkness inside. There was no sign of the tactical unit, just a small room and another open door on the other side of it.

"Sir?" Savage said, running after him.

"Stay back, Kate," he told her.

"I was about to say the same thing to you."

More shots, a cluster of sharp cracks that couldn't have all come from the same gun. Kett could hear Gorski's voice above the gunfire, and she sounded scared.

He swore as he pulled out his phone, calling Clare. The Super picked up after one ring.

"Speak!"

"Officers are under fire, sir," he said. "I think so, anyway. Something's going down."

Another shot, and more shouts.

Somebody was calling for help.

"We need medics out here immediately, sir," Kett said. "Where's the rest of the tac team?"

"With me," said Clare. "We're on our way. Do *not* engage, Kett."

Kett hung up without replying. He could hear footsteps, slow and heavy. Something was emerging from the darkness of the interior door and he stepped defensively in front of Savage.

"Need some help here!"

Gorski walked through the door, another officer stumbling alongside her, his arm around her shoulders. He was holding his stomach, part of his uniform ripped away to reveal the ballistic vest underneath.

"Jesus, what happened?" Kett said, rushing over and taking the man's weight.

"Fucker rigged an internal door," she said. "Shotgun. Vaughn here took it right to the gut. We saw him, he's still in there, ran up to the first floor, I think."

"Where are the others?" Kett asked, helping her lower the man to the floor.

"There's some kind of security door," she said. "Came down when the shotgun went off, we were separated. Solid steel, there's no way through."

"*What*?" said Kett.

"He was prepared for this," Gorski said, lifting the other man's visor. "He either knew we were coming or he was set up to push back any incursion. Maybe both."

Her radio chirruped.

"Effendi?" she said. "What's going on?"

A burst of static, then a panicked voice.

"... can't see a way out, can you..."

"Fuck!" Gorski said. She pushed herself up. "I need an ambulance."

"On its way," said Kett.

"Then watch him, I'm going back in."

She ran back through the door, checking her rifle as she went. Savage had ducked down next to Vaughn, her hand on his arm. He was struggling to get air in, but there was no blood. The vest had shielded him from the worst of it.

"What do we do, sir?" Savage asked.

He didn't know, the day falling apart around him. He could hear Porter and Duke shouting from the other side of the road, the sound of a motorbike engine.

"Sir?" said Savage.

From inside the barn, somewhere above their heads, came a scream, high-pitched and full of terror. It helped to focus him, cutting through the panic, through the indecision.

"That's Happy," he said. "She's still alive."

He looked at Savage and she looked back, both asking the same question.

Both giving the same silent answer.

"Mind if I take this?" Kett asked, crouching down and removing the crowbar from the firearms officer's equipment belt. He glanced at the pistol in his holster, then decided against it. In the darkness of the barn, he was more likely to shoot one of his own team than the Monk.

"He's a... sneaky fuck," said Vaughn, recovering his breath. "Be careful. I'll let her know you're coming in."

"Yeah, tell her not to open fire," Kett said, rubbing the scar on his chest. "You sure, Kate? Nobody will think bad of you if you—"

She was already running, heading down the side of the barn in search of another way in. Kett lumbered after her, reaching the corner seconds after Savage and peering around it. The white van was here, but there was no sign of a door.

"Check the other side," said Kett.

Savage broke into a run again. Kett rammed the sharp end of the crowbar into the front tyre of the van, air whistling out of it. He did the same with the one at the rear, by which time Savage was back.

"Door's boarded," she said. "We'll need a chainsaw to get through it."

She looked up.

"Window?"

Kett followed her line of sight to see a window almost directly overhead, maybe eight or nine feet above the ground.

"There's no way I'm getting up there, Kate."

"You don't have to," she replied. "Just give me a foot up."

He hesitated, but only until another scream tore from the barn. Kett sniffed the air, catching a whiff of something burning.

"Be quick," he said, handing her the crowbar.

He laced his fingers together into a cradle and she stepped into it. She was heavier than she looked, and it took all his strength to stand straight.

"Can you get me any higher, sir?"

He groaned, his arms burning as he lifted her.

"Close your eyes," she said.

He did as he was told, hearing the crowbar shatter the glass. Savage grunted, then the weight of her vanished. He looked up, shielding his eyes from the sun, to see her worming her way through the broken window. She appeared again seconds later, one hand to her mouth.

"Smoke," she said. "A lot of it. I can hear a fire."

"Shit," he said.

She leaned out, offering him a hand. Kett stared at it.

"Come on, sir," Savage said, managing a smile. "Thought you weren't an old man yet."

"I'm not," he growled.

He planted one foot on the wheel arch of the van, then jumped up and caught Savage's outstretched hand. She held him tight and he rooted his boot on the brick wall, scrabbling up until he could reach the window ledge. There he stopped, dangling.

"You need some more help, sir?" Savage asked.

"Nope," he wheezed. "Just give me a second."

"Not sure we have one."

He kicked his way up, Savage grabbing the back of his jacket and hauling him all the way inside. He rolled onto his back, seeing that they were in a small room stuffed with cardboard boxes.

"How on Earth did you get so strong?" he asked her.

She offered him her hand, hoisting him up.

"Wrestling Colin to stop him slobbering all over me," she said. "The dog, that is. Not the Super."

"Thanks for clarifying," said Kett.

The stench of smoke was stronger here, and Kett could see fingers of it reaching blindly beneath the closed door, trying to find them. There was definitely a fire. He could hear the dull rumble of it from deeper inside the building.

No voices, though. No more screams. No more gunfire.

"Come on," he said, picking up the crowbar and making for the door. It was locked, but the wood was old and when he braced the end of the bar into the joint and put his weight against it, the door splintered out of its frame. Instantly the smoke found them, forcing its way into Kett's eyes, into his mouth. He coughed hard, his lungs spasming painfully. Savage was doing the same.

"This is insane," he said, pushing his head into a long, dark corridor. The smoke was too thick to see much, but he thought he could make out at least three closed doors and a staircase leading down to the floor below. It was lighter down there, flames guttering.

He gripped the crowbar hard, using his other sleeve to cover his mouth as he stepped into the corridor. The heat was rising through the floor, already unbearable. The fire was downstairs, he knew, but it would spread through the old building in minutes.

It would take Happy with it.

It would take them too, if they weren't careful.

The nearest door was right across the corridor and it wasn't locked. Kett opened it to see another small room, this one packed with boxed medical equipment and stacks of shrink-wrapped towels. Savage had managed to open the next door down and she appeared again instantly.

"Ladder," she coughed, pointing.

Kett followed her finger to see a hatch in the floor, a metal ladder leading into a shaft of absolute darkness. There was no way of knowing what was down there, and the screams they'd heard had been above them, so he motioned Savage to keep moving. She opened the next door and Kett saw a cupboard that was only big enough for a hot water tank.

They moved on, reaching the stairs. Kett shielded his eyes from the heat, looking down to see a heavy steel door. He could hear somebody pounding on it from the other side —the tactical unit trying to break through. He turned to Savage.

"Go show them how to get in," he said, choking on so

many of the words that she didn't understand him. He pointed back into the room. "Get Gorski, show her the window."

She nodded, but hesitated.

"I'll be okay," he said. "Go!"

He didn't wait to see if she would follow his orders or not, ploughing past the stairs to the last remaining door. This time he opened it with his boot, the door shuddering like a KO'd boxer as it let him through.

In front of him, lit by a set of blazing halogen lights that dangled from the oak beams of the ceiling and utterly out of place here in the ancient barn, was a hospital room. It was huge by any standard, at least ten metres wide and half again as long, but there was only one bed.

And only one patient.

A young woman lay there, her body mummified in bandages and her arms and legs secured with thick leather straps. She twisted her head towards Kett as best she could, her eyes liquid with terror. A gag had been secured in her mouth, but she still managed a brittle scream.

"Happy?" Kett said, coughing the word. He took a few steps towards her, feeling like he was swimming through the smoke, through the heat. "It's the police."

If anything, her expression grew more terrified still. She stared at him as if he was the enemy, as if he was the man who'd taken her, as if—

Not *at* him, he suddenly realised.

Past him.

He spun around, seeing the Monk emerge from the shadows behind the door. Allister Colón—or the man who had been posing as him—looked nothing like the friendly doctor Kett had spoken to just twenty-four hours ago. He was dressed in a full surgical suit and mask, his eyes so cold they didn't look human. They looked like *insect* eyes, Kett thought.

The man didn't hesitate, marching towards Kett with murderous purpose, something silver flashing in his left hand.

Kett swore, lifting his arm just in time in an effort to shield himself with the crowbar. He felt something slide into his flesh, deep into the muscle, and the crowbar dropped to the floor. He wrenched himself away with enough force to rip the weapon from the Monk's grip, and it hung obscenely from his forearm, as tenacious as a tick.

Not a knife, but a *needle*.

The Monk lunged again, reaching for the syringe. Kett stumbled back, almost losing his footing. The man grabbed him around the face with a gloved hand and pushed him down onto his knees, the strength of him unexpected, impossible. His other hand bunched into a fist and struck Kett in the throat—sharp and neat, and in precisely the right place to steal the air from him.

The sun seemed to set, night falling in an instant. Kett fought his way through it, trying to claw in a breath. He ripped at the fingers around his face, his other hand flailing. The Monk was trying to grab the syringe, trying to empty it into his veins. Happy's screams were relentless, like shattered glass inside his skull. But there were words, too, full of hate.

"How did you find me?" the Monk said, squeezing Kett's head surely hard enough to crack the bones. "How did you figure it out?"

Kett felt the syringe tense, he felt the other man's hand on it.

He ripped his arm away again, throwing himself back with everything he had left. He felt the needle slide free, felt the agony of something cold inside him, some poison rushing into his veins. He pushed himself to his feet, his bones made of water, too weak to hold him up.

The Monk advanced, unfazed, his eyes utterly dead.

The syringe was still gripped in his hand, and it was almost full.

Thank God.

"You know how long I've been doing this?" he said. "Thirty years. And you think you can stop me now?"

"Not just me," said Kett, stumbling back. "This place is crawling with armed police. You end this now, or they'll take you down."

"You arrogant fuck," said the Monk. "You think I don't have a way out? You think I didn't prepare for this eventuality? Once I'm done with you, I'll even have time to finish her. Shame to waste a good heart."

Even beneath the mask, Kett could tell he was smiling.

"How's yours?" he said. "I don't usually bother with the older ones, but there might be time to take something with me. Eyes are eyes, after all. Easy enough to pluck, easy enough to sell."

Kett hit the bed, almost falling onto the young woman who lay there. He staggered to the side, his knee hitting a trolley of equipment and scattering tools to the floor. Past that was a low desk, a tattoo gun sitting on it. The Monk pressed on, relentless, the syringe held close to his face, his thumb on the plunger.

"This place is rigged to burn to the ground after the alarm is triggered," the Monk said. "And after that, you'll never see me again. I'll disappear. You'll only ever hear about me on the news, and you'll know it was me."

Something exploded downstairs, powerful enough to make the entire building shudder. The heat seemed to rise another few degrees, the room a mirage of dancing light. The Monk strolled through it, low and tense, like a boxer. Kett reached towards the trolley, desperately looking for something—*anything*—he could use as a weapon.

"You'll hear about another foot, another hand, another head," said the Monk. "And you'll know it was me."

Kett's fingers closed over something slim and sharp. He clutched it tight, pulling it close.

"And one day," the Monk went on, almost close enough now to strike. "One day, you'll come home and find your wife missing, your kids missing, and you'll know it was me."

Kett's head broke into a high-pitched whine, and for a second he couldn't feel the heat anymore, he couldn't taste the smoke, he couldn't feel the pain.

The only thing that existed was his fury—fury for Alis Sayer and Benedict Gilbert, who would have met their end right here, cut open and pulled apart, the very essence of them stolen, packed away in ice then planted in somebody else. The horror of it was too much, his rage was too much, and like the fire, it almost consumed him.

The Monk lunged with the needle, aiming it right at Kett's throat.

But Kett was ready.

He ducked to the side, ramming the scalpel's blade between the Monk's knuckles. The man's eyes widened, his breath caught in his throat. His fingers spasmed and the syringe started to fall, but Kett didn't let it. He grabbed the man's hand with both of his, twisting it back and plunging the needle into the meat of his throat.

Then he pushed his forehead against the syringe, sliding the plunger home and driving the Monk backwards across the floor like a bulldozer. Colón managed to stay on his feet for all of three paces before tripping on the leg of a pneumatic guillotine, landing hard with Kett on top of him.

"No!" he said. His voice was an old man's, nothing but dust. He clutched at the syringe, but Kett kept his hands on it, clamping it in place. "What have you done?"

Another explosion from downstairs, the floorboards smouldering as the fire raged below. Kett leaned in, ripping the man's mask away. Colón looked ancient, he looked weak, his eyes red and weeping.

"How many people?" Kett growled, barely able to get enough air in to fuel the words. "How many people did you butcher?"

The Monk batted feebly at Kett's face, at his eyes, but Kett knocked his hands away. He wrenched out the empty syringe and tossed it across the room. Then he plucked the scalpel from the man's mangled knuckles and held it to his throat.

"How many?" he demanded.

"You'll never know," the Monk spat back, his eyes rolling up in their sockets. "You'll never know."

There was so much Kett wanted to do to him, but the roar of the fire and Happy's screams reminded him he didn't have much time. He pushed himself up, struggling to see the bed in the storm of smoke. He staggered deeper into the room, finally finding the young woman who bucked and writhed in her restraints.

"Hang on," Kett said. "Hold still."

He used the scalpel, slicing through the leather. The straps were thick but the blade was lethally sharp, and in less than a minute she was free. She tried to climb out of the bed but her legs didn't have the strength to hold her and she tumbled to the floor at Kett's feet.

"Shit," he said.

The fire was spreading fast, flames creeping up the wall to his right, the floorboards blistering. The Monk was trying to move, but whatever was in that syringe looked like it was paralysing him. He stared at Kett with eyes that hung on the edge of madness, his mouth trying to shape words.

Out in the corridor, something collapsed with a sound like a capsizing ship, a wave of smoke and glowing ash billowing through the door. Kett had to hold his hand up against the heat, his skin screaming, his eyes seeming to boil in their sockets.

"Hang on," he said again.

He reached down, almost blind, finding Happy. Somehow, he managed to hook his hands under her arms and haul her onto his shoulder. He took a step, then another.

Then he stopped, because the Monk had wrapped a hand around his ankle.

He looked down, seeing the man's gurning face, seeing him wrestle up a word.

"No."

Kett tugged his leg, but the Monk's grip was still too strong. The fire was spreading fast, the building groaning as it readied itself to collapse.

"Can't... leave... me," said the man at Kett's feet. "Can't... go."

Kett didn't have enough air in his lungs to reply. He wrenched his foot free, staggering towards the door. The smoke billowed around him, the inferno doing its best to eat him alive. For a terrible moment he thought he was back inside Bingo's apartment, he thought it was Alice he held in his hands, and in the madness of it he turned to try to find his other two children in the blaze. But he couldn't see anything at all.

"Robbie?"

A voice from inside the hurricane of smoke.

"Robbie? Where are you?"

He closed his eyes, following the voice out into the corridor, just putting one foot in front of the other until he felt hands on his arms, on his face.

"Robbie, let me take her."

Savage was right there, coughing her lungs up. She pressed herself close and lifted Happy from his shoulder onto her own.

"Where is he?" Savage asked. "Is he in there?"

Kett looked back, through the dancing ashes, through the flames, and saw the Monk on the floor of his hospital room. The fire had almost reached him, the floor crumbling.

But he was alive. He stared back with wild eyes, his hand groping.

One day, you'll come home and find your wife missing, your kids missing, and you'll know it was me.

"Robbie?" Savage asked, swiping the tears from her eyes. "Answer me."

He thought again about all those butchered men and women, all those boys and girls.

"No," said Kett. "He's gone."

The building groaned again, part of the ceiling detaching and falling into the pyre. Kett fought his way down the corridor, one hand gripping Savage's sleeve to steer her. They turned into the little room they'd entered through and Gorski was there to greet them. Another officer was standing on a ladder just outside the window and Savage carefully passed Happy to him.

"Everything good up here?" Gorski asked. "Because this place is about to be the end of us all."

"Everything's good," Kett said.

"Then let's get the fuck out of here."

Savage was already out of the window, throwing a quick look back to make sure Kett was behind her. He climbed through, only just finding the rung before gravity took hold of him. Savage was waiting for him at the bottom, helping him off the ladder and wrapping her arms around him to keep him standing.

She didn't ask him if he was okay because she knew what the answer would be.

She didn't ask him if he was okay because she knew what had happened.

He could see the truth of it in her face.

"Everyone back," said Gorski. "Back, back, back!"

Kett stumbled away from the building, leaning on Savage for support. He looked back from a safe distance to see that the fire had almost finished its work. Great chunks of the barn were already lost to the flames and a pillar of smoke stretched high into the sky, turning summer into winter, day into night. The heat coming off it was unbelievable, his skin pulsing with every frantic beat of his heart.

But he was alive.

He was alive, and so was Happy Heptinstall. The firearms officer who had carried her down the ladder had removed her gag, and she uttered another panicked scream, pushing herself away from him. She limped over to Kett, falling into his arms, burrowing her head into his jacket and sobbing with such grief, such horror, that he didn't know how she could get a breath in. He held her tight, even when her legs started to fail. He held her tight against him. He wouldn't let go.

"Robbie?"

Porter bounded around the side of the barn, Duke right behind him. Both of them broke into wide smiles.

"Christ," said Porter. "Thought you were a gonner, mate."

Kett did his best to smile back, but it seemed as if the smoke had coiled inside him, filling his head with darkness.

"No sign of our suspect," said Gorski. "I don't think he made it out of the building. You had a visual?"

"Yeah," said Kett, the word like a knife in his throat.

"What happened to him?" Gorski asked, stepping in. She gave him a moment to answer, and when he didn't, she shook her head. "*You* happened to him," she said, and there was no kindness there, no relief, just anger. "*You* happened."

She walked away, talking into her radio. Kett glanced at Savage, and even though she tried to smile, she couldn't meet his eye.

So he turned back to the building, to those roaring, lunatic flames. And even though he held Happy in his arms, even though he knew it was over, he still couldn't help but think that everything would have been better if he'd let the fire take him too.

CHAPTER FORTY-ONE

For what seemed like forever, they watched the fire burn.

The barn held itself up for as long as it could before surrendering to the flames—collapsing with a roar of grief and fury that sounded almost human. Even then, the inferno showed no sign of stopping, chewing through the remains of the building, making sure every last trace of it had been reduced to ash and smoke.

Every last trace of *him*.

"He's gone?" asked Happy Heptinstall, her hoarse voice pulling Kett from his trance. He was still holding onto her, but he wasn't sure whether he was keeping her up or whether it was the other way around. Without her next to him, Kett didn't think he'd be able to stop himself from falling.

"He's gone," he said, his own voice reduced to a whisper. The smoke had clawed at his throat, every swallow like he was trying to work down a lump of molten rock.

"How did you find me?" she asked, finally stepping away.

"*You* found you," said Savage. "You had everything we needed. If we hadn't found your computers, we never would have found you."

Kett caught sight of another shimmering light, seeing an ambulance emerge from behind the tall crops. An IRV followed, then Clare's Mercedes, trying to bully its way past with its horn blaring. They stopped a safe distance from the burning barn, Clare unfolding himself from his car. He spotted Kett and gurned.

"Let's get you to the ambulance, Happy," Kett said.

"I can take her," offered Duke. Kett nodded, and the PC gently took Happy's arm.

"I can get you a stretcher?" he said, but she shook her head.

Duke led her to the paramedics. She looked back once and smiled.

"Thank you," she said.

"What happened in the other barn?" Kett asked Porter when they'd walked away.

"Nothing much," the DI replied. "One of the Monk's riders was in there. Probably the one who'd been living in the house across the way, if the smell is anything to go by. Had a go at us, Duke took him down with the Taser."

"Nice," said Kett.

"It was a good shot, annoyingly. The guy's young, just a kid, really. Isn't talking."

"You okay?"

Porter shrugged.

"This time," he said after a moment. "But if they keep coming at us, then sooner or later the answer to that is going to be no, isn't it? Sooner or later, our luck is going to run out."

Kett nodded.

"What happened to the Monk?" asked Porter.

Kett didn't answer.

"What happened, sir?" Savage pushed.

The flames shifted, patterns swirling in the glowing chaos of the barn. For a second they seemed to form the shape of a man made of fire, a man who clutched at his face and screamed, and even though the heat of it still seared his skin, even though the sun was burning through the smoke again, Kett shivered.

"I could have gone back," he said. "I *should* have gone back."

And he thought about the way the ceiling had collapsed, burying the Monk alive in a tomb of fire.

"But it would have killed me."

"Kett!" roared Clare as he closed in. The Superintendent was absolutely drenched in sweat, enough of it that they could probably have held him over the barn, given him a good shake and extinguished the fire. "What in the name of a monkey's tossknocker is going on here?"

Kett opened his mouth to answer, but there were no words—and that was only partially to do with the fact that he had no idea what a monkey's tossknocker might be. Savage touched his arm, just for a second, long enough to let him know she was there.

"We got Happy," she said. "She's alive, and she's unharmed. The Monk is dead."

Clare glared at her, then at Kett.

"It was either him or her," Savage said, nodding towards the ambulance where Happy was being helped onto a stretcher. "The Monk or his victim. We couldn't save both."

Clare chewed on it for a moment, then grunted, turning to the barn.

"Place was rigged to blow," said Gorski as she made her

way back over. She'd taken off her helmet and her balaclava, her red hair impossibly bright in the glow of the pyre. "We think he rigged up several barrels of accelerant that were triggered when the emergency door was closed. It was a clever set-up, the shotgun was mounted in a way that pushed us back, allowing the steel doors to close. He knew he'd be getting visitors one day, and he was ready for us."

"How's your man?" Kett asked.

She looked at him coldly.

"Alive," she said. "But his ribs are porridge and God knows what the shot did to his organs. He was lucky he was wearing the vest. And it's lucky it wasn't one of you. Would have cut you in half."

"The Monk is definitely dead?" asked Clare.

"He told me he had a way out," said Kett. "I don't know what, exactly, but Kate and I found a ladder leading down from the top floor."

"That would have taken him into the fire," said Porter.

"Not if it went all the way down," Kett replied. "He seems like a man who planned for every contingency. He was about to operate on Happy even as the building burned, was planning to take her heart with him."

And my eyes.

He cleared his throat, spitting black phlegm onto the grass.

"But yeah, I think he's dead."

Clare nodded, looking at Kett like he knew there was more to the story. He turned to Gorski.

"Anything else you'd like to say, Sergeant?"

Gorski tilted her head to the sky, a myriad of emotions passing through her face before settling on resignation.

"He made his choice," she said. "And he paid for it."

She turned to Kett again.

"There's *always* a price to pay."

Kett hung his head, her meaning clear. If Clare understood what she was saying, he made no sign of it. He wiped the sweat from his face, lost in the fire.

"He killed so many people, sir," Kett said. "I don't know if we'll ever find them all."

They wouldn't find *any* of them, he knew. Because he'd seen what the Monk and his assistants did to their victims—did to the bits they didn't sell, that was. Those people were lost forever, packed down drains, flushed down toilets, no chance of justice for them.

Other than *this*, of course—other than being burned at the stake, without a jury, without a judge—and Kett wondered how many of Colón's victims were gathered here now in the sunlight, in the shadow, watching their killer burn.

Christ, he was tired.

He closed his eyes, rubbed his face, and the world seemed to dance around him like a madman. He would have fallen if Savage hadn't rushed forward and taken his arm.

"Sir?" she said.

"I'm okay," Kett replied, opening his eyes, the world too bright to look at. "I think the Monk might have jabbed me with something. He had a hypodermic needle, but it didn't really go in."

"Let's get you seen to," she said, leading him across the lawn towards the paramedics. "Everything else can wait."

Kett nodded, looking to Clare for permission.

"Go," said Clare. "It's over, but I need you back in as soon as possible for a debrief. Because this..."

He looked at the barn again, the last piece of skeletal framework collapsing with a feeble cry.

"This isn't how we do things. It can't be."

"Extreme crime, sir," Savage said as they walked, Porter jogging along beside them. "Extreme measures. It's right there in the name."

They made their way in silence, watching a fire engine trundle up from the other end of the track, a swarm of firefighters descending. Kett wasn't sure what they'd be able to do, as the blaze had all but consumed itself.

"Nearly there, sir," said Savage, her hand still on his arm. "Just a few more steps."

"Kate," he said with a sigh. "I'm okay, really."

"Got an old one coming in," Porter called to the paramedics. "He's cranky, and a little hard of hearing. Gets cold easily, so maybe find him a blanket."

Kett threw the DI a look, and Porter grinned back.

"What? It's considered polite to take care of your elders."

"I'm the same age as you!" Kett protested. "Almost."

"Yeah, sir, you keep telling yourself that."

He was about to protest some more, but one of the paramedics was walking out to meet them. He looked Kett up and down, giving him a smile.

"Everyone's walking wounded today," he said. "You okay?"

"I'm fine," Kett protested.

"He might have been injected with something," Savage said. "A sedative, maybe. I don't know."

"He just needs his slippers and his pipe," added Porter. "And a good cuppa."

Kett shrugged.

"Actually, a good cuppa sounds about right."

"Well, you're more than welcome to ride in the bus,"

said the paramedic. "But it'll have to be upfront because we've got two others in a sorrier state than you."

All Kett wanted to do was go home. All he wanted to do was gather his children to him, hold his wife, and forget about everything that had happened in the last three days. But he could still feel the sting in his arm from the Monk's needle, and his fingertips felt worryingly numb.

"Sure," he said. "I'll come. But only for the tea."

"Let us know you're doing okay," Savage said.

"I will," he replied. "And thanks for coming back. Not sure I would have made it if I hadn't heard you calling."

"Always," she said, finally meeting his eye and holding it.

Kett started towards the ambulance, only to hear a furious honking from further down the track. Everyone turned to look as a small, white van rode the verge past Clare's Mercedes, then past the ambulance.

"Who the hell is that?" Porter asked.

The answer lay in the round, wide-eyed face that peered over the steering wheel.

"Oh, Balls," said Kett.

The van shuddered to a stop with enough urgency that Gorski and her team stood to attention, their hands on their weapons. And as much as Kett would have loved them to scare the strange little man away, he lifted a hand.

"Hold up, Gorski. He's okay."

Balls opened the van door and fell out—literally—tumbling out of sight before pinging back up again like a whack-a-mole. He saw Kett and started running over, wearing a pair of blue shorts that looked like they were trying to disappear up his rear end and a red T-shirt at least a size too small. The long socks and sandals completed the look perfectly, announcing his presence with a flip-flapping applause.

"Robbie!" he yelled. "I found you!"

"You found me," Kett sighed.

"Are you going to get the Monk? Are you about to move in? Let me come!"

He skidded to a halt, his hands on his knees, his chest heaving as he tried to find his breath.

"Please let me. I want to take him down."

"It's over, Balls," Kett said. "We got him."

"Darn it!" Balls wailed, his hands bunched into fists.

"How did you even find us, Norman?"

Balls tapped his nose, winking.

"I have my secrets," he said. "Speaking of which, you'll probably get a call soon from Mum, because she told me if I took Ron's van again, she'd call the police. I'd like you to ignore her."

"Can't really do that, Norman," said Kett.

"Fine, I'll take it back." Balls humphed, stamping a sandal on the grass. He looked at the fire, then at the armed police, then back at Kett. "I can't believe you didn't wait for me. Was it really him? Was it really the Monk?"

"It was," said Kett.

"I knew my detective skills would pay out," he said, beaming.

"You're not a detective," said Porter, wiping the smile from the other man's face.

"Actually," said Kett, clapping a hand on Balls' shoulder. "I'm going to let you have this one, Norman. If you hadn't mentioned the Monk, we might never have started looking for him."

"So I'm a detective?" he said, his face full of hope. "A *real* detective?"

"Just for today," Kett said.

Balls pumped a fist into the air, doing a strange little jig.

"Let's go for drinks to celebrate," he said. "My treat."

He patted his shorts.

"Actually, your treat. Mum still won't let me have any money. There's a nice pub just down the road, they serve an all-day breakfast and—"

"I've really got to get into that ambulance," said Kett, the world starting to swim again. "Or you'll have to carry me home."

Balls pouted, looking at Porter and Savage.

"Will you come?"

"Uh," said Savage. "Sorry, we need to get back to the station. Paperwork."

"And I could do with getting home," said Porter. "Another time, mate."

Balls looked like he was about to cry.

"Hey, Duke," Kett called out, spotting the PC standing beside the ambulance. "I've got a job for you."

"Oh, perfect," said Porter, grinning.

"Cruel," muttered Savage.

"What is it, sir?" Duke said.

"I need you to take Norman here to the pub down the road," said Kett. "Buy him a pint."

"And an all-day breakfast," said Balls.

"Yeah, one of those, too."

Duke looked down at Balls, his face wrinkling into an expression of distaste.

"Why, sir?"

"Because I'm telling you to," Kett said.

"Come on, Big Man," said Balls, walking off. "I've got so much I want to talk to you about. And I brought some of my folders, you won't believe what I'm about to tell you. Did you know that some crimes in Norfolk are affected by the ley lines that stretch across the county? Hidden ones. I'll show you..."

Duke grimaced as he chased Balls to his car, only looking back when Kett called to him.

"Good work, Constable. Be proud."

That put a smile on his hairy face, at least.

"Don't worry, sir," Porter said, resting a big hand on Kett's shoulder. "I'm sure Balls will still be your best friend."

"Don't push it," said Kett, forcing his tired legs to move towards the ambulance.

"Best friends with Balls," Porter went on, relentless. "I'm going to put that on a T-shirt for you."

"Please don't."

He reached the open cab door, hanging onto it and taking a moment to study Savage and Porter.

"Good work," he said. "Both of you. We got a monster off the streets, a bad one. And that's a good thing. It *has* to be a good thing."

"It is, sir," said Savage.

She cupped her hand to his face—as if she was taking in every scrap of his exhaustion, his guilt, his grief—then seemed to remember herself, pulling away.

"Go get fixed up," she said. "We'll see you when you get back."

He nodded to them both, climbing into the front seat of the ambulance and closing the door. The paramedic got in next to him, firing up the engine.

"You ready, pal?"

"Yeah," said Kett. "Is Happy going to be okay?"

"She's going to be right as rain," he said, pulling down the track. "She's champing at the bit to go home."

"Good news," Kett said, waving a final goodbye to Savage and Porter, seeing them wave back.

We got a monster off the streets, he thought as he watched the world go by. And that was true enough. But how many more monsters were still out there?

He caught sight of himself in the side mirror of the ambulance, his eyes dark, the streaks of ash on his face making him look like some kind of phantom.

How many more monsters were *in here*?

He closed his eyes, enjoying the currents of cool air from the open window, enjoying the peace and quiet. Now wasn't the time to think about monsters, dead or alive.

"Good work, Robbie," he told himself. "Good work."

And he almost believed it.

CHAPTER FORTY-TWO

"You sure you don't want to take the car, Kate?"

Porter pulled the IRV into the parking space outside his house, cutting the engine and looking across to where Savage was doing her best not to fall asleep. She yawned, stretched, then shook her head.

"HQ's a five-minute walk from here," she said. "I think I can cope."

The exhaustion on her face suggested otherwise, but he didn't push it.

"Come in for a cuppa first if you like?"

"One of yours?" she asked. "I don't think so."

"Allie can make it."

"Then definitely not," she said, laughing. "Kett tells me her hot drinks make yours seem almost drinkable."

Porter gasped, and Savage laughed even harder.

"Sorry, Pete," she said. "Thanks, but no. I'll get back, get all of this down while I remember it."

"Fair enough," he said. "Maybe for the best, anyway. Allie's still not feeling great."

"The Super's cake?"

"Yeah," he said. "Never again."

"Never again," said Savage.

She opened her door, letting a wave of sunshine roll inside the chilled interior. Porter got out too, enjoying the heat on his face for as long as it took him to remember the burning barn.

"What do you think happened in there?" he asked.

Savage shrugged.

"The right thing?"

But he heard the question in her answer, and he saw the uncertainty on her face. He couldn't think of anything to say, so he clamped his mouth shut.

He heard the front door opening, turning to see Allie there. She was dressed in her pyjamas and her dressing gown, and despite the heat—and the cup of steaming tea she held in her hands—she was shivering.

"Hey, gorgeous," Porter said. "How're you feeling?"

"I don't know," she said, something in her face that he couldn't read. She looked at Savage and smiled.

"Hey, Kate."

"Hi, Allie. Hope you're feeling better. Clare's cake took out quite a few people this week."

"It's not the cake," she said.

She seemed to be wearing a smile and a frown at the same time.

"Allie?" said Porter. "What's going on?"

"I can go," said Savage, seeming to sense something. "I'll catch you later, sir."

Porter waved her a goodbye as she made her way down the street. Then he walked to his wife, wrapping his arms around her slim shoulders as well as he was able with the hot drink between them. He kissed her on the forehead, then on the lips, when she tilted her head up to him.

"What's up?" he asked.

"I wasn't being sick because of the cake," she said. "It's not a bug, either."

"What, then?" he said, frowning. Allie laughed, a sound so rare he couldn't remember the last time he'd heard it. She reached up and touched his cheek, her fingers cold.

"Aren't you supposed to be a detective, Pete?" she said.

"Yeah, but... wait."

He took hold of her shoulders so that he could look her right in the eye.

"You're not..."

That smile grew, as bright as the sun.

"I am," she said.

"But the IVF, we haven't even started. *How*?"

Allie laughed again, it seemed to spill out of her. Her body was shaking so much the tea was leaving the cup. Porter took it from her and dropped it onto the mat.

"You're pregnant?"

"*We're* pregnant," she said.

Porter's scalp tightened, the relief and the joy rushing through him like cold water. He grabbed her, holding her so tight he could feel her laughter against his chest. She wrapped her arms around his waist, squeezing, and suddenly he was laughing too—both of them standing in the open front door giggling like children.

"When did you find out?" he asked when they'd caught their breath. Allie wiped the tears from her eyes.

"Just today. I had a hunch, but I didn't think there was any hope. I spoke to the midwife, she said these things can happen while you're waiting for the IVF to start. We got lucky. But there's a chance it might not..."

The smile dropped away, her hands pressed to her stomach. Porter rested his on top of hers, kissing her again.

"It'll be okay," he said. "There's a little Pete in there. He's going to be just fine."

"I hope so," she said, her face so full of uncertainty, so full of fear, that Porter's heart seemed to break in two. He drew her close again, wanting more than anything to pull her inside him where he could keep her safe, keep both of them safe.

"We're going to have a baby," he said, laughing again at the sheer impossibility of it, laughing at the terrifying joy of it.

And then, so suddenly it took him by surprise, the laughter turned to tears. They pushed their way up from a place inside him he didn't even know existed, a flood of them, and all he could do was bury his head in Allie's hair and let them come.

When, at last, the sobs dried up, he stood back, smudging his fists into his eyes.

"You're a dope, Mr Porter," Allie said. "But I love you."

"I love you too," he replied. "I can't wait to tell the world about this."

"All in good time, Pete," she said. "All in good time."

She took his hand and led him into the house.

BY THE TIME Kett had been dismissed from the Norfolk and Norwich University Hospital, it was coming up for five. He stopped on his way out, looking into the private room where Happy Heptinstall was being treated. She was fast asleep, but Charlie Skeldon sat in her wheelchair by the other woman's bed, holding her hand. She glanced up when Kett poked his head through the door.

"How's she doing?" he asked quietly.

"Better than I could have hoped," Charlie said. "Is it true? She was the one who hired that man to kill Andrew?"

Kett nodded.

"I told her not to," she said. "It's such a waste, isn't it? All this death. Such a waste."

She lifted Happy's hand to her mouth and kissed her fingers.

"All these bad men, but somehow we're the ones who always end up in the shit."

"You're safe now," Kett said. "Both of you."

It wasn't much consolation, he knew, but it was all he could offer.

He took a taxi back to HQ, bumping into Savage as soon as he'd walked through the doors into the Major Investigation Team's bullpen.

"Wasn't expecting you back today, sir," she said. "How're you feeling?"

"All clear," he replied. "Just came in to shower, get a change of clothes."

Because the last thing he wanted to carry home with him was the stench of smoke. It had dragged him right back to Bingo's apartment, right back to the Pig Man, and he knew it would take his kids there too.

He wasn't sure they'd make it out again.

"Boss just called," Savage said. "They found a tunnel leading out of the barn. The ladder we saw bypassed the ground floor and went straight down. There were steel doors down there, too, they would have stopped the fire spreading into the tunnel. The other end comes out in the ruins of the old priory, plenty of hiding places down there."

Kett's heart juddered, almost stalling.

"But the door in the ruins was locked from the inside," she said, reading his fear. "No sign it had been opened recently, cobwebs everywhere. He didn't get out."

"You're sure?"

"I'm sure," she said. "They found his body, too. What was left of it. But if we were hoping to find out more about the Monk and his operation, how he chose his victims, the people he was selling to, the people he was paying to help him, then we're stuffed. It's all gone."

"Shit," said Kett. "It was definitely him. I saw the tattoo gun, the pneumatic guillotine he must have used for amputations. It was definitely him."

"I know, sir," Savage said. "It was. As for the rest, we can only guess. He obviously had a list of selected victims based on their blood type, on their health. He had access to all of that as a doctor. He offered his clients a list and asked them to select a name."

"But it didn't really matter who they chose," said Kett. "Because they all would have been suitable donors."

He shook his head in disbelief.

"And it adds another layer of complicity, doesn't it sir?" Savage said. "The Monk didn't choose his victim, the client did. Makes them even less likely to talk to the police."

"Yeah," said Kett. He rubbed his eyes.

"Go home, sir. Get some rest."

Kett nodded, heading for the showers.

"Oh, Kate, what happened to your footballers?"

She grinned.

"They're all in the tank, sir. Well, Spencer and a couple of the others who copped to it. The coach is there too. He claims he had nothing to do with it, but four or five of his lads are prepared to say he did."

"That's good," said Kett.

"It is."

He made his way out of the room, only to hear her call him.

"Sir, I meant to ask, have you seen Dunst?"

"Dunst?" he said, turning back. "No, why?"

"He's gone," Savage said. "Cleared out his desk this afternoon. Nobody's seen him."

"He cleared out his desk?"

Savage nodded.

"Weird," said Kett. "Call me if you hear from him."

"Will do," she said as he walked away. "Now get home. Those girls will be forgetting what you look like. Skoosh!"

IT SEEMED that Savage was right.

Kett slid his key into the lock and pushed on the door only for something on the other side to push back.

"Password!" came a little voice.

"Evie, it's me, and I'm knackered," he said. "Let me in."

"I don't know who you are," Evie said, and he heard another giggle that could only belong to Moira. "State your name."

"Robbie Kett," he said, resting his forehead on the closed door. "Also known as Dad."

"Do you know anybody called that?" he heard Evie ask her little sister.

"No," replied Moira.

"I'm sorry, you'll have to come back later, unless you know the password."

The door of the house next door opened and Mrs Stevens walked out, throwing something into her wheelie bin. Kett smiled at her and she waved back. He had to wait for her to go back in before he answered.

"Farty butt cheese," he said.

"Is that the password or your name?" asked Evie through a ripple of laughter.

"Both," said Kett with a sigh. "So let me in, or I'm coming through the window."

"Girls!" came Billie's voice, and a second later the door opened. "Sorry, Robbie, I was on the phone."

"No fair," Evie said. "He didn't say the password."

"Didn't need to," said Kett with a smug smile. "I know the queen."

He kissed Billie as he walked inside, then scooped up Moira and Evie in one giant hug. It hurt his back to hold them, because they were getting so heavy, but he clung onto their squirming bodies long enough to blow a raspberry on their necks. He dropped them back down and they ran off, screaming with laughter.

"The farty butt cheese is coming to get us!" yelled Evie as they flew into the kitchen.

"The farty butt cheese doesn't look like he could run if his life depended on it," said Billie, smoothing back Kett's hair. "Are you okay?"

She winced, like she knew it was a stupid question.

"Don't answer that," she said, her voice low. "I saw it on the news, the fire. That man was really trafficking *organs*?"

"Yeah," said Kett.

"This world," said Billie, her mouth downturned. "I don't understand it."

"I don't think I want to understand it," said Kett.

"Go sit down," said Billie. "I'll make a cuppa."

It wouldn't fix everything, of course, but it would help.

He walked into the living room, seeing the boxes

stacked against the far wall. One of their shelves had already been emptied of books and DVDs, the other well on the way.

"Little early to be packing, isn't it?" he shouted as he collapsed onto the sofa.

"Thought I'd get a head start," she said.

"So this is really happening?"

He heard the sound of the tap, the rattle of the kettle being returned to its cradle. Billie reappeared seconds later, a smile on her face.

"It is," she said. "It can't happen quickly enough. You're still okay with it?"

"More than okay," he said.

She vanished again and Evie and Moira took her place, the pair of them running into the living room so fast Moira fell flat on her face. Kett leaned over and helped her up, and she made a beeline for one of the boxes. Evie had already climbed inside, her face alive with panic, something gripped in her little hand.

"Quick!" she said, and Kett was about to ask what the hurry was when he heard Alice stomping down the stairs.

"Give it back!" his oldest yelled.

"Evie," said Kett. "What have you done?"

"Nothing," she said, ducking down into the box.

"Put me in!" said Moira.

Kett sighed, lifting her into the box with her sister. It was just in time as Alice swung around the door, her face warped with fury.

"Where are they?" she said.

"Calm down," Kett told her. "What happened?"

"They took Slothy," she said. "I'm going to punch them."

"No, you're not," said Kett.

He turned to the box, looking at Evie with his well-practised stare of profound disappointment. She held out the cuddly sloth in surrender and he took it from her, handing it back to Alice. She looked for a moment like she was going to storm the boxes like an invading army.

"You can't get them when they're in there," said Kett. "That's a safe space."

Alice glared at her two little sisters, but she didn't make any more shows of aggression. Kett turned to Evie and Moira.

"But it does mean you'll have to stay inside that box for the rest of your life," he told them.

Evie's eyes widened, and he was about to tell her he was only kidding when he heard somebody knocking at the door.

Knock. Knock.

"Wait here," he said, pointing a finger at Evie when she started to clamber out of the box. "Do not move."

He walked out of the room, seeing Billie looking at him from the kitchen, her eyes full of fear. He peered through the window in the door, the person there perfectly recognisable even through the patterned glass.

"It's okay," he told his wife. "It's just Keith."

He opened the door to see Dunst there, the DI looking older and greyer than Kett had ever seen him. He had a lit cigarette in his trembling yellow fingers and his face was a contour map of worry.

"Keith," said Kett. "You okay? Kate told me you've cleared out your desk?"

Dunst sighed, something rattling in his throat. He glanced at Kett, but he didn't hold his eye for long, looking away and taking a mighty drag on his cigarette.

"Can I talk to you?" he said, the words made of smoke.

"Sure," said Kett, opening the door a little wider. "You want to come in?"

Dunst shook his head.

"Not here."

The old DI retreated up the path, walking along the road.

"I'll be right back," Kett shouted, closing the front door behind him.

He made his way down the path, stopping when he reached the street. He wasn't sure why he looked back, but he did, staring into the dark living room to see Evie and Moira standing up in their box, both of them watching him with the same expression of fear their mother had worn—Alice, too,. from further back. Evie lifted a little hand and waved, and he waved back.

"Love you," he said, although he didn't think they'd hear him.

Dunst was halfway down the street by now, pacing back and forth beside the parked cars and vans that lined the road. As Kett walked up to him, he took one final puff on his cigarette, then crushed it beneath his shoe. His lace was undone, Kett saw, coiled beneath him like a dead snake.

"What's up, Keith?" Kett said, breathing in the DI's smoke and feeling those same old cravings kick in. "You've not been yourself at all this week."

Dunst didn't look well, Kett thought. His skin was waxy, his hair unbrushed. When he lifted a hand to scratch his neck, it was shaking hard. Was that what this was all about? Had he been given some bad news? He was a heavy smoker, after all, and sooner or later it always caught up with you.

"Keith?" Kett said again when the other man didn't answer.

Dunst leaned against a parked panel van, rubbing his

face with both hands. When he looked up at Kett again, his eyes were bloodshot.

"I'm sorry," he said.

"Sorry for what?" Kett asked him, moving closer. "If something's wrong, just tell me. However bad it is, we can fix it."

"Not this," said Dunst. "You can't fix this."

Kett shook his head, lost. The sun was still raging, pounding the back of his head like it was trying to crack his skull open, like it was trying to get his attention. A car drove by, its windows down and its radio blaring. Further along the street a dog barked, kids laughing.

"I didn't have a choice," said Dunst. He lifted his hand, staring at the stump of his missing finger.

"What are you talking about?"

"*They* didn't give me a choice," Dunst said. "Because I know they mean everything they say. I know they don't bluff."

It was like the sun had dropped right out of the sky. Kett stepped back, shaking his head.

"Who?" he said, his voice a million miles away.

Dunst blinked up at him.

"You know who," he said. "They told me it was you or your kids and I know they meant it. They said if I spoke to anyone, then they'd take the girls. There was nothing I could do."

He reached up, his fist bunched.

"I'm sorry, Robbie."

Then he pounded on the side of the van.

"Shit," said Kett, turning.

Somebody was climbing out of the silver car behind him, a young man with a smile sharp enough to cut glass.

Even with the sun right over his head, Kett recognised him. He'd been sitting on this very street four months ago in a black Peugeot.

"No," Kett said, pointing a finger at the man. "Don't you fucking dare."

His grin widened.

"Your friend is right," the man said, his voice unnaturally high. "It's you or them. Doesn't make any difference to me, but I'd much rather it was you."

The rear doors of the van squealed open, two more men dropping out. Kett couldn't see their faces because they were wearing masks.

Animal masks.

"I'm sorry," said Dunst, backing away. "I'm sorry, Robbie. Whatever happens, I'll try to make it right. I promise."

The three men converged on Kett like a clenched fist, and before he could even raise a hand in defence he felt the punch of a cattle prod in his ribs—a brutal electric charge seeming to rip the bones right out of him. He dropped like a sack of bricks, somebody catching him before he could hit the ground.

Then there was a hood over his head, held in place by a plastic cable tie around his throat. Another tie secured his arms behind his back, sharp enough to slice into his skin.

Somebody grabbed his legs, hoisting him into the air. His muscles twitched and spasmed from the electric shock, his throat contracting—he couldn't even scream as the men threw him into the back of the van.

He heard one door close, the world dropping further into darkness. He rolled onto his stomach, trying to worm his way towards the exit, but his body wasn't letting him.

"It's time, Robert Kett," came a voice from outside. "You're finally ready."

The second door closed, another fist thumping the van.

Knock knock.

And that voice again, one final joyous cry of victory.

"Welcome to Hollenbeck!"

KING RAT

THE ELEVENTH DCI ROBERT KETT NOVEL

When you find yourself in hell,
You have to become a Devil.

DCI Kett's worst nightmares have finally come true, the mysterious group known as Hollenbeck have resurfaced. After being violently abducted, Kett wakes inside a labyrinthine warehouse with no apparent way out—a warehouse rigged with deadly traps.

And he's not alone in here.

Forced to become a rat in a maze, Kett must use every skill he has if he wants to escape. But there is a far greater price to pay if he ever wants to see his family again.

On the outside, DI Porter, DC Savage and PC Aaron Duke face a race against time to locate Kett before it's too late. But Hollenbeck are smart, and this case may prove too much even for the Extreme Crime Task Force.

Because Kett is in hell, and he's about to come face to face with the greatest evil of them all.

Relentless action, compulsive mystery and dark humour abound in the internationally bestselling series that Thrilling Fiction calls "Heart-stoppingly gripping!" from the million-selling author that James Patterson describes as "fresh and ferocious!"

Coming Soon!

ABOUT THE AUTHOR

Alex Smith wrote his first book when he was six. It wasn't particularly good, but it did have some supernatural monsters in it. His latest books, the DCI Robert Kett thrillers, have monsters in them too, although these monsters are very human, and all the more terrifying for it. In between, he has published thirteen novels for children and teenagers under his full name, Alexander Gordon Smith—including the number one bestselling series Escape From Furnace, which is loved by millions of readers worldwide and which is soon to become a motion picture. He lives in Norwich with his wife and three young daughters.

Find out more at alexsmithbooks.com

RELENTLESS
MEDIA

Printed in Great Britain
by Amazon

83478916R00274